DESTINATIONS CHANGE

S.B. GILFILLAN

WHYDE RANGE
PRODUCTIONS

Destinations Change
S.B. Gilfillan

Copyright © 2021 by Samuel B. Gilfillan

Library of Congress Number: 2021919089
ISBN: 978-0-9995320-3-4

Published in the United States of America by
Whyde Range Productions, LLC
12598 Ridgely Road, Suite 4 Greensboro, MD 21639
www.WhydeRangeProductions.com

Photo Credits: Forrest Whitesides
Cover Model: SDG
Book Design: Cissell Ink

Contents

Acknowledgments

To my amazing family and friends – Thank you for the roles you've played in my life and during the writing of this book. I love you all.

To Lois "Midge" Gilfillan, my grandmother – Your faith, love, prayers, and guidance sustain me always.

To Wadell Wright, whose tireless efforts made this a better book.

In Memoriam:
William Carl Gilfillan – Dad, the bigger-than-life man who taught me so much, you encompassed "My Way" like no other.

George A. King, Sr. – Uncle George, my other father.

Byron T. Gilfillan – Grandpap, from WWII to God's work, he served with incredible honor.

Richard E King, Sr. – Pop-Pop, you were the epitome of a true gentleman.

June Parish King – Mimi, my reading buddy, whose grace and style will live forever.

John Cramer – J.W., my stepfather and friend.

And to the others who have been lost along the way – too many, too soon.

PART I

The Morning March

The Morning March

Lori Ann hated the 5:00 AM wake-up call more than anything else about being a so-called "Navy Brat." It didn't matter if it was the sounds of the base or her dad, Chief Petty Officer William P. Morgan, you were going to be up before dawn every day. Her father believed sleeping late was a sign of laziness, and lazy meant weak, and weakness was intolerable for a man with almost twenty-five years in "this man's Navy." She had been awakened to similar sounds for as long as she could remember and never found a way to sleep through it. "The Chief" was unavoidable but she always felt the damn stomping and chanting should be something she could just ignore like the sounds of a city street, but it was not like that at all. As a little girl, she cried when the marching men came near, sometimes passing through the housing areas of the various bases her family called home. They lived in the South for the last ten years, primarily in Florida, but rarely for more than two years at one location. This was her family's second stint at N.A.S. Jacksonville, but the few friends she made during her last residence at "The Jack," as she called it, were either reassigned or had simply gotten old enough to head out on their own. Two years had passed, and in the military, that's a lifetime.

Lori Ann had never been on an unescorted date but didn't mind too much because the only people she'd ever been out with were by way of her father's introduction, guys who escorted her to some event where "The Chief" would also be in attendance, "family functions" he called them. They were sons of other families on base. Tonight, however, was going to be different. Her escort was picking her up instead of meeting her at the event, and her parents were not attending. Her father said he allowed it because the young man was as crisp as any he'd seen come out of O.T.S., "Officer Training School," and had received his first orders as a Lieutenant within Chief Petty Officer Morgan's Unit. "The Chief" couldn't attend the event because he was "non-com," not a commissioned officer.

Her father was a proud Navy man but had a rough time keeping his rank or assignments and always seemed to draw the worst duties that were of the utmost in urgency. She assumed his hard core, know-it-all attitude kept them moving, but he never discussed why an assignment would change, only that, "his expert services were now needed at a new location ASAP." She knew he tried, but he didn't have a college degree, was highly opinionated, and refused to keep his thoughts to himself. Without the ability to reach commissioned officer rank, his world was destined to remain a constant source of frustration through his final year in service to his beloved country, but his daughter could be part of the elite within his precious Navy, and it was time to see that she was properly introduced. He knew his family's remaining time in the Navy was short, and that his daughter wouldn't have many opportunities to meet an officer after his retirement, so he suggested Lieutenant Green take Lori Ann to the ball when it came up in casual conversation that the young Lieutenant hadn't met anyone on or off base since arriving only weeks before. He believed that the best option for his daughter was to become the wife of an officer, thereby securing provisions for her future, and she needed to be at events like the ball if she was to meet prospective suitors. Lori Ann would soon be an adult and out of high school; she needed a plan for her future.

"Now you be respectful of Lieutenant Green; he's a first-class sailor and exactly the kind of man you should hope to marry one day," "The Chief" advised her.

Lori Ann objected, but her mother double-teamed her. "Oh honey, have you seen the officers' quarters? My, they are so wonderful, and the wives attend the most glorious balls. You are so fortunate to be invited to such an event and you must make your father proud."

Lori Ann ultimately agreed and put on the dress her mother purchased for the occasion with little more discussion on the subject.

"You look pretty as a peach in June, my angel. You'll be the belle of the ball for certain this evenin'."

Mrs. Morgan came from a small town near Walterboro, South Carolina, and was raised in a strict Southern Baptist household. She met Lori Ann's father in Jacksonville, Florida while on spring break her senior year in high school. She used to say, "Oh Lord, your father was so dashing in his Navy Whites; how could a good Southern lady avoid losing her heart to such a gentleman? I knew he was the one the very moment he kissed my hand outside that little corner store."

It seems Lori Ann's mother and her friends were in the shop buying some suntan oil when a small group of men in Navy uniforms introduced themselves.

"We spent three days laughing and carrying on at the beach, and even in one of the gentler pubs in town." She always blushed when admitting she'd been in a pub. "We spent three days together before he finally kissed my lips."

Her mother could go on for hours about the first week they enjoyed together. On the last evening, he said he couldn't live without her and would show her the world if she'd only do him the honor of being his bride. She, of course, had to wait for her daddy's permission, but once he heard that William was a U.S. Navy man, he agreed without a formal introduction.

"We were wed that very same day, Lori Ann, and I've loved him every day since."

Lori Ann wore braces for six long years before finally, her seventeenth birthday present was to have them removed for her eventual "coming out." All the years of teasing her about her pig tails and metal mouth had caused this young flower to keep a low profile in school and at the "family functions," not wanting any more attention than was necessary. But with her braces off and hair styled up, even she had to admit that she didn't look half bad. She was over five feet seven inches tall, with sandy blonde hair flowing in full-bodied waves beyond her shoulders, and brilliant blue eyes that always drew attention. Lori Ann also shared her mother's high cheekbones, but they didn't become pronounced until her latest growth spurt. She was thin but muscular due to her father playing with her on training courses instead of playgrounds over the years, and the long jogs that helped clear her mind and allowed daydreaming about what destiny might have in store for her future.

The upcoming event was deemed so important in her household that her mother even purchased fancy lingerie for Lori Ann, a matching silk panty and bra set, saying, "A woman needs to feel beautiful when in the company of a man."

Lieutenant Green was right on time at nineteen thirty hours, just as he told "The Chief" he would be, and he was said to be "absolutely dashing in his dress whites" by her mother, adding, "I just know you'll have a grand evening, and you'll make your father so very proud."

Lori Ann felt like a present wrapped up for this guy's inspection as she came down the hallway to greet him in the tiny foyer, with her dress trailing just slightly behind as she moved in the way her mother had instructed, in the way a "Southern lady" does. It's kind of a flow more than movements, and very graceful when done right. Lori Ann's mother was as intent on instilling the best of Southern attributes and values in Lori Ann as her father was in passing along honor and love of country.

The Morgan's were wholesome and patriotic; they had dinner each evening together, discussed the day and the future of the family and the country, honored the fallen military, and gave thanks and prayed to God. Lori Ann loved her parents and valued what they stood for, but she counted the minutes to her leaving the military life and striking out on her own. Their life was admirable, and she had it better than many, but Lori Ann believed destiny had more in store for her.

Lieutenant Green was a handsome guy, but he stood just as stiffly as "The Chief," and uniforms were about as impressive to her as another field to a farmer's daughter.

"A pleasure, I'm sure." Lori Ann offered her gloved hand for the

Lieutenant to take while she ever so slightly curtsied before him. As for the gentle bow of her head, her mother was out of luck.

He took her hand in a gentle grasp. "The pleasure is all mine, and I thank you for doing me the honor of accompanying me on this fine evening."

"Shit," Lori Ann thought, "I hope this isn't going to be a night out with my mother in uniform."

His accent was so strong it was as if her mother had raised him herself. Lori Ann's accent was reduced to a minimum as one of the only forms of defiance she was allowed. After a few more pleasantries were exchanged, the couple walked toward the car at the short concrete walkway's end. Lori Ann glanced back at her parents standing pridefully on the tiny stoop and wondered what it could've been that kept her mother so happy all these years.

All the houses were the same and lined up for blocks on end: three windows in the front, one to the left of the door and two on the right, one step up to the concrete pad and then one step in. All but the end units on each block shared walls on both sides, all painted a soft shade of blue with the curtains tied back in the same fashion. The only way to tell them apart was the tin number attached adjacent to the front door or the corresponding number painted on the curbing out front.

Once in the car, her escort gave a final wave and quasi-salute to "The Chief" before pulling away.

"So, Lori Ann, do you like to party?"

She almost fell out of her seat at the shock of hearing something like that from a distinguished officer but managed to reply, "What do you mean?"

Lori Ann had misappropriated her fair share of beer over the years, and even a few "Jack and Cokes" while her parents were out in the evenings, but she only smoked pot once and it made her feel a bit dizzy and nauseous.

"Well, we're a bit early for the ball, and a small gathering has come together in the officers' club. Would you like to stop by for drinks on our way?"

"Sure." After all, her dad tried to get in that damn bar his whole life to no avail; there must be something incredible going on in such a place.

"Great, and don't worry, we'll arrive in plenty of time for the introductions."

"What introductions?"

"An Officers' Ball always begins with the introductions of the attendees, kind of like at a wedding party's entrance."

Lori Ann had never been to either.

"What do I have to do, Lieutenant Green?"

"Not a thing, Lori Ann, and please call me Greg, okay?" He concluded with a well-polished smile.

"Okay, Greg." She was feeling a great deal more at ease with the evening.

The officers' club turned out to be just a bar where only officers can drink, and Lori Ann didn't even think it was that nice of a place. Why had her dad wanted so desperately to come in here anyway? It looked like any other bar she'd ever seen through a street window. Greg was a fun guy though, and he kept her laughing while she drank several beers with the small group in the corner. They sat boy/girl around the tables that had been moved together, and all were dressed for the upcoming Ball. Lori Ann figured she was the youngest of the group but didn't feel too out of place. Greg drank vodka and tonic with lime and seemed to be enjoying the group but didn't appear to be as taken with Lori Ann as some of the men seemed with their dates. Kisses were happening all around the table and even some touching under the table. Other than kids making out in the school's corridors, she had never seen public displays of affection. Her mother would've said it was crass, but Lori Ann wasn't so uptight — inexperienced yes, but prude, no.

Lori Ann kissed a boy on several occasions during sophomore year, but the young man broke off their relationship when "The Chief" refused to let her go out on weekends unaccompanied. She'd only seen a naked man twice; once was her father, accidentally, as he stepped out of the shower, and he scolded her severely for walking into the bathroom without knocking. In fact, she was not allowed to watch TV all weekend as punishment. The second time was when Lucy, one of her wilder friends at school, convinced her to sneak into the boy's locker room with her. They went in between classes, and Lori Ann thought it would be empty during that time of day anyway. When they rounded the corner there was one kid toweling off, but the look of shock on the young man's face was much more vivid in her mind than anything else. In neither case did she think it was all that much to behold. Lori Ann did have acquaintances that claimed to be "doing it," but after using her first tampon some years ago, she decided it couldn't be as great as she'd heard.

The Ball was like nothing she'd ever seen, complete with fountains pouring drinks, waiters in tuxedos, and a jazz band. Greg and Lori Ann danced many times and even once to a slow song that made her begin to understand why a woman might like a man to hold her, but it was later that she got a real taste of what the girls had been giggling about.

The Ball ended just after zero two-thirty hours; Greg held her hand as they exited, just as he did when they arrived. Lori Ann felt a bit tipsy and thought perhaps the punch was filled with more than Kool-Aid. Once in the car, Greg asked if she enjoyed herself, to which she replied, "Very much so, thank you."

"Good, I enjoyed you as well."

Lori Ann blushed at his remark and felt faint when he leaned over and kissed her on the cheek, his lips just barely touching the corner of her mouth.

"Do you mind if we stop by my quarters for a moment on our way to your house? I need to pick something up."

"Not at all," Lori Ann agreed, excited for the opportunity to see the famed Officers' Quarters.

The main difference between the two living arrangements was size and the small stretch of grass between each house, but it was still better than where she lived.

"I'll just be a minute," Greg said as he opened his door.

"Oh..." She blushed in embarrassment as she tried to pull her door closed without completely opening it first.

"I'm sorry, did you want to come in?"

"No, that's fine."

"It's okay, really, c'mon in."

"All right." She opened the door completely this time.

"It may be a bit of a mess, so I hope you'll excuse its state," he offered while opening the door and stepping aside for her to enter first.

"It's great. You should see my room sometimes."

"Well, make yourself at home. I'll be right back."

Lori Ann sat down on the couch nearest to where she stood and looked around the room. He had several pictures of sailboats on the pale white walls, a love seat, and the couch she sat on. A television was placed on a cart with wheels, and a stereo was on the shelf below the TV. The coffee table in front of her had an ashtray, but no sign of it being used, and the Cable channel directory was on the couch by her side with the remote. If this was a mess, clean must be hospital quality. There wasn't a speck of dust on any surface.

Greg returned to the room with two glasses of wine and handed one to her. "I hope you like wine."

"Sure, do you?" She felt so ridiculous. Of course he likes wine, why else would he have it, but he just smiled and added, "I do, very much," as he sat down next to her.

He raised his glass in a toast. "Here's to the prettiest lady at the Ball."

Lori Ann almost looked over her shoulder but caught herself. "Thank you."

"No, thank you, Lori Ann. I had a wonderful time tonight."

"Me too."

"Good, I hope we'll do it again real soon."

Lori Ann started to reply but he was already kissing her, this time squarely on the lips, and a moment later she felt his tongue brush up against her own. His hand came to rest on her shoulder while her mind raced in a swirl of shock, enthusiasm, fear and disbelief. Why would he want to kiss me? Surely, he's used to older women. Am I doing it right? He's such a good kisser. But then another hand touched her knee; it shot a lightning bolt up her thigh as she gasped. Not wanting to seem inexperienced, she put her hand on his knee in return. "I'll show him I'm no beginner," she thought. They kissed for what seemed like the longest time and she was getting uncomfortable in the half-twisted position, so she broke off from their embrace and leaned back into the couch.

"Maybe..." She started to speak but his hands moved as she exhaled the first word. Now he was kissing her again, but she could feel the weight of his shoulder against her own as he massaged one of her breasts. She mused in her mind that even his hands were muscular. She had always been flat-chested until last summer, but in the space of just a few months her whole body changed. Her hips became pronounced, and a training bra was traded in for a B-cup, then eventually a C-cup. She would look in the mirror after a shower in amazement at the changes, but she didn't see much value in it until now. She was glad her body was so appealing, and he seemed quite pleased, so why not let him touch her for a while. His other hand had moved a bit as well, but it wasn't as noticeable through the heavy ruffles of the gown. She began to have sensations that were new to her, but not so strange in their feeling. They seemed to be leaning very slowly off to the side, but she'd become caught up in her thoughts about having this older man, an officer no less, show such interest in her. Once almost completely on her back, she could feel her dress move along her shin, and eventually, his hand was on her bare knee. This was a whole new sensation; no boy had ever touched her bare anything, but it was as exhilarating as it was scary, so she again decided to just enjoy. He began softly kissing her neck; it was nearly more than she could take. Her legs trembled as the sensations slammed into each other from her neck, breast and thigh. Thigh? He was caressing her thigh, and she should stop him, but it felt so good to be touched like this. Finally, a shot of adrenaline burst through her body as he slipped his hand beneath her panties; before she could react, he put one of his fingers inside her.

"Wait! We can't do this." She pulled at his arm, wriggling free of his invasion.

"What's the matter?" He asked as if he was as shocked as she was.

"I don't want to do this yet." She replied while trying to adjust her undergarment without him seeing her doing so.

"You're going to shut me down now?"

"Well, I like you and all, but I think we should wait."

"Wait for what? We're both adults, right? Do we need permission?"

"I just want it to be special and I've had too much to drink, and we just met."

"Fine, he whined, but what about this?" He opened his pants and pulled his fully erect member free right in front of her; it glistened with a clear liquid that ran down him and onto his fist. He smoothed it along his shaft as he stroked it proudly for her inspection, but he was closer than anticipated and suddenly released thick pulses of pearlescent fluid onto himself.

"Gross!" After the initial shock wore off, she started laughing as they both viewed the mess on his lap. It was soaking into his white shirt and pants while the once-solid erection began to list within his grip. It seemed the poor guy had gone a bit too far already and she only knew that no story she ever heard had that as part of it; plus, it happened without her so much as touching him.

"Screw this," he yelled, stowing the mess from sight. "C'mon, I'm taking you home little girl."

Lori Ann just got up and walked out the door. Even a "little girl" knows when to keep her mouth shut, and besides, there would certainly be plenty of time to laugh about it later.

Back at her house, Greg opened the door for Lori Ann to exit the car, but he might not have even walked her to the front door if her father hadn't been standing there waiting.

"Well, did you two have a nice evening?"

"Absolutely. I saw all kinds of new things tonight." Lori Ann answered with a little mischief in her tone.

"Good," her father said while Greg silently grimaced in fear of the underlying implications of Lori Ann's statement.

"Thank you for a very interesting evening, Lieutenant," she taunted.

"Yes, well..." Greg started, but Lori Ann interrupted. "Maybe we can do it again some time."

Her father smiled and looked for agreement from the young officer, who replied, "I'm sure I'd be delighted," and then made a hasty exit, inadvertently ignoring her father's invitation for a nightcap as he fled in hopes of "The Chief" not noticing the wet spots on his dress uniform.

Lori Ann never said a word to her parents about the true events of the evening and Greg never came to call again. But she had a story to share with the big talking girls at school, and of course, she had the memory of the fine evening at the Ball.

Lori Ann decided that her date with the Lieutenant would be the last with a man in uniform; it simply didn't align with her mental picture of life off the base, but she also thought the right boy might just be fun to have around. She began paying more attention to her appearance and learned she was becoming quite desirable to the boys in her midst.

Lori Ann's mother taught her well; she was not going to be with just any guy. Besides, she strongly believed in destiny, and she knew the right one would be obvious when he eventually arrived, so she went on about her studies and bided her time until she would be able to head out on her own. She loved to read and was somewhat interested in college, though most of the girls seemed to view the experience in terms of getting their "M-R-S degree," as they put it, which meant to find a successful husband and not use their degree anyway. In the end, she just wanted to settle down with the right guy, so where she met "Mr. Right" wasn't as important as destiny arranging it. Lori Ann's goals primarily consisted of the American dream: a quaint little house in a darling neighborhood, some kids running around, a few quality friends, and of course, a great man at her side. She was never focused on money and only aimed towards enough to be happy. Lori Ann just wanted a guy to be nice, honest, and a great kisser.

As "The Chief's" retirement neared, he bought a car and began to look at off-base housing for the first time in his adult life. He hated the thought of retiring, and leaving the base was almost more than he could stand, but Mrs. Morgan said twenty-two years was enough for a military wife, and it was time to move on. Lori Ann figured it was one of maybe two times her mother had ever been in charge of their direction, the first being when her father wanted to try again for a son in recent years, but her mom said it was too late, and they needed to focus on the traveling of the world he promised so many years ago. How could "The Chief" argue with her? She was the best darn wife in the Navy, and she was right about the promise owed, plus he had a full retirement package after the twenty-five years he served.

Lori Ann was so excited when they came home with the car. Maybe she'd finally learn to drive and get her license. Her father always said they didn't need a car and why waste the money when everything we need is right here on base? Her mother quietly went along, walking to the commissary and the exchange all these years with a small-wheeled basket to bring home the family's dinner and supplies. Now they had a used minivan her mother selected within the budget "The Chief" offered. It wasn't too bad: a dark green Dodge with tan seats and fake wood paneling on the sides. The back windows were tinted, and the front ones were power, along with the locks. The radio also played cassettes, and her mother seemed thrilled by finally having a car of her own. They rented a car for the annual journey to her parent's home, and she hated giving it up at each trip's conclusion. Lori Ann believed if her mother hadn't already had a license when she married her father, she never would have gotten one at all.

Lori Ann had never driven a car, but she did ride dirt bikes at her grandparent's home during their visits. Her grandpa bought two motorcycles for the grandchildren to enjoy and loved teaching them to ride in the neighboring fields. She loved the feel of the wind on her face, and the freedom to choose which of the many paths she'd explore with each turn through the nearby woods. Once, she was gone so long, she ran out of gas and had to push the bike home, but she didn't mind the walk through the woods and took the time to observe the things she missed while traveling at speed on her way in. She sure was looking forward to having a license; with that and a car, she could go anywhere destiny takes her.

PART II

School Daze

School Daze

The crisp morning air weighed heavy on my lungs as I walked toward the bus stop at the bottom of the only hill in Crystal Cove. If this was the magnificent new opportunity to better my life, I already missed the old days. I hadn't been on a school bus since the sixth grade and based on the preppie punks at the bus stop, my new school was going to be an adventure in abstinence from my favorite pastimes.

My mother recently married a wealthy CEO of a Minneapolis-based software company. They met in New York City through friends in the divorce circuit that must exist among the yuppie set, and although my parents split when I was twelve, Robert was the only "date" my mother ever introduced to my sister and me.

Robert was a self-made man and demanded the respect he deserved. His accomplishments in the business world were highly admirable, and to be honest, he could be a fun guy to be around. After a particularly difficult divorce, he found true happiness with my mother, and he tried harder than most to establish positive relationships between himself, his kids and us.

My mom is more of a poetic type, big heart and warm nature, but in no way short-changed in the brains department. She's a beautiful brunette with bright green eyes, educated, well-raised within a prominent family, and she managed to run a successful business while simultaneously attending to the many demands of parenting two utterly opposite adolescents since the divorce.

I'm newly released from my New Jersey reform school a year early to start over in Minnesota without my troubled past dragging me down; at least that was how they presented the move from New Jersey. I had been in several public schools in various towns, plus one of the finest private schools money can buy, and when they'd all grown weary of my refusal to toe the line, as my father put it, finally, a state-mandated reform school for the hopelessly incorrigible. I hadn't always been so bad; in fact, I largely focused my hostilities on sports until the seventh grade. And even though I was no stranger to sex, drugs and alcohol prior to then, I hadn't completely succumbed to their lure until the truly upscale version was introduced in the private school. The high school kids drove Ferraris and BMWs, had Gold Cards, and hosted incredible unsupervised parties in mansions and four-star hotels. Man, did they know how to live, and all our parents were busy pursuing the wealth that seemed to fall from the skies during the Reagan years. If you were halfway on the ball in the 1980s, you had bucks, and I intended to grab some too.

My sister, Parish, did no wrong, and felt that consistent straight A's going into the ninth grade should have entitled her to stay in New Jersey, at least until going to some top-tier college in four years. However, she would adapt. She's like my mom, but a bit more pragmatic, and a touch less of the artsy side. She's very bright, every bit of five feet eight inches tall, long and lean with sparkling blue eyes and light brown hair, athletic, but also hard-working and focused on the task at hand: her education. The divorce unraveled her as much as anyone, but she hunkered down and forged ahead in a show of admirable strength. The other pivotal woman in my life is my grandmother; without her love and prayers, I'd already be dead a dozen times over. She's the biggest ally I've ever had and the finest person I've ever known.

Lake Minnetonka is quite beautiful and was much larger than any inland waterway I had ever seen. It has over one hundred miles of shoreline twisting through subtle rolling hills and branching off endlessly into remote coves, each a private community for the wealthy who call the Minnetonka area home.

Crystal Cove is one of the smaller notable coves, well off the main lake and several miles from "7-High," which is the intersection of Routes 7 and 101, where the larger of the community's shopping malls are located. The high school is just a mile north on 101 from "7-High;" it sits overlooking the highway from an extension road that is raised dutifully above the traffic of past generations now scrambling for a better location on the lake. To date, not many outsiders were relocating into the community, a distinct advantage for a new kid, regarding the girls anyway.

The bus ride was short, for which I was grateful while observing our nation's future being unloaded into the parking lot on campus. As I wandered the halls in search of the main office, I noted my sister would be in heaven in this buttoned-down Polo world. She and I agreed not to speak at the bus stop or within the school walls, neither wanting to be connected with the other's seemingly intolerable lifestyle.

A warm-natured lady with a strong Norwegian accent in the main office provided a copy of my schedule of classes and a school map with directions to both my locker and first class; Parish received hers during the orientation I skipped. The school was a large two-story rectangular building, and except for its remarkably clean appearance, it was much like any other public school I had graciously been asked to leave.

The smoking lounge was down the main corridor on the left, an outside courtyard surrounded by three walls, with the open end being the back entrance to the student parking lot. At the time, how cold and inconvenient an outside smoking lounge would be in Minnesota had not entered my mind.

I meandered down the long hall toward the lounge for a quick smoke before first period, checking out the populous as I went. My first class was nearby, and nothing important happens on the first day anyway. I torched my smoke, looking over the few small groups of "Burn-Outs," as they were called by the "Jocks," "Brains" and "Preppies." I flicked my butt at the wall, ignoring the strategically-placed ash trays, and was heading to class when she turned the corner with the sound of an unseen Hot Rod pulling off in the distance behind her. At that moment, my destiny was locked in so solidly that the best of Alcatraz's breakout artists would've laughed at any escape I could have imagined.

She walked directly to me and asked for a light of the long, slender cigarette that was cradled in her delicate fingers. I was speechless. Laurie was five feet five inches at best, with the finest blonde hair I've ever seen, styled in gently flowing waves, with brilliant blue-green eyes and a body that frustrated the cheerleaders to cynical thoughts of her demise. Her voice was soft and smooth as silk, with a subtle French-Canadian accent to-die-for. She clearly controlled all she surveyed.

"Your name?" She asked as she casually exhaled a thin cloud of smoke through pouty lips glistening with pink gloss.

"Uh, Reno," I replied, in awe of her mere existence.

"New, huh?" An easy smile graced her blush pink lips.

"Yeah, I just moved here in July."

"Where from?" Her eyes sparkled as she spoke.

"Jersey."

"Hmm. What's that like? Do they get high?"

I had goose bumps despite the seventy-degree breeze as she paused, waiting for my response.

"Everybody I know does." Every nerve ending in my body twitched in the delight of her presence. I felt my face flush when she casually flipped her hair from her face and asked, "Have you got any?"

"Nah, I ran out a month ago." As I finished the sentence, I thought, how could I have known to save something for such a day as this? And then she spoke softly and directly, "Come with me."

Her order was the finest directive I'd ever received. I'm not one to stumble around girls, but my mind raced a thousand miles per hour trying to remain cool and collected as we walked to the far side of the student lot where a trail appeared sloping down into the woods.

"You do coke don't cha'?" She asked as she carefully navigated the rocky hill in shimmering pink pumps. I responded, "Oh yeah," wondering if all new kids were welcomed in this manner.

When she said, "Do you have a girlfriend?" my heart stopped cold.

"Nah, I don't really know anyone here."

"I meant in New Jersey, but I guess it doesn't matter since you're here now, don't cha' know." She smiled, glancing over her shoulder, her eyes twinkling within a gentle squint, and I felt instantaneous love for the third time in my young life; few moments have rivaled that instant's intensity since. To this day, the words "don't cha' know," when spoken in proper accent, still spike my heart like they were shot from a compound bow.

It's perhaps worth noting that my first love was punctuated by a "Charlie's Angels" lunch box hitting me on the head when I mistakenly served up an uninvited kiss on the cheek of my unsuspecting love interest in third grade. A wiser man would've garnered more from that experience.

In a clearing at the base of the path, Laurie produced a small, brownish glass vial with a tiny spoon attached to the lid by a little gold chain. She carefully scooped the spoon full of white powder, one for each side of her adorable little nose. I watched, jealous of the opportunity to be a part of her. She took half of a step forward and I could smell her sweet perfume mixing with an herbal shampoo. The half erection I had been struggling to conceal was now full-blown; I hoped she wouldn't notice it as she filled the tiny spoon for me.

After the second round of spoons, I couldn't tell where my lustful feelings ended and the cocaine-induced euphoria began.

"Well, that oughta do it," she said, with an angel's glow as she started back up the hill.

I gathered my head as we ascended the path and thanked her for the coke. She glanced over her shoulder and winked while saying, "You're welcome, and by the way, welcome to Minnetonka."

As per Laurie's instructions, I waited around the corner of the brick school wall for a couple of minutes before re-entering the smoking area so we wouldn't attract attention. I kept thinking about how soft her silk blouse felt against my arm and concluded that she was more stimulating than any powder could ever be.

The story goes that Laurie's family had only two things of real value in this world: Laurie and her older sister Debbie. They were both beautiful, and in their respective time at the school, each was the most sought-after girl on campus. I heard their parents divorced due to dad being a gambler or something, and that mom was a drinker, but it's all high school hearsay, potentially originating from jealous girls. One thing's for sure: They only dated guys with money, and usually older guys. It seems Debbie moved in with some super-wealthy guy no one knows much about, which was hard on Laurie because they were so close. Regardless of the facts, they simply wanted more and who could blame them. As for me, I don't think Laurie ever had a chance to find out who she really was before simply duplicating a persona that served her sister so well. At her core, as in all of us, she was probably just a scared kid trying to figure out the world presented to her, but on her terms.

To my amazement, there were still three students in the smoking area when I rounded the corner, and I could smell pot in the air. I wondered why there weren't any security guards, "bouncers" as we called them, dragging them off to class, and then remembered I was back in public school, which immediately knocked my stress level down to idle. Most freedoms are taken so lightly until they are gone.

Reform school was a crazy environment: classrooms had sofas, you could smoke just about anywhere including the classrooms, recreational drugs were plentiful, and if you had an issue with someone, you just beat the hell out of him until a "bouncer" broke it up. The two "bouncers" were gorilla-sized guys in their twenties with a demeanor similar to most of the student body, but in fairness, they had their hands full with the hundred or so juvenile delinquents inhabiting the prep school for convicts, as I liked to muse about it. Their primary job was to "disarm and redirect," remove all identified weapons, and police the halls, meaning keep them empty. If they saw you in the hall when classes were occurring, they'd grab you, physically drag you down the hall and shove you into the nearest classroom. Few were foolish enough to reenter the hall from whence you'd been tossed. Which class you were in wasn't relevant to them, you just had to be somewhere, and everyone got a passing grade anyway, as long as you didn't kill someone. These kids had run out of options in the public school system; the cops were tired of locking them up, and so they were court-ordered to attend the school as a last chance before being subjected to long-term incarceration of varying natures. Although I was considered pretty-damn crazy in public school and especially private school, I was about as menacing as a well-flung marshmallow in this place when I first arrived, and the almost daily beatings I took the first year reflected it. Taekwondo lessons during the first summer break had little impact on my self-defense capabilities among these animals, but the day I stabbed the most feared guy in the school in the neck with a pencil turned things around promptly. I'm not saying they feared me afterward, but a new level of respect was definitely afforded, and I also made two new friends that kept me out of the majority of harm's way. Having a "crew," as we referred to our mini gangs of sorts, was a necessity. The guy I stabbed, "Billy," was later jailed for life for blowing the heads off two guys at a stoplight with a sawed-off shotgun. I guess they said the wrong thing to the wrong guy on the wrong night, and so it goes in parts of Jersey.

The encounter with Laurie bolstered my desire to approach a group of guys sharing a joint in the smoking area, and as I neared them, I had beautiful thoughts of smoking the joint I would buy from them with Laurie down on the path.

"Hey, you dudes got an extra 'Bone' for sale?"

"Naw man, just this one. Want a hit?" The guy who spoke extended his hand and offered me the joint. I looked at my watch and figured a couple of hits should settle me down nicely for second period, which was rapidly approaching now.

Another guy asked, "Where you from, dude?"

"Jersey."

"Yeah, that would explain the accent. What's your name?"

"Reno." I replied with a large hit of the sweet smoke filtering through my lungs.

"Well, I'm Tommy, this is Levi and that's Ron."

"Thanks for the smoke, guys." I turned and started walking toward the doors to go inside and Tommy called out, "Hey Reno, we're goin' over to Ron's for a liquid brunch. Wanna come with?"

"I don't know, first day and all," I replied, feeling the pleasant confusion of the morning's events haze over my brain in a victory march.

"Come on, dude, no one even knows you exist yet," Tommy countered. "Why don't you come with and I'll see if I can getcha that 'Doobie' you wanted."

With thoughts of Laurie in my head, I hopped into Tommy's '69 Camaro, grinning as it roared to life. Ron leaned forward and whispered in my ear, "You might want to buckle up." Just then, an old man came out of a little guardhouse at the exit/entrance to the student lot. He was waving and shouting something indecipherable through the piercing volume of Judas Priest and engine noise. Tommy laughed out loud as we passed him in a cloud of smoke and swung sideways onto the extension road.

"So, did ya get some?" Levi asked as we walked into Ron's parent's house in Wayzata. For some reason, a handful of Wayzata kids went to Minnetonka High School. They were generally wilder than Minnetonka kids and usually not as rich.

"Get some?" I was unsure if he meant sex or drugs but sure he was referencing my walk with Laurie.

"Little Laurie, dude," Tommy said. "She usually only dates rich guys with a lot of coke, but she seems to dig you."

"Naw man, we just smoked a joint."

"Yeah, right. Laurie smokin' dope? It's cool if you don't wanna tell us. Besides, I heard she'll only fuck in a limo."

I didn't respond to Tommy; I just shrugged and gave Ron a dollar for the joint that now had greatly diminished value.

"So, ya like the Camaro?"

"Yeah Ron, it's cool."

"Fastest in town," Tommy said as he searched Ron's refrigerator.

"Really?"

Tommy snapped his head in my direction. "You got somethin' faster?"

"No, dude, I don't even have my license back yet."

Ron asked, "What'd ya do?"

"I got busted for drunk driving on a learner's permit while visiting family in Maryland."

"No shit; that's a bitch. Why don't you just go to the DMV like ya never had one?" Tommy suggested.

"Ya think it would work?"

"Sure. Why not? What does Minnesota know about New Jersey or whatever?"

A few weeks later and after a seriously ridiculous driver course, I had my license, having learned a valuable lesson about the system.

The next morning, I waited in the smoking lounge until first period ended; no Laurie. Tommy and I smoked a joint down on the path, and I attended the rest of the day's classes. In fifth period, History, I sat behind an incredible girl. I never actually met her, but she somehow stuck in my mind. Her hair was long and straight, chestnut in color. She was beautiful and intelligent, an obvious scholar. The smile she awarded me was my invitation to the road of choice Robert referenced in our long talk in New Jersey, the path of all good children, the ones with bright futures. I rarely returned to that class, and when I did, she didn't give me any more welcoming looks. When I described the girl from History to Tommy, he knew her as the future class president and valedictorian, obviously not well suited for my lifestyle.

Tommy is another story; he was raised in a nice house in Minnetonka and wanted for nothing until the day his father left them with no hope of maintaining the lifestyle they grew accustomed to. From that day forward, he was reminded how quickly things can change. He, his mom and stepfather lived in a rented townhouse in Wayzata, a far cry from his early years, and no one was pleased with the turn of events. Tommy's rage at the change in status was further fueled by a remarkable excess of drug and alcohol usage. To further aggravate the situation, Tommy believed in the folklore that certain well-known musicians rose to fame through a pact with the devil, and he pursued this track with a fury. He read books on demons and black magic and offered himself and even his girlfriend and family's souls in exchange for the bright light's gleam upon his Stratocaster, but to no avail. Eventually, his resentments grew to include the very demons he prayed to for an escape from the mundane world he despised so deeply. Essentially, he hated everyone. Tommy was the original angry young man, and I don't think anybody other than me and Missy, his first love, had ever seen the greater depth and heart hidden within him.

THE SEASONS CHANGE RAPIDLY IN MINNESOTA, AND IN NO TIME, winter was in full swing, leaving summer nights as nothing more than a pleasant memory. It was around 5:00 AM one morning when I awoke to Tommy knocking on my bedroom window. In a groggy state of confusion, I shouted, "What?"

"It's me. Open up, I'm fuckin' freezing."

"What are you doin' here man? It's like 5:00 AM," I said while getting out of bed and opening a sliding glass door to let him in.

"There's a major snowstorm going on out there. Shit, I barely made it over here in my mom's car."

He would never have driven the prized Camaro in bad weather. In Minnesota, many people buy "winter beaters" for the season to protect their nicer cars. A "winter beater" is usually a big old car, like an early nineteen seventy's sedan that can be purchased for around fifteen hundred, driven all winter, sold for between a hundred and fifty to five hundred, potentially back to the original seller, and then fixed up again for the following winter. It's kind of cool because you just bounce them off the ten-foot-tall snowbanks, and anything else, all winter, then pull out your nice car again in the spring.

"Too bad ya did, now go away so I can sleep." I was heading back to bed when he insisted, "Come on, get dressed, we gotta go."

"Are you serious? Go where?"

It's worth noting that they rarely close schools or anything else for snow; they're loaded for bear out there and can manage incredible snow volumes with ease. Only extreme cold, like dipping beyond twenty below zero kind-of-cold, can shut down things in that part of the world.

"We gotta go out in the Jeep, dude. I brought some jumper cables and a case of anti-freeze." He was rifling through my closet as he spoke.

"You're fucking crazy!" I crawled back under my covers.

"Listen Reno, it's the first storm of the year; every idiot in the state will be going to work in an hour."

"So. Who cares?"

"We do! They'll be in ditches from here to St. Paul."

"Good," I moaned in an angry tone. After all, we hardly ever called it quits before daylight was nearing, and I was only entering my second hour of sleep after the previous night's blitz.

"Exactly! How are they gonna get out?"

"I don't know, maybe a fuckin' tow truck."

"No, not a tow truck, dude. I'm telling you, it's gonna be a mess out there; it's falling at like six inches an hour and it's really cold today."

"So, you want to drive around pulling them out in the Jeep?"

"Yeah!"

"No way man, you're stoned. Wait, are you on acid or something?"

"Listen to me. These fuckers land in a ditch in their hotshot Benz and they're just sure they're gonna die out there." Tommy was full-on laughing now, saying, "They'll pay anything to get out."

The only thing he loved more than money was seeing people with it suffering.

"Really?" I still wasn't sure if he was fucking with me.

"Dude, I got out of bed at 4:00 AM to come over here. What do you think?"

"Well, you are the laziest fucker I've ever met." It wasn't true but getting him out of bed can take a crowbar and a gun.

"Exactly, so get dressed and let's go."

"How much do you charge 'em?"

"No, dude, you're missing it. It's how much have you got?" His fiendish chuckle grew louder at the thought of profiting from the privileged.

"Really?" I was getting dressed as fast as I could.

"Yeah, man! We stay on the back roads, the farther out the better. They're all alone, it's zero visibility and cold, and along we come. Ya do have a cable or some rope, don't ya?"

"There's a nylon tow strap in the garage."

"Rock and roll, dude. This is gonna be great!"

It was just like he said: well below zero with the wind chill factor, maybe a foot of snow and piling up fast, with cars wrecked on every road.

"Keep going, dude," Tommy ordered as we passed a desperate-looking commuter on the side of the road.

"But he's waving us over."

"This is a main road; we'll get caught."

"Caught by who? I'm just giving him a pull."

"Nobody but a tow truck can tow on city streets."

"Well, that's pretty stupid."

"No shit, but that's the deal."

His sarcasm was not what I needed for breakfast.

We drove until we were well into the farmland that surrounds most towns in the Midwest, drinking from the bottle of Brandy I pilfered from the house as we cruised through the secondary roads of the Heartland. The rolling hills between patches of forest were breathtaking with the fresh snow glistening along endless swirling drifts in the early morning light.

"Up there, dude." Tommy pointed out the windshield. "That's our guy; pull up next to him so I don't have to get out."

"What an idiot."

I pulled alongside the black Saab nearly on its side in the ditch. Tommy rolled down his window. "Hey! Are you okay in there?"

The guy rolled down his window and yelled, "Boy, I'm sure glad to see you fellas."

I smirked at his thinking this was simply good luck on his part, although from his perspective it certainly was.

"Do ya think you can pull me out?"

"Well, I don't know," Tommy said, shaking his head. "It might hurt the truck and..."

"I'll pay you. How much do you want to try?"

Tommy looked over at me with a devilish grin, and then slowly shifted back to look out his window. "Well, it's his mom's truck, and if we mess it up, he'll be hung for sure."

"My wife's got a Wagoneer just like it. I'm sure it'll be okay," the man pleaded.

"Well, I..."

"Look, I'll give you a hundred bucks to try."

Tommy turned to me and said, "We're in business. Put down the back window, dude," as his power window went up.

A few minutes later, the Saab was on the road and Tommy hopped in the Jeep with two fifties in his hand. "Next," he shouted, dropping the money in my lap as he simultaneously reached for the bottle of brandy I held between my thighs.

"We should do this all the time, dude." I stuffed a fifty in my pocket and handed the other back to Tommy as we pulled away.

"Nah, it only works with the first storm. They pull out the "winter-beaters" with chains, snowmobiles and all kinds of shit from here on out."

"They can't drive a snowmobile to work."

"Sure they can; it's legal from October through February or something. All you need is a tag."

"Really?"

"Yeah. It's only this good on opening day." He toasted with the Brandy bottle.

By 9:00 AM, we'd pulled seven cars out and had eight hundred in cash. One guy actually paid two hundred to get his 500 SL Benz out of a field. Man, was he screwed. He'd lost it on a corner and ended up buried about fifty feet off the road.

"Where to next?" I asked, pulling away from Lucky Number Seven, as I nicknamed him.

"That's it, man. The plows will be caught up soon, and every tow truck on the lake is out by now."

"All right, so what do ya wanna do now?"

"I know a guy in Wayzata with eight balls for two-fifty."

"That's a plan. Let's go."

I pulled a giant U-turn through a field with Tommy cheering as the front tires spewed snow and chunks of frozen earth into the air.

"We're gonna need more booze too," advised Tommy, holding up the empty brandy bottle before hurling it out the open window at a road sign.

As we headed around the lake towards our rendezvous with a different kind of snow, we came upon a person walking down the side of the road. When we got closer, the woman, probably in her late twenties, turned and put her thumb out.

"Fuck her. Don't stop."

"C'mon, Tommy, it'll be fine."

I slowly pulled alongside her; she was wearing a big army-type camouflage coat and a brightly colored ski cap, not exactly a fashion statement but winter is winter.

"Ugh, look at her," Tommy grumbled in disgust as she approached his door. "Get in the back," he ordered, emphasizing the mandate with his thumb.

"Hi, guys! Thanks. It sure is cold out there."

"Why ya walkin'?" I asked, looking at her in the rearview mirror as I pulled away.

"My asshole husband wouldn't pick me up at work when the power went out."

Tommy growled. "Fuckin' perfect."

"So, you're headed home?"

"Yeah, nothin' else to do."

Tommy threw his head back into the headrest. "That's valuable information."

"Where do you live?"

"Offa' McGinty Road; it's not far."

"What? Yeah, right, that's not far." Tommy's sarcasm was evidence of his mood declining.

"Tell ya what. If you buy us a bottle on the way, I'll bring you there."

"A bottle of what?"

"Booze! Whaddya think? This chick's unreal," Tommy replied in disbelief.

"Oh, well my dad's got booze at the house."

Tommy asked, "Where's he live, Texas?"

"No, we live with him." She was laughing, totally missing his patronizing tone.

"So, let me see if I got this put together. We're going to your house, and your dad and your husband are gonna be there. Then, you're gonna give us a bottle of dear 'ol dad's booze. Like, hi everybody, these guys want a bottle, okay?" Tommy was thoroughly amused with himself.

"No, it'll be cool, nobody's home 'til later."

"Good, so you'll give us a bottle then, right?"

"Sure, whatever you want," she offered with a cheerful tone, our eyes meeting in the rearview mirror.

She lived in an apartment complex made up of three two-story buildings just outside of some little town. We parked in the lot and walked down a half-ass shoveled walkway.

"It's up here."

We followed her up a flight of exterior stairs and entered the living room of the sparsely-furnished apartment, not a recent winner in "Better Homes and Gardens," but it was clean. The kitchen was on the left, filled with outdated cabinetry and appliances, and a well-used card table surrounded by four metal chairs with floral-print vinyl cushions. To the right, she advised, were three doors concealing the bathroom and two bedrooms down a narrow hall.

"Have a seat, I'll be right back." She exited the kitchen, walking off toward the hallway.

"Where's the booze?" Tommy asked.

"Oh, it's in the cabinet over the sink. Help yourself."

"Cool, see Tommy, this wasn't so bad."

"Yeah, yeah. Let's just get the bottle and go."

We scanned the cabinets, opened the middle one and found three bottles.

Tommy opened and smelled one of the bottles. "What's this shit?"

"Martini and Rossi."

"It's nasty."

"I know." I was holding the other two bottles; one was vermouth, it was nearly empty, the third was an off-brand vodka with maybe two good drinks worth in it.

"Did you find it?" She appeared behind us in a satin, knee-length, dark blue robe, her black hair still a mess from the hat. Her figure was now apparent in the cinched robe, and she was kind of cute, youthful looking.

"There's nothing in here. What's the deal?" Tommy was jerking one of the bottles around in menacing waves that made me think he might let it fly across the room, or worse, into her.

"What's that?" she asked, looking at the bottles we held.

"It's crap. You gotta go to the store with us to get a bottle," I demanded.

"I don't have a license."

"So?" It was obvious to us that she was over twenty-one, and Tommy was on the razor's edge; I could see the twitching of his upper lip that was like the tell of a novice boxer dropping his shoulder before throwing a punch. I knew he was ready to snap.

"They won't sell to me without one," she replied in a mournful tone.

"Let's just go." I sat the vermouth bottle firmly on the kitchen table with a thud.

"This is bullshit. You oughta blow us for this shit." Tommy snarled as he haphazardly tugged at her robe, intending to move her aside so he could pass. The robe flew open exposing her naked body to our view. We were both stunned and then erupted in boyish laughter.

She casually closed her robe. "I'm sorry. If you want, I'll try."

"Try what? You already said they won't sell to you."

"Getting served, I guess."

Tommy jumped in. "Waste of time. I'd rather have the blowjob."

"Really? Well, I guess I could. But what if somebody comes home?"

"You said nobody would." Tommy taunted her while walking out of the kitchen.

We watched him walk through the living room and into the first room on the left without saying another word.

She asked, "Is he serious?"

"I wouldn't doubt it." I couldn't help but chuckle, still a bit loose from two hours of sleep and our eighty-proof breakfast.

"He went into my dad's room."

I followed her through the living room without a reply.

"You guys do this a lot, don't you?" She turned toward me after seeing Tommy on the bed with his pants around one ankle, his other after-ski boot on the floor. I just laughed at the sight of him. He looked so serious yet was lying there half-naked.

"Yeah, we drive around in snowstorms looking for hitchhikers to give us blowjobs."

"You're not going to do anything funny, are you?" She questioned Tommy while moving cautiously onto the bed, sliding on her exposed knees.

"Gimme a break. What do you think I'm going to do?"

She looked at me still standing by the bedroom door, choking back laughter from the ridiculous scene before me, and then she leaned forward and down into Tommy's lap. He motioned to her butt with a pointing finger; it was high in the air as she bobbed up and down at the neck. I pondered the invitation, then slipped off my coat and boots, plopping down in a nearby chair to adjust my socks that were bunched up at the heels. She paused, flipping her hair over her shoulder while glancing at me with a welcoming wink. I thought, wow, looks like this chick had a plan of her own. If we'd been somewhere else, I might've accepted the invite, but it was kind of crazy, even for me. I mean, she's married and doing my buddy in her dad's room; "Ya gotta draw the line somewhere," or at least get more booze to blur it away.

"Don't stop, I'm almost there!"

She continued working on him while I carefully slipped the first boot back on; at that moment, the front door opened.

"Lorraine, are you home? Why is my cabinet open?"

Tommy's eyes met mine in horror as he tossed her over onto her back on the bed.

"It's my dad!"

We hit the floor simultaneously and were fumbling with our garments when the door pushed fully open into the bedroom. The man was about sixty years old with mostly gray hair, short and stocky, wearing some sort of company-issued overall.

"What the hell is going on here?"

Before her father could wrap his head around what he was seeing, Tommy drove him into the wall with his forearm as he fled the room. Wearing only one boot, with coat in hand, I charged out the door in Tommy's wake, laughing so hard that I almost fell as I followed him down the outside stairs. Tommy had his right pant leg and underwear balled up in his hands; his left pant leg was on.

"You better have the fuckin' keys," he yelled as we neared the Jeep.

I was searching my coat pockets for the keys and peripherally saw the silhouette of her dad falling in the snow while running down the path. "I'll kill you little bastards," he screamed while getting to his feet. He was too close for us to stop at the Jeep, so we ran past it and into the woods, only stopping when he broke off the chase and turned back toward the apartments.

"What the fuck are we gonna do now?" Tommy panted.

"I'm not sure, dude, but we won't last long out here without shoes."

Tommy was pulling his other pant leg on over a sock that was matted with snow while I contemplated our options and the recent events.

"How 'bout that chick, bro'? I think she planned that shit."

"I was only fuckin' with her, man. I didn't think she'd actually do it. What's the story with her gettin' naked in that robe?" Tommy was shivering and rubbing his foot which was now a ball of snow covering his sock.

"Fuck if I know, but we gotta go," I said, rising from my knees to a crouched position. We cautiously made our way through the woods, each with only a left boot, until we were directly across the street from the parking lot. I scanned the area. "I don't see him."

"Me either, but my foot is a block of ice, man. We gotta make a run for it."

We both sprinted from the woods and across the street toward the Jeep. Her father reappeared, hurling down the stairs just as we opened the doors and leaped in the Jeep. After starting the engine, I was laughing so hard that I almost hit him as we bounced over the sidewalk and into the street.

"I can't believe I lost my fuckin' boot," Tommy complained while looking back at the irate man running down the street after us. I slammed on the brakes. "Yeah, get mine too."

"Go! You fuckin' maniac."

Her father ran into the back of the Jeep, unable to stop his momentum on the ice. I mashed my foot to the floor and howled at the sight of him lying in the road, holding my now broken-off rear wiper in an angry fist.

"You're nuts," Tommy said just before erupting in laughter.

MINNESOTA IS KIND OF LIKE CALIFORNIA, LESS THE CLIMATE AND cosmetic wonders on the ladies; most of the girls are blonde, life is an endless party and sex is more popular than team sports, well, aside from ice hockey. Although Laurie occupied my heart, there were many beautiful girls around the lake to occupy my time. With an average temperature of twenty degrees during the many winter months, house parties become a common occurrence. These people are resourceful too; if there's no house available, they tunnel into the mountainous piles of snow in the parking lots using spray bottles with water to solidify the newly-bored corridors and open areas within the pile. It's pretty warm in there because it's a small space filled with people and there's no wind to drop the temperature below thirty-two degrees. Groups of four or more could sit in little caverns with a boom box and a bottle of booze without anyone even knowing they were there.

One of the craziest things is the tunnels along the Mississippi River that divides the Twin Cities. They were created by the Army during WWII to stockpile all kinds of military hardware that could be moved downriver at a moment's notice. After the war, the tunnels were sealed off, but industrious teens and homeless people bored through the mountain face and created little entrances to access the massive caverns within. We'd squeeze through a hole along the upper mountain face and then slide down the interior wall to the floor more than fifty feet below. I think the soil was limestone; in any event, it was sturdy but could be easily chiseled away to create footholds to climb the tall walls in the main areas. Larger cave-like openings were carved high into the interior wall faces that provided safer gathering locations for small groups while menacing marauders roamed the cavern below. The temperature inside was approximately fifty degrees year-round, which feels like summer on a Minnesota winter day. It was crazy in there, and you never knew who you'd run into, kind of like a modern-day Huckleberry Finn adventure but with more dangerous people. We'd usually go in with a group, carrying flashlights, torches, and all the booze we could haul. The homeless generally avoided us, but other groups of derelicts could be highly confrontational, so sometimes things got ugly. And of course, we always had to watch out for the police when entering or exiting. For me, the coolest thing was the vintage Army jeeps, trucks, and equipment that are entombed within the caverns, but we enjoyed a drunken brawl from time to time as well. Not many girls would dare to enter the caverns, but the ones who did were up for anything and fun to have around.

By Christmas break, I had been transferred from the mainstream curriculum into a short-day program for noncooperative students, known as micro-school; it was held in the first three classrooms just up the stairs from the smoking lounge entrance, probably to limit interaction between us and the masses. Lounge chairs, couches, and several desks made up the micro-school classrooms, and the curriculum was well reflected by the casual furnishings. It was basically reform school lite, without any real bad-asses or smoking, but they did make an effort to keep humanity's rules intact.

I loosely attended micro-school until the day I was caught with my pants around my ankles on a couch with another micro-student, her quilted dress pulled up to her breasts. That one was hard to figure out. She flashes me the "no panty" shot for an entire class, and then says, "Where you goin', fella?" as I get up to leave, but I'm the one who's told not to come back? I think the teacher was jealous; hell, with that chick, he may have been banging her too. The worst part was I wasn't even into her, and certainly not enough to go for it in the school, but I'd used three sixteen-ounce malt liquors to wash down the two valiums I had for breakfast; in that state, all bets are off.

I would later miss the advantages of wandering the halls to search out girls and the drugs of the day. Tommy was expelled about a week earlier for drug possession on school property, so we'd have to sneak in and pull a fire alarm, emptying the whole damn place into the main lot if we needed to see someone during the day. It was risky but effective. The sad thing was both Tommy and I had the ability to pass the classes, we just couldn't be bothered. We were avid readers with diverse interests, but neither was willing to sit through the endless hours of nonsense to be part of the program. Confronted with total freedom, the drugs and alcohol completely took over our daily routine. Days were now filled with intoxicated adventures and sexual deviance with most any willing participants, and the occasional narcotic-induced attempt on each other's lives.

Tommy and Missy dated off and on for years, but it seemed she finally had enough of the debaucherous lifestyle he reveled in. Publicly, he was disinterested; privately, I knew he was becoming dangerously obsessed with her. The holidays are tough enough for garden-variety, drunken, pharma-laden cowboys like us, with family pressures and personal struggles; throwing Tommy's obsession with Missy into the mix finally brought the festering to a head.

I returned from California with my family after my sister's winter break; my educational future was still perilously up in the air. During the trip, I scored some Lemon 714 Quaaludes and was in a hurry to restart the party. I went over to Tommy's to begin where we left off; instead, I walked into a highly turbulent situation.

The music from inside was even louder than usual. Iron Maiden was flooding the neighborhood, accompanied by indecipherable screaming. I entered through the garage on the lower floor, the way I always did, passing the beautiful Camaro I'd become fixated with owning. The two-story townhouse had a bedroom and a den downstairs, with a bathroom that doubled as a laundry room. Upstairs was a kitchen, living room, and a master bedroom suite with a bathroom. Upon entering, I noticed the living area was totally in shambles. Tommy's guitar was smashed into the television, its neck protruding from the imploded tube. The glass table we typically used to do coke and other assorted drugs on was shattered, and through the music I could hear Missy screaming. Missy believed she and Tommy could remain friends following their breaking up, which explained why she was there in the first place, but I viewed this as a colossal mistake. Suddenly, Missy flashed past me in the hallway and into the downstairs bathroom, slamming the door behind her. She was wearing only a bra with jeans and evidently didn't notice me in her hysteria. I was hidden by the wall of the stairs she came down. Within seconds, Tommy came down the stairs declaring that her soul was gone and now her body was to follow.

At six feet two inches, maybe one hundred and seventy pounds with long curly black hair, he was your typical "heavy metal banger." He had in his left hand a nearly empty half-gallon bottle of gin, the kind with a handle, and in his right, the huge Ginsu knife I still have a scar from due to an earlier incident.

For a moment, he stood stunned by my presence interrupting his rage as I moved into his view at the base of the stairs, but he quickly dismissed me with the ultimatum, "Leave or you'll die too," as he reached the bathroom door.

I wasn't unfamiliar with his episodes, and to be fair, we both had unsettling tempers, so I just reached into my ski parka and produced the prescription bottle that held the Quaaludes, shaking them like a maraca and shouting, "714's, dude, the real deal, all the way from California."

He paused at the bathroom door, which was riddled with indentations from the bottle, his fist, and that damn knife, just long enough to focus on the prescription bottle. Our eyes met and a smile slowly crossed his lips, replacing the expression of fury that previously contorted his face, his eyes still wide and psychotic. "Well give me some, you fuckin' beach boy pussy."

I turned and went up the stairs, leaving him yelling profanity at Missy, me, or perhaps some unknown demon that gin seems to bring to all men. By the time he reached the top of the stairs, I had turned down the stereo to a more manageable decibel range and was seated at the kitchen table, pill bottle in front of me.

"So, what's up, dude? How was your Christmas?"

"How many 'ludes' you got?"

"Enough for all!"

"Gimme one," he demanded, repeatedly glancing over his shoulder at the stairway behind him.

"Sure, dude."

"Mmm, Lemons."

"Straight from SoCal, door to door delivery. So, what's Missy doing here?"

"Fuckin' cunt's cheating on me."

"I thought you dumped her a while ago" were my words, but both of us were well aware of the actual facts.

"Yeah, well she's fuckin' that little bastard Andy and I'm gonna kill her."

"In your mom's house?"

"Why not? I oughta kill her too."

"That's cool. Got any beer?"

He sat down across the table from me and mumbled, "Yeah, in the fridge."

"Your step-dad won't mind?" I asked while opening the can back at the table. Tommy smirked while downing a "lude" with the last of the gin. "Tell ya what, dude, why don't ya kill her at her mom's house, you know, so we don't have to deal with the cops," I suggested, almost believing my own faux sincerity.

"I oughta kill that pig too."

Just then, the downstairs bathroom door flew open as Missy charged out into the garage, finally fleeing into the streets of Wayzata. I convinced him we'd go get her later, but soon after the "lude" kicked in, Tommy forgot she'd been there at all.

Missy was a case worth studying, her light brown hair so effortlessly sweeping across her shoulders and eyes the wildest shade of green. She was around five and a half feet tall and in great shape from years of various sports. I guess you could say she had natural beauty, the "Ivory Girl" look, not flashy. My favorite thing about her was her laugh, the way it was so honest. Her eyes would squint, her cheeks turned flush, and the softness of her voice would warm your heart. She was from a good family that loved her dearly, and she loved them. She was an A-student and had been a cheerleader and involved in many other legitimate extracurricular activities; but the day she saw Tommy, that was it. If he wanted rain, she'd have built a ladder to shake a cloud. I think they both fell so hard in love the moment they met that life's details were lost in an instant; but some things just aren't meant to be. Her mother hated Tommy; her dad threatened him; but she, their pride and joy, adored him. Sadly, he just couldn't accept her love for what it was and always painfully waited for her to leave. Trust just wasn't in his DNA and hope just couldn't leave hers.

MMY RELATIONSHIP WITH KYLIE ENDED ALMOST AS QUICKLY AS IT started: just two parties long. Sometimes it was hard to tell where one day ended and the next began, but parties are a good way to measure time when you're in a fog of booze and narcotics. The first party was at this guy Stan's house. Stan and his sister Jenny had a lot of parties because their parents were never around. I had been there since Friday on this particular occasion, and by Sunday night Jenny and I were sitting on her bed doing lines on her makeup mirror. During the week, Jenny was serious about school, but come Friday night, she liked to party with the bad boys who she wouldn't even look at within the school walls, namely, her brother's friends. It wasn't her fault if they were always around, or so she told her "In-school" friends.

Jenny asked, "So are you still going to Minnetonka?"

"Don't know yet. They tossed me out of micro-world."

She blushed and said, "I heard about that. You're crazy."

At that moment, I noticed the moisture on her powder blue sweatpants. Jenny was all worked up over me. There's just no accounting for chemical attraction or the lure of a bad boy.

"So, who do you go out with these days?"

"Nobody," she offered abruptly, and then in a softer tone added, "No time with school and work."

I leaned forward, nuzzling my face into her plentiful breasts, and slid my hand gently along her thigh until I felt the wet cotton of her sweats on my index finger. She leaned down and kissed my neck near my T-shirt collar after gently brushing my hair out of her way.

"I love your hair," she whispered; it was light brown and fell just below my shoulders in an easy feather, kind of like David Cassidy of "Partridge Family" fame.

When our eyes met again, we were contemplating the teenage dilemma of whether you kiss after oral sex and believing just once without a condom won't get a girl pregnant.

Jenny introduced me to Kylie, knowing she was as insatiable as I was. You see, Jenny was going to do something with her life, and so I was to settle for the occasional good fortune of a nightcap on her pillow, always on a Sunday night, always after the majority of weekend warriors had left, and always waking up alone on Monday morning. She'd of course be long since gone to school, having rejoined the real world for another week's grind. I'd look around at the many stuffed animals and little framed pictures while I dressed in silence, and then I'd just smile and close the door behind me as I left. I'm not sure where their parents were; I never saw them.

"I just know you'll get along," Jenny said as Kylie and I shook hands as if being introduced at some business function. We were both already secretly pondering where we could consummate our meeting, which is more or less par for the course with teens in heat, especially when booze is in the mix.

Kylie declared me her boyfriend as she searched for her panties in the back seat of my mother's Jeep. The next weekend my mom and Robert went away; I guess it could've been worse timing or circumstances, but I can't imagine how. Tommy quickly chased my sister and the house sitter away to a hotel with promises of upcoming satanic rituals, and the party became inevitable.

I got two kegs and sat them on the upper tier of our multi-level back deck, wrapped them in blankets as insulation to prevent freezing, and then got on the phone. When Kylie asked why I was having a party, I said, "I don't know, it's my birthday. Who cares? Just come over and bring people," in a wise-ass tone. It was not my birthday, but it takes time to learn that girls will hear what you say and not what you mean. Kylie arrived with several people, most of whom left quickly due to the riotous climate; a girl named Mallary was among them, but she remained. Kylie was petite and beautiful, a blue-eyed blonde with double "D" breasts like most of Minnetonka's Scandinavian settlers. Mallary was a tall and slender brunette, brown-eyed, and quite stunning even at just seventeen years old. After two fights, hours of brutally loud music, and a second visit from the local law enforcement boys, none but Tommy, some red-headed chick that Tommy was making nervous, and Kylie remained. Kylie told me it was time for my birthday present and that I should wait for five minutes before coming down to my room. It took me a second to recall my birthday comment, but I agreed without resistance.

Our house was a sprawling, L-shaped, two-story palace set high above the cove with the best view in the neighborhood. My room was downstairs, with its own bathroom, family room, and entrance from the yard through giant glass doors. After Kylie headed downstairs, I spent a minute reassuring the red head that Tommy had never actually killed anyone I knew of, or at least not in my presence, before locating a bottle for the impending birthday nightcap.

I entered my room with a bottle of Robert's chilled champagne after deciding to play this birthday thing to its fullest. After all, the odds of Kylie still being my so-called girlfriend when my real birthday came were slim at best; and besides, she seemed pleased with the evening's progression so far. The shock on my face must have been obvious because both Kylie and Mallary giggled gleefully as I shut the door behind me. All the surfaces in the room now had lighted candles on them. On my desk was the mirror in the shape of a ship's wheel that I often used for doing lines with friends during my more intimate gatherings. Centered against the back wall was my king-size waterbed; on it was a birthday cake with burning candles and the two young ladies lying on either side of the cake, wearing only panties and smiles.

Kylie said, "That's for you," pointing to the mirror, "You're gonna need it, honey," and then they sang, "Happy Birthday," in stereo with a Marylin Monroe-type tone.

Upon closer examination of the mirror, I saw at least two grams of coke spread out in a large heart-shaped line. I sat down at my desk facing the mirror, admiring my situation and thankful Tommy was upstairs; otherwise, he'd never believe me. I was snorting from the heart-shaped line when Kylie appeared on my left holding the cake with eighteen tiny candles burning dangerously close to the cake's top. "Make a wish and blow out your candles, birthday boy," she whispered in a sultry tone.

"What could I possibly wish for?" I replied in all sincerity and blew out the dripping candles.

"This is for later," Kylie said, placing the cake on a dresser nearest the desk.

I got up and took the mirror with me over to the bed, setting it next to Mallary's slender thigh, and then I handed my fourteen-carat gold straw to Kylie.

"I hope you'll both join me."

Mallary spoke up. "It's your night. Whatever you say goes, don't cha' know."

My heart was pounding almost audibly.

Kylie handed the straw to Mallary saying, "I've had enough," and then she turned to me and sat down on the padded side rail of the bed, pulling my shirt free from my torso, telling me, "You need to get a little more comfortable."

I slipped out of my Levi's and crawled onto the bed while carefully handing Kylie the mirror after Mallary did a good-sized line, which she placed on the desk behind her. Both girls wore white silk panties, although Kylie's had a large band of lace around the edges. This was every guy's fantasy, and these two amazing ladies had an agenda to see it through.

Mallary pulled me gently to her side; she reached across me with an arm and kissed me hard on the mouth. Meanwhile, Kylie smoothly glided into position above me, lowering herself until I disappeared within her. I climaxed quickly due to the thrill of the situation, and Kylie slipped off to one side, playfully tugging Mallary's panties off in the process, saying, "Well, you wanted to learn," as I lay in bliss.

"I hope you don't mind," Mallary sheepishly whispered as she turned around, now facing Kylie, my half-erect partner in crime between them.

"It usually takes a little while for it to get hard again, but it'll be easier at half-mast anyhow." Kylie explained, "It's just like a Popsicle," complete with a demonstration.

I noted that kissing after oral sex is definitely okay for future reference, and as my eyes rolled back with the pleasure of being the instrument of this lesson, I saw the true splendor between Mallary's thighs. I guided her leg across my chest until her sweet treasure was mine to enjoy. This was undoubtedly as close to total ecstasy as I had ever been. When I awoke to Tommy spreading the last of the heart into equal lines, I doubted that it had been real until he said, "I would have killed you in your sleep if I didn't want to hear the details so badly." A true friend would have killed me.

Kylie was in the smoking lounge talking to some friends when I arrived on Monday for a scheduled meeting with the principal. She was ranting and raving about something to one of the girls standing with her. I said, "Hey there," as I passed by the group, her back facing me as I spoke.

"You asshole! You think you're pretty cool don't cha'?"

"Me?"

"Yeah, you! Tommy told me it wasn't your birthday on Saturday; it's not even close."

"Listen, Kylie, I'm sorry about that, I..."

She interrupted me. "Sorry? You sure are sorry, you son of a bitch. I can't believe you pulled that shit on me. You think because you're rich you can do whatever you want. Well, fuck you!"

"Fine," I snapped in retaliation. "I only wanted Mallary anyway."

With that, she attacked me, punching and screaming too many obscenities to recount. I shoved her into her friends and said, "Hold her or she dies," and then started back to the Jeep having concluded this was obviously a bad day for school issues.

The Camaro was parked one row over from my Jeep. Apparently, Tommy was there to sign his expulsion papers, as he was now eighteen and it was required to keep the law off his ass. This also explained how he bumped into Kylie, whom he didn't particularly care for, and assuredly took the opportunity to antagonize her with the tidbit of knowledge about my actual birthday. I left a note that read, "Nice job with Kylie!" I placed it under the wiper on the driver's side of the car and was heading for the Jeep, cursing him as I went.

Ron was coming up from the path when he saw me walking away from the Camaro. "What do ya think you're doin', dude?"

We were less than friends by that point and had exchanged unpleasantries on several occasions. I spun around, teeth gritted, and yelled, "Fuck you," and then continued toward the Jeep. When he tackled me to the pavement, the smell of pot was powerful. After a brief struggle, I was on top. Poor Ronny was too stoned to fuck let alone fight so I got the better of him; admittedly, I was a bit overzealous about it. Chalk it up to bad timing. Ron never spoke to me again, even when he later attended a party at my house.

When my eighteenth birthday came and went without payment of my promised settlement from the car accident, I hired an attorney to look into it. I learned of Pete Wolf through a friend's father, a wealthy investment broker who did more blow than we did and let us party at his house sometimes. I think he had a brush or two with the law, and I know he lost his stockbroker's license for some less than legal moves, which is how they ended up in Minnesota from NYC. Anyway, he told me Pete was exactly the kind of legal wizard I ought to get connected with.

Pete was maybe thirty years old, single, and not your average lawyer. The first time I met him, we did lines on his massive mahogany desk. He understood what the $50,000 settlement would mean to me and quickly cut through the stop payment initiated by my mother's attorney in New Jersey. She hoped that when I turned eighteen I'd be more mature, would see the value of money, and would be in pursuit of higher education as opposed to a never-ending party. She hired a lawyer to postpone my receipt of the money when it became apparent that I had yet to see the light, but once I was eighteen there wasn't much hope of keeping me from the cash. Of course, I saw the value of money clearly, but I didn't see much benefit in higher education, especially when I was quite certain that with the money in hand, I could be making more money than most people with degrees ever would.

The papers were signed in early January and payment followed soon after. Once all was said and done, and seemingly every attorney in two states was paid, I received nearly $37,000. A $10,000 retainer was left with Pete, in addition to his fees, in anticipation of legal problems a lifestyle like mine can bring. I thought fondly of my security blanket and trusted him implicitly.

IT HAD BEEN A FRIGID OCTOBER NIGHT IN NORTHERN JERSEY WHEN Dave pulled the just completed '70 Cutlass out from the garage. After two years of knuckle-crushing work, she was as fast as she was pretty. The gold, metal-flake paint sparkled as the 454 cubic inch engine idled slightly off beat due to the oversized Cam at her core. Dave was so excited to have her running that he didn't even take the time to put the chrome wheels on. The anticipation of a Saturday night in his dream car was more than he could bear.

As the evening gave way to the twilight hours, snow flurries filled the sky. A light blanket of earthbound powder covered the Cutlass in the driveway of the best party house in Warren Township, the home of a single mother with two daughters: Allison, fifteen, and Darleen, sixteen, and mom trying desperately to stop the inevitable aging process through vicarious experiences.

Dave and I arrived at the party around 9:00 PM; I sat in on vocals for a set with the band, but after an assortment of pills, liquor and hallucinogens, we ended up leaving hastily to avoid the wrath of the massive boyfriend of the local girl who provided me with what turned out to be an ill-advised oral gratification. Dave, at the tender age of nineteen, was an accomplished veteran of the psychedelic war being waged to this day by America's youth; I, at sixteen years of age, was a recent draftee of such battles. Having no concept of the difficulty in operating high-performance chariots under extreme distraction, I trusted my fearless chauffeur in vain.

The roads were a patchwork of icy hazards not exposed to the brave pilot's vision. It's of little surprise our vessel lost its way on a corner just four miles from the safe homes we journeyed towards. One bridge, one hundred feet of fence line, and two fatefully-positioned pine trees stole my comrade's life in an instant of accelerated travel. For the loss of this fine soldier, his family was awarded a canceled insurance policy on the great machine, while I was bestowed $50,000 for pain and suffering of every nature. Dave was a good man, and like so many before and since, he is missed.

WHEN THEY RETURNED FROM JAPAN, MY MOTHER AND ROBERT were very disturbed by the news of my gathering and the actions causing the relocation of Parish and the house sitter. Tommy was barely welcome in the house before the incident; now there was talk of me being thrown out.

Robert grabbed my shirt as I entered the house, pulled me down the hall into the master bedroom, and shoved me onto the wooden chest at the foot of their bed. "Reno, before I left, I told you three things. What were they?"

"Don't buy the Camaro, go meet with the principal, and don't bring anyone into the house."

"Whose car is that in the driveway?"

"Mine."

"You bought the goddamn car. You never saw Principal Townsend, did you? And then you bring that son of a bitch, Tommy, and all your other fucked up friends into my house. What do you have to say for yourself?"

"I guess I'm out."

"You're goddamn right you're out! And, you can have your things when you pay your twenty-five-hundred-dollar phone bill from calling that fucking girl in Pennsylvania all the time. Do you understand why I have to do this Reno?"

"Yeah, can I go now?" I just wanted to retreat. He was right, of course, but the coke was clouding my thought process so badly I couldn't even stay focused on the conversation.

"You just don't get it, do you? You're missing the big picture. I told your mother I'd straighten you out, get you pointed in the right direction, but you're always high on dope. No one can reach you," he concluded as he frowned and lowered his head in obvious disgust.

"I'll bring over the twenty-five hundred on Tuesday and get the rest of my stuff."

He was silent as I left the room. My mother had tears in her eyes when I walked through the open door into my room.

"Reno, I couldn't argue with Robert about asking you to leave; how could I after all that took place? I just don't know what to do for you."

She was a caring woman, but everyone has limits, and rightfully so.

"I'm in a hurry mom. Don't worry. I'll see you Tuesday." I spoke without looking at her, pained by the moment as well but not wanting to show it. I grabbed my shoebox and a handful of clothes before making a hasty retreat from the situation.

She grabbed and hugged me as I passed her heading into the hall.

"We love you but we just can't watch you destroy yourself anymore. You understand that don't you?"

I didn't respond; instead, I pulled free of her grasp as I headed for the stairs. I paused for a moment at the top step, reviewing what the shoebox contained: the title to the prized Camaro, a bank book, all my on-hand cash, roughly five thousand dollars, and a reasonable supply of every illegal substance available in the Twin Cities. I closed the box and walked out the front door.

Eventually, Tommy and I became so crazy that even our wilder friends couldn't take it anymore. They sat us down one afternoon at a guy named Roger's house and told us they thought we were out of control, and they didn't want to go to jail or end up dead alongside us, so maybe we shouldn't come around for a while. We, of course, found their proclamation of us being too crazy to hang out with to be hysterical at the time, and in response proclaimed them all pussies of the less desirable nature. This intervention was on the heels of the story getting out about an infamous trip to Wisconsin involving a rockstar-style motel trashing with an underage girl and a roadblock at the Minnesota-Wisconsin line. It wasn't as bad as the story sounded, she was within a few months of our age and insisted on coming, even though I tried to convince her not to at the party where we met, but the fact remains we were completely out of control. Tommy had already been to rehab once, and only my drug money kept me from that or worse. Tommy and I were arrested for destroying one of several demolished motel rooms in Wisconsin, where the drinking age is eighteen, and although the whole room wasn't worth a grand, they got twenty thousand dollars total out of us from the judge, including punitive payments. We provided fake IDs, but the motel owner got the plate number on Tommy's mother's car, so it wasn't a big leap to figure out we trashed the room. It was crazy; we even brought in tools to take apart the plumbing and to get the bolted pictures off the walls. I had my half of the money, no problem, though I complained the twenty grand was way too much for the damage. Pete Wolf said, "Just pay up and move on;" he always told me that when I whined about buying my way out of trouble. On the day we walked out of court, Pete said, "Okay boys, cough up the green." Tommy had no choice but to turn over the title to the Camaro for the ten thousand I held smiling in anticipation. His only words were, "I hope you die in it." Although Tommy's mother refused to pay for the damages, the funny part was she immediately bought him the Corvette, which was probably worth more than the ten grand, so it didn't make much sense to me. Maybe the loss of the hot rod he painstakingly built with his father was the punishment, or maybe the car pissed her off because of some ex-husband relationship thing. Who knows? However, at that point, our saving grace may have been the distance created between us by the Camaro sale, otherwise, we probably would've both ended up dead.

I've always been a magnet for the craziest people wherever I go, possibly because only they would have any interest in the insanity my drug-addled, alcoholic lifestyle created. Most people just briefly stepped into my world and then quickly retreated for their own preservation, or perhaps the reality of the wild side was just too obscene for their participation. Girls, in particular, liked to visit the madness of the proverbial bad boy world, dipping a toe in the turbulent waters, but none wished to reside there.

<hr>

PART III

Wings of the Angel

<hr>

Wings of the Angel

Lori Ann looked out over the sea of orange cones in the expansive parking lot and felt a sense of pride in her father's declaration that she was ready for the test. He may not have been her first choice for a driving instructor, but his methodical approach was extremely effective in conjunction with the Florida state driving manual he ordered from the DMV.

He smiled and said, "Well, it looks as though my little Seal has grown up and become a woman." He paused, looking her over as though he was seeing her for the first time. "I know you're eighteen, but I hope you know you aren't required to move out as I was at your age. I mean, your mother sure does enjoy having you around the house, so…"

"I know, sir, thank you."

And that was it: they shared another of those rare moments when he let her know he was not only proud, but he loved her, as a father should. In his heart, he knew she'd be leaving soon but he hoped the little pecker-head boyfriend of hers was more of a man than he appeared. His career in the Navy behind him, his daughter all grown up, his wife pushing him to purchase a damn RV to tour the country, what the hell had happened to his world?

"Well, it was awfully nice of the motor pool boys to let us use the lot and cones."

"Yes, it was, very nice of them."

"We'd better get these cones up and head home. Your mom will be ready with chow at seventeen-thirty, sharp. She's one heck of a trooper, your mom. I'm lucky to have her," he concluded, speaking more to himself than anyone.

Lori Ann and Stephen met shortly after the family purchased the minivan. He worked at the Goodyear tire store in town and started talking with Lori Ann while she paced the lot waiting for the new tires to be mounted. He seemed like a nice enough guy and offered to take her to a movie on the following Saturday. Her mother, now being much more open-minded than in previous years, granted permission, and that was that. After the movie, the two went out for some pizza and sodas, and then for a ride in his pickup along the beach in Jacksonville. He was a perfect gentleman and didn't even kiss her goodnight, much to her dismay. She thought he didn't like her, and he was thinking she didn't like him very much. Later, they spoke at length on the phone and discovered they were both incorrect in their assumptions and decided to go out again. They'd been dating for nearly six months, and she made him wait the better part of three months before allowing his fingers to explore her in the way the Lieutenant took for granted. She made him wait another three weeks before she decided to spend the night with him.

Lori Ann began working as a waitress in a restaurant called The Metropolitan on the other side of town from the Base, and on most nights didn't get off until late. On several occasions, she stayed with a girlfriend, Beth, who also waited tables there. Beth's apartment was only two blocks from work, and if they'd been drinking during the clean-up, always after the owner left, she would never drive for fear of losing the license she treasured. Beth was a real party animal at twenty-one years old and loved to take advantage of the fully-stocked bar as a "career perk." She was born and raised in Jacksonville and had four older brothers who liked to get her drunk when they got stuck babysitting, just in case she decided to tell on them she'd have to tell on herself as well. She was a pretty girl: tall, thin, brown-eyed, blonde with lots of guys around, but she only slept with two of them. She'd always say, "I'll pick one, but I'm not done with the test drives yet." She started bussing tables at The Metropolitan when she was sixteen, became a waitress and moved out into her apartment at seventeen, and was just waiting for a bartender slot to become available so she could make enough to buy a little house.

The girls worked hard and made enough money to get by, but Lori Ann saved every penny possible until she could buy the Honda coupe that gave her the freedom she longed for. Her mother said the car was like wings for her angel when she and her father returned home with it. Her father made her look at countless cars and then research the safety, repair history, and fuel economy of each one she considered before buying it for fifteen hundred dollars. Lori Ann loved her car; she spent the entire first evening with it doing a complete detail inside and out before driving it another mile. "The Chief" taught her how to change the oil and a flat but wasn't truly satisfied until she could do a basic tune-up by herself. Lori Ann hated it at the time, breaking nails and cutting her knuckles, but she did like the sense of independence and especially not having to pay someone to do such tasks. Stephen said he'd do that kind of stuff for her, and she let him, but she could do it if she had to, and that mattered more than actually performing the task.

Stephen stopped by the restaurant at about eleven and asked if she would be done soon?

"We're done now, sugar," Beth replied with a knowing grin before Lori Ann could respond to his inquiry.

Lori Ann gave her a little jab.

"Just let me get my stuff and we can go, okay?"

"Cool," he answered, sitting down by Beth at the bar to wait.

Earlier in the evening, Lori Ann told Beth that tonight was the night she was going to "be with Stephen," and that he had no idea she was even staying over at his place.

"Want a beer?"

"Nah, I'm tired and besides, Lori Ann'd bust my chops if I drank and drove again."

"Fine, but I think she meant when ya can't walk."

"I could walk just fine, but she just thinks I'm drunk when I'm not. How come you girls are always talkin' 'bout guy's problems anyhow? Y'all got your own, in my opinion."

"Okay, tough guy, simmer down. Here comes our little angel now."

He just glared at her as Lori Ann reappeared, asking, "Ready?"

"Yeah, let's go."

Stephen didn't appear to like Beth very much but was actually just jealous of Lori Ann's willingness to sleep over with her instead of him.

"So, what's with the bag?" He asked as he opened the door of his pickup for her to hop in.

"Well, I thought I might stay at your place tonight, if you don't mind, that is?"

"Damn right, I don't mind. Hell, I've only been asking for months." He smiled so widely that his eyes almost squinted shut.

Stephen was about five feet ten inches tall and maybe one hundred and eighty pounds at twenty-one years old. He had a baby face, but lines were already forming around his bright blue eyes from so much exposure to the sun. His blond hair was cut short, but not in any particular style, and his belly was starting to show signs of what his beer intake would do for his physique in the years to come. He was a good-looking guy and crazy about Lori Ann but just couldn't get comfortable with his station in life. He wanted to get rich, but the extent of his plan was lottery tickets and selling pot on the weekends. He sold pot while Lori Ann worked, never involving her, as she was pretty straight about that kind of stuff. His fantasy was to be Tony Montana from "Scarface," but he had no plan for that either.

"Good, because I could stay at Beth's if you'd prefer," she added with a teasing tone.

"Bull shit!" He slammed the door after she was in, and then he grinned like a little boy at Christmas seeing the look on her face as he passed in front of the truck. He hopped in behind the wheel and asked, "So, where we off to?"

Lori Ann made a habit of leaving her car at work if she wasn't going home; she felt confident it was safe because no one had ever messed with cars that the many other employees left there as well.

"Let's just go to your place. I don't feel like going out tonight, okay?"

"Sure."

Stephen's place was a rented, one-bedroom cottage in a questionable neighborhood, but okay for a single guy. The only bad thing that ever happened to him was having his lawn mower stolen when he forgot to lock the metal shed in the yard. Lori Ann looked around the little living room as they entered; it was about ten feet wide and fifteen feet long, with a worn sofa against the front wall beneath a window; an old Army footlocker was the coffee table, and the TV and VCR sat on a small, wheeled entertainment unit with two glass front doors below the VCR shelf. There were no pictures on the walls in the living room, but a plastic framed poster of a scantily-clad girl on the hood of a Ferrari was hanging in the little connecting kitchen with a table and two chairs; there wasn't room for the other two chairs, so they were in the shed. A short hallway led to the bathroom complete with a fiberglass shower stall, a sink with a small, wall-mounted vanity unit, and a toilet. His room was about the same size as the kitchen but was filled nearly wall to wall with an enormous waterbed that had drawers built in below. You had to close the bedroom door to open the drawers, or to walk around the other side of the bed, but he loved the bed and didn't care. It had mirrors and lights in the headboard and had originally come with padding on the rails, but a mattress leak ruined the felt. Lori Ann didn't care about his house and figured all guys either had no taste or it just wasn't a priority to them. He was good to her, so that was good enough. However, if they ever did live together, not one thing from the cottage was coming with them.

They settled in on the couch with a couple of beers; he clicked on the TV while slipping off his shoes on the other side of the footlocker where his feet were hanging over. Lori Ann looked at him and smiled, saying, "I appreciate that you've never pressured me about sex."

He interjected. "Well, I..."

She stopped him, warning, "Don't say something stupid that'll ruin it," knowing boys can do that, even with the best intentions. "I want tonight to be special, so turn off the TV and let's talk a while, okay?"

"Sure." He kept his response short, heeding her warning.

When they entered Stephen's house, Lori Ann tossed her bag through the bedroom door onto the bed before joining him in the living room where they sat and talked for about an hour until she excused herself to the little girl's room, as she always put it. He loved the way Lori Ann was so ladylike and never said vulgar things like most of the girls he knew.

Lori Ann called out to him. "Stephen, can you help me with something?"

When he got to the bathroom she wasn't there. He opened the bedroom door and saw her lying on his bed in an incredible silk teddy that made him gasp. It was black and shiny, with spaghetti straps hanging precariously over her shoulders, and delicate lace trim around the deep V-line in front and the bottom at her thighs. He said, "Damn girl, you are too much."

Lori Ann blushed. "So, can you help me? I'm having a little trouble taking this off."

"Hell, I could help ya lift the house right now!"

"Come here," she beckoned in her softest of voices.

"Yes Ma'am, anything you say."

He pulled his clothes off as he moved around the door, closing it behind him before climbing onto the bed, sending a series of waves across the surface. She kissed him softly, and said, "Let's go slow. We have all night, okay?"

He just smiled, having won the biggest lottery of his life. "Sure, I'm in no hurry."

Lori Ann laid quietly looking up at the ceiling in the early morning hours, occasionally glancing over at Stephen sleeping soundly at her side. He had been gentle, and the experience was nice, although the second time was longer than the first, and she'd become a bit uncomfortable toward the end. She now knew why Beth liked sex so much, but still wondered why many girls needed more than one man in their lives. Lori Ann felt that sex was very personal, and her body was not for just any guy's entertainment. On the other hand, she had waited a long time for the right guy and was not going to be so long without this pleasure again. She knew how important sex was to men and planned to keep her man satisfied in every way possible. Lori Ann's mother said, "There may be things you won't like sometimes with men, but if your husband's needs aren't met at home, you'll always be left to wonder where they are being met." That wasn't going to be an issue with Lori Ann; so far, she liked what her man liked, and that was all the better. She moved carefully onto her side and kissed him softly on the ear as she enjoyed the faded smell of his aftershave mixing with the fragrance of the room.

Lori Ann stayed at Stephens house at least a few nights a week over the following months and worked hard to save money toward a home they would call their own. Stephen was ever diligent in chasing a quick buck, but as long as he worked hard at his day job, she didn't see any reason to give him a hard time about his aspirations for wealth the easy way. So, when he and a friend looked into ways to make some money, and he promised there would be no trouble, she left him to pursue it without interference. Lori Ann didn't use drugs at all until Stephen but had come to believe that a little recreational usage on the weekend wasn't the worst thing a couple could do; and if Stephen could feel like a big deal by selling a few joints to his friends, so what, it wasn't like he was some big-time dealer.

It was just another day when Stephen's friend Marty called him at work from Miami and said he'd found something amazing while enjoying an early morning surf. They grew up together and were inseparable until Marty moved south when his father relocated during their senior year in high school. They spoke fairly often on the phone, and occasionally a weekend road trip would reunite the boys for some "beer drinkin' and hell raisin'." This was different though; Marty sounded scared when he spoke and just told Stephen they needed to get together as soon as possible. Stephen knew Lori Ann would be angry about time off from work, but Marty said, "Big dollars, dude," and that was all Stephen needed to hear. Lori Ann argued as expected but eventually gave in to Stephen's request for a three-day leave of absence, and so he was off to Miami with a bag of sandwiches and some cookies she baked for his trip. He promised to call and stay out of trouble, and of course, he'd let her know what the big secret was as soon as he learned himself. She wasn't a distrusting sort and never felt

Stephen was less than trustworthy, but his fixation with the Florida drug dealer lifestyle, as seen on TV, in opposition to their reality began to trouble her. Her biggest concern was he might not be satisfied with the life they'd likely share, and his inability to reconcile with it was disheartening at times.

PART IV

The Party

The Party

As I pulled into the driveway of the big empty house, even the rumble of nearly five hundred horses beneath the hood of the fastest car in town brought no joy to my freedom. Dustin met me at the door, joking about hearing my car start at my old place, Robert's home, just a few miles away. He tried to improve my sullen mood with some good news as we walked down the stairs into the basement devoid of furnishings.

"We are going to party tonight, a blowout, and Laurie's coming."

The thought of Laurie warmed my cool heart and offered hope of a bright spot in an otherwise crappy day. I had a big bag of good blow and a nice house I rented and might even furnish someday. The only thing missing was a limousine, or so the stories went about Laurie.

The party was as advertised. People came at all hours for three days. Dustin was all he had promised. He was never out of my sight for even a moment. I hired him and rented the house soon after I got the insurance settlement. I was becoming paranoid from the cocaine and believed someone would kill me for my money. Dustin was an imposing guy, tall and built like a tank, and had served three years in Joliet State Prison for armed robbery; he was more than enough body-guard for Minnetonka, even without his trusty thirty-eight caliber pistol tucked in his pants. During the three days of Rock-n-Roll and sexual freebies from every coke-whore on the lake, we sold more than we consumed, which is definitely a priority if you're a dealer. I was rolling in cash.

I wondered why Laurie didn't come to the best party in Minnetonka history, but she was so aloof that it was anybody's guess. Tommy came the first night but just couldn't be around the Camaro without the keys in his pocket, even if he did have a nice Corvette now. He would only come to the house to pick me up. We never took my car on any excursions; he wouldn't even sit in it, nor did he allow me to share stories of beating other cars in street races, which was frequent because everyone wanted a shot at the renowned Camaro. My purchase of that car forever changed the dynamic of our friendship, even if he had no other alternative at the time.

The ride to downtown Minneapolis was a short twenty minutes. We enjoyed the time out of the house, and with Dustin in the passenger seat, pistol in his lap, I felt as safe as being in my own home. However, stepping out of the car in the small Columbian neighborhood with seventy-five hundred in cash made even Dustin seem insignificant; and although he'd never admit it, I saw a twinge of concern in his eyes every time we walked through the guarded upstairs apartment door. We always knew, while stepping over the passed-out junkies in the stairway, that we might have just seen daylight for the last time; but $10,000 in cash profit for ten minutes surrounded by Uzi-toting South Americans was too good to pass up.

"You sure the gun's hidden?"

"It always is, and you always ask. Just relax."

Once inside the large apartment that consumed the better part of a floor, you needed only to locate the drug you wished to purchase. In each of the doorless rooms were young men with Uzi's or sawed-off shotguns. A man either sat at one of two desks on opposite sides of every room facing each other or at a single desk facing the doorway, depending on the product they offered. The desks were either wood or metal and seemed to be dilapidated office furniture. Two wooden or folding metal chairs sat in front of each desk for buyers, and no more than two customers seemed to be allowed in a room, or more specifically, at a desk per transaction. On each desk were small quantities or samples of the drug the particular man sold, a scale if necessary, and a pistol off to one side of a plastic work surface. We walked through the first room glancing at the desktops left and right, and then continued down the hall, passing armed guards, looking in each room as we went until we saw Jose sitting at the sole desk in the center of a room's back wall. It seems cocaine always warranted its own space.

I said, "There's Jose," without looking at Dustin. They frequently changed up the rooms that each drug was offered within, but it was always Jose that had the coke. Entering the room meant passing the space's expressionless Uzi-toting guard with his back to the entrance wall, which always ratcheted my blood pressure a notch or two, even after all the others you had to go by, but at least you knew nobody would bust in and interrupt the deal.

"Hi, Jose," Dustin casually greeted with his hands held open and loosely away from his sides, his trademark smile from ear to ear. His smile and the twinkle of his deep blue eyes offset his enormous size and potentially intimidating appearance, calming people in his presence; that, and his open-handed posture, kept even these men at ease, or so it seemed.

Jose weighed maybe ninety pounds and was best described as frail, but if any fear was present, he concealed it masterfully. With a wide-open hand, I offered Jose a handshake; he accepted with a friendly smile. We knew him as Jose, not because he spoke English with any noteworthy conversational ability; he did not, but rather via the patting of his chest during our first meeting and him saying, "I Jose," and then gesturing for us to sit in the chairs in front of his desk.

Jose slid a small mirror across the desk towards us after cutting two generous lines from the mound. Dustin did his line, one shot up his left nostril, and sat back in his chair with a silent wink of approval. He said on our first visit to this place, "You do the talking and I watch your back," and this worked fine for me.

I divided my line into three sections by switching nostrils with the straw, and then, using my index finger to pick up what remained, I tasted the powder as though I just finished a candy. The quality was top-notch, just as I'd come to expect from Jose. I briefly paused, like a connoisseur tasting a fine wine, offering, "Okay," with a subtle nod. Jose gestured toward the small mirror indicating I may have another sample, but with my raised hand he knew it was time for business. Jose pulled the small mirror toward himself and gently to his right side, and then on the return motion turned on the digital scale at his left, facing it so we could both see the number display. I reached my right hand into my ski parka's inside pocket, and a sudden movement behind us had Dustin up and turned around. Jose leaped to his feet, hands held high saying, "Esta Bien, Esta Bien," repeatedly to the man now just feet from Dustin, holding an Uzi in a fully extended arm. I slowly pulled the rubber-banded roll of money out for display to Jose, also making it visible to the unnerved guard. Jose repeated, "Okay, okay, okay," broadly smiling while calmly placing his pistol down in the same location it had been. It later occurred to me, there was no commotion in the other rooms because of our exchange; they clearly didn't perceive us as any real threat, or at least not one that couldn't be quickly and deftly handled within the room we occupied. However, sensing our tension, Jose swiftly thumbed through the roll of hundred-dollar bills I purposefully placed on the desk, keeping my hands visible as I returned to my seat. He pulled out a large Tupperware container from one of the drawers. With a chrome scoop, he shoveled one hundred and seventy-one grams, just over six ounces of rock and powder onto the basin atop the scale.

Jose asked, "Si algo es aceptable?" looking for my consent.

I don't know exactly what he said but I knew he was checking my satisfaction with the deal, so I replied, "Okay," having done the quick math and seeing a clear bargain without turning to see Dustin still facing the man behind us. Dustin never went for the pistol, which is probably why we didn't die on the spot, but he also never turned away from the guard to return to the seat beside me. He just stood, casually looking him in the eyes with his hands just slightly away from his hips, a kind of prison showdown where nobody needs to move, it's all very clear, and it'll soon be over if everyone can just stay the fuck calm.

Jose offered me a tiny spoon with a long handle, intended for me to test the bulk product against the sample I had been given. I declined by shaking my head "No" and saying, "Esta Bien," one of the few

Spanish phrases I picked up along the way; with that, he removed the basin from atop the scale and poured the contents into a Ziploc baggie that he handed me, still open. I carefully folded the baggie at the top, and with thumb and forefinger zipped it closed.

To my surprise, Jose rose from his desk and followed us down to the Camaro. He pulled out a small brown glass vial from his pocket, similar to the one Laurie used that first day of school, but his had the spoon attached by a little black chain instead of gold. He handed it to me, asking, "Okay?" with the eyes of a trusted friend. I patted his shoulder and added, "Gracias, Jose," and quickly climbed into the driver's seat, pulling away on route to the freeway. Dustin grabbed the bag from me and without a word, put it in the small leather satchel I'd strapped to the springs under the passenger seat for concealed carry of various items. Not a word was spoken the entire ride home, but what is there to say when you know you could've just as easily been dead five minutes before.

I PULLED UP THE WINDING DRIVEWAY AT ROBERT'S, GLANCING DOWN at the rubber-banded twenty-five hundred dollars sitting on the passenger seat next to my shoebox. Parish stood outside near the far side of the four-car garage that constituted much of the L-shaped side of the house. She was talking to Brittany, who lived next door and appeared to be upset, judging from her body language. I didn't get along with my perfect little preppie sister very well, but I would not allow a third party to cause her angst in any circumstance. When I stepped out of the Camaro, now parked nearly dead center of the garage doors, Parish looked over at me as if she had just noticed my presence, which was impossible with that car.

"What's up kiddo?"

"Nobody's home and Robert said you're not supposed to be in the house unless they're home."

"Yeah, well, I got his money and I need my stuff, so let me in."

Brittany spoke briefly in a voice too soft for me to hear and then waved in my general direction as she trotted up the lawn towards her house. I seemed to always make her nervous, but I didn't know why other than my less than favorable reputation. Parish and Brittany must have just gotten home from school because she had to use the alarm code to get inside the house. I glanced at my watch, saw it was 3:00 PM and thought, "Where do the days go?"

I paused at the first plateau on the stairs and asked, "Everything all right?" before continuing down the stairs toward my room.

"Don't forget to leave Robert's money," she answered while heading toward the living room, oblivious to the target of my concern.

It was not apparent that my room had been searched, which I appreciated. I rifled through the walk-in closet's floor until I found my sleeping bag, grabbing some shoes that turned up in the search. I noticed moving boxes sitting in the sunken living room when I came in and chuckled to myself with thoughts of them sneaking off in the night with my stuff. After filling the bag with assorted clothing and a pillow, I pressed the intercom "all call" talk button on the wall.

"Parish, where are you?"

A moment later, her voice came through the speaker: "Kitchen."

I dropped the stuffed sleeping bag in the foyer at the top of the stairs, placing my boom box gently on top before heading for the kitchen.

"Going somewhere?"

"Fucking Tokyo."

Her discomfort in using the word "fuck" in casual conversation amused me.

"Vacation?"

I helped myself to one of Robert's beers in the fridge as we spoke.

"No, we're moving." She decided that condemning me for my drinking was futile at this juncture.

"Are you serious? Why ya goin' to Japan?"

I joined her at the table located in what's known as the breakfast nook section of the enormous kitchen.

"Yeah, next month. You'd know if you ever came over. Robert's got some great opportunity in Tokyo, and there's an American school that's supposed to be really good."

I sat silently, thinking of how, "See ya Tuesday," had turned into months.

"Robert said you could come if you straightened up your act."

I angrily considered them leaving without even saying goodbye until it occurred to me that they didn't know I was so nearby. I could have been dead for all they knew.

"Are you going to come?"

"Look kiddo, I can't go to some other country halfway around the world. They'd lock me up for sure." The latter statement was directed more to me than to her.

As I walked toward the telephone, Parish softly said, "Not if you didn't do drugs."

Ignoring her proclamation, I told her, "Here's my number; don't give it out, but if you need anything, you call me, okay? And thanks for sticking up for me. I know they'd rather have VD than me in Japan to worry about."

Parish just smiled, knowing it was useless to argue, and asked, "Are we going to see you before we leave?"

"Sure. Just call me and I'll come over, okay?"

"Okay."

I handed her the sticky note with my number at the house and "love ya kiddo" written on it, and then walked out of the kitchen without another word. I picked up my stuff in the foyer and tossed the twenty-five-hundred-dollar roll of cash on the small table in the mirrored alcove next to Parish's keys, and then took another look around before walking out the tall double doors of Robert's house for the last time.

At the top of the hill where Minnetonka Boulevard intersects the entrance to Crystal Cove, I saw Brittany standing by the stop sign. I tapped the horn and waved her over. Brittany was petite, about five feet two inches and maybe a hundred pounds. She was a cutie with longish brown hair and bright green eyes, wearing a soft-pink, down coat that hung past her knees, and tiny Nike sneakers with glimmering pink laces, triple knotted to keep them off the ground. I was shocked when she opened the door and hopped in saying, "Hi!"

I offered a smirk and asked, "Do you need a ride somewhere?"

"I was supposed to meet my friends here fifteen minutes ago but I was late. We were going to Missy's house. I think you know her."

She said this all in one breath. I hadn't heard so much from her in all the times I'd seen her with Parish combined.

With Tommy in mind, I said, "Well, I don't think you should be hanging out at Missy's anyhow."

"Why not? She's cool," Brittany defended with a sparkle of mischief in her eyes.

"Hmm, do you party?"

"Yeah, all the time. I was supposed to go to your last party but Missy couldn't find it."

I had to laugh to myself. Thank God she's bad with directions. If Tommy found out Missy was over there while Andy was there buying drugs, he might have killed us all.

"Where are you off to?" She asked while fiddling with her seat belt.

"I was going home to drop off my stuff." I pointed to where I'd just placed my shoebox with the sleeping bag behind her seat. I had been holding the box since she jumped in, nearly sitting on it in her exuberance.

"Then what?"

She was a little too nosy even for a high school girl. I looked at my watch; it was about 4:10 PM.

"Then I've got to see some people later on."

"Just 'cause I hang out with Parish doesn't mean I'm some virgin ya know. I party all the time."

"Does Parish ever party?"

"No way. We were just fighting about that."

"About what?"

"You better go," she suggested, motioning over her shoulder at the small collection of cars now waiting behind me.

The tires spun on the cold pavement as I crossed the boulevard to turn left.

"I love this car. It's so cool."

"Thanks. But I don't know if you should be at my house. You're kinda young and..."

In truth, I was only a couple of years older than Brittany, and a lot of younger girls hung out at our house during parties, but none were even casual acquaintances of my sister. Brittany pushed in the Mötley Crüe tape that was protruding from the deck, and "Red Hot" came on.

"Red Hot! I love this song. Vince Neil is way gorgeous."

In the end, she seemed cool enough, so I just headed home without real concern for her joining me. Brittany roamed around the big empty house while I put my sleeping bag and boom box into a downstairs room I used for privacy and to sleep on the rare occasions that it occurred. I was glad to have the sleeping bag because the blanket I'd been using for a mattress left a lot to be desired. I could've bought a bed, but it never occurred to me except when I laid down. I let her wander alone upstairs because there wasn't anything but a few beers in the fridge on the entire floor. Dustin and I primarily lived in the two bedrooms downstairs. We set up a wet bar in the common area to avoid the walk up two flights of stairs to the kitchen for beer. Only a big party or the occasional dope deal at home found us in an upstairs room. It was perfect for parties; people could use the rooms upstairs for sex or whatever. There was nothing to break or clean on the whole floor.

Brittany popped her head into my room. "Do you have any pot?"

"Yeah, just gimme a minute to get organized here, okay?"

"Cool, can I come in?" She asked as she padded across the room and plopped down Indian style on her coat, now in a pile on the floor. I did not respond. "Can I help?" She moved on her hands and knees next to me while I folded an Iron Maiden concert T-shirt. Tommy and I went to many concerts since I got the money, mostly front row, and often in a limo after a few instances when we were unable to remember where we parked and froze our asses off while waiting for the damn parking lots to empty.

"Thanks, but I think I've got it."

She was already straightening the piles of clothes along the wall and mumbling something about how boys can't fold. As I leaned back against the wall, opening my shoebox in search of a joint, I looked at her more closely; she was a little hottie in a pink sweater and pleated cotton pants that fit as if they were painted on.

"Have you ever done coke?" I was not in the mood for smoking dope, and it was always time for a bump.

"I tried one time, but the guy sold us baby powder or something." She rolled over ending up next to me against the wall as she spoke.

"Wow!" She was looking into the shoebox I held open on my lap. "What is all that stuff?"

"A lot of stuff you don't need in your life."

"Please tell me." Now she was leaning against me looking intently at the many various-sized baggies.

"What have you done?"

She paused and then smiled. "Oh, drugs? Well, I've smoked pot a lot and tried black beauties to lose weight. Do ya think I look good?"

"Probably too good for your age," I responded while noticing her ample breasts.

"Thanks." Her eyes sparkled. "Can you get coke?"

I had to laugh out loud at the question. After all, I was on my way to becoming one of the biggest coke dealers on the lake. "I'll let you try some but don't ever tell anyone you were even here, okay?"

"Sure, but can I come back sometime and see you?"

"We'll see."

Just then, Dustin rounded the corner, pistol in hand. "Shit man, I didn't know you were home."

He hurriedly stuffed the pistol into his pants. Brittany gasped but didn't scream, which was surprising considering she didn't even know this lunatic. When I asked her later why she didn't scream, she answered, "I knew I was safe with you." It made me feel good that someone could have faith in me.

"I parked the Camaro in the garage so nobody would know I was here."

"Should I leave or...?"

"Nah, it's cool man, we're just hangin'."

Brittany beamed at being included.

"Well, I'm not alone. Have you got a little candy for me? We'll go upstairs."

"Sure, dude, but don't feel like you gotta hide out on my account."

"Thanks, bro'."

I tossed him a full eight ball of coke from a large Ziploc baggie filled with smaller bags.

"I'll be upstairs then, okay?"

"No problem. Glad you're home, Dustin."

"I'm on the job."

He disappeared down the hall and up the stairs. My deal with Dustin was simple: For a thousand dollars a week, free rent and all the drugs you need, be my bodyguard. He loved it and had already earned his keep several times.

"Should I close the door?" She felt safe enough but still preferred to reduce the likelihood of another armed lunatic surprising us without at least a knock.

"No need but go ahead if you want to."

I laid out a gram of good coke from my uncut stash onto the mirror I picked up from the Jamesway at "7-High." I never did the cut stuff, even when offered it after a sale. My response was always, "Don't waste it on me. Enjoy." The lines were small for my taste, but I didn't want to get Brittany too high to go home. Her eyes widened as she looked at the lines.

"Twelve is a lot, isn't it?"

"Just do one up each side and see how you feel."

A few minutes later, she did two more and then asked if I thought it was hot in the room.

"Well, your sweater may be the culprit."

She promptly sat back on her shins, looking into my eyes, and without a word, pulled it over her head.

"Feel better?"

"No. You're wearing your shirt."

"I'm not hot, though."

Brittany pouted and looked down at the floor.

"Okay, okay." I pulled off my T-shirt.

"Thanks. I feel more comfortable now. How come you don't have a girlfriend?" She moved back next to me against the wall.

"How do you know I don't?"

"You do? Who is she?"

"I don't. I was just kidding." I laughed at the expression on her face.

"Don't tease me. I don't like it."

"I'm sorry Britt, I don't like it either."

"Why'd you call me that?"

"What?"

"Britt. Nobody calls me that."

"Sorry, I won't..."

"I like it when you call me that. Call me that from now on, okay?" She was glowing; her pupils dilated with cheeks flushed from the coke, but I could see earnest pleasure from being in my company. It was nice to have something so innocent in my world. Most of my experiences with girls had become very transparent, almost transactional. Her motives were genuine, and it was attractive, even if she was too young to take seriously.

"Sure Britt, if it makes you happy."

"You make me happy." She spun around, resting her head on my thigh."

"I'm glad." I looked down at her while running my fingers through her hair, brushing it away from her face.

"Do you think I'm pretty?"

"Why? Don't you?" I snapped, not meaning it to be quite so intense.

"I guess so, but there's a lot of better-looking girls in school."

"Does that matter?" I asked in a calmer tone.

"I guess not. Do you like me, Reno?" She looked so defenseless lying there, staring up at me.

"I'm not the guy for you Britt. Get a guy with a future, okay? You'll be much better off; I can assure you."

"Why, don't you like me?" Her arm was now behind her head, resting on my groin while looking at the ceiling like the stars in a late-night sky.

"Britt, if I didn't like you, you wouldn't be here, okay?"

"Good. I like you too. I always have."

"You don't even know me."

"Yes, I do. Everybody talks about you ever since you guys moved in."

"I'll bet."

Ignoring my statement, Britt asked if I wanted to see what her aunt got her for Christmas.

"Sure, why not."

She kicked off her sneakers and stood up. I could see her sway for a second from the head rush of standing so fast. Then, she slipped out of her slacks, tossing them on her coat. "What do you think?"

"Of what?" I asked, thinking of Laurie and how her trademark color was pink.

"My lingerie. My Aunt Chrissie got me four pairs for Christmas."

Her panties were soft pink and matched her bra; both had narrow outlines of white lace on the edges.

"Looks good to me." I admired her standing on display.

"You really think they look good?" She struck a smooth and probably practiced pose.

"Yeah, I really think so." I moved slowly toward her on my hands and knees, rising to my knees as I neared her.

"I'm glad you like them. They're my favorite."

On my knees in front of her, I lightly kissed her navel while slowly moving my hands upward along her calves and thighs until they rested on her firmly rounded bottom. She quivered as my tongue flicked along her torso. I felt her bra graze my back as she released it, allowing it to fall to the ground. With a gentle nudge, we moved to the wall, her back arched, head tilted with eyes closed. I nibbled at her panties as they pulled free with a tug of my fingers, unveiling her secret desires, so steamy with anticipation. As my lips met the sweet heat of her excitement, her knees buckled, and she fell into my arms. I gently guided her to the floor, holding her tightly and with great care. Her eyes were now wide open, beckoning the moment of our joining as she gazed into mine, looking up through her curls. Just as she gasped for breath in desperation, I moved up and forward, entering her in one smooth motion. Speaking in words without definition, we conveyed sincere gratitude for the pleasures we shared. Finally, we collapsed as one, spent of life and absent of cares, unconscious in our shared glory. Dustin's knock at the door woke us both.

"Yeah, what's up?" I shook off the fog I'd been blissfully resting within, trying to gather my thoughts as I felt myself slip free of Brittany's warmth, bringing a gentle sigh from her. She ran her fingers along my back and kissed my open mouth, only to taste herself on my lips. She reached down and wriggled to guide me back inside her eager depths as Dustin spoke.

"It's 7:15, dude. Are we gonna meet those guys or...?"

Brittany twitched as reality crashed through the haze, her muscles contracting and pushing me free. "I've got to get home," she said, much to my relief, because I sure as hell wasn't taking her to a drug deal, although, I would've preferred to spend the rest of the night within her grasp.

"Yeah. Eight o'clock, right?"

"Yeah. Well, it's a haul. We better get movin' if we're gonna make it."

I stumbled to my feet and opened the door. "Can you run Britt over to Crystal Cove for me so I can get my shit together?"

Britt was kneeling, wrapped in her coat, looking around in the after-euphoria of intimate pleasure and cocaine.

"Sure, dude, no problem." He was unfazed by my nudity.

"Five minutes, okay bud?" I wiped the sleep from my eyes, equally unconcerned with my state.

"Sure man, five minutes. I'll be in the car waitin' for her." He turned and headed toward the stairs, running a mental checklist for the upcoming drug deal.

"I've got to meet some people, Britt, but gimme your number and I'll call you later, okay?"

She smiled while pulling up her Christmas panties and asked, "Gotta pen?" in a sensual tone.

"It's in the box." I grinned slyly and then turned to look through the now meticulously organized piles of clothing for something to wear.

"Your whole life is in this box, isn't it?"

I looked at her beautiful breasts still exposed, so perfectly round with her silver dollar nipples now relaxed and smoothly conforming, and replied, "Yeah, I guess so," thinking no one had ever been in that box before, and judging from her glow, no one had ever been other places before either.

"Are you a virgin?"

"No." She answered without looking up from the notepad.

"No Britt, I mean before today." I moved beside her as I spoke, gently moving her hair from her face as I tenderly kissed her cheek. "Were you?"

"Not really, I did it once before, but not like that. I hope you're not mad."

I leaned in close again, taking her soft face in my hands, bringing her eyes to my own. "Of course I'm not mad. Your life is your own, as are your choices, so don't buy into anyone's bullshit judgment. Dustin will take you home and I'll call you later. I promise." I kissed her on the forehead and then softly on the lips, smiling warmly as I exited the room, nude, towel in hand.

Dustin and I returned home after 3:00 AM, kind of late to call Britt at home. Several times throughout the night, while taking larger orders and noting appointments in my little pad, I read the note by Britt's number.

Dear Reno,

Today was wonderful! Thanks for everything.

Love, Britt

555-2561

P.S. Don't call too late or my mom will flip out.

This was not the note of a little girl. She was cool, and I enjoyed her company.

At 6:15 AM I did another fat line, gave Dustin a nod, and walked out into the garage. I wondered if Britt took the bus and what Parish would say when I pulled up to the corner of Crystal Way at seven in the morning. I idled up to the street corner, just below Robert's house, trying to keep the Camaro quiet, which was an impossibility. Minnesota has no state automobile inspection, so open headers into short, straight pipes puffing bluish-gold flames from high octane fuel are the entire exhaust system of the car. The redhead from up the street was already there when I cut the motor, rolled up to the side of the road, and waited to see who'd show up next. To my amazement, when the black Mercedes stopped at the corner, after coming from Britt's house, she popped out smiling widely. She told her mom that she'd ride the bus today without mention of me. Her mother sneered at me as she turned to head off to work, or more likely to play some indoor tennis at the country club – no winter-beater for her.

As soon as the Benz disappeared, Britt trotted over and hopped into the Camaro.

"This is much better than a phone call."

"Sorry, I didn't get in 'til pretty late."

"No problem. It's great to see you. So, where we goin'?" She punctuated her question with a kiss on my cheek.

"I thought I'd give you a ride to school."

"Well, if you're too tired to play, I guess that'll be okay."

"Tired I can fix, but you should go to school."

"I'll worry about school, okay smart guy? Got any candy?"

"Sure, the box is behind your seat."

I made a U-turn and headed home, pleased to be able to let someone touch the box without worry.

***

THINGS HAD BEEN PERFECT FOR MONTHS. THE MONEY WAS ROLLING in faster than I could stash it. I placed nearly $50,000 in Tupperware containers and sealed them again in large Ziploc bags. I buried the cash containers in Britt's mother's flower garden until it came time for her to plant, but then I was forced to go back to using banks for some easy access cash, knowing the flowers in her back yard offered better security than federal insurance for the majority of the cash. I deposited nine thousand in one savings account and nearly six thousand in another bank for quick capital without digging up flowers or tipping off the IRS. I had over $70,000 in total, including several thousand in on-hand cash in my trusty box. I looked forward to hitting the $100,000 mark during the summer, and our now frequent parties provided a great one-stop shopping customer base.

Unfortunately, it all went to shit when Dustin shot a nineteen-year-old kid in our kitchen. Britt and I were spending time whispering commentary about the general population of people milling around the upstairs living room of my house during a party on the July 4th weekend. From our position in the farthest corner of the kitchen, we could see most everyone. Dustin was amped out that night; he'd been up for three days and was becoming even more paranoid than me. A friend of a friend brought a guy named Danny to the party. He was having a run of bad luck and thought stealing my now well-known box of goodies would set him up for some long overdue breaks.

Britt saw Danny coming even before I did. He moved with purpose through the crowd toward us, his eyes locked on the shoebox under my arm. Dustin was just on the other side of the counter that separated the kitchen from the living room. There were cabinets attached to the ceiling, leaving a three-foot space through which he watched me intently while chopping lines on the counter that divided us. Danny reached us just as I noticed him. With Britt saying, "Look out," Danny's shoulder hit my chest, driving me into the wall, the box popping out and into his grip. Danny hadn't even made a step towards his retreat when Dustin shot him in the lower left abdomen, spinning him entirely around as he fell doubled over on the floor. I froze solid for a moment, taking it all in on a two-second delay, and then flashed rage at the balls of the guy for trying that shit in my house; but little Britt, with tears in her eyes, picked up the box at my feet and began pulling me through the scattering crowd of stunned burnouts while I watched the aftermath unfolding behind us. Dustin slipped over the counter, screaming at Danny, who lay confused and bleeding on the floor. I regained my composure as we reached the split-level's landing at the front door, satisfied that Dustin was taking care of the attacker.

"Britt," I shouted over the music and now doubled crowd noise, "We'll never get the car out." I was motioning towards the front yard and driveway now cluttered with people and still packed with hotrods and borrowed family cars. Brittany was weeping openly as the events began to become real in her mind. "C' mon!" I took her hand and moved down the lower stairs towards the basement and out the sliding glass door into the backyard. We ran silently through yards and side streets but were still a good mile from her house when we first heard a siren. We scrambled under a raised deck as one siren turned into many. The police came down Minnetonka Boulevard from both directions until they turned on Woodview and headed for the house. In our silence, we could hear the pounding of our fearful and confused hearts. I ran the events through my mind, again and again, considering Dustin's reaction from every angle. Was this my fault? Had I created a timebomb?

Months before, Dustin and I were at a party in Shorewood one night when a stranger cornered me in a room with a knife saying he wanted my box or he'd kill me. Eventually, I made eye contact with Dustin, who was in an adjoining room, oblivious to my situation. When he saw the look on my face, he quickly pushed through the crowd, grabbed the guy from behind, and disarmed him as he entered the room. Holding him with his head snapped back by the hair, his pistol under the guy's chin, he asked, "What's the problem here, Reno?" simultaneously applying substantial pressure to the man's body against the wall.

"This fuckin' guy tried to rob me, man. He said he's gonna kill me for the box, and you're hittin' on some fuckin' chick while I'm unarmed with all this shit! You know I don't carry. This box is enough fuckin' risk without a fuckin' gun charge on top of it; that's why I have you!"

"Should I fuckin' kill him?"

"Wait a minute, dude," the guy pleaded, struggling to speak due to the pressure on his throat. "I'm not gonna kill anybody." His eyes were bulging in pain.

"You're not doin' anything mother-fucker, 'cept maybe dyin'. So shut the fuck up."

I stepped around them and closed the door, turning back to face them. Dustin threw the guy to the floor with a sideways motion, effortlessly sweeping his wobbling legs from beneath him. They hit with a thud, and on contact, Dustin began full rounded swings into his face, still holding the pistol but using it as a club. After six or eight shots to the face, the guy was nearly unrecognizable, but Dustin was relentless. "You dumb mother-fucker. You wanna fuck with me. I'll kill you!"

I grabbed at Dustin's shoulder. "Dude, that's enough, we don't wanna kill him." It was the kind of beating dispensed in reform school or jail; it was brutal, one that carries a message.

"What do you think this piece of shit would have done to you? This ain't no fuckin' game, Reno. You better wake up."

"I know, dude, thanks." He was right of course, but I also didn't need my bodyguard wrapped up in a murder charge.

Dustin leaned in close to the man's battered face. "If I ever see you again, I'll fuckin' cap you so fast you won't even hear the shot. Do you understand me?"

He did not respond; only the bubbles of blood in his mouth indicated he was still breathing.

"Let's go, Reno. We gotta bail." Dustin delivered a parting kick to the ribs of the lifeless body.

His crushed face smelled like iron from the blood when I leaned in close. "This coulda gone the other way for you mother-fucker. Be glad I let you get outta here alive." I shadowed Dustin out to the Camaro and we headed home. Later, once we both calmed down, he apologized and promised no one would ever get near me again.

"Man, I can't believe this shit," I whispered to Britt as we sat in the dirt, quietly waiting for a chance to continue our escape. "I am so fucked. The house is rented in my name, the Camaro is in the garage, and my fuckin' ex-con roommate shoots a guy in the kitchen."

Fear and anger jockeyed for a hold on my thoughts as I considered the incredible circumstances unfolding around me.

"It'll be okay. You can stay at my house. You didn't do anything wrong."

"Britt, I'm like the biggest coke dealer in Minnetonka. Shit, you don't think those punks are gonna talk when the cops start pulling bindles of coke out of their pockets? I sold over an ounce of coke tonight. The cops are havin' a fuckin' hay-day right now."

Britt smoothed the hair back from my face. "I won't leave you, Reno."

"Leave me? Are you serious? My life is over. My mom's in Japan, I haven't spoken to my dad in a year, and old 'Peetie' Wolf is gonna charge me big time for this mess, and I'm still goin' to jail. Why did he have to shoot him? He coulda jumped in and taken him down no problem."

My retainer was just about gone after I took the Jeep down an exercise path in a State Park one night. I was so drunk that when the cop asked me if I had been drinking, I held up my drink and replied, "Are you serious? You think I'd be out here at 3:00 AM sober?" Pete got me off with some fines, an evaluation of my "drinking problem," and a ninety-day revoked license, but it cost me dearly. I gave him cash out of my box the night he bailed me out, that is after he brought me back to the church parking lot where the cop let me leave the Jeep since I was so cooperative, almost jovial. He never even searched it, and the shoebox was on the floor of the passenger side the whole time.

Pete said, "It'll take five G's to get you out of this mess."

My reply was, "You got it, dude. You're holding ten on a retainer."

"No, I mean additional cash, no questions asked."

I handed him the money from the box and then he said, "Go home, be good, and call me in a week," before turning on his heel and walking back to his car.

Britt rested her tiny hand on my shoulder and tried again to reassure me. "It'll be okay."

"Yeah, your mom's gonna love this. The guy who's not even allowed in your house is moving in. Oh, and by the way, I'll be fuckin' your daughter."

Britt snapped. "Don't say it like that."

"Okay, okay. I'm sorry Britt, but honey, I'm under a little stress here, so give me some room, all right."

"What about all the money in the garden?"

"Yeah, that's the last money I'll make sellin' shit in this town."

When I woke Brittany up, it was almost daylight. I sat up all night looking out over the lawn from under the deck and doing spoons from Jose's little vial. She fell asleep on my lap, looking so peaceful and innocent. Shit, she was so innocent. What the fuck was I doing with this kid hanging around my insanity? It was just a matter of time until she got hurt by my recklessness and it had to stop.

"C'mon, we gotta go," I whispered, nudging her gently.

Once at her parent's house, Brittany let me in through the window in her bedroom saying, "I should've done this a long time ago," as she grabbed at my pants button.

"No, not now. Wait until everyone leaves."

I crawled under the bed and stared at the backside of the dust ruffle, afraid to make a sound. Mrs. LaBeau came into the room around 7:00 AM to get Brittany up for some family outing we knew was planned. I lay silently, holding my breath while they bickered about Britt's not going, her mother telling her, "No more late nights for you, young lady," as she walked out.

Once I heard the automatic garage door closing, I waited five minutes for the forgotten-item syndrome. When they did not return, I slid out from under the bed. As I sat against the wall watching Brittany sleep, I wondered if she was the proverbial "one" and maybe I was just missing it. Just then, I thought of Lynn.

In many ways, I loved Lynn without even having sex with her. We met during the summer we moved to Minnesota from New Jersey, while my sister and I were staying with family near Pittsburgh to allow my mother and Robert to handle the move. I was physically stunned when I spied her across the parking lot sitting with her friends at a picnic table. A group of my cousin's friends were playing basketball in the lot behind an elementary school, but all I saw was her and I was instantly consumed with desire, wanting nothing more than to be with her. After the two weeks passed and Parish and I went on to Minnesota, we talked on the phone most every night for hours, hence the twenty-five-hundred-dollar phone bill at Robert's house. I'd call late at night, after being out drinking on our boat or later partying with my newfound friends, and she'd stay on the phone with me until she had to go to school. Early on, I thought once I got the money, I could get her and we'd run off to some island, happily ever after — what a concept. Eventually, Lynn set me free to live life in the reckless abandon I was accustomed to, saying she could never live in my world regardless of her feelings towards me. By that point, I'd become distracted by Laurie and my lifestyle anyway, but she'd been special to me no matter how you cut it.

I walked from Britt's room knowing what had to be. Once outside, I quickly found the little shovel I used on the frozen ground and again just recently in April before Mrs. LaBeau planted her precious flowers that were now in full bloom. As I dug, carefully piling the uprooted flowers off to my side, I thought of Britt. I had treated her well; money was no object. She even had a pair of two-thousand-dollar diamond earrings I bought her after disappearing for three days. I was at the Le Luxe Hotel with a twenty-five-year-old coke-whore who taught me exactly how to please a woman in exchange for the half-ounce of the good stuff we freebased in her pipe. I told Britt I was jailed for being in First Avenue underage, a rocking nightclub in the heart of Minneapolis that was featured in Prince's Purple Rain movie, and I couldn't reach Pete to bail me out until Monday, the day I got home. When she asked why I didn't call her, I said I was embarrassed to have been caught and knew she couldn't bail me out anyway. Britt wanted so desperately to believe me that she just did, and that was the end of that, although the tears she shed when I gave her the earrings may not have been from joy.

When I hit the first container, I was almost surprised as if I had found someone else's buried treasure. I carefully removed the four containers and stuffed the empty Ziploc bags back in the hole. They were nasty from the mud and time; the Tupperware was still perfect.

I took a small backpack out of Brittany's closet before going outside with my shoebox in hand. A T-shirt probably used for gym class was in the pack; it smelled like Britt, so sweet it made me sad. I laid the shirt out flat on the grass and placed fifty hundred-dollar bills divided into two stacks on it, and then rolled it up and folded it in half. Five thousand dollars should buy her a nice first car in case Mom and Dad weren't feeling generous when she got her permit in December. I would have given her more, but I didn't know when I'd be able to sell again or even if I could get my money out of the banks.

I considered the pack that now contained $48,000 in cash, nearly an ounce of uncut blow, a quarter ounce of good pot, several bags of pills ranging from Black Beauties to Valium, the Camaro title, my note pad and pen, and two bankbooks. Forty-eight thousand dollars was a good stake to hold me over, but man I wanted my car back so bad I could taste it. I sure did love that sweet Camaro.

I snuck back into the house, leaving the pack by the garbage cans on the side of the garage. I tossed the little shovel in the trashcan along with the shoebox just to punish Mrs. LaBeau for being such a bitch. I went into the kitchen, washed my hands, and picked up the phone. "You better be home," I mumbled as I dialed. On the eighth ring, I heard his voice, but it was his answering machine saying, "You called me, so tell me what you want and maybe I'll call ya back." Nice, I thought.

"Beep."

"Tommy, pick up the phone. C'mon, dude, I gotta talk to you."

"What the fuck do you want? It's 9:14 AM; this better be good."

"I need you to sit up and listen to me." I said this knowing if he was still under the covers of his waterbed, he wouldn't get up even if he wanted to.

"Yeah, that's likely," he joked, still groggy.

"Tommy, I'll give you a thousand dollars if you get up and pick me up at Crystal Cove in forty-five minutes."

"Hold on a second."

I could hear the bed sloshing; this was a good sign.

"Now, what did you say?"

"I said it's almost 9:15 AM and..."

"I know that," he interrupted.

"Shut up and listen."

"Fine, shit."

"At 10:00 AM, exactly, I need you to be parked below Robert's old house by the boat dock. I'll meet you there on foot. Be there and I'll give you a grand. Okay? Can I count on you?"

"Where's the Camaro?"

"It's gone, man. Look, I've gotta go. Will you be there or not?"

"What do you mean it's gone?"

"Jesus, Tommy!"

"Okay. Have you got any blow?"

"Gimme' a fuckin' break." The last of my patience was exhausted.

He said, "I'll fuckin' be there," and then slammed the phone down.

I was confident he'd show up, and probably on time, but I should have asked him to get a newspaper so I could see what was in the morning news about the party and the dumb-ass kid who got himself a bullet.

I snuck back into Britt's room with the rolled-up shirt full of cash in hand. As I walked past the bed and carefully opened the bottom drawer, I thought about writing her a note, but what would I write? "I'll miss you. Good-bye." It's not like we were in love, although I did care for her, but she was a sweetheart and I didn't want to hurt her any more than I had to. At that moment, I almost woke her to say, "C' mon, let's go, I'm taking you with me." I had to chuckle to myself, feeling like a character in a bad movie. Suddenly, a way to at least leave her with something heartfelt popped into my mind. In the back of my pad, late one night, I wrote a poem thinking I was going to OD and die. Before I left, I would give it to her since it was kind of like a goodbye note, and a lot sweeter than anything I could pen in the moment. I placed the shirt full of cash under a pair of her jeans and quietly closed the drawer.

After quickly removing my clothes, I slipped into her bed; it was a canopy style with white frills draped along all the sides. Brittany asked me many times to have sex with her in this bed; I always declined, unsure of when her mother might return. She was wearing an extra-large T-shirt to sleep in as many girls do. She stirred slightly when I eased the big shirt upward exposing her fuzzy little friend, as she coyly referred to it. I always enjoyed performing oral sex on her for extended periods, but today I was pressed for time. So, as she awoke, I moved lovingly, removing the shirt and resting my weight on her naked body. She quickly orgasmed, probably from getting her wish fulfilled in this manner, but who knows with women. Anyway, we men are just lucky to be any part of their anything. My orgasm came moments later as I gazed into her soft green eyes, concurrently wishing I wasn't privy to my plan.

"Mmm, I wish I could wake up like this every day."

"Why don't you get in the shower?" I tried to pull free but she held tight with her entire body.

"Oh, don't go yet," she softly pleaded as she moved the sheets away, climbing on top of me. How could I deny her anything on this morning? I felt like, somehow, she should know, like the deceit in my eyes would give me away. With her tiny hand, she guided my half-relaxed member into her saturated depths, renewing my erection in short order. Afterward, I felt so guilty, laying there wrapped in her warmth, her breath smoothing across my chest once she'd fallen limp in conclusion. I glanced at the clock on her nightstand: 9:51 AM.

"C' mon Britt, hop in the shower, I've got a lot to do today."

She slid herself free of our bond and in one motion, spun sideways and rose to her feet. She grabbed a robe from her closet and turned to me. "Ya comin'?"

I said, "No, I'll take one later," now sitting at the edge of the bed.

"Okay. I'll be right back."

She walked out the door, her effortless little sway tearing my last heartstring. Guilt is a useless emotion, but when you're wrong, you're wrong and there was no way around my being all kinds of wrong on this morning.

The clock read 9:54 AM as I tied my second sneaker and dashed through the house out to the backpack; I fumbled through its contents until I found the pad, flipped to the back, and tore out the poem on the last pages. I sprinted back to the room with the backpack in one hand, pages in the other. The shower was still running in the bathroom just next door; the clock read 9:56. I sat on the bed and placed the pages on her pillow, smoothing the pillowcase in lieu of her hair in my final goodbye. As I headed down the hall, passing the bathroom, she turned off the water. I felt a wave of nausea rush through my body. In just moments, I was out the back door passing beneath her window and then charging through Robert's old yard. I leaped off the tie wall that formed the sweeping driveway and was at the dock entrance right on time.

Seconds felt like hours while waiting for Tommy to arrive, and I had just decided to go back to Britt and explain my leaving in person when the black Corvette sped around the corner and rotated one hundred and eighty degrees in a perfect skidding stop within twenty feet of me. As I climbed into the car, my emotions took over, guilt washed over me, and my eyes welled with tears. Tommy was looking past me, out the passenger window and said, "What the fuck is this?" I snapped my head to the right and saw Brittany running barefoot through Robert's yard, her robe flailing about from her stride down the hill.

"Go, man. Now!"

Tommy slammed the accelerator to the floor, howling in laughter as the car lunged forward leaving a cloud of smoke and dust in its wake. "She must really suck in bed if you'd pay a grand to sneak out."

I hung my head in my hands as we raced along the windy lakefront road, wishing a big tree would end my misery.

Brittany collapsed in the grass on the edge of the road, trying desperately to finish reading the small pages she grasped in her hands through the tears in her eyes.

I thought I'd smiled in the sunshine, I thought I'd cried in the rain
I thought the wind was an angel, who'd come to take my pain
But now I have awoken, and I remain the same
Once I came across a lady, she was all that she could be
And as I grew to know her, she shared her gifts with me
Lovers are like fortunes, quickly found - more quickly lost
The thing to know of lovers, your heart must always pay the cost
You see, life is like a rainbow, ends cannot be seen
And to the one who reads this, you know just what I mean

She was lying on her side, curled up like a child in the throes of life's pain when a police detective pulled up.

"Are you all right?"

"Leave me alone."

"Miss, are you sure you're not hurt?" He stepped out of his unmarked patrol car.

"Just go away."

"Miss, you're not clothed. I, uh, can't leave you here like this."

"What are you talking about?" She looked up at the older man, clad in an off-the-rack suit.

"Uh, well you're exposed Miss, and I, uh, are you sure you're okay then?"

Brittany looked down at herself, exposed by the robe pulled behind her waist. She quickly wrapped up as she stumbled to her feet on the sloped lawn. "I'm sorry, I didn't know. I wasn't, I mean, I've gotta go."

"Miss, excuse me. Miss," he called to her as she started up the lawn. "I'm detective Brockway. Do you live here?" He held up his police badge as he spoke.

"No, I live next door." Her eyes were tearing up again. "No one lives here anymore. They moved."

As part of his new hire package, the house had been purchased by the corporation Robert was working for in Japan and they hadn't sold it yet.

"Miss, may I ask your name please?"

"Britt."

"Miss Britt, do you know..."

"No, Brittany, Brittany LaBeau."

"Oh, Miss LaBeau..." He cleared his throat. "Actually, it's you I wanted to speak with. Is there somewhere we could talk for a few minutes? I just have a couple of questions if you don't mind."

"Well, I, what's the problem officer?" She was regaining her composure.

"It's Detective, Miss. Is that your house?" He gestured up the hill to the second house on the left.

"Yeah."

"This will just take a few minutes. I'll pull my car up if it's okay with you?"

"Sure. Let me get dressed and I'll let you in through the front, all right?"

"That'll be fine, sure."

As Brittany turned to walk up the lawn, he noticed her putting the small, crumpled papers into the pocket of her robe.

Tommy was still amusing himself as we pulled up to the townhouse.

"So, what? She wouldn't swallow and you just had to go?"

"She did everything right. Can we drop it?"

"Sure, sure. Hey, dude, where's your magic box?"

"Huh? Oh, It's in the bag. Everything's in the bag. I hope you've got some booze in the house."

"Yeah, we'll hit mom's cabinet. They're out of town 'til tomorrow." He unlocked the front door as he spoke.

"Good. I need a drink."

"Rough night, huh?"

I did not respond, nor did I notice Missy's car parked on the street out front. He grabbed a bottle of tequila and sat it down in front of me.

"So, what's worth a grand to get away from?"

"Oh, yeah." I reached for the bag.

"Forget it, man, but I could use a jump start to wake me up. I can't believe it's only ten o'clock, on a Sunday no less."

"Let me get my head right and I'll fill you in. By the way, where were you last night?" I handed him a large baggie of coke from the pack.

"Wow, dude! Obviously at the wrong spot. I went to a party with Missy in Excelsior."

"Now I really need a drink. She's not dead, is she?" I asked only half-joking.

"Nah, she's asleep downstairs. I didn't know what you were into, so I left her here."

I took a long swig of the bottle and almost gagged. "Are you ready for this?"

"Yeah, shoot." He looked up from the long lines he was spreading on the table, oblivious to the irony.

BRITTANY OPENED THE DOOR, LETTING IN THE DETECTIVE. HE carried a notebook and manila file with him.

"So, what's this all about Detective?"

"Is there somewhere we can sit down, Miss LaBeau?"

"Sure, right through here." She led him into the kitchen and sat down at a small table in the corner.

"There was some trouble at a party last night; it was near here, and I was wondering if you could clear a few things up for me."

"Like what?"

"Did you attend a party last night, Miss LaBeau?"

"Yeah, obviously you know I did or you wouldn't be here askin' questions about it, right?"

"And was Mr. MacNab there?"

"Yeah. It's his house. Could you get to the point please?" She was more angry than nervous.

"Yes Ma'am. And at what time did you leave this party?"

"I wasn't wearing a watch."

"Okay. Did Mr. MacNab leave with you?"

"No. I left alone."

He looked at some papers. "Hmm, are you currently dating, uh, Reno?"

"We broke up." Her tone turned sad again.

"Is that why you were so upset this morning?"

"I guess so."

"And what was the break-up about?"

"Are you serious? That's none of your damn business."

"Well, yes, I am serious. Are you aware a young man was shot at the party you attended?"

"No. Who was shot?" She tried her best to look shocked.

"Did you know many people at the party?"

"I knew some. It was a big party."

"Do you know where Reno MacNab is now?"

"No."

"When was the last time you saw him?"

"Last night."

"At the party?"

"Yes." She was getting restless.

"Do you know what time you last saw him? Perhaps there was a clock on the wall."

"No, there are no clocks on the wall."

"I suppose that's true. Why do you think he has such a large home with no furnishings?"

"I don't know. Why don't you ask him?"

"Perhaps you'd be more comfortable if we continued at the police station?"

"Are you arresting me?"

"No, no. I'm just trying to locate Mr. MacNab so I can ask him some questions."

She pulled out a cigarette. "I told you I don't know where he is."

"You know, you really shouldn't smoke Brittany."

"Are you through then?" She flicked her cigarette firmly into the soda can on the table.

"Just a few more questions please." He reviewed his notes and then continued. "How long did you two date?"

"Not long. Why?"

"Are you aware that he's known to be a drug pusher?"

"A drug pusher? Man, are you serious?" She laughed with a nervous smile. Although "pusher" was a funny term, the truth remained, and she knew I was in deep.

"Do you use drugs and alcohol, Miss LaBeau?"

"Yeah, I'm on heroin right now."

"If that's true, it would explain this morning and I'll have to take you into custody."

"Look, officer, I don't do any drugs, okay?"

"It's Detective, and would you be willing to submit to a drug analysis?"

"Ya know, my father is a lawyer downtown and I don't think he'd appreciate you accusing his daughter of being a dope fiend."

"Do your parents know about your relationship with Mr. MacNab?

"Of course." She lied.

"When do you expect your parents to return?"

"I don't know."

"Would you tell me if this description of Mr. MacNab is accurate, please? Five-foot-eleven inches tall with brown hair worn beyond his collar, blue eyes, and approximately one hundred seventy-five pounds."

She did not respond, thinking of how he felt on top of her earlier that morning.

"Would you say that is an accurate description of Mr. MacNab, Miss LaBeau?"

"I guess so." She wandered off in thought again.

"Do you have any idea where Reno is, Brittany?"

"No idea at all."

"Here's my card. If you hear from him, you'll call me, won't you?"

"Sure."

"Also, please have your father call me at his earliest convenience, okay?"

"Why him?"

"Just do it, okay? I need to speak with him today."

"Yeah, fine."

"Just one more thing, Brittany. Do you know a Mr. Cascella, Dustin Cascella?"

"No."

"Okay, Miss LaBeau, thank you for your time. I'll show myself out."

Britt was silent. After he left, she put out the cigarette under the faucet while looking at the business card: Detective John Brockway, Minnetonka Police Department. She picked up the phone and called Missy.

"Hi, this is Missy. Leave a message and I'll call ya back, I promise." "BEEP."

"Missy, this is Brittany. Call me as soon as you get this message. It's Sunday about 10:00. Bye."

It was almost noon when Missy came up the stairs wearing one of Tommy's concert T-shirts.

"Tommy, have you heard from Reno today? Oh!" She was startled seeing me sitting at the table with Tommy. Britt had not recognized Tommy's car in her emotional state; she'd probably only seen his car once or twice and didn't make the connection, so Missy had no idea we were together.

"Brittany just told me about the party. What cha' gonna do?"

"I didn't hear the phone ring," Tommy interrupted, accusingly.

"She left a message at home and I called her back. She said the cops were at her house today and I'm supposed to go get her."

"Why ya checking your messages? Fuckin' Andy-boy 'sposed to call you today?"

"No! You know my mom leaves me messages on my machine before she goes to work."

"Relax Tommy, she's here with you. So, what did the cops want?"

"Brittany said they were there forever but basically they just wanted you."

"Tommy, we gotta get outta town, man."

"Go where?"

"I thought I'd get a room downtown at Le Luxe."

"Can we meet you guys later?"

"I don't want to get Brittany involved in this shit, well any more than she already is. She's a sweet kid but I think it's best if I don't see her again."

"Brittany won't come here. She said to tell you she understands why you left now and that she misses you."

Tommy was eyeing her. "Then who is 'we' Missy?"

I sat silently, feeling some relief that Britt understood my choices.

"Oh, Laurie's heading downtown to her sister's place, and I told her I'd get her later anyway, so I thought we'd come over and hang out for a while."

I spoke up, rejoining the conversation. "Laurie who?"

"Laurie Borne." Missy grinned as she said Laurie's name, fully aware of my history with her.

"Get a limo!"

"That's not true, Tommy, but she does like you, Reno, and Brittany was too young anyway you cradle robber." She looked at me sweetly with a little chuckle to lighten the moment.

"We'll be at the Le Luxe Hotel under the name Reno West and you're welcome anytime."

Reno West was the name on the fake ID I purchased through one of Pete's contacts; I swear it was a real license, and it should be for the one-thousand-dollar price I paid. In hindsight, West was a dumb choice of surname, but the guy put me on the spot and that's what popped into my head.

Missy kissed Tommy on the cheek from behind and then winked at me. "I'll see you boys later."

"Tell Britt, tell her I'm sorry."

"She knows, Reno. And she also knew it was only temporary with you; how could anyone think otherwise? It'll be okay. So, keep your chin up." She headed down the stairs to be on her way.

"I gotta take a shower, dude, and so should you," Tommy said while getting up from the table. I'm sure I was ripe after my night and morning. "You can use my mom's, okay?" He paused on the third step and added, "If you need clothes, help yourself in my room," and then continued down the stairs.

I leaned back in my chair thinking Britt was more of a woman than anyone gave her credit for, especially me. She'd be okay and was far better off without me, plus I think what we shared was primarily just lust and a convenience of sorts. I needed some kind of stability, any kind, and she needed an escape from her strict household, a perfect fit for the moment, and I believe she quickly came to the same conclusion once the flash of fear from each other's security blanket being pulled away passed. I wondered if I should call Pete Wolf today at home or wait until tomorrow at his office. I decided today had been enough already, plus I didn't need him bitching about Dustin again, especially since now he had a good reason to complain. I did a big line cut from the pile still on the table, grabbed Britt's backpack and headed for the shower.

Tommy and I drove past my house around 2:30 PM; I glanced over at the empty garage and unmarked cop car parked on the street out front.

"The assholes took the Camaro."

"You left it, fucker."

"Yeah well, if I didn't, they'd have me and the car."

"How much cash you got anyway? You know this place ain't cheap."

He was right and it reminded me of the banks.

"Go to '7-High'." I figured they would soon find the bank accounts, but they couldn't have gotten that far yet.

"I thought we were going downtown."

"I've got to empty my accounts before they seize my cash too."

"How much is in the bank?"

"About fifteen-grand between 'em." I started digging in my pack for the bankbooks.

"Holy fuck! You still got that much?"

"Yeah, plus twenty-grand in here." I lied reflexively without even thinking about it.

"Wow! Thirty-five grand. Let's go to Hawaii!"

I thought for a minute: sixty-three thousand is what I will actually have in cash. I could go anywhere. I wasn't so big that the cops would be at the airport, and with my fake ID I could hop a plane easily, although it occurred to me that it was stupid to use my real first name on the ID too. Anyway, an exit absolutely deserved consideration.

"Let's just hit the bank first, okay, big spender?"

"I'm on it."

Tommy's mood was seriously improved as was mine. Although I was scared when I learned I'd have to go inside to empty my accounts, the banks gave me no trouble. After all, it was my money.

We checked into the hotel a little before 5:00 PM. I went directly to the concierge desk and handed him five one-hundred-dollar bills folded in half in a quasi-handshake. "I need a large and very private suite with two bedrooms for a week to start; is that something you can help me with?" The purpose of this was to avoid the usual data-grab at the front desk. In the '80s, the concierge was like a brothel Madam: all about discretion. The concierge smiled and placed the bills in his center desk drawer. "I understand, sir." He picked up the phone and spoke softly for a few moments. When he hung up, he produced a key card from the drawer in his desk.

"I have a suite that will serve nicely, sir, and we can attend to the registration at a later time. You may call me directly with any needs you have during your stay."

In this case, registering later meant never as long as the cash keeps flowing.

"We need more than one room, dude," Tommy complained, obviously not paying attention.

"It's fine, Tommy."

Holding a large handful of one-hundred-dollar bills, I asked, "How much?" the acid test.

"Four-thousand five hundred dollars will cover your first week, sir, and I'll establish a rate for you beyond that. All right?"

He charged me fairly, considering, but didn't provide a discount upfront, probably covering any potential damage expenses in case this was a hit and run, especially since I was paying in cash.

"Thank you."

I handed him forty-five crisp hundreds and he handed me the key card.

"Oh, and sir? What name will your room be under?"

"Mr. West."

"Very good, Mr. West, and thank you for choosing Le Luxe. If you take that bank of elevators," he pointed across the expansive marble lobby as he spoke, "up to the eleventh floor and proceed left, you'll find your suite is the last in the corridor."

I started to cross the lobby but paused, turning back towards him. "Excuse me, sir."

"Yes, sir," he replied, looking up from his desk.

"I'll need two extra key cards, okay?"

"Two, sir?"

"Yes, please."

"I'll give you one now and have the other brought up to your room shortly if that will be acceptable?"

"Fine, thanks." I took the second card from his extended hand.

"Oh, and sir?"

"Yes?"

"The master bedroom will be on the right."

"Thank you."

Tommy was grumbling as we entered the elevator. "What a dick."

"He was fine."

I pressed the button for the eleventh floor after double-checking the envelopes that held our key cards. Ours was the last door in a long hall, with large spaces between the doors; eleven twenty-four was the room number.

Tommy said, "Holy Shit," as I swung the door open.

There was a large foyer with white marble tiles that ended with three stairs into the sunken living area. A pair of sliding glass doors bordered either side of a big-screen projection TV centered on the wall directly in front of us. An expansive wet bar covered half of the left wall; next to it was an open door revealing a large bedroom.

"That's yours." I pointed to the far room.

The living room had a huge sectional in a horseshoe shape with a coffee table on each of the three spans; to its right was a dining table with six chairs surrounding the sizeable, beveled glass top. Closest to my right were French doors with smoked glass insets half-opened, exposing an overwhelming bed with thick wooden posts jutting up from its corners. Also inside the master bedroom was a round glass sitting table with four chairs. To the right of the bed was a wall with a large dresser flanking the bathroom entrance. An enormous shower, twin vanity sinks, and a large elevated hot tub filled the principal space; the commode was stowed behind a pocket louvered door. After surveying the entire suite, including the bar, I spoke softly to myself. "I'm home." It was even bigger and nicer than the one I spent the weekend in with the club girl. I pushed the guest services button on the phone.

"How may I direct your call?"

"Concierge desk please."

"Thank you."

"How may I be of assistance, Mr. West?"

"I'll need the bar double-stocked with full-size bottles and an additional refrigerator brought up as soon as possible, stocked with several cases of Beck's Light."

"Yes, sir, I'll see to it personally."

"Also, I'll need two dozen long-stemmed roses; one dozen with a card reading: 'For my Sweet Missy, with Love, Tommy;' the second card reading, 'I've missed you, Yours, Reno.' I need these double-quick. Oh, and I'll pay cash for all, no room charges, okay?"

"Right away, sir. Oh, and Mr. West?"

"Yes."

"Please accept two complimentary bottles of champagne to be sent with the roses, on behalf of Le Luxe."

"Thank you."

I had only seen Laurie a few times over the past few months, whereas prior to my relatively brief stint with Britt, I'd occasionally run over and take her here or there in the '69 Jaguar XKE she admired so greatly. It was also Robert's pride and joy, so only she could've convinced me to take it out at all, much less in a snowstorm at one point, which ended with us in a snowbank. Fortunately, no real damage occurred on that ride, but I spent hours sitting on the garage floor with a hairdryer and toothbrush getting the snow and grime off each wheel spoke. I'd have done anything for that girl, but I just couldn't hold her attention for more than fleeting moments, especially since it was constantly vied for by older and much wealthier suiters. If this was my one real shot, I was going all in.

PART V

The Miami Run

The Miami Run

Stephen was blown away when he saw the size of the plastic-wrapped bricks of cocaine on Marty's kitchen table, but even more amazed by his story. Marty was sitting on his surfboard about a hundred yards offshore when something bumped his leg. He thought it was a shark at first and started paddling with all his might until he glanced over his shoulder and realized it was just a black, plastic-covered block bobbing in the surf. As Marty caught his breath, the bag floated within a few yards of him, so he eased over to it for a look. "Ya never know what'll wash up in Miami but it's usually just trash from a Cruise Ship or some asshole's Yacht," he explained. When he felt the weight of the bag and its density, he was surprised it floated at all, so he balanced it on the board and paddled in. Once back at his car, he peeled back the black plastic and found a wall of about four-inch-thick Styrofoam surrounding bricks that were duct-taped too tightly to open by hand. He needed a knife to check it out. He brought it home and cut one open while eating a bowl of cereal at his little kitchen table before work, and here is where it sat ever since.

"Holy Shit, dude! Is this coke? It's pink! Are you sure it's coke? Do you know how much is here?"

"Yeah, it's coke. I tasted it. And it's a lot, that's how much."

Marty's eyes shifted quickly around the room and to look out windows as he spoke.

"Hell yes it's a lot! It's fucking pounds, dude! Don't you have a scale?"

"No. What do I need a scale for? I didn't buy it, I found it."

"Who's is it?"

"I don't know but I'll bet they want it back."

"Yeah, well fuck them. They can buy it back or they can piss-off." Stephen was already picturing the Ferrari and coastal home of his dreams.

Marty interrupted Stephen's daydream. "Look, dude, that's why I called you. Do you know someone who could buy it? I'll split it with ya even up, but I want it outta here today. Stephen, people wash up on this beach too ya know, especially people who steal coke from other people."

Stephen thought for a moment but disregarded Marty's concerns. "I know a guy," he lied. "We'll call him later but let's try some of it."

"No! I already tasted it and my mouth was numb for an hour. Take it and go if you want, but I want it outta here today. I'm serious, dude, like now."

"Relax man, I just got here."

Marty was already putting more tape on the incision he made in one of the blocks. "If you don't get it outta here, I'll flush this shit."

"Flush it? Are you fuckin' kidding me? This shit's worth huge cash, dude; why would you flush it?"

"I've been sitting here staring at it since yesterday and then I started thinking about the shit on the news every day: dead guys all over the place, drug-related dead guys. I just want it outta my house and outta my life." Before Stephen could speak, Marty added, "Just tell me what ya get for it and send me my share when ya get it, okay?"

"Can I at least call Lori Ann before I go?"

"Fine, but don't tell her about it on my phone. I mean it, Stephen. It goes today, not tonight."

"Relax, dude. I'll head out after I call her. By the way, do ya have any beer? It's been a long ride."

Marty pointed to the fridge and handed him a cordless phone

before going into the modestly furnished living room to watch the story he was half listening to on the news. The story was about a gang-style killing of four men, and the probability that it was drug-related was being investigated by the Miami-Dade authorities.

Stephen telephoned Lori Ann and told her he'd be home tomorrow, but he had to wait until he got back to fill her in on the details. She wasn't too happy about the secrecy but was glad to have him coming home, so she just told him to be careful and not to be drinking beer while driving. She didn't understand why he'd be driving all night to come home, especially when he just got there, but one thing she knew for sure was not to argue with your man when he's coming home; arguing was for when he's not coming home.

Stephen settled in for a beer and pondered how he'd spend his newfound fortune until reality sunk in: who would he sell this much coke to? The only customer base he had were small-time pot smokers and none would have anywhere near the cash or need for so much coke. He wandered through his mind as if flipping through an imaginary Rolodex but couldn't come up with a single name, and then it hit him: his old buddy Jeremy had gone off to college in Minnesota two years ago and constantly called with stories of beautiful girls and great drugs. Jeremy claimed to know a guy who got the best blow anywhere, and maybe this guy would have the contacts to move such a quantity. Stephen figured he'd call him once he got home, but first, he'd weigh it up and try it for his own quality test. After finishing the beer, he put the four bricks into a paper grocery bag and walked through the front door being held open by Marty.

"Dude, ya really need to relax a little."

"I'll relax when you get it outta my house and preferably outta this state."

"Fine, dude. I'll call ya soon."

"Good. Be careful." Marty scanned the street before closing the door.

Stephen began to feel the exhaustion setting in after being back on the road for an hour or so and realized he'd never make the return trip without some rest. He looked down at the bag sitting on the floor of his truck and thought a little pick-me-up may do the trick. He pulled off into the next rest area and looked around at the others in the parking lot. A few families were walking dogs, a young couple sat in the grass on a blanket, eating, but no cops or security were in sight. He took one of the bricks out of the bag and cut a small incision in it with a razor blade he found in his glove box. After one more scan of the lot, he carefully scooped a small amount onto one of his keys and snorted it, and then he repeated the same process, filling his other nostril. The wave came over him before the second drip ran down his throat, flooding his body with a warm sensation he never felt before. It reminded him of the way it felt to have Lori Ann go down on him, but it added a sense of heightened awareness.

"Wow. This shit is amazing." He did two more small scoops from his key. "I'll bet it's not even cut at all," he said out loud as if talking to someone else in the truck. He carefully placed the brick back into the bag so it wouldn't spill out and pulled out of the rest area and onto the highway again. He knew he could easily make the trip but did worry about keeping his attention on the road. His eyes seemed to wander without regard for the task at hand.

Lori Ann went directly to Stephen's house after work and straightened up the mess he left in his haste to leave on his trip. She was glad he was coming home early and just figured he and his buddy had an argument or something. She never gave much consideration to his "get rich quick" schemes and knew they were on track to being able to get a little place they could call home. He wasn't perfect but things were good, and she planned on making his homecoming a memorable one. She bought a new negligee and would greet him at the door no matter how late he returned.

Stephen arrived home sometime after two in the morning, and due to four more pit stops along the roadside, he was anything but tired when he bounded in the door with the paper bag in his embrace.

"Hi, honey! Wow, what a trip," he announced as he swept her off her feet with one free arm.

"Boy, I thought you'd be a bit less energetic after ten hours of driving." She giggled as he swung her.

"Hell no, I'm not tired at all, and you won't be either after you have some a this." He gestured to the bag after freeing her from his grasp.

"What is it?" She began to worry a bit about how much energy he was displaying.

"First of all, don't think I didn't notice how incredibly hot you look in that teddy, but this stuff is something you gotta see."

Lori Ann smiled, blushing, and said, "Thank you. So, let's see what you've got."

Stephen pulled all four bricks out of the bag and placed them in a row on the kitchen table. Lori Ann stood looking at the taped bundles without a word while Stephen used a steak knife to further cut the one he opened earlier, allowing its contents to be viewed.

"What is it?"

"It's coke, tons of pure coke," he shouted with an ear-to-ear grin and wide arm gesture.

Lori Ann felt a chill of fear sweep through her body. "Where did you get the money for this?"

"It's free and it's all ours."

"Free from who? And why is it pink?"

"Marty found it, and it's pink cause it's pure, at least that's what I think. We're gonna get everything: the house, cars, money, all of it!"

"Stephen, what do you mean he 'found it'?" She asked nervously, knowing this much of anything valuable doesn't simply get gifted or discarded.

"Don't worry, honey, it's cool. He found it in the ocean; shit just floated by his surfboard, and he picked it up."

"Okay, so why did he give it to you?"

"Ah, he's all scared, so he gave it to me. We're gonna split the money once I sell it."

"You're going to sell it to who? How much is it worth? Why didn't he sell it and keep all the money? Why you?" She rattled off question after question as they ran through her mind.

"Settle down, honey. I'm gonna call Jeremy; he knows a guy in Minnesota that'll buy it."

"But that still doesn't..."

Stephen interrupted her. "I told you, he was scared, so he gave it to me."

"Scared of what?"

"I don't know. I guess the guys who lost it."

"Who are they? Stephen, what aren't you telling me?"

"I'm telling you everything. He found it and nobody knows who's shit it is, and that's all there is."

Lori Ann sat down at the table, looking at the brick-shaped packages and the glistening pink flakes and powder in the cut-open one that reminded her of a split baked potato. She didn't want to get into a fight with him, but this was a lot different than the usual little bags of pot he bought and sold.

Stephen was cutting a row of small lines on the table, glad for Lori Ann's temporary silence. His mind was spinning too hard to have an in-depth conversation about anything, especially one where he didn't have the answers. He rolled up a dollar bill into a straw and did one line up each nostril before looking up and extending the bill to Lori Ann. His eyes watered and rolled slightly back into his skull as the rush overtook him. Lori Ann took the bill from his hand, dabbed at one of the lines with a finger and tasted the powder while looking at him. The numbing sensation was instant and seemed to spread along her tongue while the chemical taste caused her to react as if she'd eaten a spoon full of peanut butter, smacking her tongue against the roof of her mouth. She looked at Stephen's glossy black eyes; his pupils were fully dilated from the drug. She tried coke once before at the bar but wasn't terribly impressed with the effect. She leaned down toward the table and placed the straw into her tiny nostril as she drew the powder into her nose. She sat back for a moment and then leaned in and repeated the process in her other nostril. Once the rush took hold of her, she slumped down in the chair and found an involuntary smile crossed her lips. Her nipples became firm under the weight of the satin garment she wore; she could feel herself becoming aroused in a way she'd never been before. It was like she'd been touching herself, or maybe it was like when Stephen caressed her, but the feeling didn't seem to come from any particular part of her body. It was like a ghostly stimulation moving without direction through her entire body and mind. She couldn't focus on a specific feeling or thought; this wasn't at all like the coke she tried in the past. Lori Ann wasn't sure if she liked it or not, but she did want to ride it out for all it was worth, even if she never did it again.

Stephen moved to her side of the table and began smoothing his hands along her negligee. His touch was familiar but somehow simultaneously foreign. Her body temperature rose, and moisture formed on her brow as well as more delicate areas. Stephen's hand found her steamy excitement and began focusing on her heated curls until she could stand it no longer and pulled him to the floor right there. Her hunger was insatiable, like nothing she'd ever known; she just couldn't stop orgasming, wouldn't stop riding him, even when he could no longer get hard. It was as though he was a sex toy like a vibrator or something, separate from the person beneath her, which was both concerning and exhilarating. The only break she took from grinding on him was for more lines until they both succumbed to dehydration and exhaustion, unable to go on for another moment.

The next morning, they awoke in a state of delirium, relaxing once they realized they were safely in his bed, but the tension returned as Lori Ann spoke. "Stephen, that was the most incredible night of my life, but I don't like it one bit. I want you to call Jeremy or whoever and get rid of it right away, okay?"

"I'll call him this morning, honey, don't worry."

"Let's not do any more of that stuff, okay?"

"Why? You said yourself it was the best night ever. We'll just keep a little bit for special occasions, okay?"

"Fine." He was right about that; she never orgasmed like that before, and they did seem to be all right this morning. "But only for special occasions. I don't want us getting strung out on that stuff."

"That's cool. I'll go call Jeremy and you get the paper."

"Why the paper?" She asked as she looked down at her body, reminiscing about the way it felt to be a complete animal last night, and feeling a twinge of concern that sex without it could be less exciting.

"So you can find us a house!"

She jumped up and pulled on an oversized T-shirt to go out front for the paper. Maybe this was a blessing after all, she thought, as she kissed him while passing into the hall.

Jeremy woke to the ringing of his frat-room phone, answering on the second ring.

"It's early; this better be good."

"It's real good, dude. You won't believe how good."

"Hey, Stephen. What's up?"

"Dude, do you remember telling me about that guy who gets the best blow you've ever seen?"

"Yeah, so what? You wanna buy some?" Jeremy answered in a tired voice, now sitting up and lighting a cigarette.

"No, dude. I wanna sell some. Actually, I wanna sell a lot."

"What do you mean, 'a lot'?"

"I haven't weighed it yet but I'm guessing it's about four keys."

"C' mon, dude, it's too early for bull shit. Do you really wanna buy some or not?"

"Jeremy, I'm serious. I need to sell about four kilos of uncut shit."

"Where'd you get it?"

Stephen told Jeremy the story and asked if he thought the guy was a player?

"It's really pink?"

"Yeah man, it's pink, and it's amazing, like nothing I ever heard of, man."

"Well, I don't know. Let me ask him and I'll get back to ya, okay?"

"Today?"

"Yeah. Fine. Today."

"Cool. I'll be home waitin' for your call."

"Hey."

"Yeah?"

"What do you need for it?"

"Shit. I don't know. What do ya think it's worth?"

"I have no idea but it's a big number for sure. I'll ask around and then call ya back."

"Cool. Later."

"Later."

"So, is he gonna sell it?" Lori Ann asked as she sat at the table with the coke laid out in front of her.

"He's gonna call me back but it sounds good."

"Good, 'cause this stuff makes me a little nervous too."

"It'll be all right, honey, don't worry."

But for the first time, his reassurance didn't ease Lori Ann's mind.

Jeremy called back late in the afternoon and woke Lori Ann and Stephen from a nap on the couch. They napped on and off all day long, completely spent from their night of debauchery. Stephen had a brief conversation with him as Lori Ann listened from the living room. Stephen kept saying, "really, here, and when?" When Stephen hung up, Lori Ann asked, "What's up?"

"The guy wants to fly down here from Minnesota to check out the stuff; he'll be here tomorrow."

"Really?"

"Yeah, and then we'll meet again to make the sale." Stephen was playing it cool, but Lori Ann could sense a bit of uneasiness in his body language and tone.

"Why twice?"

"I guess he's just checking it out. This other guy is the buyer."

"Another guy in Minnesota?"

"No. The buyer is some guy in LA."

"California?"

"Yeah."

"He's coming here too?"

"Nah. If it checks out okay I gotta bring it to him in LA."

"I don't know..."

"He said if it's as good as we think, it's worth about a hundred grand."

"A hundred..." Lori Ann trailed off as the magnitude of his statement sunk in.

"Yeah! A hundred grand."

"I don't like this, Stephen."

"You don't like a hundred thousand dollars?"

"Don't be an ass. You know what I mean."

"An ass?" His amusement from her use of profanity was evident by the twinkle in his eye.

"Yes, an ass. Do you know who buys that much coke? I'll tell ya: the mob, that's who, and they'll kill you before you get a penny." Lori Ann's voice was shaking.

"Calm down Lori Ann. I won't do it stupid; I'll make sure it's on my terms all the way."

They argued for hours about how the deal should go down and "if" it should go down at all before they finally agreed on a way it might be safe. Neither of them knew LA, so they'd have to go out a day early and check into two hotels; one to stay in and the other for the meeting. They would arrive in the second room just before the meeting and leave at the same time the buyer did. They would go back to the other room, get their stuff, and take a cab to San Diego to fly home. The buyer wouldn't know any of their plans, and the movements would keep anyone from knowing what they were doing. Stephen repeatedly appealed to her dream of a lovely little house in a safe neighborhood and offered the promise that he would never again get involved with selling drugs to anyone, even though it seemed like his dreams of being in the big time were right in front of him. He imagined striking up a relationship with these guys and getting "plugged in" to the business and lifestyle.

Lori Ann considered Stephen's assurances after he left to meet the man, wondering if he could keep a promise to never get involved with drugs again after such a huge deal. He drooled over "Miami Vice" and "Scarface," boisterously rooting for the drug dealers and cursing the cops, pointing out how he'd do it better and not ever get caught. He romanced the thought of being a South Florida dealer since she knew him, fantasizing about a waterfront mansion and exotic cars. She felt ill about this entire situation and wished she'd stopped him from going to see Marty in the first place. Their life wasn't perfect, but they worked hard toward carving their little piece of the American dream, and she felt like he might already be abandoning their shared dream for his fantasy. She felt placated, her concerns ignored in favor of his rapidly unfolding plan. Lori Ann hadn't heard any of the calls, been part of any of the discussions, and now Stephen was off meeting another stranger to make a deal in LA.

Raul flew in from Minneapolis and met Stephen at the Waffle House on Academy Drive at 3:30 PM; they talked over coffee and after sampling the coke in the parking lot, Raul agreed to set up the buy for the following week. Stephen would have to get to LA and then call a number Raul provided to arrange the meeting time and place. Stephen suggested meeting at the hotel but that would be decided in LA. No concrete plans were to be made until the day of the buy. Stephen, usually an overconfident young man, found himself intimidated by Raul and his directness. Raul filled a small brown glass vial to enjoy on the trip home from the eight-ball-sized paper bindle Stephen provided as a sample, and then put the lid with its small spoon back on before folding the bindle of cocaine back up.

"That's cool," Stephen noted, thinking Lori Ann would love the vial with a tiny spoon attached by a fine gold chain.

"What's cool?"

"The vial."

Stephen pointed to the vial in Raul's hand.

"Si, sus cool?" Raul looked at the small vial, thinking about the triviality of the item in his world, a trinket, readily available at the house where he picked up cocaine from the cartel.

Raul handed Stephen the vial along with a small piece of scrap paper with a number written on it, explaining that it was a gift. Before Stephen could say thank you, Raul continued, advising him that a call must be placed to this number from LA at precisely 3:00 PM on Thursday or the deal would be off. The man he would be dealing with would be named Carlos, and if the product were different in any way from the sample Raul was bringing with him, Carlos' reaction would be swift and harsh. Stephen just nodded and agreed to the requirements of the deal. He breathed heavily as if he'd been underwater for too long after Raul finally got out of the truck.

Lori Ann hung up the phone and said, "This will almost break us."

"What?"

"The plane tickets are $2,500, Stephen. We only have $3,900 in our savings and checking combined; that's almost one-third of the $15,000 down payment for a $150,000 house."

"Not for long."

"So you actually want to go through with this?"

"Hell yeah. You're the one who needs to have the nice house.

You're the one who talks about this life we can't afford all the time and how long it'll take to save up enough money for the down payment. This fell in my lap and I'm taking it. I think you should stay here; I'll run out there and do the deal and then it'll only be twelve-hundred for one ticket, and I'll be back the next day."

"Okay Stephen, we'll do this deal, but I'm going."

Lori Ann looked at the small vial with the cute little spoon held on with a gold chain Stephen brought back from his meeting with the Minnesota drug dealer. Every nerve in her body tingled with anxiety; even the little vial felt threatening in her hand. She ran scenarios through her mind: Who were these people they'd be selling to? Where did this cocaine come from? Why was Stephen so blind to the danger and how could they possibly survive this drug deal? Her thoughts began to wander beyond the deal into their relationship. Was Stephen really her destiny? Was he the one she was meant to share her life with, or had she clung to the first man who entered her life outside of her father's world? Perhaps she'd been viewing him through the proverbial rose-colored glasses, confusing her feelings of joy related to her adult freedom with her feelings for him. Had she recklessly given her heart to the man who was given her virginity, and for no other reason than timing? She shook off the feelings, thinking destiny was destiny, of course he and they were in the right place at the right time; that's destiny in a nutshell.

They agreed not to talk about it to anyone, not even with Marty or Jeremy until it was over. They went about their business and requested three days off work to go to the Keys together on a romantic getaway. Everything was in place, but Lori Ann just couldn't shake the awful feeling that they were in way over their heads.

Stephen was the only boyfriend Lori Ann ever had and she wasn't interested in dating a bunch of guys for the fun of it. She preferred to accept Stephen as is and hope he'd mature and grow into the kind of a man who would embrace the simple but fulfilling life she wanted. She watched his eyes grow wide and intense during the episode of "Miami Vice" on TV that evening, occasionally looking over at her with a gleaming smile as the show progressed. The flashy, plastic world that was temporary at best, even for the good guys, had no appeal to her, so she daydreamed about thirty-three percent down and a solid nest egg while the cigarette boats and Ferraris raced across the TV screen with a backdrop of bikini-clad bimbos, each no more important to the story than the next tank of fuel.

They wouldn't fly as a couple, and each would check one bag with two bricks onto the flight. They bought cheap suitcases; Stephen fitted them with false bottoms made of plywood; Lori Ann made matching linings for them on her mother's sewing machine. They started to feel like secret agents and began to enjoy the preparations. They bought their tickets in cash on two different days and from different travel agents across town. Each packed two days of clothing and Lori Ann added a sexy garment for their celebration after the deal was done.

When Wednesday night rolled around, they were all set to go. Everyone wished them well on their romantic trip to the Keys, and they went home to relax and go over the plan once more. Stephen would arrive at the airport first in his truck, park in the long-term lot and head to the gate. Lori Ann would get there thirty minutes before the flight's departure via taxi, and they would not communicate at all in any way until outside the terminal at Los Angeles International Airport (LAX) at the taxi stand. They took a couple of grams from the opened brick and had been using little lines every other night to heighten the sex, but never used it during the day, and agreed that when it was gone, they would put the cocaine behind them, even though both secretly hated to see it leave the bedroom.

CARLOS PACKED A BAG IN HIS MINNEAPOLIS MANSION, FEELING pleased with himself as he took only five thousand dollars from his wall safe for travel money. There would be no payment for the pink cocaine from Florida. Deborah's ticket to Vegas had been purchased, the hotel reservations made in Los Angeles and Las Vegas, and soon Carlos would have four kilos of his competitor's cocaine for free. He loved it when life handed him bonuses out of the blue. Deborah complained about him going to LA without her, but he again reassured her that he would meet her in Vegas the following day and that it was just business, nothing that would interest her and nowhere near the beach.

If all went well, Carlos would give Raul a nice little bonus for his part in this very profitable deal, and some time in Vegas afterward with Deborah would be a nice break from the daily grind of running a drug empire. His spirits were high, and business was excellent, as usual.

The limousine would be arriving soon to take them to the Minneapolis-St. Paul Airport. First, drop off Deborah for her gate, and then he was off to his private jet where he'd meet Raul and the two local girls who'd be keeping them company on their flight to LA. He never flew commercial, especially with big money or coke, though you could still check stuff through in those days, but why risk it? Deborah had a fear of smaller private planes; she preferred flying commercial jets, first-class of course, so no problem there.

PART VI

The Limo Ride

The Limo Ride

At 6:00 PM, the knock on the door was a small army of bellhops accompanied by the concierge and another man also in a suit. I showed them in and they went to work, stocking the bar with liters of top-shelf vodka, gin, whiskey, bourbon, tequila, vermouth, and assorted mixers. They took the mini bottles of booze with them as they left. I knew better than to tip them individually with the concierge in the room; he'd take care of them at his discretion.

The roses were in vases, one pale blue, the other soft pink. Laurie's note was within the flowers of the pink one. I thought: This guy is good. After the last of the bellhops left, the concierge spoke.

"I hope all is satisfactory."

He was approximately forty years old but didn't seem offended by some kid flashing big bucks.

"It's fine." I handed him five hundred in cash folded in half. "Will this cover it?" Without counting it, he nodded, placing it in his outer suit pocket. "And this is for you." I handed him another two hundred folded on all corners to contain the gram of rock cocaine inside. I figured it's the '80s; everyone was coked out or at least knew someone who wanted to be. In the worst-case scenario, he'd have it for some other use as a well-connected concierge.

He accepted the gift graciously with a modest tilting of his head. "This is Anthony, my assistant; he's the night concierge. He'll be here until midnight if you should require anything else."

I said hello with a nod but did not shake his hand. Instead, I pulled a large wad from my front pants pocket, stripped a hundred-dollar bill from the top, folded it longways and held it up between my index and middle finger in front of me. "Anthony, are you familiar with Fantasy Limousine Service?" I knew the company from concert rides and nights on the town when we rented a limo to go into Minneapolis and hit the clubs. If you showed up in a stretch limousine, you were escorted straight through the velvet ropes without any lines or ID checking. The few super-clubs downtown had a kind of contest to see who had the most limos lined up out front on any given night; it was a great look, and they overlooked quite a bit to accomplish it. Those were crazy nights filled with twenty-something-year-old girls who went crazy for cocaine and limos.

"Yes, I am."

"Good. I need to speak with the owner as soon as possible. Can you arrange that?"

"Yes, sir. Right away." He disappeared out the door with the cash in hand.

"Sir, please allow me to more formally introduce myself. My name is James." He handed me a card with his off-hours number, a room extension in this case. He informed me that he resided on the first floor and that I shouldn't hesitate to call him twenty-four-seven if I should need anything.

"Thanks, James, I will. Enjoy your evening."

"And you as well, sir." He turned and walked out the door, closing it softly behind him.

The card read, "James Myers, Director of Guest Services."

Tommy watched the entire process without expression until they left, and then a look of scorn crossed his face.

"What?"

"What a bunch of shit. Those guys think we're a couple of punks who hit a liquor store or somethin'."

"Bullshit. Robert showed me that if you know the game and are respectful, they don't care how you look." Under my breath, I added, "A big tip helps too."

"Yeah, whatever." Then, in a softer tone, Tommy said, "This place is awesome," as he scanned the room a second time.

Fifteen minutes later the phone rang.

"Hello."

"Mr. West?"

"Yes."

"Sir, this is Anthony at the concierge desk. I can connect you with Mr. Maxwell from the limousine service. He's not the owner but says he can help. Is that okay?"

"That's fine, thank you," I replied, already missing James' attention to detail.

I could hear the transfer taking place. "Mr. Maxwell?"

"Yeah, this is Bobby Maxwell. How can I help you, Mr. West?"

"Well, Mr. Maxwell, I hoped to speak with the owner. I've used your service before but this time I'm interested in a twenty-four-hour rate."

"The owner is on vacation but I'm his brother and I can help you. When did you need a car?"

"Well, I was hoping to get a black stretch Lincoln. You see, I'm currently without transportation and I need this limo at my disposal twenty-four hours."

"For how long, Mr. West?" He asked with a tone of disbelief.

"At least one week."

"How did you plan on paying for the, uh, car, Mr. West?"

"Is cash okay?"

"Hell yes, it's okay." He sounded out in joy before changing back to a business tone. "I mean we do accept cash, sir."

I decided to take it down a notch. "Look, Bobby, don't call me sir, okay? It's Reno."

"Okay, Reno. Well, I do have a car like that, but I don't know if it has any bookings this week. You did mean this week, right?"

"Listen, Bobby, it's July; this ain't prom season, so how much?"

"Well, let's see." He began computing out loud. "The ten-pass stretch, twenty-four hours a day, times seven, that would be, uh, $21,000 plus fifteen percent is…"

"Hold on, Bobby. Are you familiar with the term 'A rate'?"

"Well yeah, of course. But I don't…"

"I'll give you seven thousand for the week, plus a good tip; that's a grand a day, Bobby, and the car will be parked most of the time. Your brother will be thrilled."

"Yeah, I guess, but…"

"Last chance, Bobby."

"Okay, I'll take it." He was still unsure if it was a good deal or not but knew there were no commitments for that car all week.

"Oh, and Bobby?"

"Yeah?"

"You'll be my driver, right? I don't want some ten-dollar-an-hour flunky."

"Do I have to park at the hotel all day?"

"We'll work it out, but I need you here tonight at 10:00 PM."

"I'll be out front of the hotel at ten, but I need the fee upfront for the week on the car."

"Fine, you've got a deal. And Bobby?"

"Yes?"

"Jeans and a sport coat, okay? No suits."

"Works for me. I'll see you at ten." Bobby's mood improved dramatically when the formality of his role was relaxed, plus I was right, they were slow, and his brother would be thrilled with the revenue.

"Fine." I hung up the phone, another check on my mental list.

"Laurie in the limo, Laurie in the limo," Tommy chanted. "You lucky bastard!"

Before I could respond to his teasing there was a knock at the door.

"What now?" Tommy asked, looking up from the small pile of coke on the coffee table facing the left side of the sectional.

"It's them, dude. Not a word about the limo."

When I opened the door, my entire body and all my senses tingled. She was like a work of art, perfect in every way. She wore a white satin slip-dress that ended at mid-thigh, with thin straps that followed the lines of her shoulders as precisely as the garment covered every contour of her body. Her stockings were sheer and matched her tan like a finely blended oil work. I caught my breath when noting a slight rise from the garter straps hidden just above the dress' seam. I was no stranger to the finer things, and this girl knew how to dress. Her shoes were soft yet shimmering white pumps, at least three inches high. At just eighteen years of age, she put to shame any top model in the business. My heart was pulverized. I'd do anything for her.

As I let them into the suite, all the money I spent was justified by Laurie's statement: "This is first class, Reno." Her voice dropped to a whisper as she added, "I am impressed," directly into my ear before softly kissing my cheek. My knees went weak from her fragrance and touch, just as they had every time I was so blessed to experience them.

"Thanks. I figured on staying for a while, so..."

"Where's my room?" Missy interrupted, kissing me on the other cheek before scampering down the stairs behind Laurie in her effortless charm.

"Back there, if you're good." Tommy responded with his thumb over his shoulder, pointing to the second room.

"I could stay here," Laurie concurred as she peeked into the master bedroom through the French doors.

"Stay as long as you like." Immediately, I wished I hadn't shown so much enthusiasm. She just smiled, closed the door, and asked, "So how does a girl get a drink around here?"

"Wait 'til you see the back of that bar. We've got everything," Tommy proclaimed with a joyous tone.

"What would you ladies like?" I was following Laurie en route to the bar, holding a beer in my left hand.

"What have you got there?" Laurie asked regarding the greenish bottle.

"Beck's Light." I raised the bottle for her inspection as another knock paused the room. "Hold on." I retraced my steps across the back of the room toward the door. The girls were at the bar, Laurie in front and Missy looking through the vast selection of liquor from behind as I opened the door. A man in a polyester uniform stepped into the room with an ice bucket in each hand. "What's this?"

"Compliments of Le Luxe, sir. Our finest house champagne. Where shall I put them?"

"Over here," Laurie replied, with a smile that was as evident in her tone as upon her face. She was holding her card from the roses that were placed on the bar.

"You boys are full of surprises," added Missy, now holding her card.

The man sat the stainless-steel buckets on the bar. "Shall I open the doors, sir? It is a lovely evening."

"Yes, thank you, but don't draw the drapes."

"Of course, sir." He accepted the challenge with a forced smile.

Missy took control of the bottles as soon as he sat them on the bar and was peeling the foil from one as he moved toward the balcony doors. I handed him a fifty-dollar bill as he passed by me to leave the room.

"Thank you, sir. That's very kind, and please enjoy your stay at Le Luxe."

When I turned from closing the door behind him, Laurie was right behind me. She kissed me again on the cheek, this time more solidly, with more contact of our bodies, exhaling just slightly in my ear. "Thank you, the flowers are lovely."

I thought I'd fall over. No other person could've taken me from the hopelessness I'd been entrenched in just hours before to the heights of exhilaration I felt in her presence.

"Well, Prince Charming," Missy asked, looking at Tommy sitting on the sofa, "are you gonna open these bottles or should we just look at them?"

I said, "I'll get it."

"No, no. I'll do it. I've been sittin' here too long anyway."

Laurie took a seat at the dinner table and asked, "Does anyone want a line?" She usually had a little stash on hand, especially after seeing her big sister who always had more than enough to share with the little sister she adored.

"Sure, I'd love one," Missy answered." Use those glasses, Tommy," she added with a gesture toward the champagne flutes while walking from behind the bar.

"Yeah, yeah." Tommy grunted, sounding like an old married man.

"How about you Reno. Interested?"

"Sure, Laurie, thanks."

"Tommy?"

"Nah, I'll pass," he replied and then asked, "What?" after noticing our stunned expressions.

We laughed and Tommy mumbled expletives under his breath, followed by the boyish, self-deprecating grin that was so seldom seen, a rare glimpse into the guy Missy was so crazy about.

"Well, that's that." I poured the last of the second bottle of champagne into Laurie's glass.

"What should we do tonight?" Missy asked, rhetorically, and with a hint of mischief. I always liked Missy, and although we never spent much time conversing one on one, I felt we shared a bond of sorts that was of value.

I looked at my watch; it was 9:45 PM. I thought, "How do I do this casually?"

Missy broke the momentary silence. "When does the limo get here?"

"What the fuck, Tommy?"

"I didn't say a word, Reno."

"I was only kidding; did you really get one?"

"Well, I was car-less so I booked it twenty-four-seven thinking I might need..." I was stumbling through an explanation when Laurie said, "We've got a car, plus Tommy's. Do you want to cancel it?"

"No worries. I just needed transportation until I get some wheels." I wanted to remove any association between the limousine and her; I sure as hell didn't want her to think I got it in hopes of the stories of her and limos being true.

"Geez, what does that cost?"

Laurie shot a look of displeasure at Missy.

"What?"

"That's very impolite."

Missy pouted and sighed. "Sorry, Reno." Much of her charm was in her innocence, and she had plenty of class for this group or any other in my opinion.

"It's cool; forget it. So, does anyone want to hit a club?"

"A club? Look at this place. We've got a full bar, a big-screen TV and a bag of coke that could kill a horse. I'm not goin' anywhere," Tommy replied while stretching an arm across the sofa back.

"Well, I've gotta go down and meet the driver. I'll just get his cell number for future needs."

There was modest flushing of Laurie's cheeks when she asked, "Wanna go once around Lake of the Isles?" She had the slightest hint of reservation in her tone, not wanting to sound forward but hoping to get me alone sooner than later.

"Sure, why not," I agreed. "You guy's into it?"

"You two go ahead," Missy answered, looking at Tommy's scrunched-up facial response and reflecting on her conversation with Laurie on the ride over. Laurie confided that she'd always been into me, but never had an opportunity that felt right to do something about it. Missy told Laurie I was really into her as well but playfully pointed out that I'd been somewhat of a popular sport among the girls since arriving on the scene, which brought a frown from Laurie, and also a challenge to lock down this playboy once and for all.

"I'll be ready in a minute. He's here now, right?"

"I'm sure he is."

"Good, then you'll excuse me for a moment?"

Even Laurie's posture was alluring. I mean, she could melt a guy with a glance. The subtle tilt of her neck and squint of her eyes was paralyzing and I'm fairly certain she knew it. She locked eyes with me for a moment as she headed into the master bedroom, and I got light-headed as my manhood swelled until Tommy snapped me from my trance.

"Hey dude, will ya get some munchies while you're out?"

Missy said, "There's a ton of stuff behind the bar, next to the glasses."

"Forget it then."

Tommy got up from the couch and headed for the bar. He's the only guy I know with an appetite even cocaine can't kill.

"Leave us some blow though, okay?"

I plopped a large rock on the table as Laurie came through the double doors, saying, "Ready?"

"Sure, let's go. You kids be good."

I zipped the baggie closed and dropped it into the pack before following Laurie out of the room through the door I held open. My pulse quickened again as I opened the gigantic, brass-trimmed glass door to the left of the revolving doors for Laurie to exit the hotel. Everyone in the stylish lobby looked as we passed through; one woman even smacked her husband's arm for stealing more than a reasonable glance at the vision that was Laurie. If Laurie noticed the attention, you would never have known it.

The limousine was spotless, long, and black with the interior done in black leather and deep burgundy crushed velour. Inside was a bar stocked with vodka, gin, and whiskey in crystal decanters. A TV and VCR were at our end of the long "J" seat that spans the left side and beneath the divider, hidden by a wooden rollaway shield. The vast sunroof was centered above the back seat that had a cellular phone and flexible reading lights mounted behind it below the rear window. Mobile phones had just started appearing in cars, and it was a cool concept when you consider that Cable TV was still a new thing. The glass was tinted dark black from end to end, and the indirect lighting encircled the car around the mirrored ceiling and in highlights around the bar and window trim. The intercom, stereo, sunroof, and partition controls were located in an overhead panel, and two partitions divided the driver from the passenger area; one was clear glass and the other solid with crushed velour and the Lincoln symbol embroidered in its center. It was a suite on wheels.

Bobby gave me an approving nod as he opened the door for Laurie. I handed him a large roll of hundreds, seven thousand dollars held together with a rubber band. He looked shocked as he accepted the money. Laurie silently witnessed the transaction as she entered the car.

I stepped into the limo from the other side, sat back, and tossed the pack onto the left side forward seating, behind the TV console. The right side of the car consisted of the bar, glasses, and an ice trough. Laurie looked amazing in the limousine, the soft lighting accentuating her tan. She was so at ease, legs crossed exposing a fraction of her upper stocking's lacy ring.

"I took the liberty of picking up a bottle of bubbly for our maiden voyage," Bobby declared as he reached through the open divider, bottle in hand.

"Thank you. I'll get it Reno, you relax." Laurie placed her hand on my thigh with a pat as she rose.

"Thanks, Laurie."

She had to crouch as she moved forward through the car to retrieve the bottle. I adjusted my instant erection while admiring the split-second image of her semi-exposed buttocks. She wore a floss-thick G-string, pearl in color, that widened just at the moment of desperation to cover what the soft blonde curls surrounded so perfectly. Any guy in Minnetonka would have sold his soul to be present for this view.

The glass partition slid upwards as Bobby's voice came over the intercom. "So, where are you two off to tonight?"

I pushed the talk button to respond. "Once around Lake of the Isles for starters and then we'll go from there."

The interior lights shut off and only the soft indirect lighting remained as the solid partition rose in silence.

"Why don't you get us a couple glasses," Laurie suggested while removing the foil wrap from the bottle.

I dropped to my knees, reaching the champagne flutes from a foam-lined drawer beneath the rack of less delicate glasses housed in lighted wooden holders. Handing the glasses to Laurie, I took the bottle, hit the sunroof open button, and shot the cork out of the opening sunroof as the tinted glass top disappeared into the roof; she quickly offered a glass to catch the initial flow of champagne. I filled the glasses and placed the bottle between my legs instead of having to get up to place it in the ice trough.

Laurie toasted, "To our maiden voyage," as she gently tapped our glasses together.

I just looked directly into her brilliant eyes ever so fondly. After finishing the small flute, she reached for the bottle to refill our glasses, gently grazing my near fully erect member in the process.

"Oh," she coyly remarked, now leaning against me with her right breast pressuring my shoulder as she changed the radio station on the overhead control panel to soft rock from jazz. "That's a good sign," she added with a schoolgirl's giggle.

"Sorry..." My erection was now complete.

"I don't think sorry's the right word. Sorry is for when he doesn't wake up."

"Well, I meant..." I started to explain but she interrupted me.

"I liked you that first day Reno. You didn't bullshit me or even make a pass at me on the path. Don't you find me attractive?"

"Everybody thinks you're gorgeous, Laurie."

"That's not what I asked you, Reno."

"Yes, I think you're absolutely exquisite; I always have." I was sincere in my response, and it showed.

"That's sweet. I think you're a very handsome man, but more importantly, a warm man, and I'm glad we're here."

"Thanks, me too." I said it with a broad, "cat that ate the canary" smile.

Laurie had a way of exuding class and sex appeal simultaneously, an ability that, like all her other wonders, came naturally.

"Are you still seeing Brittany?" She asked semi-casually.

"No. It was wrong to get her tangled up in my problems."

It was true enough, and even though I cared for Britt, in some ways it was always a bit unclear exactly what I wanted with her from the beginning. I mean, we could never have been in a "serious" relationship. Hell, her parents never even knew we saw each other; she always told them she was with someone else when she was with me. I never took her anywhere; we just hung out at my place a few times each week. So, whatever relationship we did have was just between us. I guess I never really thought it through, but I did have feelings for her, in my own way.

"I don't think you caused the problems at all, but I'm glad you're free again."

"Did you hear about last night?"

"Yes, I heard all about Dustin."

"Well, I just hope he's okay."

"Who?"

"Dustin. He's screwed and there's not a damn thing I can do about it." I couldn't care less about that dumb ass who got popped for his ridiculous move on me in my own damn house.

"You have a big heart, don't you Reno?"

"Yeah well, don't let it get around, okay?"

"Your secret is safe with me."

It was nice to be with Laurie again. I missed our little trips and the easy conversation.

When the bottle was empty, I leaned forward and wedged it upright into the ice trough.

"Have you ever made love in a limousine?"

I almost choked on my last sip of champagne. "Huh?"

"I'm sure you've heard I like sex in limousines, right?"

"Well, I, uh..."

"That rumor was started by my date to a senior prom. I was a freshman and wouldn't sleep with him, so he told everybody the next day we had sex in the limo. Do you believe me?"

"Of course. Guy's like to talk, and..."

"You're not like that, are you Reno?"

"Well, I try not to..."

"Why haven't you made a pass at me, Reno?"

I pressed the driver call button and Bobby responded, "Yes, sir?"

"Where are we, Bobby?"

"We're on the south end of The Isles, approaching Lake Calhoun, sir."

I looked at my watch: 11:20 PM.

"Bobby, go around Lake Harriet, then back to the hotel, okay?"

"No problem, sir."

"Thanks, Bobby; and Bob, please stop calling me sir."

"You got it Reno."

I was laughing when I turned my attention back towards Laurie from the overhead microphone until I saw the shoulder straps of her dress draped along her arms, only her supple breasts holding the dress in place. Through an ear-to-ear smile I said, "Man, you are absolutely spectacular."

She slipped the straps from over to under her arms, releasing her perfectly symmetrical breasts into the soft light. I gently took a breast into my hand; it was warm and firm within my grasp. She leaned into me, and as I tasted the sweetness of her velvet tongue swirling past my lips, I dropped my hand onto her thigh and then ran it slowly upwards until reaching a downy cushion, fully exposed to my touch. She must have removed her panties while I was taking a much-needed pit stop earlier along the lake's shore. My middle finger slipped into the warmth, her inner muscles embracing its entire length, and then I pulled back, more surprised than even she.

"I can't."

"What do you mean?" Laurie asked looking more hurt than anything else.

"I can't make love to you for the first time in a car, no matter how nice it is."

"You're incredible."

"I'm sorry Laurie, but I..."

"And now you apologize for it?"

She leaned across me, still mostly exposed, and pushed the intercom button. "Take us back to the hotel now, Bobby."

Bobby's voice came over the speaker. "Is everything okay?"

"It's fine, Bobby, just take us back now," I replied.

"Sure, right away."

I looked back towards Laurie. "Look Laurie, I'm sorry, I didn't mean..."

"No guy has ever talked to me like that in my entire life." She placed the straps back over her shoulders. "Tonight, I'm going to make love to you like no woman has ever made love to a man."

I was in total shock as she unbuttoned my jeans, simultaneously pulling my shirt up. She swung to the floor, pulling my pants and underwear to my ankles.

"You sit back and enjoy the ride home while I reward your golden heart."

It was like a dream sequence, watching her take me beyond her pouty lips, feeling the sensation of her slender fingers along me, and then seeing her capture the last of my release with a flick of her tongue. In the midst of the indescribable pleasure, I brought my hand to my face taking in the spectacular fragrance that was her, tasting the exquisite traces on my fingers before returning to the privilege of running them through her hair while she exceeded fantasy in reality.

"Was there some problem? It's early, maybe I could..." Bobby spoke as he held the door open for us at the hotel entrance.

Laurie interrupted him. "The problem is I'm going to need more room to make love to this beautiful man tonight, so we need to get back to the suite. You understand don't you, Bobby?"

She glanced back and looked into my eyes as she gracefully exited the limo. Bobby was stunned and did not speak. I broke the silence, feeling more powerful than any head of state. "Do you party, Bob?"

"Yeah, but I..."

"Would you like to come upstairs for a while?"

"Now?" He was clearly confused by this turn of events.

"Sure. Just leave the car here. I'm sure they won't mind," added Laurie as she took my hand.

Bobby swatted the rear door closed as he headed for the front of the car. He shut down the engine and appeared at the lobby entrance with keys in hand. Bobby's mind spun as he wondered what the hell he was getting into with these two. His brother told him you never know what'll happen on a limo run, but this was turning out to be one for the books. I mean, this chick is maybe the hottest little thing he's ever seen in heels, and they want him to come upstairs while she gets more room to do this rich kid. "Must be good to have money," was all he could conclude, and thank God he agreed to take the job in the first place.

As we passed through the lobby, I turned towards the pillared opening of the hotel lounge. Upon entering, the attractive woman in her thirties I observed from the lobby approached to inform us that they already had last call. She wore a polyester waitress uniform; the skirt was ruffled but accented the low-cut top nicely. Her name tag read "Sally."

"Sally, I'm Reno, this is Laurie, and Bobby here owns that super-stretch limo out front. Do you think it'll be okay out there?

While looking at her watch, she said, "It's late; I'm sure they won't mind."

"Good. I don't mean to sound forward, but we're having a small get-together in suite eleven twenty-four and thought you might like to join us."

"Well, I don't know." She answered as she looked down at her cocktail outfit.

"Attire is very casual, as you can see. We'd love to have you join us," I said, gesturing to point out my jeans, Vans, and a Mötley Crüe concert T-shirt, regardless of Laurie's dress and Bobby's sport coat.

"Well, I've got a couple more things to do before we lock up."

"Perfect. Bobby has a key and will wait for you here if that's all right?"

"Maybe I should wait over by the elevators, so you don't get into trouble," Bobby added, finally catching on to my efforts on his behalf.

"Why not. I'll be about fifteen minutes, okay?" Sally replied while looking at Bobby more closely. He was a handsome man in his mid-thirties with jet-black hair and brown eyes. His build was muscular, his smile warm, a man of obvious Italian heritage, regardless of his father's surname.

"Great, then we'll see ya upstairs," I concluded before kissing Laurie on the cheek as we turned toward the elevators.

Bobby joined us at the elevators, just a moment behind.

"What was that room number again?"

"Here's the key. It's eleven twenty-four. We'll see ya up there soon." I simultaneously handed him the small envelope containing the key card. Just then, the elevator doors opened; Laurie and I stepped in with her saying, "Good luck Bobby," in a teasing tone.

"Thanks. I'll be right up."

Bobby had to laugh at a conversation he had with his wife about taking this job when the construction work he was doing slowed up. She said, "I know you'll miss hanging out with all your beer buddies after work, but maybe this is just what you need to get a little responsibility. They'd been together since high school, and after seventeen years he still loved her dearly, but also felt he was entitled to a few of youth's pleasures he missed out on because of the relationship.

Bobby checked his hair in the brass reflection of the elevator door and then felt silly when he saw the mirror only feet away.

Tommy was watching a replay of a NASCAR race on the big screen. Missy came in from the balcony as we entered the suite and asked us, "How was it?"

"Wonderful," replied Laurie, releasing my hand and walking toward Missy, now near the bar.

"Did you get a paper?" Tommy asked about the newspaper as he looked over his shoulder at me still standing in the foyer, admiring my temporary home.

"Nah, I forgot," I responded without a care.

"I had one brought up; it's on the table if you want it."

"Not now, but thanks. I'll look at it tomorrow." I didn't want to bring my mood down on this evening.

Laurie was listening to the exchange and spoke up from behind the bar, her voice sultry and provocative. "What can I get for you, big boy?"

Tommy's jaw fell slack as his head snapped back and forth between us. He wanted to say some rude comment but thought better of it after looking at Missy's preemptive stern expression.

"Just a Beck's Light, please." I may have been blushing, if such a thing is possible for me, but I enjoyed it nonetheless. It's amazing how empowering a woman can be to a man; she can make or break him in a moment, and the saying about a woman being behind every successful man is true more often than not. I sat down on the right side of the sectional and thanked Laurie when she handed me the beer. Missy and Laurie joined us with some bizarre-looking cocktails in daiquiri glasses.

"The driver and a waitress from downstairs will be here soon. They're pretty cool, so I invited them up."

"Works for me, dude."

Bobby and Sally arrived a few minutes later. Sally commented that the room was awesome; Bobby just asked, "Where's the booze? I'm needin' some refreshment."

I introduced them to Tommy and Missy as they crossed the room and added they should help themselves to anything they needed. Tommy whispered, "Do they party?"

"I don't know. Hey, do you guys want a line?" I asked while opening the backpack.

"Really?" I think Sally was a little shocked.

"I told you he was cool," Bobby reiterated while looking for a beer glass, and then asked, "What can I get for ya Sally?"

"A beer will be fine."

"No problem. Let's see what we've got here," he said, turning to the refrigerator. "Holy Shit! Plannin' on stayin' a while or what?" He gasped as he opened the larger of the two refrigerators, finding it filled with beer.

"I'm the thirsty type," I replied with a smirk.

"I guess so," he added, approaching the sectional.

Laurie and I sat on the right with Tommy and Missy in the center; Bobby and Sally joined us on the left span of the sectional.

"Is this your room, Reno?"

"Well, he does have company," Laurie responded to Sally's inquiry, sounding more defensive than she intended.

"Oh, I didn't mean anything like..." Sally started to explain before being interrupted by Missy. "Okay, okay, who wants a line?"

After several grams of coke and a substantial amount of booze, I declared, "It's 3:00 AM and I'm hittin' the pillow," taking Laurie's waiting hand as I stood and helped her up.

She grabbed the pack from under the table along with her small purse and followed me into the master bedroom. "See ya in the morning."

The conversation never skipped a beat other than Missy's snide remark: "You kids sleep tight now."

I closed the French doors behind us, softening the relatively loud Van Halen video playing in the living room. When I turned around, Laurie was stepping free from her dress that now lay on the floor at the foot of the bed.

"Come here," she softly directed as I took in the vision before me. I moved closer and stood toe to toe with her as she whispered, "Take off your clothes and get into bed; I'll be right back." She then kissed me on the lips as she grazed my body while heading toward the bathroom. She was braless and had left her G-string under the seat in the limo knowing she'd get it back later. She was still wearing the pearl-colored garter belt that attached to her stockings by way of narrow straps, both front and rear. The muscles in her legs and buttocks flexed as she crossed the room, still in the heels she slipped back on when we got up from the sofa. Turning on the bathroom light just before she closed the door, I caught another glimpse of the diamond-shaped space between her thighs, the shimmer of light on blonde curls adding to the breathtaking vision before me.

Obliging Laurie's request, I disrobed and crawled under the sheets. Using the remote by my side, I turned MTV on quietly before lighting a cigarette. When Laurie entered the room, I could see by the light of the television she was completely nude. She crawled like a cat stalking prey across the king-size bed, pulling the sheets down and exposing more of me within each stride.

"Tonight, your wish is my command," she said in a most seductive tone, now straddling me. She grinded against me in a circular movement, smearing me with her anticipation as she whispered, "What do you desire me to do?"

I almost exploded on the spot.

With a devilish grin and a wild gyration, she asked, "Well?"

"I really wanna go down on you."

"Anything you want," she replied, pushing hard from her pelvis and sliding off to my side. Her silken hair cascaded onto the pillow as she came to rest beside me. I rose to my hands and knees in a twisting motion and then leaned forward to kiss her waiting lips. Our tongues danced like some tribal ritual in and out of each other's mouths as my body came to rest upon hers. Kissing and flicking my tongue along her butter-smooth skin, I descended her body, pausing to tease her tempered nipples with slurping actions, each time releasing the vacuum of my lips to watch her breasts quiver in their liberation. I probed her deep, oblong navel while she wriggled in pleasure before finally reaching my destination, parting her with a deep swipe of my tongue. Laurie gasped an inward breath and uttered a muffled, high-pitched squeal. I nipped, kissed, and explored, flicking in a controlled motion along her satin boundaries until focusing on her pleasure center in a swirling motion. She bucked and pleaded for mercy through a series of convulsing orgasms until finally going limp in my grasp.

I moved slowly up to again rest upon her, kissing her softly on her lips, cheek and ear, and then slipped carefully to her side, holding her tightly in my arms and whispered, "You've been in my heart since the first time I saw you."

With a single fluid movement, she thrust me to my back, straddling me as I sunk to her core. With pain and pleasure blended like a fine wine, she rose and dropped solidly, her hips rocking and guiding me within her, our fingers locked in a white-knuckle grasp. Her muscles clamped rigidly with each motion of her body until I released like a shattered dam, embracing her as the spasms subsided.

"You're in my heart too. I just had to wait for you to find your way to me," she declared in a soft pant before we drifted off to sleep, still joined by our passion.

We woke to the phone ringing at noon followed by a knock at the bedroom door. I responded to the knock by asking, "What's up?" while looking into Laurie's eye's just inches from my own.

Bobby's voice came through the door. "They need me to move the limo. Do ya mind if I run home for a shower and some fresh clothes?"

"Not at all. Just leave a number where I can get you later, okay?"

"My card is on the bar. I'll see ya later." After a short pause, Bobby added, "The key card is on the bar too. Thanks for everything."

And then, another voice came through the door; it was Sally. "Why don't you guys come down to the lounge tonight and I'll buy ya a drink. I start at five o'clock. Thanks for last night, it was fun."

Laurie giggled shyly in the ensuing silence and then suggested, "How about a shower, lover?"

"Sounds great, but first I need a smoke to kick start my day, okay?"

She kissed my forehead and then added, "I'll see you in there," before crawling out of bed and going into the bathroom, this time leaving the door open behind her. After my smoke, and the last lines from a pile on the bedside table, I joined Laurie in the shower. She looked so sexy, all sudsy and wet. As I entered the shower that was perfectly sized for two including two showerheads and a bench, Laurie took control.

"I'll do the honors."

She proceeded to wash my entire body, pausing only once to pleasure me with another oral treat. The combination of the hot water, steam, and her prowess was beyond description.

As we toweled off, she said, "I have to go home and change clothes, but if you like, I can pack an overnight bag and come back later?" She was not the type to simply invite herself anywhere, although you'd be hard-pressed to find a destination where she'd be unwelcomed.

"Why don't you pack a big bag and stay every night?"

"Are you sure?"

I just looked at her, deep into her eyes now just inches away, confident my feelings had to be written all over my face.

"Well, okay then, perhaps you need a little lingerie show tonight in this big 'ol room of yours."

I kissed her hard and pulled her body forcefully into mine. Our towels fell to the floor as she hopped onto the counter between the sinks; one hand tugged me close as the other guided me in from my standing position. She arched her back toward the expansive mirror, head rocked back with wet hair nearly reaching the countertop, eyes closed as her chest heaved with each deep breath while I gazed at her body under the bright lights; even her neck was sexy enough to make me throb, and I reveled in true bliss as I watched myself disappear into her glistening curls with each slow movement, taking in the grandeur of her body and the divine fragrance that was her. "Who in their right mind would ask Laurie to leave anywhere?" I was in heaven, and she was the stars in the sky.

<hr>

LAURIE AND MISSY LEFT IN A SOFT CLOUD OF GIGGLES, WHISPERING to each other as they waved goodbye, passing through the doorway and into the hall. I gave Laurie the room key from the bar top; now she, Tommy and I each had one.

I opened yesterday's paper while seated at the dining table after retrieving a cold Beck's for breakfast. Tommy came into the room, his long, wavy hair dripping water from the shower.

"How was the limo ride, you lucky fuck?"

"It was great. You should've come," I absent-mindedly replied, still looking for the story in the paper.

"Yeah, right. I don't think I need to see ya get that one, ya fuckin' whore. So, what's up with that Sally chick?"

"Huh?" I looked up from the article I was reading, titled, "Shooting At Local Teen Drug Party."

"The waitress! Did you forget?"

"I know who she is. What about her?"

"Didn't you hear her?"

"Apparently not. What happened?"

He was laughing again as he joined me at the table, now with a beer as well. "It was around 6:00 AM, but I'm sure it wasn't as good as the music you were makin'."

"Yeah, yeah, what about Sally?" I just wanted to get back to the story of my life being over.

"Well, we're all sittin' on the couch when Sally gets horny or somethin' and starts rubbin' that Bobby guy's balls, sayin' how she wants him and wants to suck his dick. Man, it's like we're not even there, ya know?"

"C' mon, are you serious?"

"Yeah. So, Bobby wants to go to her place, but she wants it right now." Tommy's laughter was getting louder as he continued. "So, she tries getting his pants open but he's sayin' 'not in front of them,' and finally she says to me and Missy, 'Do ya mind if I blow Bobby?' and she means it."

"No shit?"

Tears start to fill his eyes as he goes on. "Well, that's it. I'm like on the floor laughin' my ass off and Missy says, 'Let's go to bed,' but I don't wanna miss this shit, and it keeps getting better."

"So, what? Did she blow him or not?"

"Well, Missy got pissed and so we go in our room but like five minutes later, Sally's howlin' like a dog, 'ooowe, ooowe,' for like fifteen minutes. You really didn't hear her?"

"No. I must have been out of it. So, where did he fuck her?"

"Fuck if I know, but boy did she like it." Tommy let out another chuckle in hindsight. "Hey, if the chicks don't come back tonight, I think we oughta double team 'er."

This was said in jest but was by no means out of the realm of possibility in his mind.

"I'm not cheatin' on Laurie with some barking waitress."

Tommy's face dropped. "What do ya mean cheatin'? Are you guy's some kinda thing now or what?"

"Yeah, man, Laurie's awesome. Like you'd walk away from a chick like Laurie."

"No shit, dude, I'd kill to fuck 'er, but look at this place. We could fill it with chicks like Laurie."

"Yeah well, I'm pretty happy with the one I've got."

"You're killin' me, dude. Why do ya think she did you in the first place? It's the suite, the car, the whole deal you've got laid out here."

"Maybe so, but I waited a long time to get a chance with her and I'm gonna go with it. Besides, I've had the money and drugs for months and she never came around before."

"A road trip in the limo, that's what we need to get your Jersey-gangster ass back in line. You're going soft, Reno. Used to be you'd a had three chicks in here of your own, and we'd a still found time to slip out lookin' for trouble."

"Sounds good, but not today. Okay?"

"Fuck it. Ya got any blow left?"

"Yeah man, I'll get it." I folded the paper as I got up to get the pack from my room and then tossed it on the bedroom's glass table as I entered thinking I'll get the bad news later. What would a few hours change in the realm of things? There was a knock on the door as I pulled the pack out from under the bed. Tommy was letting the maid into the room as I came out of the bedroom.

"Hi. Just sheets and towels today, okay?"

"Yes sir."

She was gone in about five minutes.

"Tommy, come here a second."

"What?" He turned the corner from his room and walked behind the bar.

"We gotta go to Little Columbia for more blow, dude." I was

looking at the dwindling pile of cocaine I dumped on the glass table in front of the couch.

"Why don't you get Laurie to get it for ya?"

"Ya know, she does get good stuff; maybe I will call her."

"Are you serious? Man, you're so far up her pussy you can't see fuckin' daylight."

"Give it a rest Tommy. At least she doesn't need a gun to score the shit."

"What gun?"

"Man, you've never seen Jose's place. It's pretty rough."

"Fuck that! The little bastards ain't gonna fuck with me," he said as he walked across the room with the "JD" bottle in hand. We weren't much for glasses if the whole bottle was at our disposal, especially if it was just us.

"What's Missy's number?"

"Why?"

"So I can see if Laurie's with her."

"Bullshit. Let's go!" he demanded, waving the bottle wildly.

Not wanting to further alienate him, I agreed to go, taking twenty-five hundred dollars from the pack before sliding it back under the bed, but warned, "Don't get loud on these people, Tommy, or they'll fuckin' plant us both. And leave the bottle here."

"Yeah whatever, let's just go." He sat the bottle on the table by the door.

When we parked the Corvette in front of the building, I reiterated, "Please don't say anything inside, I mean to anyone, okay?"

"Yeah, yeah."

"Just be real cool, okay?"

Tommy swatted at the wino on the steps as we entered the building.

"You've gotta settle down, dude. These people don't fuckin' play."

I opened the door and walked in, looking over my shoulder for some kind of reaction from Tommy; he exhaled a muffled "Holy shit" as the situation suddenly became clear. As I turned back from him, there was some commotion in the room. The Columbians were talking loudly between the rooms and responses were heard from unseen persons. I got nervous when Jose appeared and took my arm, quickly pulling me to his desk in the next room, saying, "Esta bien, esta bien," to each person we passed, gesturing dismissively at those who came near. Finally, he addressed me with two words: "Denero rapido." I don't speak Spanish, but everyone knows certain terms, and the tension of the room was no less than palpable. I tossed the money on his desk and did not sit down, mostly because he was still standing. Tommy stood behind me, facing the men with Uzi's pointed at us.

"Geez, you weren't kidding."

I whispered, "Shut up," as quietly as possible and without looking back at him. My heart pounded as Jose said, "No mas. No mas, comprende?" while handing me a large baggie but without weighing it.

"Si, comprende." I responded without losing his eye contact. He grabbed my arm and whisked me through the house and out to the car, repeating, "Esta Bien, esta Bien," as we went. Tommy remained right on my heels during our brief journey. An older man, more formally dressed, followed us out and stood at the stairs; he continued talking to Jose in excited Spanish while we were shoved toward the car with Jose saying, "Vaminos rapido!" As we got into the car, he shouted, "No mas, amigo."

Tommy turned the key and before the engine even came to idle, he was smoking the tires and trying to maintain control as we slid sideways through an intersection.

Tommy was screaming, "You're fuckin' crazy," as we ran the stop sign.

I said, "Don't speed," in the calmest voice I could muster.

"Fuck you, don't speed."

"Do you wanna go to jail?" I held up the big bag of coke.

"Shit, man." His eyes were wild, but he slowed down. "That was fuckin' nuts, Reno."

"I know."

"Why do you go there?" He was finally starting to calm down.

"It's not usually that bad," I replied, also thinking of Jose's words: "No mas, Amigo."

"That bad? Shit, this ain't Jersey, motherfucker; we don't usually see

Uzi's in 'Tonka Town'. So, what, I guess they usually have pistols instead of machine guns?"

"They know, dude. Don't ya see what's goin' on?"

"Know what?"

"About Dustin, man, the party. I buy a lot of shit down here; don't ya think they might have had a little interest in knowin' who the fuck I am?"

"Oh, shit." I could see Tommy working through the connection while I began to wonder how safe I was in Minneapolis. Perhaps a road trip was in order. I looked out at the city as we entered the freeway on-ramp and then realized he was going the wrong way.

"Where are you going?"

"Sorry, dude. I was goin' home. I'll get off up here and flip a U-turn."

"It's over, try and relax." I tried to not sound patronizing.

"Yeah, sorry, dude." His mind was still spinning.

We were silent for the rest of the way back to the hotel.

James' voice startled me as we walked through the lobby. "Good afternoon, Mr. West. Is everything all right today, sir?"

"Huh, oh yeah, fine. Thanks, James."

"Excellent, sir." He looked back down at his desk. I figured I must look like I feel.

Tommy asked, "How would they know? The newspaper?" as we sat down on the couch in the big room.

"I'm not sure but they do, and that's that."

We examined the Ziploc bag sitting on the table between us.

"How much blow did you get?"

"Well, twenty-five hundred should be a heavy ounce of the good stuff, but this looks heavier than that."

"Looks more like a couple ounces to me, dude." With all the bags he'd seen in my possession over the months, I'd say he was as good of a judge as any.

"Gimmie somma that." I referred to the bottle of Jack he retrieved on our way through the door.

"Knock yourself out, dude. Ya want a beer to go with it?" He handed me the bottle on his way to the bar.

"Yeah, thanks. And call Missy."

"Why?"

"To tell her to stop by your place and grab the triple beam on her way over." I always kept a scale at Tommy's place in case I needed to make a sale on the fly.

"Oh yeah. Good idea."

Two hours and the bottle of Jack later, the girls arrived. They each had a bag in hand. Missy produced the scale from her duffel bag while Laurie opened her garment bag on our bed before joining us in the living area.

I was carefully adjusting the weights on the scale when Laurie sat down next to me on the sofa with a kiss and asked, "Have you read the paper yet?"

"Nah. It's in the bedroom."

"You should," Missy suggested.

I asked Laurie if she read it while looking more closely at her adorable little pink outfit, noting tears forming in her eyes. "Yes, I have; it's sad."

"Well, are you going to tell me or what?" I was becoming more concerned by the second.

"Don't you want to read it?"

"Just give me the highlights, Laurie, okay? No sugar coating."

"Bottom line," Tommy said, "You're wanted for questioning in the attempted murder of some kid. They know you're a dealer, so anything in the house is being seized including the fuckin' Camaro."

"And?"

"And there's some kinda reward if someone turns ya in and they arrest you."

"Convict you," Missy said.

"You mean if somebody turns me in, they get paid?"

"Well, yeah. Somthin' about a new program to stop drugs."

"Well, that's good news. If I run outta money, I'll just turn myself in."

Laurie said, "That's not funny."

"Don't worry honey, I'm like Tony fuckin' Montana in this joint. They won't get me."

"Be serious, Reno," she pleaded.

"No! You guys lighten up. I'm in the fire not any of you, so let me deal with it."

"I think you should..." Laurie started but I cut her off. "Laurie, you know how I feel about you but if anybody feels the need to discuss this further, I'd appreciate them not doing it around me, okay?" The room fell silent until I said, "We've got nearly two ounces of high-quality blow and a fully stocked bar. Does anybody wanna get fucked up?" Three hands went up, classroom style, and I laughed out loud.

With the room relaxed and before I could stop him, Tommy suddenly blurted out, "Man, you should've seen the shit we went through today. They were gonna shoot ol' Reno in the back with a fuckin' Uzi."

"What?" Laurie was shocked and obviously concerned.

"Nice work Einstein. Nothing happened, we're not going back, and it's over."

Laurie hugged me firmly. "I can't leave you alone for a minute, can I?"

"Then don't," I whispered back, kissing her ear.

While the girls unpacked their bags, I asked Tommy what the paper said about Dustin.

"They got him at the house. He's locked up again and probably won't ever get out after this stunt."

I shook my head, pointed towards the pile of coke on the scale and said, "You see where all this shit leads don't ya?"

"Yeah, but fuck it."

"Well buddy, here's to fuck it." I punctuated the moment by knocking the bag from the scale to the table with the bottle of beer in my hand. Tommy ignored my point as he grabbed the empties from the coffee tables.

"I'll reload the beer situation."

"Thanks, dude," was all that was worth saying as I sat back into the big couch and reflected on just how fucked my situation had become. Robert's prophecy had come to fruition like forecasting a breeze on his boat. I could almost hear him: "You'll be dead or in jail inside of a year and I'm not keeping you around to watch." I wondered if there was any way to change course at this point in my life and then blew it off as self-pity.

"Hey, Laurie?"

Her response came from the bedroom with a subtle jest. "Yes, honey."

"Do you want me?"

"Always," she replied, now peeking out the double doors with an irresistible smile.

"Good. Just checking."

"Prick."

A minute later, Laurie called out. "Are we going to Sally's lounge tonight?"

"Nah, I don't think so."

This had Tommy busting up and Missy yelling at him to shut up. I suddenly felt as though I had a family again.

Laurie joined me on the couch after unpacking her bag. "Tomorrow, let's go shopping for some new clothes, okay?"

I took a break from shaping a heart out of the cocaine on the table and looked down at yesterday's borrowed clothes I was still wearing.

"Sure honey. I guess I could use some." Everything I owned was either in the house or likely thrown away by the Tokyo crew. I waved an arm over my design on the glass. "This is my heart; don't break it."

"You're the second man I've ever said I love you to, and I meant it both times." She ran her fingers softly through my hair and then clinched it in a fist, making me look into her incredible eyes.

"I believe you Laurie and I'm sorry I didn't say it back last night but it's like my world is goin' so fast I can't even see what's goin' by. I've wanted this opportunity with you since the first time we met and now I've got it and don't know why."

"You'd better believe me. I've wanted you since the first day too, but I had to let you find your way. You were so handsome and seemed sincere when we talked. When you didn't hit on me, I knew I wanted to get to know you but the opportunity to spend some time together didn't come until yesterday."

"What about when I'd give you rides in the Jag?"

"Reno, you never made any move; it was always like you weren't interested in being more than friends so I thought that's what you wanted, and I only had so many rides I could ask for in hopes of you seeing through it. I've been watching you, waiting for the right opportunity, and when Missy told me you were here, well, I jumped on the chance to get you alone somewhere other than a little sports car."

She suddenly seemed more vulnerable than you'd think a girl like her could be.

"Thanks, Laurie. You had my heart the moment we met; I just didn't have the courage to pursue you, especially with the stories of older rich guys being all you were interested in."

"Don't believe everything you hear about people; it's not always true, and I'm not some man-eater. Hell, I've only had three boyfriends in my whole life." She concluded with a giggle.

"Yeah, me too."

"I said I think you're wonderful, not virginal, and you may be in my heart but I'm not stupid. Remember, I've been watching you."

Tommy leaned over my shoulder and said, "Where have I seen that before?" referring to the heart on the mirror. He had changed into some clothes Missy brought from his house and was holding a clean shirt, underwear and socks for me. Laurie was, of course, oblivious to the meaning of his comment; I did not respond except to thank him for the clothes.

Over the next few days, we hardly left the suite, other than a chauffeured shopping spree to the tune of about four thousand dollars and my much-needed haircut. I looked as good as I've ever looked; my mom would've loved the style, even if it was a blend of nightclub and gangster. James attended to our daily needs, but by Friday I thought I better call Pete Wolf to find out how deep I was really in due to this latest shitstorm of trouble.

"If this is life on the lamb, I'm on the wrong side of this business," Pete said as he entered the suite late Friday afternoon. I introduced him to everyone and then he and I sat down at the table in the master bedroom to discuss my situation.

"When I saw the story on Monday, I took the liberty of starting a file on your latest tangle. It could be worse you know." He thumbed through some papers as he spoke.

"How's that?" I was sincerely perplexed by the thought of a worse scenario.

"Well, they didn't get you at the scene of the crime; this allows a shred of plausible deniability even with a dozen witnesses. Your friend, on the other hand, is gonna do two years back in Illinois for parole violations and that's before he even answers these latest charges. I told you he was no good."

I ignored his comment while my head clouded as I thought of Dustin being locked up for defending me in our own house.

"Not to worry. There's always a solution, so chin up Reno." Pete took a long swig of the bottle of Beck's Light he was given when he arrived, and then continued as my mind tried to stay in the moment and not wander to thoughts of Dustin. "Here's the deal: twenty-five thousand in cash on Monday plus my fees and expenses and you won't even go to court."

"No way!" I was elated by the thought of this just going away.

"Slow down buddy; the bad news is next if you can call it bad in the face of this latest shit you've stacked up."

"What's the bad news?" I asked with a growing sense of confidence.

"You've gotta leave the state. Hell, I'd leave the Midwest if I were you."

"Why?" I jumped out of my seat in protest.

"Because the money isn't buying you out; it's more or less putting you on a shelf. If you so much as get stopped for jaywalking in this state within the next ten years, you'll do serious time; and that, my friend, is a bankable promise." He paused to give me time to absorb the newest reality in my world.

Pete's father was a major league judge who'd risen through the ranks during his career that began at Yale, and he was born connected at all levels of government just by association. He went on to solidify the network to serve his clients very well, but even high-profile connections can only make so much happen when you're guilty as hell.

"I thought you'd be happy. You do have the cash, don't you?"

"It's not the cash, Pete. Fuck the money." I shook my head in defeat.

"Then what?"

"Well, Laurie and I…"

"Hey! Forget about pussy. This is your ass and it's non-negotiable." Now holding my forearm tightly, he continued, "You don't have choices, my friend. I'm sorry, but that's that." He patted my shoulder and added, "Look, buddy, you're in great shape, so let's get out of this dark room and celebrate." He stood and started for the door.

"Wait." I reached under the bed for the pack and placed it on the comforter. "I'll pay you now."

"If you want, but Monday is fine."

He watched me dump the contents of the pack onto the bed and stood silently as I counted out twenty-five thousand in cash, wrapped the bill stacks in rubber bands, and handed it to him. He slipped the money into his now open attaché case, dropped the lid, and clicked the locks with his thumbs in a sweeping motion. He grabbed the handle, jerked the case from the bed and said, "It's good to be free, anywhere, and don't you forget it. Hey, bud, it's not the end of the world, just another chapter, so wrap it up and head out while you still can." As he finished his last words he turned and walked out of the room.

Laurie came into the room a few minutes later and asked, "Should Bobby take Pete somewhere or…"

Bobby had picked up Pete a few blocks from his office, which can be done without ever walking outside in Minneapolis via the above-ground skyways that connect so many of the downtown buildings and parking garages. Pete was concerned the police may be watching him to find me. He'd represented me repeatedly, so he didn't want to drive his car to see me.

I was standing at the drapes that blew gently in the breeze, looking out over the balcony when Laurie walked up behind me after I didn't reply.

"Are you okay?" She snuggled against my back with her arms around my waist.

"Can we talk about it later?"

"Sure honey, whenever you want." After a kiss on the back of my neck, she was gone.

From the doorway, Pete asked, "You don't mind if I stick around for a while, do ya?"

"Of course not, Pete. You're always welcome. I'll be right out."

"You got it, buddy." Pete quietly pulled the French doors closed.

I stepped out onto the balcony, looking at the city I'd grown to love. My legs became weak, and I slumped down against the wall, weeping like a child. About an hour later, the French doors opened; a few moments passed, and then Laurie stepped out onto the balcony.

"I put your stuff back in the pack; it's under the bed, okay?" I remained silent, staring out into the distance. Laurie moved in front of me and leaned against the railing. "I'll be here for you no matter what happens." I got up without a word, lifted her little pink skirt, and pulled her panties to the side with my thumb while she fumbled with my zipper and underwear. As we made love, her butt balanced on the railing, I thought for a second that if I leaned just a little farther over, I could die happy; but life just isn't that easy.

"Let's rock and roll," I shouted, waving the baggie of coke into the air as Laurie and I entered the living room through the double doors.

"Top of the world!" Pete toasted from the couch where they all sat like some kind of cocktail party.

Besides Laurie and me, in the room were Tommy, Missy, Bobby and Pete. By the time Bobby left to take Pete home, we had gone through more than a quarter ounce of coke and almost emptied the remaining bar stock.

"Call James..." I said to no one in particular, "...and tell him it's time to reload for round two."

"Yee-ha!" Tommy cheered like some cowboy on the first night back from the range before leaping for the phone to carry out my bidding.

I sat back on the couch, thinking of Pete's parting words spoken into my ear as he rubbed my shoulders. "Stop by the office on Monday but be sure to come in through the mall. I want to see ya before you go, okay?"

Now that I agreed to the deal, I had a couple days to vacate the state, but it was still best to avoid seeing any cops.

At 8:00 PM, Sunday night, James Myers was let in the door by Laurie just minutes after his call asking if he could come up.

"Excuse the intrusion sir, but I need to speak with you. Is there somewhere we might talk?" He spoke from the foyer as he entered; I sat alone on the couch.

"Of course, James, please join me."

Tommy and Missy were gone in search of limes and little umbrellas for the upcoming tequila-fest we planned to celebrate one week in the palace. Laurie followed James and sat down by my side after his polite refusal of the drink she offered. A stack of cash sat next to a moderate pile of coke and my bottle of Beck's from Friday's replenished supply.

"Sir, the weekly rate I can offer you at this point is three thousand five hundred. Will that be satisfactory?"

"James, this is Laurie." My speech exposed my level of intoxication.

"It's a pleasure to make your acquaintance, Miss." He responded with a fatherly warmth.

"I think I'll marry her, James." I slid the just counted thirty-five hundred towards him on the table. "What do you think?"

"A fine choice, I'm sure." James ignored the money; he just looked at me with concern in his soft brown eyes.

Laurie leaned over and kissed me, saying, "Don't tease me," in the softest of tones.

"You're awful good to me, James." I leaned back deeply into the sofa and stared at the ceiling. "I really like this place, ya know."

"Thank you, sir. You're a well-liked guest." James retrieved the money from the table while standing with a hand outstretched to receive mine. He looked at us affectionately before adding, "You'll call on me should you need anything, won't you?"

"Sure. Thanks, James."

Laurie led him to the door and then returned to my side.

"Laurie, Pete said I've gotta leave town tomorrow."

"Then why would you pay for another week?"

"I've got over twenty thousand dollars, the most beautiful girl in the world, and this suite that's fit for a king, not to mention a limo out front. It's kinda hard to go."

"What's the deal from Pete?" She was still glowing from the compliment as she asked.

"If I go tomorrow, they'll put my file away for ten years and then lose it; but if I get caught here, I'll go to prison for a long time."

"The room is for me?" Her eyes turned deeply mournful.

"What else can I do?"

"Why can't we go together?"

"I can't do that to you. Look at me. I'm a mess."

"I think you're wonderful and I'll decide what's done and not done to me."

"What would we do for money?"

"I'll model, I've had offers, or even wait tables if I have to, and you'll write a book about all the crazy shit you get caught up in."

"No. I'll sell drugs and go to prison and then you'll be alone and far from home."

"You didn't fuck up, Dustin did, and I'm not paying the price for his mistakes."

"We'd need more cash."

"Missy and I can sell in Minnetonka. In a week, we'll have more than enough cash."

"I haven't got enough blow to make a big enough hit, and I can't go back to my guy, so where will I get the coke?" I was cheering up just a bit as a ray of sun broke through the clouds of my life once again.

"I'll make a call to Deb and get us a 'key' for ten grand, at least I think that's what she said anyway."

"A kilo for ten G's?"

"Isn't that enough?"

"Enough? That's a hundred grand on the street; we'd get at least seventy-five grand back even if we didn't even cut it all."

"Perfect. I'll call her tonight."

Laurie's sister had called from Vegas to say her boyfriend Carl got some awesome coke out west that was selling cheap for some reason; you could get a whole kilo of the stuff for ten "G's."

"Wait a second. Do you know how much coke a kilo is?"

"Just over two pounds, right?"

"Right. One thousand grams! You couldn't sell that much blow in a week if the whole lake lined up to buy it."

"Well, then we'll have to sell to other places too." She was not to be defeated.

I thought for a minute and then it hit me. "You're right! I can unload half of it from right here. I know a guy in Jersey who'll take a no-risk kilo at that price all day long. Shit, he'd pay twenty grand for it no problem, and then if you guys can sell another thirty grand in a week, we'd have another fifty grand to go with."

"But you said you'd sell him the whole thing. Where do we get the other stuff?"

"If it's as amazing as your sister says, I'll cut it by a hundred percent, that makes two 'keys' baby." I punctuated the statement with a wink.

She tackled me onto the sofa, saying, "I love you," while yanking at my fly. I pulled her panties out of the way just as she crashed down on me, nearly injuring us both. She rode me like a rodeo star, yelling, "CA-LI-FOR-NI-A." I was still inside her, lying beneath her collapsed body when Tommy and Missy came in.

"Oh, sorry." Missy apologized.

Tommy just ignored us on his way to the bar as we fumbled like a couple of kids caught by her parents. After explaining the situation to them, and our plan, Tommy said, "Let's blow this frozen hole and get 'Cali' bound!" I noticed during the excitement that a Jimmy Buffett video was playing on MTV; the song was "Margaritaville." I turned up the volume on the big screen and we sang along, further fueling our electricity. "Wastin' away again in Margaritaville. Lookin' for my lost shaker of salt."

We drank and snorted to our future adventures until the exhaustion of the day finally sent us to our rooms. Much later that night, I lay awake in bed with Laurie's warm breath on my chest as she slept beside me with her head tucked into my shoulder. I wished I was strong enough to slip away into the night, to save her from the cloud that darkened my every step, but I remained, disappointed by my weakness as a tear of doubt ran down my face and into her golden locks.

When I told Pete Wolf of my plan for one more score before leaving, he said, "Good luck my friend. I'll miss you," as he tore one of his business cards in half, handing the pieces to me in place of a handshake. He sat back down at his desk and continued to read from an open file. I stopped at the door and looked over my shoulder at him. He's been a good friend. As I walked out the door, I heard the words "top of the world," unsure if they'd been spoken. I passed through the reception area silently without stopping and merged into the masses traveling from one building's interior to the next. I heeded his advice to come and go through the mall as opposed to directly into his building from the street. I'd been given until tonight to split town per the court's sealed agreement, and Minnetonka was thirty minutes from downtown, but it was still best to use every precaution.

Once back in the limo in the underground garage several blocks from the office, I drank directly from the whiskey decanter while Kansas' "Dust in the Wind" played mockingly on the radio. We drove under the skyways of the great city watching the people crossing through the elevated tubes. I felt encapsulated by my actions, trapped in an endless tunnel. The sky was as sooty gray as my tortured soul; it loomed in warning of the inevitable storm to come.

I decided not to pay for another week of the limo, to save money and lay low. After opening the door for me to exit the car, Bobby warmly said, "If ever you should need the services of Fantasy Limousine again, don't hesitate to call on me." He paused sadly when I didn't respond, apparently missing his humor, and then added, "I'll get you a rate," as he swatted the door closed behind me.

"Thanks, Bobby." I wore a forced smile as I handed him a small roll of five one-hundreds.

"I can't take this from you."

He was holding the money outstretched to me. We'd had an amazing week together and he grew to appreciate me and the way I treated the people around me. "Yes, you can. Don't insult me."

I had already turned to walk away when he asked, "Are you okay, Reno?"

"Top of the world, man." I waved without looking back as I pushed through the revolving door with a slight stumble.

A voice called out while I passed through the lobby. "Reno." It was Sally; she was working an early shift and offered to buy me a drink while complaining that Mondays were always slow.

"Sure. Why not?" My speech slurred as I turned toward the lounge.

"Great. What can I get you?"

I stepped onto the carpeting from the marble-tiled lobby. "Well, I've been drinkin' whiskey all day but it ain't workin', so why don't ya get me a bottle a tequila and I'll buy." I headed to a corner in the back of the place; the quarter-round booth I chose faced the whole room, but the bar was obscured by a mirrored support pillar. Neil Diamond serenaded the empty room with "September Morn" while the bartender focused on some sports highlights show on the screen over the bar.

"Mind if I join ya?" Sally was filling the two shot glasses she placed on my table.

"Help yourself." I slid into the corner to provide her some space in the booth.

"I'm glad I saw you." She was jovial, completely carefree, but I couldn't help wondering if Tommy's story about the howling waitress was exaggerated. As she poured me another shot, she asked, "Are you still staying here?"

"Yeah. You still work here?"

"Huh? Oh, I guess that was a stupid question."

I did not respond but instead drank the shot and followed up with a long drink directly from the bottle.

She filled my shot glass again. "Is Laurie still here?"

I drank the shot and then replied, "Yeah," as I sat the glass down hard, indicating it needed to be refilled.

"I'd like to thank you for the other night," she said while honoring the requested refill.

"Great. Then keep my fuckin' glass full."

She scanned the lounge before sliding her hand onto my crotch with a firm squeeze. "I'll do more than that." She slipped under the table, unbuttoned my pants and pulled them open with a tug. I tossed my head back into the red velvet cushion and laughed at the absurdity of the event. "Quiet," she warned, now holding my half erection in her hand, but I continued laughing as she consumed me again and again, apparently not loud enough to attract attention even when the sound of her head occasionally hitting the table was added to the clamor. I thought of how insane and depraved my life had become; even the orgasm was unpleasant within the stream of thoughts and guilt. The only pleasure I could muster was prolonging her fear of being caught. Finally, I released the last of my worldly cares with each pulse of would-be carnal pleasure.

What the hell had happened to me? I wasn't the guy I knew or wanted to be, and money and drugs just made it worse. I was so caught up in staying one step ahead that I forgot to keep in touch with the moment at hand. I didn't want to cheat on Laurie, and I sure as hell didn't give a shit about this waitress, nor did I even want the act she performed to take place; yet just like everything else in my world, it seemed to just happen. I felt like a bystander in my own life, unwilling to put forth the effort to try and control what happened to and around me any longer.

Guilt, confusion, and fear of so many things kept my head spinning, and the booze and drugs made it impossible to find even a moment of clarity, so I simply forged ahead as each new event unfurled like some fucked up movie on fast forward.

PART VII

The Broken Wing

The Broken Wing

The California sun was every bit as hot as Florida's, but the heat was arid and felt scorching on Lori Ann's exposed skin. The humidity was gone from the air, and most of the insects were nowhere to be found, but the same charge of life filled the general atmosphere and all those she encountered. The same underbelly of society was ever-present as well, but this place had a feeling of raw uncertainty like anything could happen at any moment. Lori Ann wondered if that was how the locals felt or was it just the possibility of earthshaking quakes that kept them on their toes? Either way, she'd be glad to get back to Florida and put this snapshot of big-time moving and shaking behind her. All she wanted was to get the money and go house hunting where picket fences line the streets instead of topless bars and junk cars on blocks. Stephen, on the other hand, seemed to be loving it.

Their taxi driver was nice enough, especially since he had been offered no specific destination; still, she felt completely at his mercy as they drove down West Century Blvd with LAX disappearing into the background. They had no problem getting the luggage, even though they both got pale while waiting at the turnstile for their respective bags to appear.

They looked out the windows in silence while scanning hotels and motels as they traveled the city streets. Stephen saw a motel a half block away and told the driver to pull in. Lori Ann waited in the cab while Stephen checked in; upon returning, he explained to the driver that it was a dive and they needed to keep looking. The driver grumbled but continued through the city, pointing to every hotel and motel as they neared. Finally, Stephen saw a Holiday Inn and told the driver to drop them there. After checking into the room, Stephen called a Pizzeria for delivery and settled in for the evening. Lori Ann unpacked the meager supplies they brought, putting personal items in the bathroom and hanging their clothing in the closet. It was a long night with little conversation and no discussion of seeing any sites beyond the room.

In the morning, Lori Ann asked, "So, when do we meet them?"

"We don't, I do. It's nothing for you to get involved with."

"I thought we agreed to do it together?"

"We are doing it together but one hour of this deal will be me alone. I'll need to focus on the deal and not have to worry about you. I'll be back in no time and then we'll leave and go home."

"Fine, but you'll come right back and then we go." Lori Ann didn't want to meet these people anyway, so she avoided a fight and let it go.

"Absolutely."

That was good enough for her, so she sat waiting beside him for three o'clock to come.

Carlos woke up late and asked Raul to arrange for the girls to be taken to the airport for their commercial return flight to Minnesota. At first, they argued with Raul about being in LA and not seeing anything, but quickly realized a free ticket home after one hell of a night was by far the best option before them.

When 3:00 PM neared, Carlos pulled the cell phone out of the room's bedside drawer and pushed the on button; it was fully charged. It was more like a small briefcase than a phone, with the handset connected by a spiral cord and an antenna that unfolded to extend for reception. It had been left in the drawer by the associate who rented the room and was the local number given to the young man from Florida as a contact number. One phone call was all that would be received from this phone and then it would be destroyed, even though the phone was worth more than a thousand dollars.

At precisely three o'clock, Stephen called the number on the scrap of paper; it rang only twice before being answered by a man with a strange accent. He could have been English or maybe even Spanish, but the speech was very elegant and precise in its delivery.

"Who is calling?"

"It's Stephen, I was told…"

"I know what you were told. Where are you?"

Stephen looked at the card from the cheap motel and read the information out loud. "The West Coast Motel, forty-three hundred West Century Boulevard, room number twenty-nine."

"I see, and you will be there in thirty minutes as well?" Carlos asked while writing down the information on a hotel notepad.

"Yes."

"Fine."

Carlos hung up the phone and tossed it to Raul. "Dispose of this properly and have the car out front immediately."

"I've gotta go," Stephen said, jumping to his feet.

"Who was it? What did he say?"

"It was the Carlos guy; he's meeting me at the other room in thirty minutes. I've gotta go." He was scanning the room wildly and patting his pockets in anticipation of leaving.

She looked at him and began to worry again. "It's not too late to just bail out on this deal."

"I'll be back in a couple hours max and then we'll get outta here in plenty of time to catch the flight in San Diego." Stephen leaned over, kissed Lori Ann on the cheek, and handed her a thousand dollars in cash, keeping only a few hundred for himself. It was the balance of their life savings, but he insisted on having the cash on hand.

"Please be careful, Stephen, and call me if you need me, okay?"

"No problem. It's three o'clock now; I'll see ya by five."

"Be careful."

"I will, honey. I'll be back in a flash with the cash."

And he was gone.

Lori Ann watched out the window but only saw the roof of taxis passing by. She wondered how it would go down and if these people were simply the businessmen Stephen thought they'd be, honorable in their dealings with each other. She paced for a few minutes and then she saw it. The little coke vial with the spoon attached by a gold chain was laying on the dresser. Her stomach dropped as she thought of who these men must be, men who can come up with so much money in such a short time and have the means to sell such a quantity of cocaine. Maybe it was the men who lost it to begin with, or perhaps it was some gang that would kill him for the drugs. If people die in big cities for a pair of sneakers or a jacket, certainly this much money is worth killing for. There was no one to call, no way to help him, and nothing to do but wait.

"Carlos and Raul." These were the only names she knew; one from Minnesota, the other from LA, maybe. She was getting too worked up and had to calm down, but she couldn't go for a walk. What if Stephen called while she was out? She turned on the TV but it was a feature on a hijacking in the Middle East, so she shut it off. It was a world filled with violence and death. She looked at her watch: 3:15 PM. He'd be back in an hour; she just had to calm down.

Lori Ann began packing the suitcase Stephen left behind, carefully folding the clothing and placing it on top of the false bottom. Again, she looked at her watch: 3:17 PM. She turned the TV back on and flipped through the channels without paying attention to the shows as they blinked past on the screen.

Stephen arrived at the motel at 3:20 PM, slipped into the room, and sat the suitcase on the dresser next to the TV. As soon as he sat down on the bed, there was a knock at the door; it was two solid raps in quick succession. He felt his mouth go dry as he stood up. His palms filled with moisture as he reached for the door handle. He took a deep breath, turned the handle, and opened the door.

Raul smiled at him and extended his hand in greeting, saying, "Good to see you," as he pushed his way past Stephen and into the room. Carlos entered on Raul's heels and looked over the room without saying a word.

"You must be Carlos; it's nice to meet you." Stephen offered an outstretched hand.

"A reasonable assumption," Carlos replied, looking him over without shaking his hand. "So, where is the product you discussed?"

Stephen pointed to the suitcase; Raul opened it and said, "Esta bien, Don Carlos."

"Good," Carlos responded to Raul and then asked Stephen, "Are you here alone?"

"Yeah, but I've gotta get goin', so..." Stephen hoped to move the conversation to money.

"I see. So, you wish to be paid now, am I correct?"

"Well, yeah. I mean, like he said, uh, the stuff's right there, and so..." Stephen was finding it hard to swallow but believed he looked calm on the outside, so he didn't panic, yet.

"You don't think I'd walk around with such a large quantity of cash on me, do you? Stephen, the world is full of dangerous men who would kill someone for far less."

"Well yeah, but I thought..."

"Did you presume how I run my business?"

"No, I just thought..."

"You thought I was some kind of fool?" Carlos loosened his tie. "Is that what you thought?"

"No. I just wanna get my money so I can go." Stephen looked over his shoulder at Raul, who had closed the suitcase and was now holding it at his side.

"Go where? I thought you were traveling alone."

"Nowhere, I mean, I need to go home."

"I see, and where is your suitcase?"

"Raul has..."

"No. The one with your personal effects in it. You know, like a toothbrush or perhaps some clothing. You are in such a hurry, but I don't see another bag here in your room. This is your room, is it not?"

"No, I mean yes, it's my room, but I don't have another bag."

"So, your plan is to carry one hundred thousand dollars in your pockets?"

"No, I was gonna..."

Carlos asked, "Who is traveling with you and where are they now?" while indicating to Raul to check the bathroom.

Raul looked in the bathroom, closet, and under the beds and then said, "Nobody and no stuff."

"So, Mr. Stephen, you came all the way to LA from Florida alone and without even a clean shirt or toothbrush? That is very interesting indeed."

"I..."

"I find it very upsetting when people lie to me, Stephen, very disheartening indeed."

"Look..." Stephen began but was interrupted by Raul this time.

"Where is she? Don't fuck with us."

"Raul, such language."

"Pardon me, Don Carlos."

"So, Stephen, there is a woman traveling with you, but she is not here, so where is she? In another room in this place?"

"No, she's, I mean, she's at home. Look, can I just have my money now?"

"Now you're calling me a liar?"

"No. What?"

"I told you I didn't have the money with me, but you think I'm lying?"

"No, I just thought we could get it now." Stephen could hear his voice breaking, and the sweat was running in his eyes causing a sting and blurred vision. He hadn't turned on the air conditioning when he came in; the room felt like a thousand degrees.

"Well, Stephen, I'm afraid I may have left something at home as well. In fact, I'm quite certain of it. You see, I have forgotten your money at home, just as you left your girlfriend at home."

Stephen's fear and stress level got to him; he lost his temper and screamed, "What the fuck does Lori Ann have to do with my money?"

Raul grabbed him around the neck and pulled him close in a tight headlock before Stephen knew what happened. From the corner of his eye, he could see the gun being held to his temple and didn't have time to flinch before his stomach collapsed under a blow from Carlos.

"Where is she?" Carlos delivered another blow to Stephen's stomach. Stephen expelled fluid and chunks of pizza down his chin and shirt front after the second impact. "You'd be amazed at how long I can do this, Stephen. Are you listening?"

"I, oof..." Stephen attempted an answer but was interrupted by another more severe shot, this time to the ribs.

Raul pulled tightly against Stephen's neck, whispering into his ear, "We're not fucking with you amigo. Where is your girl?" He eased the vice grip just enough so air could be taken in to speak.

"Well, at least tell us her name. Stephen, you can at least do that, can't you? Lori Ann who?"

Carlos pulled a pistol from inside his suit coat and a silencer from a trouser pocket, putting them together while Stephen watched, and then added, "Stephen, I'm growing tired of your refusal to cooperate with me. Now, what is her name?"

Stephen squeezed his eyes tightly shut in defiance of Raul's grip but opened them again while screaming as a bullet exploded his knee.

Carlos leaned in closely, holding Stephen's bobbing head up by his hair. "Tell me her name and where she is, or I'll kill you and your entire family."

"Morgan! Christ! You can keep the money."

Carlos laughed out loud. "Well now, Stephen, that's more like it. Now you're being both cooperative and generous; these are traits that I admire." Stephen's head fell forward again as he struggled with consciousness. "No, no, no, Stephen, not yet. I need to know where you and Ms. Morgan are staying, then you may pass out but not before."

Stephen knew now that he would never leave this room and that Lori Ann had been right all along. She begged him to just work hard and save money, to stop looking for shortcuts, but he never listened. He looked up at Carlos and whispered inaudibly causing Carlos to lean in closely to hear the words. Once Carlos was just inches away, Stephen spat blood and saliva all over his face before saying, "Fuck you, spic!" Raul reacted instantly, pulling the trigger on his nine-millimeter, sending a bullet through Stephen's temple, covering all three of them in blood.

"Raul! What are you thinking?" Carlos admonished him as he

wiped the chunks of brain matter from his face and hair. "How are we going to walk out of here looking like this?"

"But Don Carlos, he called you…"

"I don't care what his words were; in fact, it shows courage on his part that few of my own men possess. Raul, we have a problem now that we were not prepared for. So, how do you propose we deal with it?"

"I don't know, maybe…"

"Maybe? Okay, Raul, this is what we're going to do. I'm going to clean up in the bathroom and leave this place while you decide how to deal with this body and our missing girl."

"What if she's not here?"

"Raul, she is here. Find her!" He shouted while walking into the bathroom, growling in disgust as he looked at the condition of his suit. "Check his wallet for a picture, Raul."

"What?"

"La catera!"

"Si, Don Carlos."

Lori Ann paced the room wildly, staring at the clock on the bedside. 4:47 PM. Where was he? He said that if he wasn't back by five o'clock, she should go to San Diego and catch their return flight alone; he'd get a later flight and see her at his place, so she shouldn't hang around the room waiting. Why would he say that? Was there something she didn't know or maybe he knew something was going wrong? Maybe he planned to take off with the money all along. Maybe he'd grown tired of her resisting his desire to be a big-time drug dealer. The life she wanted wasn't aligned with his kingpin fantasy and this was his chance to enter that world. Maybe there was more to the Miami story and she'd been in the dark all along. Her mind raced in too many directions as the clock's digital numbers flipped to 4:52, and still no word.

Carlos reappeared from the bathroom soaking wet. He had stripped down in the shower, scrubbed all the blood and gore from his clothing, skin and hair, and then toweled off after dressing to reduce the appearance of being saturated.

"What is your plan, Raul?"

"I have it covered, Don Carlos. You need not worry."

"Is that so?" Carlos replied with a tone of disbelief as he picked up the suitcase from the bed, examining it for blood splatter. "Did you clean this?"

"I looked it over; my body must have shielded it from the blood."

"Fine. Now you will see to it that this room is clean as well before leaving, right?"

"Si, Don Carlos."

Carlos opened the suitcase and examined the contents before closing it again. He scanned the room for anything that might tie him to the place, running through a mental checklist. He hadn't touched the door while entering or anything in the room, other than the incidental contact with the body and the shower that he wiped down. The only other thing was the suitcase, and that would leave with him. The room was clear.

"Raul, you have done well in this matter, but see that you follow through on your obligation to finish the job."

"Si, Don Carlos. I'll take care of it."

"Fine. I will speak to you upon my return home, and you will also locate Ms. Morgan, correct?"

"But?"

"She's here, Raul, and may have seen us. And if not, you must go to her in Florida. Raul, she is the only link between this situation and us. Do you understand the importance of what I'm telling you?"

"Si, Don Carlos. I'll find her and take care of it."

Carlos handed Raul a roll of bills, two thousand dollars. "You may need some additional funds to be sure this is done correctly."

Raul smiled widely and accepted the money knowing this would not cost him ten cents to clean up and he would be reimbursed for any expenses anyway. "Thank you, Don Carlos."

"I must go now. I can see this is well in hand, Raul."

"Thank you, Don Carlos."

Carlos opened the door with a wet handkerchief, looking carefully beyond the threshold as the opening broadened for his departure. He did not look back as he heard the door close behind him; instead, he focused on the waiting car parked just a few spaces away on the street. His drivers knew better than to open his door in less formal settings, as he avoided drawing attention through such trivial luxuries. Within moments, the black Town Car was pulling onto the street and disappearing into the afternoon traffic.

"Go to the airport, Julio, and we're in no hurry." Carlos settled into the leather seat, his arm resting on the suitcase at his side.

Lori Ann was in tears as the digital clock radio flashed 5:57 PM. She knew she should go, but where? She grabbed her suitcase and headed for the door. As she glanced back at the room and the clock, she noticed the little vial on the nightstand. The maid would find it and they'd know who was in the room last and have them arrested. She went back and slipped it in her pocket and headed for the door. Once in the lobby, she asked the front desk attendant if he could get her a taxi.

"Of course. Just tell the doorman and he'll flag one for you. Thank you for staying with the Holiday Inn."

Raul was still wiping up all the blood when he noticed the wallet lying on the floor; he picked it up and reviewed its contents: three hundred and forty-nine dollars, five Florida lottery tickets, a house key, a condom, several business cards, and a picture of a girl. He flipped over the photo; "Lori Ann 5/29/84" was written on the back. It was her! He put the money and the picture in his pocket and flipped through the business cards: one from a tire store in Jacksonville, Florida; one from a restaurant in Jacksonville, Florida; one from the motel he was in right now and another from a Holiday Inn on Sunset. "That's it," Raul shouted. "She's at the Holiday Inn."

Raul stuffed the card in his pocket and ran out the door, sprinting into the street and in front of a passing cab. "Taxi! Stop!"

The cabbie slammed on the brakes to avoid hitting him; Raul jumped in shouting, "Holiday Inn." He gave the driver the address and finished with "Hurry!"

"You should be more careful. I almost ran you down my friend."

"Yeah. I said hurry, okay?" Raul realized he didn't need to be any more memorable than he already was, so he decided against threatening the man. A few minutes later, Raul asked, "Is that the Holiday Inn?" as he pointed down the block ahead.

"Ah, yes. That is the Holiday Inn."

Lori Ann walked out into the sunlight and asked the doorman for a cab to San Diego Airport. He waved a taxi into the "standing lane" in front of the hotel, but the cabbie was driving too fast and had to lock up his brakes in front of them. She glanced at another cab that also had to slam on brakes to avoid hitting hers. Her heart raced even harder for a second, but she calmed as the doorman opened her taxi door and told the driver the San Diego destination.

Raul's taxi was pulling up to the hotel behind another cab in traffic, but that cab stopped short, so he jammed the breaks as well to avoid hitting it and said, "My goodness, that man is not paying attention to his driving; we nearly collided with him. He added, "Your fare will be sixteen dollars," with a friendly smile.

Raul was flipping through the bills in his hand, looking for a twenty with one hand while opening the door of the moving car with the other when the tires chirped to a stop. He braced himself with a forearm, looked up at the driver, and was handing him a twenty when he saw her getting into a cab. She glanced up after hearing the squeal of the tires before climbing into the taxi. She looked familiar to Raul, a standout in a sea of young and beautiful California girls, perhaps a model or a girl he'd seen on some sitcom; and then it hit him. He pulled the picture out of his pocket; it was her, Lori Ann! He slammed the door shut. "Follow that taxi."

"Oh, my friend, you have been seeing too many movies."

"I said follow her, I'm serious."

"But sir..."

"Please!" Raul forced a smile as he tossed a one-hundred-dollar bill onto the seat beside the driver.

"Well, if you insist." The cabbie chuckled and pulled out behind the exiting cab.

"I don't know where these towelheads get their licenses," Lori Ann's driver said with a nearly toothless grin while looking in his rearview mirror at both her and the cab that pulled the seemingly erratic maneuver behind them.

"Yeah," Lori Ann replied, already nauseous from the smell of the man. She glanced over her shoulder as the other cab passed the hotel's entrance without someone exiting or entering the cab.

"So, how come you don't just fly outta LAX? It's right down the road."

"I'm meeting someone in San Diego; he's already there." She answered him while keeping her eyes on the taxi behind them, now wondering if it could be Stephen.

"Stay with her," Raul cautioned.

"I am doing my best but some of these drivers don't obey the laws."

Raul threw another hundred onto the front seat. "Here, I'll pay the ticket."

"Oh no, I have never been issued a citation for such behavior." He put the money in his shirt pocket with a smile.

"Just don't lose him."

Lori Ann sat sideways to look at the pursuing cab and asked the driver if he would mind turning left at the next light?

"That's not the way to the Freeway." He smiled a predator's grin.

"Just go around the block and then we can get on the Freeway, okay?"

"Anything you want, honey."

Lori Ann focused to catch a glimpse of the passenger on the first turn but couldn't see him; the second and third turns were no better, but on the fourth turn back onto their original course she saw him. He was looking at her as well and seemed to be arguing with the driver in his car. It wasn't Stephen. It was a man in a suit, a man of Spanish descent. He was a large man with black hair and big hands banging on the window as he pointed in her direction.

Lori Ann asked, "Can you lose that taxi?"

"Lose him?"

"Yeah, you know, lose him in traffic."

"What's he? Some ex-boyfriend or somethin'?"

"Yes, and he's following me, so can you please speed up and lose him."

"Sure, darlin', but I could get in trouble ya know."

"I'll pay the ticket if you get stopped."

"Shit, I don't care about money. If I did, you think I'd be a cabbie?" He took a few quick turns but the other taxi was hanging with him.

"This guy really wants you, darlin'. Do ya owe him money or is it just that great little ass he can't get over?"

"Just lose him!" Lori Ann began to consider the possibility that it was one of the men Stephen met with; but how could they know her or where to find her? Surely Stephen wouldn't have told them.

"They're speeding up! Don't lose them," Raul ordered.

"Sir, I am already exceeding the limit of speed for this area and will surely be risking a citation if we continue."

"You listen to me, motherfucker. If you lose that taxi, you'll have bigger problems than a fucking ticket."

Lori Ann was terrified now, pleading with the driver. "Please go faster."

"Okay sweet thing, but what do I get if I do lose him?"

"Anything you want, just lose him." Lori Ann reached into her pocket and pulled out the money while watching the other cab slowly slip further behind as her driver slid around corners and accelerated through intersections.

"You're fucking losing them," Raul shouted as he reached for his gun in its shoulder holster.

"I cannot drive this fast. We will crash." Raul's cabbie began to slow. "Maybe another taxi will drive faster for you." He pulled up to the curb and looked over his shoulder just in time to be shot through the neck and into his chest. The driver slumped forward as Raul squeezed through the plastic partition opening he shattered with the shot, shoving the driver's body out of the way as he took over the car's control.

Lori Ann's driver flashed a disgusting grin in the rearview mirror as he flew through a red light and darted in and out of cars. "He pulled over, sweetie. I guess he gave up."

Lori Ann's mind raced wildly. Maybe they knew about San Diego and maybe even about where she and Stephen lived. She couldn't go home, not until she figured out what happened.

"Where's the Bus station?"

"I thought you wanted the airport?"

"I changed my mind. Just take me to the bus station."

"In LA or San Diego?"

"Here! Just take me there!" She was frantically looking at every cab in traffic.

"Settle down, darlin'. It's just a couple miles from here. We can be there in about ten minutes."

"Make it five." She tossed two one-hundred-dollar bills through the partition.

Raul smoked the tires, lurching back into traffic, and began scanning streets as he crossed intersections but couldn't find her. He sped up to taxi after taxi but no Lori Ann, punching the corpse as he went. "I fucking told you not to lose them!"

"I told you I didn't care about money." Lori Ann's driver chuckled as he tossed her money back at her. "I just want some of that sweet ass."

Lori Ann reached up through the partition opening and took his ear in her fist while driving her index finger into the side of his eyeball. "Look, scumbag, you take me to the fucking bus station or I'll leave this piece of shit with more than just your eyeball. Understand?"

"The Chief" had shown her several self-defense moves over the years, and the Navy Seal's moves were among the best. He loved those guys, hung out with them at every opportunity, and probably would have attempted becoming one had his life gone differently.

"You fuckin' cunt!" He was unable to break her grasp by swatting at her hand. His eyes and nose ran fluids at incredible rates, and his ear burned like a branding iron was being driven into it.

"Are you going to behave and keep that tiny little shoehorn in your pants, or do I need to pull your ear off your greasy fuckin' head?"

He was as shocked by her ferocity as she was. She could only guess that hearing those drill sergeants hammer away at the recruits sank in a bit over the years. "Fine! Just fucking let go."

"Not until you promise to be a gentleman and watch your filthy mouth."

"My filthy mouth?"

"Yes." She dug into his eye again and added a twist to the grip on his ear. "Your filthy fucking mouth."

"Okay, okay, please let go."

She eased her grip but didn't release him completely until he stopped at the bus station in central LA. He made it in less than five minutes, taking shortcuts and speeding the entire way. "How much do I owe you?" She asked in a forced pleasant tone.

"Just get out!" She released her grip, and he leaned into his hands to comfort his pain and check for missing parts.

Lori Ann hopped out of the cab, pulling her suitcase with her in one fluid motion just in time for the cab to speed away in a cloud of dust, slamming the door shut from the acceleration. The driver screamed, "Fuckin' slut," as he vanished in the distance. She scanned other cabs for the man that was following her. He was nowhere in sight, so she hurried inside the terminal and began reading the destinations and departure times.

Raul drove around for nearly thirty minutes before giving up and heading back to the motel. He parked two blocks away in an alley and stuffed the driver in the trunk before walking back to the room. He didn't see any cops, so he assumed that no cleaning lady had stumbled upon Stephen yet. He carefully crossed the small parking lot and went into the room.

Carlos touched down in Las Vegas just forty minutes later and slipped into a waiting courtesy limo from the casino that took him to his hotel. Deborah was gambling at the twenty-dollar blackjack table and appeared to be having a nice time, so he told the concierge to wait half an hour before advising her that he arrived. He wanted some time to shower properly and change out of the very casual clothing he changed into on his plane. He hated to rush back to Minneapolis, but business came first and there were some loose ends to be tied. He already wished he'd passed on the free score and felt as if the product he obtained must have been stolen or lost by a competitor. There was no way a kid like Stephen would legitimately have so much pure cocaine, and now he wondered just who it did belong to. He needed to be careful in the resources he selected to distribute it.

Deborah arrived back at the suite within the hour and inquired why he came directly to the room. He pointed out the pink product on the table and offered her a sample. After she expressed delight at the color and quality, he asked if she might know some people who would be interested in purchasing some of the amazing surprise. Carlos always had incredibly high-quality coke, direct from his cartel's fields, but never would distribute anything so traceable as a pink supply, even if it were highly profitable. Only the Peruvians had pink product, and he always felt it was obnoxious. He had tried the famed pink Peruvian flake on several occasions, but never felt the high-profile product was worth the risk.

"Hell yeah, I know people who'd want it. How much do ya have?"

"Deborah, please refrain from the usage of such language in my presence; it is neither ladylike nor attractive. I have quite a bit and wish to be rid of it in a timely manner. For this product only, and subject to change, I will sell ounces for one thousand dollars and kilos for ten thousand dollars."

"No shit? Oops. I mean, wow, that's cheap."

"Yes, it is an astonishing bargain, so if you'll be so kind as to speak to your friends when we return tomorrow and let me know if any interest is found. Needless to say, I do not wish to be involved in anything less than the sale of kilos, and perhaps not even then."

"Okay, but why are we going home so soon? You just got here."

"I have business to attend to and must be rid of this particular product posthaste."

"Why? This stuff is awesome." She could feel the rush warming through her body.

"There were some complications, and a girl has information that is most unfortunate, so I'd like to distance myself from the product."

Carlos hated explaining himself to anyone, but Deborah had always been given special privileges. Perhaps it was her beauty, an American prize to say the least, but more likely it was her endless nagging that made it easier to just tell her enough to satisfy any curiosity upfront. Deb thought about it and decided she didn't care, so she went back to the pile of coke and dropped the inquiry.

Lori Ann didn't know anyone outside of Florida except her grandparents, so she began looking elsewhere. It needed to be close but not too close while she figured this out. "Vegas," she unintentionally said out loud, "Hmm, that might be good." Vegas is near but not too near; millions of people are there all the time, and she could blend in easily. If Stephen left a message for her at home and it turned out he was still in LA, they could still meet up. She would check into a hotel and just sit for a few days and wait it out; that was the only real choice.

Debbie called her sister Laurie from the room while Carlos was getting in a few hands at the high-roller game that was still going on after ten in the morning. She caught her as she was heading over to some guy's hotel room in Minneapolis. She told her about the pink stuff, but Laurie didn't need any right now; she'd let her know if she came across anyone. Laurie assured her big sister that all was well and that she was fine with her friends at the Le Luxe. They would talk again when she got home that afternoon.

Debbie was extremely protective of her little sister and wanted to meet this man who had her in a hotel room downtown. She didn't care how rich or good-looking he was; she'd decide if he was up to par, and besides that, it seemed to her that she'd heard this name Reno before but couldn't remember from whom or why.

Raul finished cleaning up the room and sat back to wait for dark. Dealing with the persistent maid had been a chore; in the end, he had to let her in and strangle her. He'd dump her and Stephen's body in a dumpster and then take the cab down to East LA where some gang-banger would muddle it up with fingerprints while looking for anything of value. Lori Ann was another matter; he needed to come up with something to tell Carlos other than he lost her in a damn taxi race. He already called associates in Florida, of which they had many since that's where their shipments entered the States, and provided a description of the girl to two men; one would meet all flights landing in Jacksonville from LA, Ontario, and San Diego airports in the next twenty-four hours while the other man would stake out the address on Stephen's license. Surely, she'd turn up sooner or later; he just needed it to be sooner.

Lori Ann boarded a bus to Las Vegas at 6:47 PM and was on The Strip just after midnight. She wandered briefly, finally checking into the Aladdin Hotel and Casino. She took a shower to help wash the memory of the taxi driver and bus from her mind. She wondered how long it would take to hear from Stephen and decided to check the answering machine at his house. He had a number you could dial that allowed you to listen to messages on the machine when you weren't home. There was nothing from him, just old messages from work and Marty.

"That son of a bitch Marty started this whole thing." She cursed the situation and him in general, and then started thinking about the man in the taxi. Who was he and why was that driver helping to chase her down? She got a real good look at the driver and certainly saw enough of the passenger's face to know it wasn't Stephen.

Lori Ann knew she needed money, especially if she had to stay awhile, so she decided to look into a waitress job in the morning. She was wiped out from the day and needed to rest. Although she was exhausted, she tossed and turned all night long, thinking about Stephen, Raul and Carlos, and the man in the taxi; it was just too much to sink in so fast.

After dark, Raul deposited the maid and Stephen's stiffening corpses into the nearest dumpster, drove the taxi down to East LA, and parked it. He walked about six blocks before spotting a gypsy cab that picked him up and returned him to LAX for an overdue exit from the city of lost angels. His friends would probably have Lori Ann by sun-up and then he could go back about his business. He hadn't worked this hard to rise to this level just to have some Chica take him out. The only other loose end was Jeremy at the University of Minnesota, the one who connected Raul with Stephen in the first place, but college kids disappear and overdose all the time at big schools; no worries there.

Lori Ann awoke startled and gasped for breath until realizing she was in Vegas. A wave of sadness overwhelmed her. She wondered if Stephen had checked in yet, so she tried calling the house but still no message. She was getting angry again thinking he may have taken off with the money, but why would the man be chasing her? She'd secretly questioned Stephen's interest in her aspirations over time and occasionally thought he might just be with her because of his physical attraction to her, but she couldn't fathom him being involved in doing her harm. All his friends seemed to be amazed that she stayed with him. Maybe she was nothing more than a hot piece of ass to show off to his friends. Lori Ann hated thinking this way, but one thing is for sure: You can't put anything past anyone in this world, and he was clearly into something heavy that she knew very little about. She still believed in destiny but began to question whether Stephen was her true "meant to be." Maybe he was just supposed to get her away from her parents and the base. Thinking about it made her sadder and more confused; she decided to go downstairs to get a newspaper. If she was on her own, she better start acting like it.

LORI ANN WENT INTO A LITTLE SHOP INSIDE THE CASINO AND bought the local paper and the LA Times, just in case. Nothing in the Times about anyone she recognized, so she went to the local classifieds. Waitressing wasn't exactly her dream job, but it paid cash on your first night and she was good at it. There were many listed but one caught her eye: "Waitresses and Entertainers needed, up to $1,000 cash per shift. See Danny at the Black Stallion." A thousand cash per night, now that was money. She wondered how so much money could be made and then worried it might be too expensive to stay in Vegas. Certainly, she needed to get out of the hotel room; it was over one hundred dollars a night, and no way to cook meant eating out for every meal.

Lori Ann put on her only other outfit, aside from the negligee, and headed over to the Black Stallion in search of Danny. The place was big, bigger than she expected, and pretty nice considering it turned out to be a topless bar. Danny greeted her by asking, "Where ya dancin' now?" with a look in his eyes that made her a bit uncomfortable, even after all she'd just been through.

"I'm not, I mean, I'm here about the waitress job. Is it still open?"

"Hmm. Where ya from?"

She thought for a few seconds before answering. "San Francisco. I just moved here." She wasn't going to provide any real information unless she had to. Who knows what big-time drug dealers are connected to, but a strip club in Vegas wasn't a big stretch of the imagination.

"What's your name?"

Lori Ann hesitated and then saw an advertisement for the Desert Casino on a wall and said, "Desiree."

"Are these questions too hard?"

"Not at all. So, is the waitress job available or not? I need work."

"Ya know, you'd make a lot more money dancing. Are those real?" He pointed toward her breasts as if she was holding something not attached to her.

"Yes, they're real and I think I'll stick with the waitress job if you don't mind?"

"Too bad. Ya got a nice ass too." He looked her over like a slab of beef.

"I'm sorry I took up your time. I've gotta go." She started walking toward the door but he stopped her.

"Wait. Hold on. Yeah, you're hired. Waitress job is yours. When can ya start?"

"I can start today." Lori Ann was unsure if this was a great decision but certain she needed the money.

A red-headed dancer walked by as they were speaking; Danny called out to her. "Whitney, come here."

She frowned. "No, I won't have a threesome with your new friend."

"Fuck you. I wouldn't want your tired ass anyway. I need you to show her where the applications are."

"You're the manager, why don't you show her?"

"Because I want you to do it. Is that a good enough fuckin' reason?"

"Yeah. Fine. It's this way, honey." She turned and headed back in the direction from which she came.

"Well, she won't carry ya over to 'em."

Lori Ann thanked him and then went after the redhead before she disappeared into the darkness of the room.

"Yeah, you can thank me later." He muttered under his breath as he wandered off to discourage a guy from snorting coke off another dancer's breasts.

She followed the redhead into a small office and watched as she rifled through the drawers of the desk, eventually pulling out a handful of free drink coupons and a two-page job application. Whitney pulled her panties outward and carefully placed the little coupons over her meticulously manicured patch of pubic hair and then covered them with her panties, and said, "Pure gold."

"What?" Lori Ann was a bit shocked by this girl exposing herself to a stranger.

"Free drink coupons. The customers earn them for spending big bucks but we get most of them back as tips. Drinks are even expensive for us in this hole, so we get 'em when we can."

Lori Ann was still staring at the bulge in her panties and Whitney caught her looking and asked, "Are you a diver?"

"A diver?"

"Yeah. Are you a muff diver?" She pulled her panties down in illustration as she spoke.

"No! I mean, I guess it's cool if that's what you're into, but I..."

"Relax sweetheart, I'm not either unless the price is right, that is. I like guys too, just not any I've ever met in these places."

"Doesn't it bother you to show yourself like that?"

"Nah. I do it all night long during private dances. You will too if ya want the big tips. I don't let 'em touch it in here and they pay dearly when they do."

"They try and touch you when you're dancing?"

"Listen Cinderella, they try everything and some of the girls let 'em do more than touch it if the price is right. I only do outcall for that kinda stuff. It's more money anyway."

"Outcall?"

"Yeah, outcall. Is this your first time dancing?"

"Oh, I'm not a dancer. I'm a waitress, but it's my first time working in a strip club."

"That's a shame. You'd be a big draw. Do you shave?"

"What?"

"Are ya bald down there?"

She asked while poking at Lori Ann's crotch with one hand. Lori Ann jumped back and said, "No, and it's none of your business."

"Relax Cinderella, I already told you I'm not a diver. You see, the boys like it when a young one like you is shaved. Brings more tips."

"I told you I'm not a dancer, I'm a waitress, and I'm not interested in any guy who'd want a little girl with no pubic hair."

"Yeah, me too, until I saw the first dancer in a Porsche, and then I traded in my Subaru and my bra for one of my own."

"You have a Porsche?"

"Honey, I was speaking metaphorically. I drive an Eldorado, but it's brand new and I paid for it in cash."

"In cash?"

"Everything is cash here, honey. Money talks and bullshit walks."

"How long did you have to dance to save that much money?"

"Two weeks and one very long weekend at Bernie's."

"Bernie's? Is that another club?"

"No. Bernie is what we call our customers on an outcall. This Bernie owns the dealership where I bought my 'caddy' and we kinda made a deal on the price."

"You had sex with him, and he gave you a car?" Lori Ann was blown away.

"No, but he gave me one hell of a discount. Ten grand cash and a weekend at Bernie's condo for a twenty-thousand-dollar car."

"Wow!" Lori Ann considered making ten thousand dollars cash in two weeks; it was almost inconceivable to make that much in such a short time. In fact, it was nearly half of her annual income as a waitress.

"Wow nothin'. I like sex; men do too. Instead of buying me dinner and jewelry for two weeks before I can let him fuck me without being a slut, we just cut to the chase and everybody's happy." Whitney's expression revealed her amusement with her description. She added, "Well, back to the salt mines," before checking her panties one last time and leaving Lori Ann alone in the office with the application in hand. A few seconds later, Whitney popped her head back in the door and offered a few words of wisdom: "If you stay in Danny's office too long, you'll end up seeing a lot more than my little bush when the next undies drop." She cracked up as Lori Ann grabbed the door and walked out behind her.

"You're not some kinda virgin are ya?"

"No, of course not, but this is a bit much all at once."

"Look, Cinderella, I'm Whitney, and if ya have any questions just ask me, okay? I won't steer ya wrong."

"Thanks, and my name is Lori Ann. Why do you keep calling me Cinderella?"

"It's not personal. We call all the new girls Cinderella until they have their first ball; then, you're just one of the girls."

Whitney looked her over again. "Is Lori Ann your real name?"

"Yeah."

"Well forget it. Don't tell anyone else what it is and use a fake one on the application too, and a bogus address, or else Danny and every other swingin' dick in the place will stop by for unannounced wake-up calls."

"I told Danny it was Desiree."

"See, you've got good instincts. You'll be fine."

"Thanks."

"See ya later. Gotta move in before Lips sees that one." Whitney was referring to a man just being seated at a table in a corner by a topless hostess.

"Lips?"

"Yeah, Lips." Whitney pointed to a girl squatting in front of a man who was seated at another table; it was obvious she was going down on him, but the room was so dark you'd never notice them. Lori Ann scanned the room more closely, trying to see what else she missed while following Whitney into the office. It was a large warehouse-type building, divided by mirrored partitions and carpeted pillars. There were at least six elevated stages with lights shooting up from the floor, down from the rafters and at the sides as well. A brass pole, or in some cases two of them, went from floor to ceiling, and chairs lined the perimeter of all the Grecian-shaped stages with a narrow bar surface around their perimeter. Small tables were scattered around the entire room and tucked into corners along the wall. Other than the stage lighting and the neon beer and alcohol lights, black lights were the only illumination in the place. It made it easy to see up close but difficult to see any distance, and made everyone in the place look tan. White shirts glowed like moving signs as people moved throughout the place. She saw a waitress go by and wondered if she danced too. Her outfit was so tiny that Lori Ann could see the white cotton panties she wore without even trying, and only the nipple itself was covered by the low-cut top. Her heels looked to be at least six inches long and her fingernails were nearly as lengthy. When she served drinks, she bent at the waist and the puffy skirt rose exposing her entire bottom and maybe more if you were closer. Lori Ann couldn't imagine herself wearing such an outfit in public, especially when she noted the hands of one of the customers all over the girl's butt. The waitress just smiled and replaced empty glasses with full ones, even as the man pulled her panties out to insert money in them.

"Done yet?" Danny's voice startled her.

"Huh?"

"The application. Is it filled out?" He pointed at it in her hand.

"Ah, I don't know…"

"Look, I can see you're too innocent for the waitress role in a place like this, but you'd do great as a dancer."

"If I can't handle waiting tables, how could I dance?" She asked incredulously as if it were the dumbest thing she ever heard.

"Because, sunshine, nobody can touch you on stage. You'll make more money too."

"Then why would anyone wait tables?"

"The waitresses think the dancers are sluts; dancers think the waitresses are fools, so pick your label and your paycheck. The bouncers are told to watch the dancers a lot more closely and it's up to you if you have any contact with the customers off stage."

Lori Ann considered what he'd been saying, and Whitney's words as well and then asked, "Are there different applications?"

"Nope. Is that one complete?"

"No. I need a pen."

He reached into his shirt pocket and handed her a pen. "You can start as one and switch to another position any time you like. Either way, I'm sure you'll do well here." He looked her up and down again. "What size are you?"

"A three-four in most stuff, but…"

"Three-four?" He laughed with a snort. "No matter, they all wear the same uniforms. Let me know when you get it filled out."

"Thank you."

She sat at the table nearest her and wished she had on jeans and a

T-shirt instead of shorts and a tank. She felt like every guy in the place was looking at her until she looked around at all the scantily clad and topless girls and realized she was being ridiculous. Who'd be looking at her in a room full of half-naked girls? She finished the application, giving all fake information except the home address of The Aladdin Hotel, but that would change. She found a payphone and tried the answering machine one more time; no word from Stephen.

"Prick." She hung up in disgust and went up to Danny's office door and raised her hand to knock but stopped when she heard a girl making sex sounds on the other side of the door. She wondered if he was watching a dirty movie but got her answer when the door flew open and one of the waitresses barged past her, adjusting her white cotton undies, saying, "Bitch."

Danny howled as he rocked back in his chair and told Lori Ann to "C'mon in" while tucking his button-down into his pants.

"Look!" She tossed the application on his desk. "I'm here to make money, not to screw my boss or anyone else for that matter. So, I don't care..."

"Relax..." He glanced at the application. "Desiree. She came to me for money and then she came back to work it off. Both times she came to me."

"If these girls make so much money, why do they need loans that get paid off in back rooms?"

"Nobody makes enough money to support her habit, honey." He winked as he wiggled his nose with his index finger.

"Oh. Well, there's my application. When can I start?"

With a fiendish grin and tone, he asked, "Which position?"

"I'll try it as a waitress if you don't mind and see how it goes."

"Sure." Danny pulled a tiny little one-piece outfit from the filing cabinet to his left and tossed it to her. "Three-four, right?"

"Right."

She frowned at the tiny outfit and started to speak but he interrupted her, answering the question before she could ask. "Now, you start now."

"Don't I need some kind of training?"

He stared at her breasts and then at her groin. "No. I'd say you're an expert. Just take section three; the bartender will show you the grid and the girls will show you the ropes. Hey, dancers don't like waitresses and vice versa, so stay close to who's on your side."

"Thanks." She looked down at the little outfit. "Where do I change?"

"Right here if you like." Before she could bite his head off, he raised his hand in defense. "The girls all share the dressing room and showers; they'll show you. Now get to work."

Lori Ann walked out of the office and looked around at the big room while her eyes adjusted to the lighting. She saw a waitress coming in her direction. "Excuse me, where can I change?"

The girl stopped cold in her tracks. It was the same one who had blown past her in Danny's office. She looked at the outfit in Lori Ann's hand, smiled and said, "Sure honey, it's in that far corner. Sorry about that back there but I thought you were a dancer. I'm Kelli, welcome aboard."

"I'm Desiree. Thanks, Kelli."

"Maybe this won't be so bad," Lori Ann thought as she crossed the room and entered a door marked "LADIES ONLY!" She walked in and was shocked to see the room filled with girls, some in no clothing at all, but nearly none fully dressed. An older woman in what appeared to be a robe asked, "Are you new?"

"Yes, I just started."

The room was small, about the size of the motel in LA, but with a bench running from end to end of two walls, and mirrors over the counters running the length of the benches. A passageway led to a small row of three stalls, and a row of hooks was just above a knee-wall of square lockers, some with locks, but all with graffiti scrolled on the doors. The only other things were a chair that the older woman sat in, and a payphone mounted next to the doorway leading to the restroom.

The older woman asked the room, "Hmm. What do you ladies think?"

One replied, "Too soon to tell. Could be a popper."

The older lady shook her head. "I doubt it, but let's have a look."

Lori Ann looked around, thinking perhaps they were talking about something or someone else, but they weren't.

This time, the older woman addressed Lori Ann directly with a spinning motion of her finger. "Well, let's have a look."

"I just came in here to change but maybe the lady's room would be..."

"This is the lady's room, and the only place we're allowed to change."

The woman spoke with an easy expression that didn't match her tone. Whitney was one of the girls in the room but remained silent, just offering Lori Ann a nod and a wink as if to say it was a rite of passage and would be fine. Lori Ann looked at the outfit she held and noticed it was all one piece, even the white panties. She decided it was no big deal to change in front of a group of women, especially since these girls not only got naked for a living, but half of them were nude now. She slipped off her tank top, exposing her breasts, and heard one girl say, "Told ya they were real." Another replied, "Mine are still better." Lori Ann ignored them and slipped out of her shorts and panties in one motion and then stood up as she stepped through the top of the outfit, wiggling her hips to seat the bottoms without having to touch herself. The girls shouted in unison, "Dancer," and the older woman agreed, saying, "So, why are you joining the fools who give up gropes for nothing? You have what it takes to be a money machine."

"I told Danny I'd try waitressing first and see how it goes."

Lori Ann noticed some of the girls were touching each other and two were kissing with no regard for the others in the room. "Well, I'd better get to work."

One of the girls said, "I'd like to get to work on you too."

Lori Ann ignored her and glanced back at Whitney who gave another nod of approval as Lori Ann left amid the catcalls of the room. She walked across the bar and over to the payphone and called once again using the phone card her dad gave her; that and a few dollars were the only things she brought from her hotel room. She had her clothing in her hand and realized after making the useless, last-ditch call to check the machine that she'd have to reenter the changing room in order to start work. She rolled up the clothes and walked boldly into the room once again. "Where may I put these things during my shift?"

"Give them to me, love, I'll watch after them." Lori Ann took a step forward and handed them to the elder woman, who unrolled and proceeded to neatly fold them on her lap one article at a time until she came to her panties; she held them in a ball and brought them slowly to her face. Lori Ann flinched as the woman said, "Absolutely divine."

Lori Ann shook her head and left the room that echoed with comments like, "I want to be next," and "No, it's my turn." She cursed Stephen once more under her breath as she made her way to the bar to find directions to section three and hopefully some guidance on how she was to perform her duties as a waitress in a strip club. "The money had better be pretty damn good," she thought as she walked up to the service bar and introduced herself to the barmaid.

Lori Ann finished her shift just after 4:30 AM and was feeling quite confident that having men paw at her for hours on end was not going to be a sustainable career choice. However, when she finished counting out her tips in order to tip out the barmaids, she was shocked to see she cleared four hundred bucks. She asked Lisa, one of the barmaids, "Is it like this every night?"

"No, it's usually much better."

"Better?"

"Or worse, depending on your perspective. It gets much busier and we make more money, but we put up with a lot more shit too."

Lori Ann couldn't imagine a busier night or worse behavior from grown men.

Most of the girls were going out partying but Lori Ann just wanted to hit her pillow. She was so tired that it didn't even faze her to witness the antics of fifteen drunken and mostly coked-out bisexuals taunting each other as they changed into their street clothes. They kissed and fondled, sometimes getting extremely personal with each other, and two were going at it full tilt in the three-person-sized shower stall Lori Ann hadn't noticed earlier. She'd never seen a woman going down on another woman and was blown away by how open they were about it.

On her way home, Lori Ann stopped for a bite at a local's diner off The Strip with Whitney. She declined the second invitation to go to some party in a residential section of Vegas, an area that's not part of the tour for visitors, which ranges from dripping wealth to absolute poverty, just like any other city. Instead, she soaked her weary body in a hot shower for what seemed like an hour and then slipped into bed and fell instantly asleep. She even forgot to try the answering machine at Stephen's house.

Whitney told Lori Ann of an apartment for rent in her complex; it was a thousand dollars per month and the deposit was one month's rent on top of the first month's rent. Whitney offered to loan Lori Ann the money but insisted that she try dancing; it was more money and she'd be manhandled a lot less. That sounded good. She'd already had quite enough of men poking at her undergarments when she bent down to deliver drinks. Lori Ann was up early the next day, called Stephen's number from the room to no avail, and then checked out of the hotel by eleven o'clock. She took a taxi to Whitney's complex and signed the six-month lease on the spot, which was the shortest one they offered. She didn't see another option since the casino's hotel room would be three times the cost, and if Stephen turned up they'd just have to work out the lease problem.

The apartment was small but clean; it was a studio but had a great bathroom and a partial wall dividing the kitchen/dining area from the main room/bedroom. It also came furnished; that was the real clincher since Lori Ann had nothing of her own. The sofa opened into a bed, and a television with Cable included was hidden in a decent-looking cabinet along the far wall. A small table with two chairs sat in the corner of the dining portion of the kitchen, and a microwave, refrigerator, and stove with two burners surrounded the sink and few cabinets. The bathroom was the jewel; it had a nice tub with jacuzzi jets, a small shower stall, and a vanity over the sink. The commode was stowed in a smaller space behind a pocket door, and a deep but narrow closet was hidden behind louvered doors. It was Lori Ann's first place of her own, and it made her feel like the crappy job might be worth it for a while.

She walked back down to the office and used the payphone out front, but still no word from Stephen. Her mother had left a message, Marty left two, and Jeremy called saying he'd call back the next day but hadn't.

"Fuck those guys," she thought, hanging the phone up solidly on its cradle. She looked around the complex's parking lot and the pool fence but decided to go back to her new home and do a thorough cleaning with the supplies she found under the sink.

Later in the day, she called Danny, explaining she would try a shift working as a dancer; he replied, "Good, I was wondering when I'd get to see those tits," followed by cynical laughter.

"That's why I'm doing it, Danny, so you can see my tits."

"Yeah, yeah, I'll see ya at nine. And don't forget to bring back the waitress uniform or I gotta charge ya fifty bucks."

"No problem. See ya tonight."

Lori Ann borrowed fifteen hundred dollars from Whitney to pay her first month of rent and deposit but figured she could pay her back with a couple of nights' work and get started on savings right away. She also missed her car but didn't see any way to get it just yet. She was too scared to call home for fear of what she might hear from her parents. There was no reason to worry about her parent's wellbeing; they lived on a Naval base surrounded by some pretty badass people, and "The Chief" would be more than a handful for anyone who'd come looking for his daughter, but what would she tell them? It's better that they think she's at Stephen's or still in the Keys.

Whitney stopped by with some slinky clothes after finding the note with Lori Ann's unit number in her mail slot. Lori Ann tried on several outfits but only borrowed one, a see-through white mesh bikini with a tiny little cotton panel so small Lori Ann had to practically shave herself bald to wear it without showing the forbidden pubic hair; the rest were even more revealing in that area and Lori Ann just couldn't bring herself to shave completely. She also had the little teddy with matching panties she brought to LA.

After buying Lori Ann several shots of tequila at the bar to loosen her up, Whitney announced that Desiree had joined the dancer ranks as they entered the girl's lounge.

"Okay ladies be nice. Desiree is one of us now and we need to show her the ropes."

One of the young ladies shouted, "I've got something to show her."

Before Whitney or Lori Ann could respond, the older woman spoke up. Her job was "house mother," a position created to keep the girls from killing each other and from going too far in any number of ways within the club. She was an ex-dancer who understood the issues faced by the girls in the lifestyle they chose. "Now, now, settle down ladies. She's one of us now and if she wants to tickle your critter, I'm sure she'll let you know." Her words drew a cheer from most of the ladies but a frown from the girl who made the comment.

"Miss April, this is Desiree. She's losing her cherry tonight," Whitney announced as an introduction to the house mom.

"Nice to meet you, Desiree." Miss April extended her hand for Lori Ann to shake and then continued speaking. "Desiree, this is our family, and we hope you'll feel at home here. Allow me to introduce your new sisters: This is Candy, Starla, Jewel, Dusty, Snap..." Some winked or half-heartedly waved, while others ignored the process altogether. "And Gem, Darlene, Mercedes, Annie, Bobby, Toni, and you already know Whitney. We have very few rules in our house, but here they are: No violence of any kind, no stealing of anything, no men in here, ever, no un-showered dancers on the floor; we call the main area of the club the floor. You must be here thirty minutes before your shift and must leave within thirty minutes after your shift. If you are into girls, even part-time, that's fine; if you're not, that's fine too. There is no pressure." Miss April looked over the faces in the room and then continued, "I repeat, no pressure to have any sexual contact with anyone in this building or within our family at any time, right ladies?"

They all answered in unison. "Yes, Ma'am."

"Desiree, we also do not allow the usage of drugs on the floor and prefer you keep any usage to yourself, although some of my girls do insist on challenging that rule. Please make no mistake, if it happens in here, it stays in here, but if it happens on the floor, you'll find your cute little ass hit by the door. Got it?"

"Yes."

"Good. Welcome to our family." She scanned the room again. "I am here if you have any questions about anything, and the girls will be happy, yes, I said happy to offer support as well. And why is that?"

Once again, they answered in unison. "Because we were all cherries once."

"Right. Now, the club's rules: You may show your breasts, including your nipples, but you may not display any pubic hair or genitalia within the building. You may not exchange phone numbers with any customer. You may not arrange to meet or otherwise have contact with customers outside of the club, that includes email addresses, right Toni?"

A tiny brunette with huge implants replied, "Yes Ma'am," while blushing.

"Customers may not touch your nipples or genitalia at any time, even with foreign objects, right Mercedes?"

"Yeah, right," a tall blonde with exquisite features said in a snotty tone.

"Excuse me?"

"Yes Ma'am," Mercedes answered, sitting up straight and revealing that she was pleasuring herself with a narrow pink object.

Miss April shook her head and sighed before resuming. "You may not have direct contact with a customer's genitals at any time and may not promise to do so either. The police feel that an offer or suggestion is qualified as solicitation, and you will go to jail if you slip up. Did I miss anything?"

One of the girls said, "Danny."

"Ah, yes, Danny. Danny is the manager of this club and I manage the girls. I set the schedules and deal with the problems we face. Danny may not fire you without consulting me, even though he broke the rules by hiring you without my approval. He and I will discuss that later, but I need to know if you have had or promised to have any kind of sexual contact with him?"

"No way."

"Good Desiree, see that you don't. I don't like him fucking my girls; it confuses the chain of command. Besides, he gets enough pussy from his little army of waitresses. Ladies, anything else?" The room was silent. "Fine. Desiree, you go on behind Mercedes on stage two. Get ready when her name is called, not yours. You dance two songs back-to-back; during the second song, you may remove your top. It's not required but it greatly improves your tips. See Johnny in the DJ booth with any special music requests, otherwise, I don't like to hear bitching about his choices. You may also bring your own albums or cassettes, but I suggest taking them home at night after your shift. You've got fifteen minutes between sets and may come in here, sit at the bar but not at a table, do lap dances at tables or in the champagne room, but you must be on stage for your next set, no exceptions. The girls will explain the rest. Good luck and don't worry about the customers; our boys will bounce them on their non-functional heads if they get out of line while you're on the floor. If not, they'll deal with me."

"Thank you." Lori Ann sat down in the space vacated by three girls heading out to work a set. One of them was Mercedes, who dropped the dildo in Lori Ann's lap as she passed. Lori Ann picked it up with two fingers and tossed it back to her. "Thanks, but I prefer a pulse in mine."

Mercedes scowled, tossed it on the bench, and walked out into the club. Whitney smiled and said, "Mercedes doesn't even have a pulse of her own."

Lori Ann stripped down and changed into the white outfit she borrowed from Whitney. "Whit, do I look okay?"

Whitney nodded and Candy added, "Desiree, as good as you look, you could wear anything."

"Thanks." Lori Ann was beginning to relax a bit and accepted the cigarette offered by Darlene.

Next, Snap approached and asked, "Are you a diver?"

"No, sorry."

"That's cool, but if you ever want a lesson." She concluded with a wink.

Lori Ann looked at the deeply tanned hard body standing nude before her, and the perfectly formed implants and piercing blue eyes of the young girl. Her teeth gleamed white behind the gloss of her full lips, and Lori Ann couldn't resist asking, "Why don't you like men? I mean, you could have any guy you want."

Snap smiled widely. "Have you ever gone down on a man?"

"Yes." Lori Ann answered reluctantly.

"And?"

"It was okay."

"And has a guy ever gone down on you?"

"Yes." Lori Ann's face flushed from having a conversation like this with a total stranger.

"And?"

"I liked it," Lori Ann admitted with a schoolgirl smirk.

"Do you remember how you reacted when he did it?"

"Yeah, I guess."

"And do you think guys are as good at touching you as you are?"

"What?"

"You know what I mean. Do they know your parts like you do?"

"Well..."

"Exactly! And imagine if that kind of knowledge could be used when someone went down on you."

Lori Ann thought about it for a second but couldn't come up with an argument.

Snap stuck her tongue out and fluttered it. "Girls know what makes a girl cum and that's all there is to it. Don't get me wrong, I like boys too, they pay for my whole world, and once in a while, it's nice to have your brains fucked out. But when it comes to lovin', I like girls."

Lori Ann tried to imagine her face between this beautiful woman's thighs, but reality sunk in. "I think I'll stick with guys, even if they are assholes."

"Too bad, you don't know what you're missing." Snap turned and headed into the shower with Jewel hopping up to follow her, also nude, patting her on her bottom as they went.

"Desiree, you're on in one," Miss April said. "Remember, you follow Mercedes. Don't make me chase you."

Lori Ann replied, "I'm sorry," and looked herself over before heading out the door into the club. She saw Mercedes bending over in front of a man seated at stage three and then walked in that direction. Lori Ann watched the way she moved from man to man, allowing them to put bills in the strings of her bikini bottoms, and the way she held eye contact with each of them, just long enough for the transaction and then moving on slowly, turning and bending to touch her toes or looking at each man from between her legs as her hair swept along the floor of the stage. Lori Ann looked at another stage and watched as Bobby sat on her high heels, clapping her thighs on a man's face while he smiled and held up a bill in each hand as if he were signaling a field goal.

The song ended and she heard the DJ announce the next perform-ers, and then she heard it: "And for the first time anywhere, the Black Stallion is proud to introduce DESIREE on stage three! Check her out boys. She's direct to you from San Francisco, California, and she is smokin' tonight!"

Lori Ann said, "Oh shit," as she walked up the three steps onto the stage with Mötley Crüe's version of "Smokin' in the boy's room" blaring from the many speakers on the walls. She felt she'd step right out of the white six-inch pumps Whit loaned her but gathered herself together by holding the pole as she walked around it. The music drowned out the sounds of the men's voices, but their lips moved as they all cheered and yelled indistinguishable comments about her body and movements. Lori Ann stayed close to the pole for reassurance during the entire first song, catching her breath while moving in a gentle sway as the second song started with the DJ talking over the music.

"C'mon boys, I can't hear you. Desiree's gonna need some noise to show you some skin. Who wants to see some of that Bay Area babe flesh?"

With that prompt, the room roared. Men were seated and standing all around the stage, and the DJ came in over the sound of Ted Nugent doing "Cat Scratch Fever," shouting, "It's gonna cost some money boys. Who's gonna see that kitty tonight?"

The music pounded, the men shouted, vying for her attention as dollar bills, five-dollar bills, ten-dollar bills, and even twenties began to fly like confetti while Lori Ann spun on the pole, hanging on for dear life. Finally, she stopped herself by planting one foot solidly on the stage and threw back her hair while taking a deep breath. In that moment, everything slowed down; she could see Danny standing next to Miss April and a group of the girls watching from their doorway. She saw Whitney giving her the thumbs up and motioning for her to take off her top by lifting her own. Lori Ann reached over her shoulder and grabbed the string of the skimpy top, pulling straight up and removing it in one motion as if it was someone else's hand. She was standing topless in front of hundreds of people, frozen in the strobe light flashing in her face. She opened her eyes and took a deep breath while looking at the sea of smiling faces surrounding her until all at once, she heard the crowd noise; it was like the music stopped and the only sound was the roar of cheers. She exhaled the big breath she held and flashed a smile in relief from not dying on the spot; the crowd went wild as she began slowly moving her hips and upper body to an unknown beat in her head until the music came back at full speed. Men leaned in toward her with money in their hands, reaching out to hand it to her as she grinded against the pole. She leaned forward and took a bill from an outstretched hand, and then another and another until finally, she was a dancer.

Between the faces crowding around the stage, she caught a glimpse of Whit's face looking back as she walked toward the dressing room; the look was of an approving mother.

At the end of the night, she counted the money in Whit's Cadillac as they drove down The Strip. "I made twelve hundred dollars tonight." She handed Whitney a thousand dollars of what she borrowed the previous day. "Thanks, Whit, thanks for everything."

"No problem, darlin'. Next, I'll show you how to make the really big bucks."

"This is more money than I ever dreamed of making in one day."

"My biggest night to date was five thousand and you'll beat that one day soon."

Lori Ann gasped. "You made five grand at the Stallion?"

"No honey, on an outcall. That's where the big bucks are. It's two hundred just to show up, and then it's tip as you go."

"Tip as ya go?"

"Yeah. You wanna play with my tits, that's two hundred more; touching my little coochie is five hundred, and if any part of me takes him on, well that's a grand. My biggest night was a little Japanese businessman, and I mean little." She used her thumb and index finger to show just how little. "He had a roll of cash that would've choked a horse. This guy has me put on his suit and then he takes it off me real slowly, and then we do it right on his thousand-dollar jacket; boom, five-grand cash. If he didn't roll over when he was done, I'd have thought he hadn't started."

Whit burst into laughter. Lori Ann giggled, thinking about the night of the Officers' Ball and how silly men can be sometimes. "I think I'll stick to the dancing. It's more than enough money for me."

"What's enough?"

The next night, Lori Ann made over nine hundred dollars and paid off her debt to Whitney. The following night, it was packed; she made fourteen hundred and bought a little used Honda Civic five-speed from Whit's friend, the car dealer. The price on the window was thirty-nine ninety-five but Whit had a talk with him in his office while Lori Ann looked over the car with a salesman and took it for a drive. Lori Ann planned to apply for a loan but when she pulled out the thousand-dollar down payment, he handed her the title.

Whitney was connected all over town and could get into any high rollers game, private club, or restaurant with just a wink in the right direction. Lori Ann was amazed at how Whit got men to do whatever she wanted, but she preferred the distance the stage provided when dealing with men herself. Most of the girls had special customers and all of them saw them after hours, but no one talked about it in a way that suggested it was a rules violation. Danny introduced Lori Ann to several men as time went by, but she just did her dancing and went home each night.

Her calls to Stephen's machine ended when she called and it was gone, just no answer. Lori Ann was on her own and she might never know the truth about Stephen. She called her mother once, just to say she was all right and not to worry, and that she decided to extend her stay in the Keys indefinitely, alone, but would keep in touch.

PART VIII

The Price

The Price

"It's about time. Where ya been hon?" was Laurie's salutation as I opened the door and walked into the big room with my tequila bottle from the hotel lounge in hand. Tommy and Missy sat on the couch, their backs towards me; Laurie and a beautiful girl in her twenties sat to their right.

"This is Debbie, Reno, my sister I told you about."

I raised my bottle in a quasi-wave. "Hey, Debbie. Another babe in the house. Tommy, what are we gonna do with all these hot chicks?"

Laurie rushed over and hugged me. "Settle down now, she is my sister ya know. And take it easy on that stuff; you've got somewhere to be."

Debbie was a taller version of Laurie with darker hair that accentuated her bright blue eyes.

"Sorry honey, I'm jus' tryin' to douse the flames," I said, again waving the bottle.

"Stoking the fire is more like it." Laurie tenderly corrected me.

She took my free hand and pulled me toward the couch where I plopped down next to Debbie and said, "Hi, sis'."

"It's nice to meet you, Reno, but we should really get going."

"I don't wanna go." I whined, comically stomping my feet. "I just got here."

"He's a real piece of work, Laurie, but cute."

"Yeah, well he's mine so you get your own lunatic." Laurie was now standing behind us.

"We're gonna be late," Debbie cautioned, glancing at her watch.

"Reno, you've gotta go get the 'key' with Debbie, okay? We'll wait here."

"Well, then I'm gonna need some money." My level of intoxication was obvious, and playfulness replaced the forlorn weight after being reunited with my friends.

"Here, and you better take this for the ride. It'll sober you up." Laurie handed me an envelope with $10,000 of my cash in it and her now-filled vile with the spoon.

"You're so good to me." I pawed at Laurie's breasts over my shoulder and then took a long swig from the bottle while Tommy chanted, "Go, Go, Go."

"That's enough of that. Let's go," Debbie commanded, removing the bottle from my hand and placing it on the table, and then she pulled on my hands as Laurie pushed on my back to lift me from the couch.

"Look at this, Tommy. There's two of 'em."

Missy cut off Tommy's, "I wonder what else...," mid-sentence with a jab to his ribs.

"Okay, okay, I'll go quietly."

"Be careful." Laurie kissed me and added, "And tuck in your shirt."

"Nag, nag, nag."

Waiting for the elevator, I fixed my shirt and ran my fingers through my hair, conscious of the requirement to remain upright. "There, how's that?"

"You look fine, just relax."

"I'm always relaxed."

Debbie looked me over while stepping into the elevator. "I believe you."

"You hungry?" I was holding the little gold spoon, pretending to take a sip of something.

"What if somebody comes."

"Who?" I looked around the elevator as if some unknown threat may have slipped in unannounced.

"Just wait 'til we get in the car, okay?" Her stern expression now softening as she began to see the charm Laurie claimed I exuded.

"Fine, spoilsport." I put the small vile back into my pocket.

As we passed the lounge, I saw Sally curiously looking at us. "She just blew me before I came upstairs," I halfheartedly disclosed as if recalling what I had for lunch.

"Yeah, I'm sure." Debbie glanced at Sally as we passed. "Laurie was right about you."

"What do you mean?"

"She said you're a handful."

"That's not what she meant." I laughed out loud as I held the door for Debbie to exit the hotel. Once in her car, I dumped the contents of the vile on a cassette case. Using my license, I divided the powder into two long, beefy lines. I held the case while she spun a hundred-dollar bill into a straw. "Ladies first."

She snorted half of her line up each nostril and handed the bill to me; I snorted mine quickly up my right nostril and sighed as I felt the all-too-familiar chemical drip.

She asked, "Ready?" while checking her nose for loose crystals in the rearview mirror.

"I am now." I sat back into the handstitched leather of the seat. "Whose car is this?"

"My boyfriend's."

"Not bad. What's he do?" I asked absentmindedly while admiring the magnificent quality of the Bentley.

"I forgot to ask." Her smirk widened. I felt like I was looking at a version of Laurie through a time warp as the black sedan sped through the city streets. "We'll go slower on the ride back."

"I didn't say a word."

"I appreciate that in a man." She patted my knee in a friendly manner.

"This city is beautiful," I said, mostly to myself as I enjoyed a good view of the IDS building.

"You like it here?"

"Well, less the weather."

"I'm not much for the cold myself."

"You know what amazes me?"

"What's that?" She asked with a tone of "this ought to be good."

"It's so clean. I mean, no graffiti on any walls or trash on the road-sides, and I love those things; it's like 'The Jetsons.'"

"The skyways?"

"Yeah, skyways. I met the guy who designed them; he's a friend of my stepdad's and a pretty cool dude. He and his wife are always nice to me, even though they know I'm nothin' but trouble. I think he did the architecture for the IDS building too." I watched the buildings fade away in favor of the approaching, more rural lakes area.

"Is everybody from New Jersey like you?"

"You mean fucked up?" My boyish grin gleamed.

"You're like an eternal child, aren't you?"

"Yeah well, I've seen the options."

"Listen, when we get there, I'll do the talking while you sample the stuff, okay?"

"Are you always this bossy?"

"Yes, so do what I say."

I just sat back and enjoyed the ride; a few minutes later, we pulled into a driveway.

"Okay, this is it, we're here."

"Nice place."

"Well, forget you saw it, okay?"

"What's this guy's name again?"

"I'll do the talking. Where's the cash?"

Carlos requested that she bring Laurie's boyfriend to him so he could decide if I should be allowed to make such a substantial purchase. It was important that this product didn't end up in the wrong hands in this quantity, and he didn't want any more people than necessary, even his own, tying the product to him in case word was out on the streets that it was missing. Enough reward money might persuade a lower-level man to take a chance, and he certainly wasn't going to go out in public with that much cocaine. Carlos liked Laurie, and in some ways thought she was more responsible than Debbie. He even contemplated a scenario where Laurie might replace Debbie at some point in the future, so this was also an opportunity to peer into her personal life. Up to this point, he only knew her through relatively brief visits to the mansion. Perhaps most interesting about this young man was him living in a suite at a very nice hotel, traveling in a limousine, and having enough cash on hand to purchase a kilo of cocaine. Carlos wanted to size him up as a client but also as a potential competitor, in which case this man should see who he's dealing with.

I handed Debbie the envelope; it was business-sized with Le Luxe Hotel embossed on the top left.

The house was enormous, a Gray Stone structure almost Gothic in appearance, with cast-iron railings and concrete outer stairways. Sharp concrete edges protruded from the corners with gargoyle-looking creatures perched on the peaks. Unseen were the men with AK-47's lurking in the shadows behind the beasts, in addition to the men just out of sight around the corners of the mansion. The windows were massive and radius in type but not modern at all. The few lights around the property were tucked under the mighty shrubbery that lined the estate and sealed the cobblestone walkway from any that would steal a glance.

As we approached the front stoop, a pair of dim lights came on at either side of the solid, possibly hand-carved, massive double doors. I noticed the flexing of Debbie's muscles as she transferred her weight from leg to leg in anticipation, each rounded cheek snapping to attention beneath her skirt. She was just like Laurie, rock-solid and perfectly proportioned. As the door opened, a Clark Gable-looking man stood before us in a burgundy smoking jacket, complete with a hanky in the pocket. I almost busted up until he spoke.

"Yes, may I help you?"

For a moment, I thought we were at the wrong house.

"Relax Carlos, this is Laurie's guy, Reno."

Debbie pulled me past him with a back-reached arm. I followed her through the Tara Plantation-style foyer; the staircase was an awesome sight, with its tremendous sweeping expanse into the enormous space. I was thinking, "Does this guy know what year it is?" as we passed through a wide double doorway on the left that was like twenty feet tall, entering a formal library. Burgundy leather wingback chairs mated with small coffee tables were scattered throughout, and centered in the room was a massive and exquisite conference table surrounded by intricately carved wooden chairs that matched the legs of the table.

"Sit here," Debbie directed, pulling the chair first to the left of the head out for me. As I sat, she moved opposite me and sat looking into my eyes without a word.

"This place is really somethin'."

She immediately shot me a stern look.

The two sidewalls were shelved to the toe of the vaulted ceiling; books filled every available space, many seemingly in series like encyclopedias. Long wooden ladders were hung on tracks from above the shelves at all four corners of the room. I was just getting uncomfortable in the unpadded chair when Carlos entered.

"Thank you."

"Excuse me?"

"I was not addressing you, Deborah." He took his place at the head of the table. "This home has been unchanged in my family for greater than three generations. I'm glad you approve."

I missed Jose.

He produced, from a closed hand, a small vial with a spoon attached by a fine gold chain, just like Laurie's. The one I got from Jose had a black chain. Without looking at me directly, more like through me, he placed the vial in front of me. "I'm sure you'll be pleased."

I unscrewed the lid and snorted a spoonful of pinkish-tinted powder up each nostril, and with a quick breath, I pulled a third into my mouth. My whole face went numb. As I sat back, an amazing euphoria calmed my body and mind.

"They say Peruvian is like none other." He was right. "Of course, the pipe is the true test," he added, pulling a small glass pipe and a cool little torch from his pocket. He placed them in front of me. "Just a spoonful," he cautioned.

"I don't need to cook it first?"

"No, my friend. There are no impurities to be removed from this product."

I plopped a spoonful in the pipe and reached for the torch. He intercepted my hand, saying, "Allow me," as I held the pipe to my lips. He ran the pointed blue flame slowly under the bowl of the pipe while I watched the powder melt until a puff of white smoke rose and I quickly drew it back through the stem. It tasted smooth, no bite at all. I exhaled and my head tingled from the inside out as the body rush started expanding from my torso through every inch of flesh. Finally, I settled into a deep comfort zone that can only be compared to the embrace of a beautiful woman. I was unaware of my gaping expression until I tried to speak. Softly, I mumbled, "It's like an orgasm."

"I'll assume that means your findings are acceptable." His expression never changed as he reached under the table and ripped a large block in the shape of a brick free from the packing tape that held it in place. He carefully folded the tape around the block and placed it in front of Debbie. As she handed him the envelope, he said, "I've enjoyed your company immensely, but all things must conclude in their time," before rising from the table and disappearing from the room.

Once he was gone from sight, Debbie said, "Put that stuff in your pocket and let's go." I must have been too slow because she grabbed the pipe and torch in one hand before I even screwed the top on the vial. She waited impatiently as I stood up and then, taking my arm, led me quickly out of the house and into the car. Before the engine had even set to idle, she slipped the wood and chrome shifter to reverse and blindly bounced backwards onto the street. The big car jumped forward with a roar from the twelve-cylinder engine as we headed off in the opposite direction from which we had come.

"I need you to do me a favor."

"Sure." My head was still euphoric from the freebase.

"I wouldn't ask but you owe me one."

"Sure, Deb. You want candy for your stash?"

"That would be nice, but I need something else first."

"Just name it."

She was turning down so many streets that I was hopelessly lost; eventually, she pulled off to the side of the road into a small open area surrounded by trees. I could see water at the edge of the grass to our left.

"Do you remember what you said back there?" I shook my head, puzzled. "What you said at the house about the freebase rush?"

"Oh yeah, that's incredible. I can't believe..."

"Have you ever wondered what a woman's orgasm is like?"

"Of course, but I..."

"That's it! The body rush is the same basic thing."

"Really?" I felt like a spy uncovering some secret plan to rule the world.

"Yes. Now I'm sure you see my point."

"So, you wanna get high?" I pulled out the little vial to offer it to her.

"Yes, but." She paused. "I love my boyfriend, but he doesn't entertain certain concepts, if you know what I mean. If you could double the intensity of your orgasm..."

"You wanna have sex while we're high?"

"Well, not exactly. I want you to go down on me and I'll take a hit just as I climax."

"Yeah, right." I recoiled, feeling a trap about to spring.

"I'm serious."

"I get it; then you'll tell Laurie, right?"

"Don't be ridiculous. I'm asking you, remember? And besides, I don't want to steal you, I just want the rush."

"Well, I dunno." I looked around nervously. "Right here?"

"In the back seat. It won't take long from what Laurie tells me." She was smiling now.

"What do I get?"

"You get my sister. Again, I'm not trying to steal you, Reno. No offense, but you can hardly offer me what Carlos does."

"He's your boyfriend?"

"Forget it!" She reached for the car key.

"All right, I'll do it."

"Is it really that bad?"

"No, I'm sure it's not." I was still unsure of her motives.

She climbed between the large leather bucket seats and took the vial from my hand as she went; I crawled through after she was seated.

"Give me your shirt."

"For what?" I started unbuttoning it before she could respond.

"A cushion. I hate all the wood in this car."

I said, "This is a beautiful car," as I handed her my shirt.

She gave me the vial's lid, complete with the small gold chain connecting the spoon, and requested, "Three scoops, please," as she kicked off her pumps. I carefully scooped from the vial in her left hand and dumped three spoonfuls into the pipe in her right hand. She handed me the vial; I replaced the lid and set it on the center console armrest between the front seats.

"Did you have this done?" I referred to the dark-tinted glass on the back windows.

"Don't be a wise ass." She jammed my shirt deeper into the hand-crafted armrest, and then carefully twisted sideways, watching the pipe as she leaned back. One stocking-clad foot was placed on the seat headrest behind me, the other on my lap. "Ready," she announced in anticipation.

Her pale blue spandex skirt rose to her hips as she raised her buttocks to help me slide it up. I was wide-eyed; I'd never seen a girl completely shaved before. I was glad I shaved to go see Pete as my lips touched hers with a sweeping glance.

"Just get me off, okay lover?"

"Don't tell the artist how to paint."

"Okay, okay. I'm sorry. Do it your way."

About three minutes later, I heard a click and then the sound of the flame pushing through the air. I worked hard on her as she wiggled and twitched and then went limp as her orgasm subsided. She sighed softly and said, "Thank you," as she rolled, somewhat twisted onto her side, tucked lightly in the fetal position. I gently probed her with a finger, feeling small muscle twitches. She turned her head to look at me. "Do you want to fuck me?"

"Of course. Who wouldn't? But I don't know…"

"Don't worry honey, I'll clean you up, and I can assure you that it's a one-time thing."

I wondered how two sisters could be so fucking amazing in every way. After I climaxed, without even a kiss from her, she pushed me off her to a sitting position and as promised, cleaned me completely with her mouth.

"We'd better go." She handed me my shirt and climbed back through the seats. She was sitting with a spoonful waiting as I tucked in my shirt, now sitting in the front seat. After I snorted two spoons, Debbie leaned over and kissed me on the cheek. "Laurie's a lucky girl. You take care of her, okay?"

"I do love her, ya know?"

"I'm sure you do. This was sex, sweetie, not love, so don't stress."

I'm not sure I'll ever understand the people in this world, including me, and moreover, I'm not sure I truly care to. As we drove through the city streets, I looked out the window, flicking the ashes from my cigarette out the crack at the top. I wondered where Dustin was and if he blamed me for running; after all, he did shoot the guy in my defense.

<hr>

"HI DUSTIN, I'M DETECTIVE BROCKWAY. HOW ARE YOU TODAY?" He took a seat in the small interrogation room where Dustin was taken without explanation.

"I'm great, dude, just fuckin' great." Dustin's tone was that of a hardened convict as he squirmed on the metal chair.

"Well, your buddy cut a deal today."

"What buddy?"

"Mr. MacNab, of course."

"Good for him."

"Very good for him, I'd say. He's walking on the whole deal."

"So?"

"So, how come Reno has some big-time lawyer cut him a deal from heaven while you get a nickel for backing him up?"

"What's your point, man?"

"No point, it just doesn't seem fair to me. I mean, him leaving his right-hand man all alone while he splits the state."

"He's gone?"

"Well, that's the deal anyway."

Dustin sat thinking, aggravated further by his shackles.

"You see, he's gotta split today or else we can grab him, and then he gets the whole load: distribution, sales to minors, accessory to attempted murder, and so on."

"So, where'd he go?"

"Well, Dustin, I don't know. How much money do you figure he had?"

"I dunno. Why?"

"You see, I figure this deal he got cost him plenty, so now he's gonna need to make a couple bucks before he goes anywhere."

"Yeah, well fuck him and fuck you too."

"I see your point, Dustin, I really do. But what if I was to tell your parole officer how you helped me get this big-time dealer who sells mostly to high school kids, and how about me telling the local judge the same thing? I bet he'd love to get this slippery fucker into his court with no deals available."

"So, what's your offer, man?"

"Oh, I can't make a deal, you know that. But I'd sure be on your side during these nasty parole hearings we all hate so much."

"Fuck, he could be anywhere by now."

"Yeah, that's for sure, could be anywhere. But if he did stick around, where do you think he might go for help. Remember, he's in a tight spot. Who could he trust?"

Dustin thought about it. "Tommy. He'd go to Tommy for sure."

"Tommy? Do you know his last name?"

"No, but he drives a mint Corvette. Oh!"

"What Dustin? Is there something else?"

"Yeah. He's the guy who sold him that sweet Camaro of his."

"No kiddin'? That is a nice car. Why do you think he'd go to this Tommy fella?"

"Tommy's his best friend, that's why."

"Do you happen to know where Tommy lives?"

"Well, kind of. It's in Wayzata. I've only been there once." Dustin sat back in deep thought, staring at the gray block walls.

"Thanks, Dustin. You've been a big help and I'll pass that along to the proper people. By the way, do you know a girl named Brittany LaBeau?"

"Yeah, she's his little squeeze. She was there too."

"Good, good, Dustin. I'll be in touch." Detective Brockway got up and walked out the door as a guard walked back in.

Dustin wasn't a rat, but Reno hadn't even offered to pay for a lawyer for his defense, so fuck him. As for Tommy, he didn't like that hard ass anyway.

The desk officer answered the phone at the precinct. "Minnetonka Police."

"Hi, Jim. This is Brockway; I'm over at county holding. Can you do me favor?"

"Go ahead."

"I need the DMV history on that Hot Rod Camaro in impound, with addresses, okay?"

"Sure. Gimme an hour."

"I'll call for it later if that's okay?"

"Fine."

They both hung up, the Detective thinking, "I just know you're too arrogant to believe you have to run off that quickly."

***

DEBBIE GAVE ME THE BRICK INSIDE OF A BAG IN THE PARKING LOT OF the hotel, saying, "Cut this stuff heavy before you sell it. We don't need a bunch of people overdosing on shit they're not used to."

"You're not coming in?"

"No. I've gotta get back."

"Okay. Thanks." I stepped out of the car feeling somewhat relieved about her leaving.

"Reno."

"Yeah." I had just closed the door when the power window went down next to me.

"I meant it about you taking good care of Laurie. Don't fuck up."

Before I could respond, the black Bentley sped off into the night.

Laurie greeted me with open arms as I walked into the suite. "Hey, honey. I missed you." After a big hug, she stepped back and asked, "Where's Debbie?"

"She had to go."

"She's cool, huh? But how 'bout that Carl?"

"He's something else all right."

"What did you think of the house?"

"You mean the one that's been in the family for three generations?" I mimicked Carl.

"Yeah, he's a trip." She giggled, kissing me again, from up on her toes to reach my lips squarely. I looked around the empty room.

"Where are Tommy and Missy?"

"After you left, he dragged her into their room; I haven't seen them since. Do you want to drag me somewhere, cutie?"

"Always, but let's look at this first." I held up the shopping bag.

After wiping down the glass dining table with a damp washcloth from the bathroom, and Laurie's retrieval of a razor from the coffee table, I carefully cut along the packing tape that covered a thick plastic material and then dumped the whole thing on the table. We stood silently looking at the deep pile of flaky rocks. Laurie broke the silence. "It's pink. Why's it pink?"

"It's Pink Peruvian flake." I was in awe of the quantity that had come from the package; it fluffed up and expanded substantially.

"That's good, huh?"

"Yeah, it's the best, as far as I know."

I began thinking this guy Carlos is not your everyday drug dealer; he's more likely the kind of guy who supplies everything in Jose's armored row house, but why is he selling this amazing product so cheap, and why to me? I'm a believer in the adage that when something is too good to be true, it is.

"Let's try it. I can't believe it's pink."

"We've gotta be careful, Laurie."

"Why?"

"It's really strong. Shit, it's probably right off the boat."

"I'm sure it is. That's what Carlos does," she said while comparing the color to her soft pink nail polish.

"Carlos?" My brain was in such a fog that I didn't piece it all together: Carl, Carlos, Debbie's boyfriend with the money and the kilo of pure coke. This guy was a serious dude

"Yeah. Carlos Montello, that's Carl's name."

I sat down in the chair at the head of the table, staring into the pile, unable to believe the day I had. She was smoothing her fingers along my face while asking, "Are you ok, honey? You look pale."

"Where's Carlos from, Laurie?" I was becoming concerned about my latest deep dive into the underbelly of the world. Jose was one thing, and I'd seen some pretty rough people in New Jersey and New York City, but this was a whole new level of bad to get tied to.

"I guess he's from here, why?"

"Where is his family from?"

"Oh, Panama, or maybe Columbia. Yeah, Columbia. He and Debbie go there a lot."

Just then, Tommy and Missy came out of their room looking like "who did and ran," saying a barrage of things like, "Wow," "Look at that," and "Holy shit." After the "oohs" and "aahs" were over, I put half the pile in a big Ziploc freezer bag, which it filled, and declared, "This goes to Jersey, once it's cut; and that, pointing to the remaining pile, gets cut by one hundred percent and sold here."

I called my friend in New Jersey.

"Yeah?"

"Vin?"

"Yeah."

"It's Reno."

"Yeah."

"It's coming to you red label, packed in a ten-pound box." This meant ten thousand dollars was still the price.

"Fine. Where should I send yours?"

"To Reno West, at the hotel."

"Thanks."

We hung up. We went over the entire deal except the final figure when I used a payphone on the street about a block from the hotel to call him at the auto parts store where he worked. It made me nervous standing out in the open like that, but it was better than calling from the room to discuss the deal. We would each have a full "key" of very good coke after adding the cut for a bargain price of ten thousand. Of course, mine would end up being free.

On Wednesday, around noon, a bell boy dropped off a box sent from an auto parts store in New Jersey; inside was a garbage bag filled with coffee grounds surrounding a Ziploc bag with a hundred one-hundred-dollar bills in it. I did the same thing except I marked "Improper Parts" on my box in black letters addressed to the store. He saw it, and in his car trunk it went.

I cut the coke I shipped and most of the stuff we kept with manni-tol, a B-12 substitute powder that was harmless, and it diluted the color of the coke so some snoopy prick wouldn't see new stuff hitting the street. Even with the cut, it was better than ninety percent of what's on the street. Laurie and Missy showed up around nine o'clock Wednesday night with another ten thousand between them. So far, they had sold three ounces: one from Jose's stuff, plus another ounce in eight balls yesterday and yet another today for twenty-four hundred each, hitting the big spenders first. I had over $31,000 in cash and still over thirty ounces of the best coke to ever hit my hands, worth another $75,000. We were on our way to paradise in the fast lane.

Tommy and I drank quite a bit throughout the day, and he was in a real mood by the time the girls got back, which was evident in the mean whisky voice he used to question Missy. "Where you been?"

"Huh?"

"I said where the fuck have you been?"

"Get off my back! I was selling this shit so we can go to California or Mexico or wherever the fuck you wanna go today."

Tommy was changing his mind about our destination almost on the hour it seemed, including places from San Diego to Australia and all points between. After another long gulp of Jack Daniel's, he continued the interrogation. "How much did Andy buy today?"

"He bought it all, then I fucked him all day, are you happy now?"

Tommy yelled, "Fuckin' whore," while leaping over the couch, heading toward Missy, bottle still in hand. I deflected his attack by stiff-arming him from my position in front of the girls. He was knocked off balance and stumbled due to his awkward landing and then crashed head-first into the wall to the right of the foyer, the bottle breaking on impact. He rolled lifelessly onto his side, bleeding from his scalp. Missy sneered at him as he twitched slightly, his brain trying to regain consciousness.

Laurie grabbed Missy's arm and spoke with justifiable concern in her voice. "You better go, Missy, before he gets up."

"I've had it with him." She headed for the guest room.

Laurie asked, "What about our plans?" while stepping carefully over Tommy as she followed Missy.

I was sitting on the floor after picking up most of the glass, dabbing a wet bar towel on Tommy's head. I couldn't see a big cut, so I assumed he'd be okay even though his attempts at speech were garbled. The girls came out of the room, Missy with her bag in hand. She said, "I'm sorry, Reno, but I've gotta go. He'll never change; you know." She leaned down, kissed me on the forehead and added, "Love ya honey. Good luck with this one." Tommy was just starting to make sense when he spoke; his "Fuckin' whore" comment was still somewhat inaudible.

Missy said, "I know, honey, I love you too," and then hugged Laurie, saying, "I'll see you tomorrow."

"Ten o'clock," Laurie whispered.

I looked down at Tommy, his face still bloody and contorted with pain. I knew he loved Missy, but they would never make it while he was drinking. I felt sad for him as the door closed along with the final chapter that included Missy in his life.

Tommy didn't recall my role in his fall as he slowly recovered throughout the night, which was nice because I didn't need a brawl with him on top of everything else. By morning, we were all pretty drawn out from the endless lines and booze that now greeted the day with us. I squinted at the light and asked Laurie what time it was.

"It's like 7:00 AM and I need a shower. Care to join me?" She slowly rose from the couch as she spoke.

I looked at Tommy. "Are you sure you're okay, dude?"

"I'm fine, for the thousandth time."

He had a bump on his forehead, but the bleeding stopped. I got up and followed Laurie into the bathroom.

"You gonna wash my back?" I asked in a baby voice.

"Of course I will, honey."

She slipped out of her clothes, leaving them in a pile on the floor. No matter how many times I saw her naked, my heart always doubled its rate as I took in the image of her exquisite beauty.

"I just wish I was a better..." I began, in a rare verbal expression of my feelings.

"Come in here," she interrupted, stepping into the shower after turning on the water. I stood watching the water cascade over every curve of her body, entranced by her beauty. She caught me staring from just outside the open glass door. "Get in here you nut."

I stepped in and pinned her to the wall, my entire body against hers, only the hot water finding secret paths between us. Ultimately, I broke the sweet silence we shared. "I don't ever want to be without you." She pushed me back into her view and passionately countered, "Then don't you ever leave me," and with that, we began making love. Maybe there was hope for me, hope for us, hope for anything better than the cloud of bullshit overshadowing me.

Laurie and I fantasized about private bungalows in Tahiti and hanging out on deserted beaches with locally sourced tequila and cocaine as I filled baggies for her to sell. I gave her several ounces with hopes of them being sold to some friends of hers that had more money than sense. These girls had older boyfriends who gave them money like it was air to spend as they pleased in exchange for moments of recaptured youth while their wives had drinks at the country club.

I put the rest of the coke, over twenty ounces, back in the pack, and then gave Laurie five hundred dollars.

"What's the money for?"

"I just wanna make sure you're covered." The thought of Debbie saying how little I had to offer got to my ego.

Tommy and Laurie left around 9:30 AM; he was to take her to her house before 10:00 so she could drive her mother to work in order to have a car for the day. Missy and she were meeting at Laurie's at 10:00 to go out and see potential customers together, but she didn't want to see Tommy. In addition to Laurie's stash, Tommy had a bag for sampling. He was to set up a big deal for the next day and then go back and get Laurie later in the afternoon. I couldn't risk being seen in Minnetonka, so I needed to lay low in the hotel.

"Will you miss me?" she asked while standing at the doorway in a pink skirt with a spandex bodysuit underneath.

Her words shot an icy quake through my body before I could say, "I miss you already." I wrapped her up in a tight embrace and kissed her passionately until Tommy interfered.

"Holy shit, some fuckin' gangster you are. You'll see her in a few hours. Why don't you give it a rest?" He was always busting my chops because of my Jersey, he claimed New York City, accent and attitude.

We parted with a last peck, and I closed the door behind them knowing he was right, the chill in my bones passing with the reassurance.

As I sat alone in the big room, I thought of how nice it would be once we could go out to dinner and clubs without the fear of being arrested on some bullshit charge. A local arrest could lead to my being identified and imprisoned for the many pending matters now on a shelf. The more I thought about it, the more paranoid I became. What if I get caught before we can leave? What if Laurie gets busted, or Missy or Tommy?

I took out the pack from under the bed and dumped it on the carpet. I sat looking at the contents for about five minutes, just thinking about the entire situation. There were several banded stacks of money, a large paper bag holding ounce-sized baggies of coke, a smaller bag containing nearly an ounce of pure pink Peruvian coke, the now useless title to the Camaro, Laurie's white G-string from the limo, and an assortment of pills. Another chill rattled my bones. I put all but the coke back into the backpack and reflexively stuffed the bag of uncut coke in my underwear. Looking at my watch reading 12:34 PM, I got up and began pacing the room, eyeing the paper bag filled with baggies of coke.

I grabbed the G-string from the floor and walked into the main room. Sitting down on the couch, I took a long swig from the tequila bottle that was left on the table. As I sat, running her garment over my pant leg, the wintry feeling swept through my body again.

"Fuck it," I thought, "We're going today." I'll have over thirty-five grand in cash tonight if the girls sell out; that's plenty to split with. We'll leave the rest of the blow with Tommy to sell and hop a plane to California. I can rent a room for a week, and when Tommy shows up, we'll all go south of the border and live like kings in a hut on some remote beach. I've always loved the Baja Peninsula, especially the places that remain untouched by the tourist scourge.

I ran into the master bedroom, grabbed the paper bag of coke, and stuffed it under the mattress. I got Laurie's garment bag, packed us both a few changes of clothes, and brought that and the pack to the foyer. After sitting the bags down, I picked up the phone and called Bobby on his company cell phone.

"Hello."

"Bobby?"

"Yeah. Who's this?"

"It's Reno, I need a favor."

"If I can, you know I will."

"Good. I just need a ride to the airport tonight. Obviously, I'll pay ya."

"Sure, glad to, and you're not paying for a twenty-minute shuttle. What time?"

"Can I call you later?"

"Sure. I just need thirty minutes' notice to get there."

"Are you sure?"

"Yeah, man. I'm off today. My brother finally came home and we're slow."

"Great. I'll call you later."

"Cool. Bye."

I hung up, reached into my pocket, and pulled out a wad of bills. Seven hundred dollars wasn't enough for on-hand cash. I went into the pack and pulled out another grand and then closed it up and went back to the couch, stuffing the money in my pocket as I walked.

"Okay, we're all set."

I drank the rest of the tequila while watching MTV on the big screen, occasionally pacing the room or doing a line from the pile on the table, trying desperately to shake this damn feeling. As I headed to the fridge, I looked at my watch: 5:04 PM. We'd be on our way soon. I rubbed the silky panel of the pearl G-string on my cheek and said softly, "I'll never be unfaithful to you again. Please hurry home."

As I crossed the room with a beer in my hand, the G-string hanging from my pocket, the phone rang.

"Hello."

"Reno, it's me, Bobby."

"What's up?"

"I called the airport for you; there's a 6:05 PM flight non-stop to John Wayne International in Orange County. Will that work for you?"

"I don't know, why?" John Wayne Santa Ana was the right airport; it serves Newport Beach, which was just as good as San Diego from my perspective, maybe better because we wouldn't be hanging around the border town we'd cross from when Tommy arrived.

"Well, my brother has a last-minute gig for me tonight at 7:30. That's the last flight I can get you to."

"Shit. Really?"

"Yeah, I'm sorry man, but I gotta take it, ya know?"

"Okay, okay, I'll let you know."

"Okay, but let me know soon. It's after five."

"Fine. Wait!"

"What?"

"Just come over now. Maybe we'll make it."

"Ok, I'll be out front."

"No, don't do that."

"Why not?"

"'Cause, I'm going to leave the room for Tommy 'til Sunday. So, can you park out back, maybe by the pool?"

"Whatever you say, dude."

I hung up.

"C'mon Laurie, hurry up," I called out to the empty room, and then I thought Tommy could take us if it's too late for Bobby, although three in the 'Vette is a stretch, plus the bags. "Okay, calm down. We could take a cab." I tried to reassure myself while pacing around the space. "It's going to be okay. They'll be here any minute."

The phone rang again a few minutes later.

"What now, Bobby?"

"Reno..." It was Missy and she was crying.

"Missy, what's wrong?"

"Tommy's. He hit..." She was too hysterical to talk.

"What about Tommy? Did he hit you again?"

"No. They were at '7-High' and..."

"Who was at '7-High'?"

"Tommy and Laurie. I saw them at the light. I was going to get Laurie and I saw them. They were going so fast..."

"What are you talking about? Where are you?" I was pacing wildly. The phone base fell off the bar and I dragged it by the long cord as I listened.

"The cops were chasing them. They crashed. They hit the divider at '7-High'."

"Are they all right? Why were the cops chasing them?"

"The cops said they're gonna get you too, Reno. You gotta go!"

"Where are you, Missy?"

"I can't tell you. They'll get you if you come. Reno, he's dead!"

"Tommy's dead?" I dropped to my knees as if struck from behind. "What about Laurie?"

"They don't know, Reno. The cop said she's bad. They found the coke..."

Suddenly, another voice was talking in the background. "Are you okay, miss? Miss?" The voice was now speaking directly into the phone. "Hello. Who is this? Hello. Who's on the line?"

I could hear Missy crying in the background as I hung up. I was dead still for a few seconds as reality took hold before screaming, "No, no, no," while pounding my fists to the floor. I stumbled to my feet, swiping bottles and glasses from the bar in rage. "No!"

The phone rang again; I dove on it, the G-string falling from its precarious position halfway out of my pocket. "Missy?"

"No, it's me, Bobby. There's a bunch of cops out front. Is everything okay?"

"What? Where are you?"

"I'm out back over by the pool now."

I dropped the phone while scrambling to my feet and then ran full speed, crashing into the table by the door, falling onto the bags in a contorted position. Before my motion stopped, I grabbed the straps of the pack with my left hand as I lunged for the door handle with my right hand. I charged across the hall and burst through the stairway exit door, taking each flight of stairs in one leap, falling several times against the block walls as I went. Finally, I stumbled out of the first-floor door into a group of businesspeople in the hallway, several of them catching me, standing me up in the process. I shoved them clear, bolted out the glass doors into the pool area, and darted into the parking lot. The black limo raced toward me, screeching to a halt. I flung the driver's side rear door open, yelling, "Go! Fucking go," as I dove onto the seat and rolled to the floor. The door slammed shut from the big car's acceleration.

"Stay down!" Bobby shouted through the open partition as we cruised slowly out the side entrance and headed down the street away from the hotel. "I'm taking you to the airport and you're catching that plane."

"No, Minnetonka." I moaned, still lying on the floor in a ball of physical and emotional pain, my mind racing in so many directions that I couldn't focus on any one thought. Tommy; Laurie; the cops; It was so surreal.

"Bull Shit! You're outta here now."

"I have to see Laurie." I groaned in pain.

"Look, I don't know what's going on, but you've got two choices: The airport or you're out here." The limo tires howled as he accelerated through a turn; my battered body ached from the force. Minutes later, I crawled onto the seat as we entered the unloading area of the Minneapolis-St. Paul International Airport. Bobby hung up the phone and said, "I just bought you a one-way ticket to California; your ticket is at gate thirty-four in the Delta terminal. You've got ten minutes to make it, so run!" The big car slid to a stop at the front doors of the terminal. "Go man, now!"

I stepped out onto the street as the limo's tires squealed and the door slung shut. After getting the location of gate thirty-four from a baggage check guy on the curb, I ran as fast as I could through the crowds. When I was stopped at the security checkpoint, I realized I had left the pack in the limo. The security guard yelled, "Slow down and get in line," as I neared the metal detectors. "Sorry, I'm late," was all I could muster through heaving breaths. The shock and adrenaline mixed with the days of drugs and alcohol to create a bewildered state that left only core functions intact as I went through the motions of navigating the airport. I followed the numbered signs to gate thirty-four and showed my ID to the agent.

"Here's your boarding pass, sir. You just made it." Bobby bought me a first-class seat.

I drank heavily during the entire flight, hardly speaking to a sole, only holding my empty glass in the air for complimentary refills after the initial order: Jack Daniel's straight, and then Wild Turkey when the Jack ran dry. My wounds stiffened during the flight, so I struggled to rise from the seat into the crowd exiting the plane. People thought I was just drunk and whispered about me as I wandered aimlessly into the terminal, with no bags, no destination. I walked out the upper-level doors and hopped into a cab that was waiting to pull out after unloading his previous fare.

"I can't get a fare here," the driver said as I pulled the door closed behind me.

"Just go to the beach." I threw a one-hundred-dollar bill over the seat.

"Fine, but which beach?"

"Any beach."

"Newport is the closest; is that okay?" We entered the traffic flow onto McArthur Boulevard as he spoke. I didn't respond; instead, I looked at the sky turning from orange to red through the palm trees reaching past the rooftops of the smaller buildings lining the airport's perimeter. A short time later, the driver said, "Just say when, okay?" as we passed fifteenth street on Balboa Boulevard heading south.

"The pier."

"Sure. You got it. Balboa Pier is right up here." I was looking through the windshield when he stopped. "This is it. Balboa Pier."

"What's that?" I pointed to a bar located just ahead of us on the backside of the parking lot.

"Oh, the Studio Café. It's a jazz bar; you might like it.

"Where's the closest bar that can't see the beach?" I couldn't bear to stare at the beautiful sunset on a beach without Laurie.

"The Pub is a good one, but you're a bit overdressed for a surfer joint. It's right over there." He pointed away from the beach toward an intersection. "Do you want to go there?"

"Yeah, that's fine."

Two and a half blocks later he pulled over again. "Here you go. The Pub is right there."

I stepped out of the cab and looked into the bar's giant window as he pulled away. My watch read just after 11:00 PM; I realized it was probably wrong but didn't fix it. I entered the open door and made my way through a light crowd engaged in various activities, noticing a bouncer breaking up a scuffle by a pool table as I sat down at the bar.

"You look like you need a drink. We have beer and wine coolers, but I need an ID for either."

I slapped my fake ID on the bar with a one-hundred-dollar bill from the folded stack in my pocket and said, "Budweiser," as he slid the license back to me.

"It's three beans for the brew." He sat the bottle on a napkin he'd just placed along with my change and followed with, "This your first time to the Zoo?" referring to the local's name for Newport Beach: "Zooport." I just stared out the window without responding and then left a five on the bar while picking up the balance of my change as I stood. I wasn't ready to engage people, and the sunset was fading as a weather front rolled in bringing an early dusk, so I headed for the door.

The bartender yelled, "Hey, dude. You can't leave with that," as I approached the door.

I stopped, chugged the beer, and then sat it on an old safe by the door as I exited.

Someone seated by the bar said, "Man, that guy's really fucked up." The bartender added, "Yeah well, lots of people get lost in the Balboa Triangle," as he wiped down the bar where my beer had been before tossing the five-dollar tip into the big jar to his left.

I walked the two blocks back to the beach and then wandered through the sand until the whitewash splashed off my suede shoes and up my pants. I thought of Tommy and the shit-eating grin he probably had as he sped through traffic away from the cops. He was as crazy as me and always just a moment away from that last bad move. But Laurie?

"Laurie, Laurie!" I called out to the heavens while falling to my knees, hands held to the sky. "Laurie, I'm sorry." I fell to my side, whimpering like a child for a lost puppy. "Oh God, not her. Why not me?" I was the one with the deadly lifestyle. Tommy was the lucky one; his suffering was over. Why did I let her go with him? I should've known better. I was always hurting the ones who cared for me. I wanted to swim out beyond the break and just let the water wash it all away and end my pointless existence. I couldn't. I knew I'd turn back for the shore at the critical last moment, always on autopilot to survive. I also believed deep inside that I couldn't go on much longer at this pace of drinking and drugs without my body giving out; in that, I found a delusional comfort: my eventual demise and an end to the pain of living with so many regretted choices. There's an endless circle in alcohol and drugs: the more you do, the deeper you get; the deeper you get, the more you do, and death is the only end. My only prayers were now for the tide's mercy to wash me away into the oblivion I chased for so long.

I mumbled, "Laurie," as the surf swept around my numb and spent body.

PART IX

Lost at Sea

Lost at Sea

One evening, both Lori Ann and Whit were off work and Whit stopped by unannounced. Lori Ann was sitting on her front stoop catching the last worthwhile rays of the day when she jogged up the walk.

"Hey, tonight's your night sweet Desiree."

"My night for what? I'm not goin' to some diver party, Whit." Lori Ann passed every night on the extended party scene and tonight was her first night off since starting at the Stallion. She worked two weeks straight and was starting to put away some money, her primary focus.

"How'd you like to make some serious money?"

"Doing what?" Lori Ann asked with a suspicious tone.

"I've got a Bernie that wants me to bring a friend."

"No way! You know I don't do that." Lori Ann got up and folded her aluminum lawn chair before heading inside.

Whit continued, "It's two thousand guaranteed and no monkey business. If you like him, great, if not, well then, you'll get paid two grand to hang around for a few hours. No harm, no foul. But if you do like him, well the skies the limit little sister."

"I don't know, it sounds too creepy."

"Look, you owe me, and I'll have a terrible time finding someone of your caliber on such short notice. Please. You might make enough to go see Jerry."

Jerry was a land developer building condos on a golf course; Whit had already put her deposit down: ten thousand dollars.

"I don't know, Whit. I just can't see doing it with a stranger, even for a condo."

"Then don't, but come along and get paid a couple grand to enjoy yourself. It's probably dinner and drinks, maybe some casino time, or a private striptease. How bad could that be?"

"I don't know. How bad?"

"I need this favor, Lor. Please help me out. I promise, if you aren't happy, you can split any time you want, okay?"

"I can go whenever I want, and I don't have to do anything?"

"Yes. I promise."

"What would I wear?"

"Take a shower and I'll be back in an hour. I've got ya covered on the outfit. Cool?"

"Fine. I'll do it for you but only this once and I'm not fucking him."

"Thanks, hon. I'll see ya in an hour." Whit darted out the door before Lori Ann could change her mind.

After a quick shower, Lori Ann opened a bottle of wine while she put on her makeup and had three glasses before Whitney returned with her wardrobe. She opened the door and let her in after the second knock.

"You scared me, honey. I thought you slipped out the back."

"No, but I should've." She took the hanger and shoes from Whit.

"C'mon, it'll be fun!" Whitney tried to convince her but it wasn't working. Lori Ann tossed her robe on the sofa, slipped into the dress Whit brought, and stepped into the all-too-familiar white pumps she wore that first night on stage, immediately aggravating the spots they wore raw that night.

"You look great!"

"Yeah, yeah." Lori Ann dumped her purse out on the coffee table and dropped select items into the matching bag Whitney provided. She put a small pile of crumpled up money and a bank card into it and then added her keys, the little vial she hadn't snorted from since

Florida but seemed to carry almost absent-mindedly, and a tube of lip-gloss.

Whitney handed her a condom. "Here, take this and don't bitch; ya never know. Girls gotta be prepared. I remember one time…"

"Don't! I don't want to hear some gorilla suit story right now. Let's just go." She tossed the condom in the purse.

"Okay, okay, just relax. It's gonna be fun."

As the girls drove down The Strip, Whitney rambled on about all the wonderful dinners and events Bernie's had taken her to, but Lori Ann wasn't feeling good about it at all.

"Try and lighten up. Shit, you've had half a bottle of wine."

"I should've had the other half."

"Why don't ya have a little blast from your hitter?"

That didn't sound like a half-bad idea, so Lori Ann dug it out of the bag and snorted a spoon full up each nostril. Immediately, she felt the warm rush through her body; it made her miss what used to come next, sex with Stephen, but at least it loosened her up a bit. She'd forgotten just how excited it made her and feared she might actually go through with this. Lori Ann Morgan a hooker? "Oh, God. Where is my life going? I can't believe this is my destiny. What I dreamed was so different." She was still lost in space when they pulled up to the valet at the hotel.

"You ready?" Whitney asked with a grin.

"I guess so. Let's just get it over with."

All Lori Ann could think about as they walked through the casino and rode up the elevator was some little old man lying on top of her; there was no amount of money that could make her do it.

⁂

I must have passed out from the exhaustion of seeing my world collapse before my eyes; that, combined with jet lag and God only knows how much alcohol and drugs was enough to bring anyone to his knees. As I woke from my brief reprieve, cold and wet on the shore where the surf abandoned me in its tidal retreat, it took several minutes for the reality of the recent events to again come clear. I looked out over the water at the lights of an island off in the distance and raged into the abyss. "What the fuck Tommy, ya couldn't just stop? Why are we so fuckin' insane?"

Staring up at the stars through tears, I spoke to the heavens. "Laurie. It all happened so fast. What could I do?" Her words, "Don't you ever leave me," just hours old, resounded in my head. I stood up unsteadily in a fog of torment, asking aloud, "What the fuck am I gonna do now?" with the self-pity of a hopeless drunk who's dug a pit from which he can see no light. I staggered toward the parking lot by the pier, still mumbling to myself while pulling the saltwater-matted money out of my pleated pants pocket. "God, I need a drink." I looked at the soaked handful of cash, shaking my head as I pushed it back into my pocket. My mind, struggling for clarity, reviewed my situation. This morning I had everything I could ever want; now I have nothing. I anxiously glanced at my watch trying to slip some reality into the moment. It was 3:00 AM.

I called out to a young couple making out in the sand. "Hey, do you know what time it is?"

"It's one o'clock, dude. Go home."

I don't have a home, I thought, and continued on, resetting my watch as I stumbled through the sand. My mind wandered in the fog of current events looking for a trajectory. If I jumped the next flight back, they'd have me before I could even get to Laurie's hospital room. My options were so few that it was almost more perplexing than having many. After looking in the darkened windows of the Studio Café, I walked toward the inner harbor and The Pub I'd been in just hours before. I was passing an alleyway when I saw the bartender from The Pub; he was talking to an older man just outside the back door to a bar called Dillinger's. He yelled, "Hey, dude" after noticing me standing in a daze on the sidewalk fifty feet from them.

I raised my hand in a half-assed wave of acknowledgment and asked if The Pub was still open.

"No, but this place is, come on in."

The older man turned and walked off into the darkness. When I got to the door, the bartender asked," So, you on vacation, or what?"

"I guess I live here, for now anyway."

He cracked up while holding the back door open for us to pass through. "You sound like a local already."

"What'll you have, Stihl?" the Dillinger's bartender asked as we sat down.

"Double scotch, and don't be shy."

"You know this guy?" The bartender looked me over with an air of distaste.

"Yeah, he's okay. I saw his proof."

"Okay, what can I get ya?"

"Cuervo Gold; bring the bottle." I put a soggy fifty-dollar bill on the bar.

"Why don't you try it a shot at a time?"

"Don't mind Larry, he's always on the rag. So, I'm Stihl. You're?" He asked with an outstretched hand.

"Reno."

"Oh yeah, I remember from your ID. Good to meet you, and good town too." We shook hands and he added, "That's really your name?"

"Huh?" I was concerned that he meant my fake ID was no good.

"Reno? Not a lot of guys walkin' around with that one."

"Oh, yeah, my dad was a mountain man; woulda probably been Sierra if I'd been a girl. How about you, Steel? That's a first."

"Yeah, it's spelled S-T-I-H-L but pronounced like the metal. They say it's German for peaceful. So, ya ever been up there?"

"Reno? Nope, never been."

"Well, you should go; it's fuckin' lawless and damn beautiful up there."

The bartender placed the drinks on the bar and took my fifty. "You buyin'?" He asked without pausing before turning toward the register.

Stihl thanked me for the drink; I just nodded, drank my shot without a verbal response, and sat the glass firmly in request of another.

"So, where ya staying?"

"I don't know."

"Hmm, have you got a car?"

"Nope."

"Well, this town's probably booked solid. If ya want, I can give you a ride to a motel in Costa Mesa."

"Thanks, but I'll just crash on the beach." I was sure the courage or ignorance to drown myself could be found in a bottle of Cuervo's best.

"Not in Newport you won't."

"Why not?"

"The Newport KGB will lock you up for sure, brah. These rich folks don't take kindly to what they perceive as vagrancy."

"I'll take my chances."

"Do ya toot?"

"What?"

He leaned closer and spoke more softly as he repeated himself. "Toot. Do ya do coke?"

"Yeah." I realized at that moment that the Ziploc baggie in my pants was what had been poking me.

"Cool. I just scored a halfer. You want a line?"

"A half-ounce?"

"Yeah, right. No, a half gram."

"Oh." I looked around the dark room; some old men were scattered at the bar and a middle-aged couple sat at a table on the far side.

"Well, do ya want one?"

"Sure, right here?"

"No. Where are you from?"

"Jersey."

"Well, in California it's illegal, so we go to the growler."

"The growler?"

"The bathroom, brah." His eyes smiled in amusement.

Once in the bathroom, he poured the contents of a bindle out on the porcelain lid of the toilet and then licked the paper before dropping it in the water. He divided the powder into four lines, snorted two, and handed me a rolled-up bill, telling me, "Easy come, easy go." I snorted the lines he left for me and returned his rolled-up bill.

"Thanks, man."

"No problem. I just wish there was more."

"That's all you have?"

"Yeah."

"Why'd you split it with me?"

"Why not? It's only drugs." His warm tone relaxed me for the first time all day.

"You want another one?"

"Do you have some?" He looked puzzled as I reached into my still-damp pants and pulled out the baggie, holding it up to his view. "Holy shit! I guess you do."

After I laid out a pile and did my full gram line with the dollar he offered again, I stepped back and handed him his bill. "You're up." I left him a pink line at least eight inches long.

"What's this? It's fuckin' pink."

"It's Peruvian, and that's your line."

"Shit, the whole thing?"

"Yeah, go for it, but brace yourself 'cause it's good."

Small rocks were falling out of his nose when he stepped out of the stall. With a finger to my nose, I said, "You got a landslide man." He pinched his nose to stop the coke from falling out, ran some water over two fingers and his thumb on his other hand, and then snorted the water from the tips, just as I had done moments before. When he finished, I added, "Thanks, dude, really, I mean it."

"You're thanking me? Man, that shit's incredible." His face and throat numbed as the warm rush moved through his chest and mind. He was no stranger to good cocaine in "So Cal" but this stuff was exceptional, not the kind of blow just anyone can get and most definitely not in that quantity.

"You shared all you had, your last, with me; that means a lot."

"Look, why don't you crash at my place tonight? It's only a few blocks from here." There was brotherly concern in his voice. He wasn't sure who the hell I was just yet, but he knew the local cops would have a field day with me if I was out wandering around at all hours.

"Well, I don't know." My hazy thoughts were still intent on the awaiting abyss.

"Dude, if Newport's finest catch you sleeping on the beach with that bag, you'll get locked up forever."

"Okay, but I wanna get a bottle first."

"No problem. I'll get Larry to sell us one to go."

After a brief argument with the cranky bartender, he agreed to sell me a bottle of tequila and a bottle of Seagram's Seven for Stihl. As we walked down the concrete path that divides the houses from the beach, Stihl asked, "Did you get that stuff here?"

"Nope."

"How long you been in town?"

"Today."

"Yeah, you look a little drawn out, and wet too. Bad flight?"

His jest implied a crash landing, but it went over my head. I burst into laughter; not at his joke, I'd finally snapped, stumbling to my knees into the sand, crying uncontrollably.

Stihl nervously scanned our surrounding area while asking, "Dude, are you okay?" I couldn't answer. I felt as if I was purging myself of all that was left of my very being. Suddenly, an icy feeling ran through my body followed by a peaceful sensation of release, like being awakened from a deep sleep or maybe falling into one. Through the mental haze I heard Stihl saying, "Man, you gotta pull it together. Somebody'll call the cops. Dude, can you hear me?"

"Huh? Yeah, I'm fine." I rocked slightly on my knees like a cattail in a breeze.

"Man, you had me worried. I thought you'd gone over the falls."

I stood up, looking directly into his eyes. "Man, nothin's worth a fuck anymore."

He looked back at me uneasily, forcing a tense smile. "Well, now I know you'll fit in around here."

"What a fuckin' day."

"Must've been."

"You wouldn't believe me if I told you."

"Brah, ya act like you killed somebody or something." He was clearly apprehensive about my potential response.

I said, "At least two," in a distant, raspy voice, counting myself along with Tommy.

"Here?" He was beginning to re-think his offer to have me stay at his place, at a minimum.

"Nah, it's not what you think." I proceeded to tell him about my day, sitting down in the sand as the story unraveled. He didn't speak until I finished but sat down with me and opened the Seagram's Seven bottle, taking long drinks without moving his eyes from me.

We sat silently for a full minute after I concluded until he broke the sullen mood. "Look, if you need a place to crash for a while, you're welcome at mine, but you should definitely be layin' low."

"Thanks. I'll let you know." I looked at him closely for the first time since our meeting. He was in his late twenties, maybe early thirties, with longish, sandy blond hair, blue eyes, and a medium build. As we stood up, I noticed he was maybe five feet eight inches tops, definitely a handsome surfer boy type with a sincere smile, but not flashy, just California casual.

Once we began walking again, I asked, "How long ya lived here.

"Twenty-eight years."

"That's a long time in one place." I felt almost envious.

"Too long. I'd rather be in the mountains. Tahoe's for me, just across the lake from your namesake."

"Yeah, well, I'm tired of cold places. I'm gonna end this lousy ride in some sunshine."

"Well, we've got plenty of that," he said in a less than enthusiastic tone.

He stopped at one of the short narrow paths leading to the beachfront homes, this one ending at a dilapidated wooden gate. Stihl spoke while opening the latch. "I don't know who'll be here, but it's my place so don't worry."

"What do you mean?"

"Well, my ex-girlfriend's kid kinda lives here; she doesn't like her dad's new wife, and nobody knows where my ex, her mom is, so she hangs out here most the time."

"How old is she?"

"Tammi's like a junior or maybe a senior, high school age, ya know, but she's okay. It's just that her friends get a little tiresome from time to time."

"A party house, huh?"

"Pretty much, I guess. Just watch out for the little girls around here; they're gonna love you."

"That's not that young." I almost slipped and gave up my age.

"Maybe not for you but I'm pushin' thirty."

We climbed up two stairs and entered through the back door. Top-Forty music played at a reasonable volume from behind the first door on the right.

"That's gonna be Tammi, and who knows who else." He pointed to the closed door and then toward the door on our left with his thumb as we continued through the hallway. "That's my room." Finally, he tapped another door on the left, saying, "And here's the head." The hallway opened to an empty room that was intended to be both a living and dining space, more or less divided by the front door.

"This is the living room; there used to be a couch, I think. Anyhow, over there is the kitchen; there may even be a beer in the fridge, and that's the tour." He sat down against the wall facing the two windows and the front door. "It's not much, but if it was, the landlord would sell it, and we certainly don't want that." His smile was sincere and welcoming.

The irony wasn't lost on me, having traveled two thousand miles and the first house I enter has no furniture either, just like home.

"Can't beat the location."

"That's the truth, but I'm not here very much, especially if I get a better offer. You can sleep anywhere you want; I'm not sure why I usually land here."

"Thanks. Have you got a phone?"

"Don't say that word around here. They'll run up a bill on the concept alone." He laughed at his own quip. "And there's clothes in my room, so if you need to borrow a shirt or something, go ahead."

The phone bill comment brought a twinge of loneliness for the Tokyo crew. I hadn't spoken with them since before they left for Japan, and it was even longer for my dad. I guess my end will be the final disappointment for those who only wanted the best for me. At some point, I decided I just wanted to go out in a blaze of glory, but it's looking like it'll be more of a whimper as the sea swallows me like so many grains of sand. Not that it matters either way, any more than whatever set me off on this path so long ago. I've hidden within the bottle and drugs for a very long time, and it seems I'll be hiding until the end. To be clear, there is no excuse for many of the things I've done, but sometimes you can only see so far ahead, and things either look a lot worse or not quite as bad as they really are; both ways are equally fucked when contrasted by reality, and hindsight will always be twenty-twenty. I always chose the easy path, even when it was harder; now I just wanted to hit the wall at the end.

A girl stepped out in front of us from the hall where we were seated against the wall. She was short, maybe five feet two inches, and thin. Her hair was black and long, her eyes were bright blue, but her braces distracted from them when she smiled. She fidgeted while she stood and asked, "Who are you?"

Stihl jumped in, sounding somewhat fatherly. "Don't be so fuckin' nosey."

"Okay. I'm Tammi, and you are?"

"Tammi!"

"It's cool, Stihl. I'm Reno, nice to meet you, Tammi."

"Ooh, deep voice, and he's not from here. He's cute."

"What do you want, Tammi?"

"How about him for starters?"

I looked at Stihl and asked, "Are all Newport chicks like this?"

"Pretty much."

"Where are you from?"

"That's enough, Tammi!"

"Sorry, but he can sleep in my room if he wants," she added before retreating down the hall.

"Well, I guess you're set for pussy."

"I thought she was like your kid or somethin'."

"She's not my kid, she just hangs out here, rent-free I might add."

"Got it." I pulled out the bag of coke. "Do you want a line?"

"Sure, twist my arm."

"Is it cool, I mean with her and all?"

"Relax. Tammi's seen it all with her mom, and she's probably too ditsy to notice anyway."

"Got a mirror?"

"I've got a picture around here somewhere." He got up and headed down the hall; two minutes later, he appeared with an eight-by-ten framed picture of Lake Tahoe. "Will this do?"

"Sure, it'll work."

A short time later, Tammi came back into the living room with a super-hot blonde who epitomized California girls in every way: long, lean, tan and tone, with a strut and attitude they write songs about.

"Reno, this is Dakota. She wanted to meet you."

"Hi, Dakota."

"Nice to meet you." She leaned down and shook my hand. She was several inches taller than Tammi, with bright green eyes and a hard body that wouldn't quit. A telephone rang from the back of the house and Dakota quickly turned and sprinted down the hall. Tammi plopped down Indian style in front of us. Both girls wore surfer style short-shorts and equally tight-fitting, sleeveless cotton shirts; we call them "guinea T's" in Jersey.

"She's got a mobile phone?" I asked in disbelief, thinking of how expensive they were.

"Yeah. Welcome to Newport, dude."

"What are you boys up to?" Tammi asked, looking directly at me. I glanced at the bottle in my hand and told her, "I'm just drownin' the day, babe."

"I like that." Stihl held up his bottle in a quasi-toast.

Dakota reappeared with the phone bag in her hand and blurted, "He's such a jerk," as she sat down on her knees, resting on her heels. Among many other things, it's always amazed me how many positions girls can sit in comfortably.

"Dakota, can I use your phone? I'll give you twenty bucks for the charges."

"Here." She tossed it toward me and it hit the floor with a thud. "I don't pay for it so neither do you."

"Thanks. You're a doll."

"I'm a doll." She giggled. "He talks like a mobster." Dakota was beaming but Tammi made a face and said, "You're somethin' all right, and he's not a mobster."

It was about 3:25 AM when I fumbled through my money to find Bobby's card. All three of them gazed inquisitively at the pile of cash, mostly hundred-dollar bills, and the substantial bag of cocaine now sitting on the floor between my outstretched legs as I pushed the buttons on the handset. The phone rang at least four times before a groggy female voice answered.

"Hello." She was awakened by the phone.

"Hey. I'm sorry to call so late, or early I guess."

"It's 5:30 in the morning. Who is this?"

"It's Reno. Is Bobby there?"

"Reno! Are you okay? Bobby told me what happened." She never met me but grew attached through Bobby's stories about the crazy young client he befriended.

"I'm fine but I left something in the limo today."

"I know. It's right here."

"Is Bobby there?"

The girls whispered amongst themselves as I spoke.

"Sure, hold on."

Bobby's sleepy voice came on the line. "How's the beach?"

All three of them were now looking at me as if they were seeing an apparition.

"It's fine Bobby, thanks."

"I've got your bag, dude, but you've got a problem."

"Oh yeah, what's that?" I was slurring my words and sounding a bit more Jersey-Italian than I might've if even slightly less drunk and weary.

"The cops found the stuff in the room, Reno. They came to the office last night asking about you."

"What'd ya tell 'em?"

"I told them I hadn't seen you in days, but they've got a line on your fake ID, bro', so don't use it."

"Shit! You used that name for my flight, man."

"I know, but they still think you're here."

"Are you sure?"

"Yeah. Do you need the pack?"

"Listen, take cash for the ticket and a grand for your troubles, then send the rest of the cash to me. You can keep the pills and dope too, but lose the Camaro title and the pack, okay?"

Stihl scolded the wide-eyed whispering girls. "Shut up, you two!"

"I don't want your money, bro'. Where should I send it?"

I handed the phone to Stihl. "Tell him this address and then hand the phone back to me."

Stihl said only the address and handed the phone back, looking at me the entire time.

"Bobby?"

"Who was that?"

I ignored the question. "Put the money in a big Ziploc and then put that in a garbage bag filled with coffee grounds. I want you to overnight it to me, okay?"

"I'll do it this morning."

"Thanks, Bobby. And Bobby?"

"Yeah?"

"Did you hear anything about the others?" I was unable to speak Laurie's name.

"Man, Missy called me last night asking about you. Reno, they didn't make it."

My hand fell to my lap, still holding the phone handset. I pressed "END" and let it fall to the floor. My jaw was locked, and tears overflowed my eyes as I stared into the darkness through the windows and struggled to take a breath. The room was dead still until Stihl picked up my tequila, removed the top, and slid the bottle upright between my thighs.

"They fuckin' killed her." I slurred as the breath left my body in a rush as if it would never return. I raised the bottle to my lips and chugged the remaining third without pause, and then, unable to function in any way, I rolled onto my side and lost consciousness with the bottle still in my hand.

The three of them sat motionless watching me until Stihl shattered the silence. "You saw nothing, you heard nothing, and it's time for bed." The two girls walked quietly down the hall without argument, whispering amongst themselves as the door closed behind them.

———

THE NUMBERS FLASHED ABOVE THEM ON THE STAINLESS-STEEL WALL as each floor passed while the short ride to the eighth floor seemed like an eternity wrapped within the implications of what awaited her. Time slowed down and Whit's rambling faded into the background with the noise of elevator Muzak. Lori Ann viewed a time-lapse chronicle of her life in her mind's eye. Images of her youth, family, adventures, and mundane events streamed by as the box that carried her climbed toward the next chapter in her destiny. Stephen's snapshots seemed dim and cold by contrast to so many others, and her resentment of his role in her situation hardened her heart against his memory. The wine and pink cocaine added layers of haze to her trance as she pushed away the memory of his touch, replacing any gentleness with a razor's edge, questioning his motives and her perspective until his face blurred into the murk of the background.

The doors opened at the sixth floor, where a young couple peered in, exchanging words with Whit before stepping back to await another car that would take them down instead of up. Lori Ann looked through them as if they were transparent, hearing only snippets of the brief exchange, wishing she too was going down instead of up; but destiny's hand held her in place, having led her to this upward journey, to a room where she would know an experience that was beyond her conception, just as being a dancer had been only weeks ago. How could she have gone from "The Chief's" "little seal," her mother's "angel," to an escort in a Vegas casino? She felt as though she might vomit as the next scene was beginning to unfold, but the film was cut short when the doors opened again at the eighth floor with Whit's voice obliterating the clouds that carried the cinematic stream of her life. "Hey, are you in there? This is our floor."

The hall looked endless and seemed to narrow in the distance as they walked toward room eight-forty-four. Lori Ann glanced at Whit, who looked unburdened, as though she might be venturing to pick up a loaf of bread as opposed to having sex with a man she's never met and will never see again. How could she get to this place, a place where you'll allow a man inside you for mere money? What would you sell next with only your soul left to trade?

Whit shared her story with Lori Ann over breakfast one morning after work. She came to Las Vegas from the Midwest. A man had wronged her, just as Lori Ann ultimately concluded about Stephen's disappearance, but this man took Whit's infant child while she struggled with an addiction, and the courts gave her no path to get the baby back in her life. She returned to the comfort of drugs and alcohol after a brief attempt at sobriety in an effort to regain custody, finding her resumed way of life better suited for Las Vegas than the quiet town she grew up in. She came to Vegas with a friend who was quickly swallowed up and found dead while using street prostitution to feed her habit. Whit, who never shared her real name, saying that girl died a long time ago, tried various jobs like at a carwash and a fast-food joint, only to be underpaid and taken advantage of by slimy managers. She was on the verge of being evicted from a low-rent motel when an opportunity to dance at one of the shadier clubs presented itself; she never looked back. A few name and hair color changes put her on track to where she was now: in control of her destiny, at the expense of men, where she held all the cards and used them for her benefit. She saw herself in Lori Ann and wanted to help her avoid the pitfalls of starting out without a mentor on the streets of this desert cesspool by fast-tracking her to what she viewed as an eventuality for her.

I AWOKE TO A HAND IN MY POCKET AND SOUNDS OF CATCALLS AND whistles in the distance.

"What're ya doin'?" Through one blurrily-opened eye, I could see Dakota leaning over me.

"I'm putting your stuff in your pocket. People are coming over and I thought..."

"Where am I?" I closed my eyes again and gravity pulled my heavy head back to the floor.

"You're at Stihl's place. Go back to sleep." She kissed me softly on the side of my head and then stepped toward the front door.

Stihl mumbled, "Fuckin' kids, no mercy in 'em at all," from behind me.

I struggled in pain to sit up against the wall. "My world for some fuckin' shades man." I tried to adjust to the bright light streaming through the curtainless windows.

Stihl said, "Breakfast of champions," as he slid the bottle of Seagram's across the short distance of carpet and into my leg.

Dakota stood by the front door looking at us with pity in her eyes. She greeted Stihl with a cheerful "Good morning." He followed with a foggy "What time is it?"

"About noon, sleepy." She rocked on her toes as she talked, wearing a scant bikini and white sneakers with ankle socks that had lace ruffles at the top. She was tan and built like a gym commercial.

"Is there any beer?" I hoped out loud, now holding the Seagram's bottle in contemplation.

"I don't think so," she sympathetically replied.

"Perfect. Well, here's to a quick end." I saluted as I spun the cap free with a flick of my thumb before taking a long swig.

"Pass that here, dude." Stihl moaned as he managed to sit up against the wall. I looked over at his deeply bloodshot eyes and began to put together where I was through blurred mental glimpses of the previous night. I handed him the bottle, comforted by the knowledge that he was kindred spirit.

Tammi came into the front room from the hall, saying, "That came for you," pointing to a box on the floor by the front door.

"When? What is it?"

"It came this morning. I don't know what it is." She picked up the box and handed it to me. The return address was in Minnesota. My mind struggled to construct a timeline. I just called Bobby; how could this be here so soon? Then, I saw the orange sticker and read it out loud: "Saturday delivery?"

"Yeah, it's Saturday, brah. You slept straight through."

"Really? But the bottle was empty?"

"That's from last night. Time marches on." The world and recent events slowly came into focus as I opened the box. "I was gonna wake you when I got in, but you were so wiped out I figured you needed the sleep more than I needed a line."

"What? Dude, you could've done some. I wouldn't have cared."

"Sure, tell me now." He joked in a hungover, gravelly voice.

They watched as I pulled the bag of money out of the coffee grounds.

"Who are you, dude?" Stihl asked.

"I think he's a mobster," Dakota speculated.

"No, he's not," Tammi said, in my defense.

I opened the plastic bag, dumped the money between my legs, and counted it while the girls stood guard at the door without being asked.

"Twenty-seven-three. He didn't even take any."

Tammi gasped. "Twenty-seven thousand?"

"Yeah, it won't go far."

I pulled the other cash from my pocket and counted it while Tammi and Dakota whispered to each other. Stihl was quietly chopping lines on the glass frame.

My mind was in its ready-standby-survival mode as I worked it through out loud. "I've got a little over twenty-eight grand; I need wheels and an ID to start." I just wanted an end, but I only knew how to do one thing: Go fast and don't look back. Even in my pain, my ingrained survival instinct took over just as it always does. Just keep moving until it's fucking over.

"To start what?" Tammy was puzzled.

Stihl shot Tammi a "stop asking questions" look and then snorted a line. I leaned back against the wall and tried to wrap my head around my new situation. Thoughts of Laurie, Tommy, the cops, California and so many other things competed for my attention until my mind fogged over and my skull ached as if it would split open. "What the fuck am I doin' here?"

"From the looks of ya, you'll probably be running the place in a month," Stihl replied, only moderately in jest.

I looked down at myself as if to get another opinion. I wore gray, pleated slacks of a silky material, a black alligator belt, charcoal one-piece Oxford dress shoes, and a slate blue, collarless, button-down shirt with matching socks. Shit, I even had a two-tone Swiss watch, gold chain, bracelet, and a monogram ring; no wonder they called me a mobster. Stihl had on knee-length pale blue shorts, a faded Cabo San Lucas T-shirt, and flip-flops. I was gonna need some local color or the cops would have me before I crossed the curb.

"If I give you girls some money, will you go pick me up some clothes?"

"Where?" asked Tammi.

"Just hit one of those surf shops by the pier. All I need is one outfit like Stihl's." A whole wardrobe seemed pointless since I didn't know where or even if I'd be tomorrow.

"Why would you want to change? You've got a totally rad look." Dakota was sizing me up as she spoke.

"Because I look like I'm walkin' into a downtown club instead of onto the beach."

"Yeah, totally, but it's way hot." She curled her lip in a kind of accidental-seductive way. "So, what are your specs?"

"You mean my size? I'm like a thirty-two waist. Just get a large shirt and shorts, and some size ten and a half shoes. Two hundred'll cover it, right?"

"Sure." Tammi was stoked about the mission.

Dakota ran the numbers in her mind. "It'll be close."

"Close? How could it be more than two hundred for shorts and a T-shirt?"

Dakota replied, "I could score ya two-hundred-dollar Jams."

"Are you serious? What's fuckin' Jams?"

"Yeah, she is." Tammi agreed in a "what's wrong with the world" kind of way.

"Forget it. Here's two-fifty; get me one outfit. Okay?"

As Tammi took it from my hand, I winked at Dakota, who winked back and said, "Give us an hour." She reminded me of Laurie in the way she was so self-confident but not a snob about her beauty. I watched them walk down the stairs and turn right on the sidewalk toward the pier. Once they were out of sight, I asked Stihl, "Are you legal?"

"What do you mean?"

"Your license and all."

"Yeah. I've never had a ticket."

"Nice! How is it you've never gotten a ticket?"

"I don't drive much, I guess, and I'm not usually in a hurry." His laid-back California attitude was almost Zen in comparison to the people I grew up around.

"Where's your car?"

"It's at a friend's place on the island."

"What island?"

"Balboa Island. It's right over there." He pointed out the front windows, adding, "Well, you can't see it from here, but it's there," realizing all we could see were the houses on the other side of the divided street.

"What do you drive?"

"A '70 Cougar."

"No shit? With a 351 Cleveland under the hood?"

"Nope, a 289, but it still sucks gas."

"I was thinking of gettin' a bike." I'd been watching people ride by since I woke up. There was no helmet law here and a high-speed crash always seemed an alluring demise to me; this image was amazingly untarnished by the losses of Danny, Laurie, Tommy and others over the years. Hell, I almost died a few times myself, but blistering speed was a whole different kind of intoxicating.

"Did you see my bike?"

"No. Where is it?"

"At The Pub, chained up outside."

"A bicycle?"

"Yeah, a mountain bike."

"I meant a motorcycle, Stihl." I started to doubt if I could fit in.

"I could see you on one of those racing bikes."

"Can I put it in your name?"

"I guess so." He nervously agreed.

"Just 'til I get some ID, then I'll change it. Okay?"

"Do you think they'll come after you?"

"Who?"

"Whoever. It sounds like you've got a hell of a mess back there."

"I don't know, man, but I'll be gone before it gets too hot."

"Stay as long as you want. Just be careful, okay?"

"I don't care anymore, ya know?" I answered with a flat tone and vacant eyes.

"I can see that. She didn't make it, did she?" He asked very softly with obvious concern for her and possibly himself for asking.

"She was so amazing. I'm just no fuckin' good." I gazed out the window at my inexplicable past and present melding into an inescapable future; Stihl sat quietly as if trying to see what I saw. "It all died with her bro'. I swear, I've got nothin' left."

"Here, have a drink."

"That I will do." I took a long swig and turned to Stihl. "Please don't bring it up again." I had to hide from the pain or I wouldn't even have the strength to drink myself to death.

"No problem, dude. I'm sorry."

We sat and drank from the bottle, occasionally doing lines until the girls returned. I took a much-needed shower, put on my new surfer-dude outfit, and we headed out on foot to get his car.

"When are you guys coming back?"

"Soon, Tammy. Thanks again, ladies."

"You're welcome." They responded in stereo followed by an exchange of catty looks at each other.

"THIS IS COOL," I SAID, AS THE FERRY REACHED HALFWAY BETWEEN the peninsula and the island.

"Beats the long way around," Stihl replied, lighting a cigarette.

The view was exhilarating. There were too many boats to count, most large enough to be classified as yachts; they lined both shores, docked in front of beautiful homes and a variety of businesses that make up what's known as the "Fun Zone" and inner harbor. I was as at peace as my anguished soul would allow, although, to some extent, I might've still been in a state of shock, my mind simply not acknowledging the recent events until it could process the extreme data. Regardless, it's truly amazing how the water can have such a calming effect on one's being. I think it's magical and shouldn't be ignored nor dismissed lightly.

I was surprised by his car's condition. "She's a real cherry, Stihl." It looked new; the white paint and chrome sparkled in the sun. If you want a car pristine, let it live on a shady street in Southern California.

"Yep, and she only has twelve thousand miles. I don't drive much."

"No shit? That's amazing."

As we crossed the small bridge leaving the island, I felt at home. I wished Laurie were there to see the unique shops and the beautiful man-made landscape dotted with palm trees.

We came to a stop at a red light. "What kinda bike are ya lookin' for?"

"My last bike was a Suzuki, but it was a motocross racer. I think we should start with Honda. Is there a dealer nearby?"

"Very maybe. I think there's one on sixteenth street in Costa Mesa."

"Ha! Very maybe there is." I shook my head thinking they had their own language in "Cali."

At the next light, after driving up a winding road that followed the water separating the island from the mainland, Stihl said, "Over there is Fascist Island," pointing to a group of tall, modern buildings set above Pacific Coast Highway (PCH) and practically overrun with purposefully placed palm trees creating the oasis effect. "A pair of fifty-dollar shades will cost you a hundred for the prestige of the bag they come in."

"I'll bet." I looked at the sign over the grand entrance nearest us that read, "Fashion Island."

We followed the Pacific Coast Highway past the exotic car dealers, exclusive restaurants, and the other pricey retail offerings that litter its path. Finally, we exited onto Newport Boulevard and found the bike shop to be just a couple of blocks away. I took out five thousand dollars and placed the Ziploc bag of cash back under the vinyl seat, feeling upbeat about having something to look forward to, anything to look forward to. Time and space were again lost on me as drugs and alcohol blurred reality into waves of unforeseeable emotion, or lack thereof.

With one foot out his opened door, Stihl asked, "How are we gonna do this, brah?"

"Just follow my lead." I stepped out and walked up to the row of new bikes lining the front of the building. "Sit on this one, Stihl." I pointed to a new Honda Interceptor 750; it was red, white, and blue with a removable café racer seat cap to limit it to one rider for racing. It was revolutionary in its advancements for the street and was essentially a Grand Prix racing bike with headlights.

A salesman walked toward us, giving us the "here we go" look. "Can I help you fellas? Please, don't sit on the bikes."

I placed my hand on Stihl's shoulder, preventing him from getting up, and asked, "How much for this one?"

"That's a 1984 VFR 750 Interceptor; it's priced at forty-nine ninety-five plus prep, tax, tag, and title."

"I tell you what, he'll give you five grand cash and you throw in one of those racing pipes."

"Well, that's a nice offer but..."

"That's our only offer."

"Well, I'm not authorized to..."

"Then who is authorized?"

"Well, only my boss can..."

"Get him."

"He'll never make that deal."

"Let's go Stihl." I turned and started for the car.

"Wait. When did you need the bike?"

I pulled the wad of money from my short's pocket, holding it up into his view without turning around. "Now."

"Okay. Let me get my boss."

"Fine. But maybe we should look at Suzuki first, Stihl. What do ya think?" I asked loudly for the salesman to hear.

"Well..." Stihl started.

I gave the salesman a dismissive wave to go see the manager, and said, "Hurry up or we're lookin' at other options?"

"I'll just be a minute."

As the man disappeared, Stihl asked, "What if he says no?"

"Then we'll go to Suzuki or Yamaha. I'm sure someone wants to make a deal."

The salesman came back with his boss who greeted us with a cheery, "So, who's looking for a bike today?"

"Look, my friend here wants that bike; five is his final offer, take it or leave it."

"That would be plus tax and tags. Oh, and Paul here says you want an after-market pipe too, right?"

"Here's the deal: You put a pipe on that bike right now and we'll take it for five grand total, out the door."

"You're asking me to take a loss on this deal. We're only a few hundred apart; surely you can meet me halfway, right?"

"Look, here's the cash, five grand in my hand; take it or leave it."

The manager told the salesman, "Write it up," and then turned and went inside without another word.

"You fill out the paperwork, get the pipe on it, and we'll be back in a little while. Here's a thousand-dollar deposit."

I handed the salesman the money, walked away, and got in the car. Stihl hopped in less than five minutes later saying, "Well, you didn't make any friends here."

"Fuck 'em. Let's go get a bottle." I flicked my smoke out the window as Stihl backed out of the parking spot.

"Okay, boss."

"Did you give him your license?"

"Yeah, he copied it."

When we returned, the bike was at the front of the line with a "Sold" tag hanging on it. After ten minutes of paperwork, we walked outside.

"I'll drive it home, okay Stihl?"

"Yeah. You wanna follow me?"

The salesman took one more shot at me. "I'll need your license too if you're going to take it. Who owns this bike anyway?"

"He does, and he wants me to drive it home. You gotta problem with that, pal?"

The salesman frowned, and after a brief tirade about what laws must be followed, finally walked away. I gave him a Jersey-style "Have a nice day" as he departed.

I turned the key and pushed the start button; it roared to life and the pipe made it sound like an "Indy" car. My smile grew wide as I pulled the clutch, dropped it in gear with a crackle, and revved it up. I'd owned motorcycles since I was a kid and driven a couple of street bikes including a first-generation "crotch rocket" or two, so this was no big stretch of my ability, although it was quite a machine.

I wore Stihl's Ray-Bans to comply with the glasses law until we stopped off at a little beachfront sunglass shop where I bought a pair of Vuarnet Legends and some Croakies to hold them on. Fortunately, the girls bought me a pair of slip-on Vans instead of flip-flops. The sales guy would have lost it if I tried to ride away with open-toe shoes.

When we arrived at the house, a group of maybe ten kids charged down from the porch where they were sitting to look over the bike. The girls argued over who'd get the first ride while the guys contemplated how fast it could go.

"Don't touch," I warned as Stihl and I went inside.

He had the bag of money and bag of coke under his shirt; it made him look pregnant, but he was rightfully paranoid about walking around with so much cash and drugs in the open.

"That bike's somethin' else, dude," Stihl said as we sat down on the floor, referring to me weaving back and forth behind him as we traveled, emphasizing the occasional wheelie and bursts of speed.

"Where's the bottle?"

"Shit, it's in the car. Tammi!"

She shouted, "What?" from outside.

"Get the bottle in my car!"

Thirty seconds later, the whole crowd came pouring in.

"Hey, you know the rules. No kiddies in the house when I'm home."

They filed out, leaving only four girls behind. In addition to Tammi and Dakota were two more bikini-clad little cuties.

"A guy could learn to like this," I admitted as Stihl handed me the bottle.

"I'll bet. You've been here two days and you've already got a new bike and a harem," he mused while the girls frowned and went back out on the porch.

About 5:00 PM, Stihl got up.

"Well, I'm off to work. Stop down later if you want."

"What time's it get goin' down there?"

"It's always busy on the weekend but come down about ten or so. It'll be crankin' by then."

"I'll see you there."

He looked at Tammi and Dakota sitting Indian style in front of me in their bikinis and added, "I won't be hurt if you don't show," as he walked out the door.

Tammi was talking to Dakota. "I'm supposed to go out to dinner with my 'rents."

"When?"

"Your 'rents?"

The girls laughed at me, saying, "Parents," in unison.

"Ahh."

"I'm supposed to go at 7:00 but I'm gonna get out of it."

"Why?"

"You just got here."

"Go out with your parents. I'm not going anywhere."

"Then you have to come, too," she ordered Dakota.

"Not likely! They don't even like me. Why are you startin' a row?"

"You guys are gonna have sex while I'm gone."

I burst into laughter and asked, "What if we did? And what's 'a row?'"

"I don't want you to. And it's a fight, silly."

"Okay. I like you Tammi, but today won't be the day you start telling me who to sleep with, okay?"

"I'm sorry."

"It's cool. So, why don't you take a ride with me to the liquor store."

"On the bike?" She jumped to her feet.

"Yeah. You can hold the beer on the way back and maybe teach me this language of yours."

"Is that safe?"

Dakota said, "I'll totally go."

"No. I'll take you for a ride later. Let's go Tammi. Geez, it's like talkin' to twin Spicolis."

They replied in stereo. "Eww! That's so Valley."

The liquor store was less than a mile away, but Tammi was thrilled; after all, she did get to be first.

The three of us sat in the living room, Dakota and me drinking beer while Tammi drank Pepsi until her dad pulled up and honked the horn of his BMW. She jumped up, saying, "Don't have sex while I'm gone. Only kidding," before walking away as if marching off a cliff, out the front door, looking back three times as she went.

After Tammi left, Dakota asked, "So, who do you like better?"

"Dakota, you're both great. You're more my type but I'm not plannin' to get involved with anyone."

"You're gonna be like celibate?"

"I doubt it, but no more relationships; there's just nothin' left."

I could see by the look in her eyes that she took my words as a challenge. She was too young and too pretty to have ever heard a guy say he wouldn't be falling for her; most guys were busy professing their love while trying to get her bikini off.

"So, when do I get my ride?"

I took the last swallow of my beer, stood up and said, "Let's go." I grabbed the two baggies, one of cash, the other of coke, and dropped them in the paper bag the beer had been in, crumpled it up, and threw it in the garbage can in the kitchen.

"What are you doing?"

"Don't worry about it."

A few seconds later she said, "Oh, I get it."

"Good, now forget it."

"Do you think I should wear something else?" She stood in front of me in a skimpy, bright purple bikini with a thong bottom, barefoot.

"Well, shoes for sure."

"Okay. I'll just be a minute."

She trotted down the hall and I waited while one minute turned into ten. I was sitting on the idling bike, smoking a cigarette after taking the seat cap off when she came bounding out the door. She had put on her sneakers and a cut-off T-shirt that hung just above her navel, fixed her hair, makeup, and who knows what else.

"What do I do?" she asked, standing beside the bike.

"Put your left foot on that peg, swing your right leg over, but be careful, the pipe is hot."

"Owee!"

"I told you."

"Sorry."

Her hands were resting on my shoulders.

"Wrap your arms around my waist and hang on."

"Okay. Let's go!" she cheered as she squeezed me with a full-body embrace.

I pulled a U-turn at the first opening between the lanes and then headed north off the peninsula. I called out over the roar of the motorcycle, "Tell me where to go."

"Go straight."

"I know that. I mean PCH or what?"

"Yeah! Take PCH."

I was charmed by her enthusiasm, even if her directions were less than helpful, and have always felt better in the presence of palm trees and water; it was a nice moment. She rested her head sideways on my back and squeezed me tightly as we accelerated south on PCH. Her firm breasts crushed against my back with all her weight, in part due to the seating position on a racing bike. Her embrace felt good; it made me feel almost human again. She was pretty quiet until we passed through Corona Del Mar; just as we went through the last light in town, she yelled, "Go faster! It's okay here."

I dropped from fourth gear to second, twisting the throttle hard. We accelerated through all three remaining gears as the coast became visible far below, the front tire rising from the ground at each shift. The speedometer read one-forty when I glanced down. "What a bike!" I yelled to all that could hear, but of course, only Dakota could.

"Yeah, totally rad!"

We drove down to Laguna, taking a right at her command, and stopped at a scenic overlook nestled on a small piece of property between two magnificent cliff-front homes. We walked over to the rail and looked out from atop the mighty cliff. I was struck by the stunning view. "It's beautiful."

"I'm glad you like it. We call it 'Top of the World'."

She wrapped an arm around my waist and nuzzled her face into my chest. Her words triggered a twinge of pain as I was reminded of Pete's "Top of the World" declaration in the hotel, his being a loose reference to my situation looking like something out of the movie "Scarface," but nonetheless, a flashback to what already seemed like another lifetime.

"Thanks, Dakota. It's some view." I kissed the top of her head, pulled my cigarette pack and lighter from my shorts' pocket, and sparked a smoke, no small task with her unrelenting grasp; but the truth is I needed the human contact, and her embrace brought a level of peace and comfort that was more than I imagined possible, so I wasn't pushing her away either.

I exhaled while gazing at the horizon, speaking to no one and everyone. "We just couldn't have been what he had in mind."

"Who?"

"God." I replied solemnly as the flaming sunset touched the Pacific's abyss.

"How old are you, Reno?"

"Why?"

"I've never met anyone like you before. You look so young but act like you're much older."

I twisted free of her embrace and held her exquisite face in my hands. "Don't fall for me, Dakota. I've got nothin' to give back. I'm sorry, I really am." I kissed her on the forehead and headed toward the bike.

"Are you leaving me here?"

I laughed at the concept. "Of course not. Let's go."

She climbed on the bike behind me; I fired it up, looked over my shoulder, and told her I was twenty-one as we pulled away.

She held me snugly in her arms, massaging me with a thumb. I drove between the cars as the traffic grew denser approaching Newport. She squeezed her thighs tightly into mine for fear of hitting a car's side mirror as we passed. I reached back with my left hand, patting her taut little ass, and said, "Don't worry."

She grabbed my hand in return, pushing it between us and into her groin. I lost balance, almost sideswiping a car, but then I relaxed and regained control, slipping my fingers inside her suit. She wiggled and adjusted until my finger slipped inside. "Wow, I guess you do like the bike."

"It makes me horny."

She pulled my arm free from between us and ran one of her fingers along my lips; it was warm and slick with her desire. The fragrance and taste were spectacular, and my shaft strained to break free of the surfer shorts' Velcro fly. I guess it's just genetic. When men touch, smell, taste a lady, everything else goes out the window. I couldn't imagine having a connection with someone, but the caveman urge to fuck remained.

We rode home and went straight to the back room.

There were two dressers with clothes folded on top of each and several sleeping bags spread out on the floor of the room Stihl referred to as Tammi's. A radio sat on the floor by the wall next to a pile of dirty laundry and shoes.

"Let's do it now." Her shirt was over her head before she finished speaking.

"Are you sure?"

"Yes, hurry, she'll be home soon." She released her bikini top to the floor and sat as she removed her thong in a single fluid motion that I couldn't accomplish on my most limber day. I looked at her leaning back on her elbows, legs idly drifting apart and together with an impatient look on her face yearning for the inevitable. I removed my clothes while admiring her perfect tan lines; it looked like she still had a swimsuit on. The tiny patch of her chestnut hair extended from soaking wet curls to the gentle rise of her pubic bone. Her hip bones rising from the depressions between her pelvis and hips created a perfectly crafted, rolling hill of flesh that only God could've imagined. The abdominal muscles encircling her deep and round belly button fell just short of the lower ribs defining yet another swooping curve of perfection. Shallow rib lines disappeared at the point where her breasts formed symmetrical perfection offering erect nipples begging for attention. Her slender neck rose to a sharp jawline with dimples and extraordinary cheekbones highlighting brilliant blue eyes framed by sandy blonde hair swept back over diamond-studded ears sparkling in the light. What could be more spectacular than a woman's body, and what better example than a California girl in July?

The sex was amazing but couldn't compare to the emotional high of being with Laurie; I was glad to feel that way. If someone this perfect doesn't stir me emotionally, no one will.

I kissed her softly on the lips, one of the very few we exchanged, and then got up to put my clothes on. She seemed content as she got dressed, so I went out to the kitchen, grabbed two beers, and pulled the paper bag out of the garbage before I sat down on the living room floor. She dropped to her knees as I handed her a beer and then she blew my mind. She bent over, kissed my relaxed organ through my shorts and said, "I really liked that," and then sat down next to me and took a drink of her beer. I was so excited by her candor that I pulled my shorts to below my knees and pushed her over, guiding her onto all fours while she was still holding her beer. This time, I admired her perfect little apple ass as I slipped inside her again while she held her suit to the side with her free hand. I was rough, driving myself deep inside her with all my might, hands gripping her razor hip bones, her moans and gasps encouraging me to pound her harder with each thrust. When I was through, she rolled to her back and ran her index finger along and within herself before licking it clean, saying, "Mmm, let's do this a lot, okay?" I was exhausted yet somehow exuberant at the concept of an open invitation to take out my aggressions within her silky walls of joy.

"You've gotta deal." I agreed in a pant as we toasted our beers.

After a while, sex becomes kind of like a beer or a cheeseburger: it's just another thing, emotionless, but a fantastic diversion and the ultimate release of life's stress. I had nothing left in my heart, at least as far as I could feel, but the physical contact reminded me that I was still alive.

She was looking me over with a bit of mischief in her eyes and asked, "Have you ever been to Vegas?"

"No."

"You should go. You'd love it. It's wild, like you."

"Maybe I will."

"Just make sure you come back. I'd miss you."

"Are all the girls here like you?"

"I don't know, but I saw you first, and that ragin' cock is mine!"

"Yes, you did." I chuckled as I slid my hand down her thigh and purposely grazed her saturated bikini with a forceful nudge.

"Are you ready, again?" She asked with insatiable teenage hunger in her eyes just as Tammi's voice could be heard saying, "Thanks, see ya soon," followed by a car door closing. Moments later, Tammi burst through the door. "Did you guys have sex?"

We both erupted, amused and bathed in the scent and memory of our evening tryst.

"We just went for a ride." I shook my head at her ridiculous entrance.

Dakota asked, "How was dinner?"

"I hate them."

Tammi sat down next to me and the three of us talked until the beer was gone.

"Well, it's time to clean up and hit The Pub." I glanced at my watch as if it mattered.

"You don't have to go." Tammi protested.

"Maybe not, but it's after ten and I'm outta here."

I headed for the bathroom to take a quick shower; when I returned to the living room, Dakota asked, "Are you coming back?"

"Unless I meet an untimely demise, but I'm just not that lucky."

Tammi said, "Be careful. Maybe you should walk."

I laughed so hard I almost fell down the stairs on the front porch as I headed for the bike.

"Make Stihl bring you home" was Tammi's last effort to ensure my return. I just shook my head as I started the bike.

"You kill me, Tammi."

I turned the bike around, now facing the street on the narrow walkway, and called for Dakota to come over; both girls came to my side as I straddled the bike. I pulled Dakota close by slipping a finger inside the side string of her bikini bottom and tugging. "Go get my bag."

She returned in a flash with the paper bag. "Here you go."

I took the bag of coke and two thousand dollars out of the paper bag and asked her, "Are you staying here tonight?"

"Probably."

"Well?"

"Definitely." She beamed with anticipation.

"Good. Guard this with your life. It's got over twenty grand in it. Do you understand?"

"Yeah. Yes."

"Why don't you let me watch it? I think you two fucked while I was gone."

"Because you'd probably invest it for me while I'm gone. Oh, and who I fuck is none of your business so cut that crap out." I shot her a grin and then yelled, "Later ladies," as I rode off.

———

I WEAVED IN AND OUT OF THE LANES WHILE TRAVELING DOWN THE boulevard, enjoying the handling of my new toy until I saw a cop. My heart skipped a beat as I slowed down to the posted "25 MPH Speed Limit," and to my relief, when I looked back, he was gone. I went straight to The Pub thinking how badly I needed a local license and feeling overwhelmed by the masses of beach people milling around. I parked next to the bicycle rack on the side of the building and walked up to the front door.

"I need to see your ID, dude." The doorman was around twenty-three, tall and cut, probably Italian.

"Stihl knows me." I tried to catch Stihl's eye behind the bar through the crowd of drunken beachgoers. I wasn't in a hurry to have too many people associate me with the name on the license.

"Yeah, well, I don't. So, let's see it."

Fortunately, I had been spotted before I had to pull out the ID.

"Tony." Stihl yelled from the bar. "He's cool."

"Okay?" I asked, not wanting an enemy at Stihl's bar.

"Go ahead." He frowned and stepped aside.

"Thanks, dude." I slipped by him and forged a path through the tanned mob and up to the bar.

"Reno! What'll you have, buddy?"

"Bud's cool, thanks." I slid sideways between two people's stools and put a twenty-dollar bill on the bar.

"One Bud for my bud." He got a bottle from the glass-faced cooler, placed it in front of me, shoving the twenty back in my direction.

"Reno, this is Joey. She's the best bartender from here to there." He had to yell to overcome the music and crowd noise, pointing to her and then the end of the bar behind her.

"Thanks, dick head. Nice to meet you, Reno."

She was a typical California girl with a "rockin'" hard body, nice tan, a carbon copy of the masses, but she was a brunette, making her unique. There are so many hot blonde babes, mostly bleached, with tanned, sculpted bodies, often surgically enhanced, that it takes a lot to stand out in any way, so any deviation is welcome. She had a gymnast body, compact and muscular, just like half of the population; the other half are over five-nine and weigh ninety-nine pounds from starving themselves, so take your pick.

"Nice to meet you too. Cool name." I shouted back over the head of a now annoyed patron seated at the bar between us.

"Wow. Manners. You're a friend of his?" She warmly shoved Stihl.

"Joey, take Reno up to the office."

"What?"

"Reno, should Joey show you the office?" He rubbed his nose.

"Sure."

"Joey, show him the office."

"Okay." She finally caught his drift.

The guy seated at the bar between us was now looking up at me with a crooked neck and a menacing face. He was about my size, probably in his late thirties, with deep lines on his face from too much time in the sun. I looked him right in the eye, leaned in close, and said, "Don't let the fruity outfit fool ya; I'll carve your fuckin' eyes out if you move on me," in my harshest Jersey tone. He was visibly stunned to hear those words coming from someone who looked as I did at the time. His look of shock was slowly replaced by a more formidable scowl as he turned back toward the bar; seconds later, he stole a glance in my direction that I met with an expressionless glare. Just then, Stihl slapped the bar in front of him, saying, "Barton, you don't even wanna try so settle down or hit the current." The guy was facing him when Joey reached us and nudged me in the direction of a ladder. I winked at Stihl, who was now consoling his friend with one hand on his forearm and another reloading his draft. Stihl didn't know much about me but seeing my potential for rage wasn't how he wanted to open the next chapter.

Directly above the bar was a loft and a door leading to the office over the bathrooms. The loft was a storage area for an old desk and some miscellaneous non-valuables; inside the office were two desks and a small couch surrounded by cardboard boxes filled with files and random papers. After we climbed the ladder that's built into the wall, she opened the door with a key and walked in.

"Can you sell any?"

"Not this stuff, but soon." I pulled the bag from my pocket.

"Wow, it's pink. You won't sell a halfer out of that giant bag?"

"A half gram?"

"Yeah."

"I'll give you that."

"What?"

"It's my way of sayin' nice to meet ya." I poured two piles on the first desk.

"No way! You're full of shit."

"Just take care of me at the bar, okay?" I asked without looking up.

"You won't be buyin' a beer on my watch."

Using my fake license, I chopped two huge lines from one pile and then tore a piece of paper from a legal pad sitting on the desk. I scooped the second pile onto the paper and folded it into a bindle. "This is for you."

She had a cut-off straw in her other hand that she offered to me.

"Ladies first. Take either one."

"Of those?"

"Yeah, but it's good, so go easy and split it up both sides, okay?"

She leaned over the desk and snorted the lines and then handed me the straw. I did mine and then asked, "Ready?" She looked a little unstable on her feet, so I stepped closer and put a hand out to catch her if she went down.

"Ready for what?"

"To go back downstairs. You look a little tipsy."

She snapped out of her daze. "This is amazing coke. Holy shit, thanks."

"You sure you're okay? Ya wanna sit down?"

"No, it's just really killer blow, maybe the best I've ever had. It's like my whole body is flushed."

Her blue eyes were almost completely black from the pupils, but she looked like she was settling into the buzz so I backed up a step and said, "I'm glad you like it, but I need ya to do me a favor."

"I knew it. Here it comes."

"What?" Just don't tell anyone where you got that, okay?"

"That's it?"

"Yeah. What's up with you?"

"Nothing. I'm sorry. Let's go."

I stopped and looked over the rail of the loft. There was a pool table by the massive front window, several small round tables filled the space in front of the bar on the side of the room, and furthest from the ladder was an open area for shooting darts. A jukebox was to the right of the dartboard on the rear wall between a side exit and the hall leading to the bathrooms.

"So, you're really not tryin' to fuck me?"

"What?" I turned to face her, not quite sure I heard her correctly.

"You don't expect anything from me, do ya? Where are you from anyway?"

"No, I'm not tryin' to fuck you, but I don't expect twenty questions either."

She hugged me. "I'm sorry. I'm not used to gentlemen."

"Look, I'd love to bed ya down, sweetie, but I don't need to use drugs to get laid."

"I like your style." She replied with a more confident grin and then patted my crotch like a football player might pat a teammate before heading down the ladder. I watched her descend and wondered if those below got a good view up her spandex skirt.

Stihl gave me a wink as I sat down on a stool that just opened about halfway down the bar.

"Ready for a beer?" Stihl noticed mine didn't make it back from the office trip.

"Load me up." I slid the baggie across the bar and onto the floor at his feet.

"Dude!"

"Go for it."

"You're a dangerous man, Reno." He picked up the bag and put it in his pocket as inconspicuously as possible.

Joey, Stihl and I took turns doing lines in the bathroom all night while I switched to Beck's Light from Bud and got blissfully drunk. At 1:30 AM, they yelled last call and by 2:30 it was just us. Even Tony, the doorman, was gone. He, apparently, didn't do coke.

I said, "We need a bottle," without looking up, my head resting on my forearm while choosing songs on the jukebox.

"You need a bed, cutie," Joey said, watching me from her barstool.

Stihl popped his head up from behind the bar. "Sounds like an offer to me."

Joey threw a handful of napkins from the bar into Stihl's face. "Okay, metal man, try to keep it in your pants."

"Metal man? He's 'The Man of Steel,' able to leap tall buildings and so on."

"In The City" by the Eagles played on the jukebox as I walked to the bar and took a seat next to Joey.

"I don't feel like Superman around this one, more like a Clark Kent."

"Poor Stihl. Is this young stud showin' you up?"

"I could still handle you, Joey." Stihl held his pecker through his shorts as he gyrated his hips.

"Should I leave you two alone?" I teased them while rising from my barstool, but Joey pulled me off balance by my shirt, caught me in her arms, and said, "You're corrupting this nice young man."

Stihl's laughter was borderline hysterical while I snuggled my cheek into Joey's ample breasts, faux begging, "Save me from the bad man."

While running her fingers through my hair, she said, "Maybe you're more dangerous than I thought."

Stihl pointed at his nose and then at her, choking on his laughter and violently nodding his head yes.

She was looking down at me still nestled against her. "He's too cute to be that bad."

That was it for Stihl; he went down on one knee gasping for air. "Stop. Stop. I can't take it!"

She pulled the bindle I gave her from her purse on the bar. "Whatever, let's just do a line."

I rose from her lap and returned to the stool beside hers, eyeing her skirt; it was pushed up during my fall and snuggling. Her black lace panties were now visible to me. She adjusted it and asked, "How's the view?" with a little edge.

"Looks good from here."

"I'll bet," Stihl added as he came around the bar with the cash register's drawer.

He passed us and headed up to the office. "Can I trust you two while I stash the cash?"

Joey looked up from the lines on the bar and said, "Just do it wise-ass."

As soon as the office door banged closed, I leaned over, slid my hand up Joey's skirt, stopping at her panty line to run my finger along the seam at her thigh.

"Well? What now?" she asked, looking directly into my eyes. "Are you gonna take me right here?"

I stood up facing her, standing between her knees. "If you let me."

"Well?"

I pulled down my shorts and with both hands slid her butt to the edge of the stool. She wiggled her skirt up as she moved and I started to remove her panties.

"We don't have time." She swiftly pulled them to the side. As I entered her, enjoying the all-too-familiar steamy temperatures that the Peruvian marching powder seemed to generate in women, I looked out the big front window; a few skater kids were passing by and pointed at us from the sidewalk. I stroked her as hard and fast as I could, rocking the stool so violently that she had to grab the bar with one hand and my shoulder with another to keep from falling. As her orgasm forced mine with muscle contractions deep inside, I realized she was looking out the window too, through the reflection on the mirror behind me. I reveled in the realization, enjoying the spasms within her until Stihl's clapping startled me. We both jumped causing her to release me from within.

"You asshole!" She quickly adjusted her panties and skirt.

I was casually pulling up my shorts, stowing my three-quarter full erection in the process and wiping the juices from my hand on my shorts.

"Relax. I couldn't see you. His ass was in my way."

"Why were you watching?" She sat back down, now facing the bar in disgust.

"I'm sorry, Joey. Can I be next?"

"Good luck."

Stepping from the ladder to the floor, he added, "Can't blame a guy for trying."

"And you! I hope you liked it; it was your last."

"What'd I do?" I was unable to wipe the amused expression from my face.

"Like you didn't know he was there."

"He was behind me."

"I thought you were different."

"I am."

"Yeah. You're worse."

Stihl made an undecipherable comment while passing behind us.

"Joey, I really didn't know." This was the truth.

"Just forget it."

Stihl, now behind the bar, broke the tension. "Who needs a beer?"

She snorted a line, got up, and said, "I'm outta here. There's a line for each of you."

Stihl and I looked at each other and in stereo replied, "Bye, Joey."

"Fuck you both." She stormed out the front door with a slam, we both erupted, and he slid a bottle of Beck's my way.

"For two years I've been trying to get with her; you show up and fuck her on a goddamn barstool the first night."

"New guy syndrome." I raised my beer in a toast. In my life of various schools and places being called home, I've always had one thing that interested women: the allure of the new guy. Oh, and the bad boy thing goes a long way too.

"Yeah, but the first night?"

"By the way, I had Dakota earlier today too," I added, rubbing salt in his wound.

He threw a bar rag in my face. "Fuck you. Get out!"

"Think I can catch up to Joey?" We both erupted again. "I'll bet you get tons of chicks in this place; missing one won't kill you."

"Yeah, but I have to put up with her shit; the least she could do is gimme' some."

"Well, I'll put in a good word for you."

"Oh great, that'll do it for sure. All I need to know is was it good?"

I looked at him squarely with a dead straight face. "The best I've ever had."

He was still for a beat and then said, "You prick," as he noticed the grin appearing on my face.

We sat drinking, talking, and joking until after 4:00 AM; finally, he said, "Let's go," staggering from his stool.

"What's open?"

"My house. I'll get some beer."

He loaded fourteen beers into a plastic garbage bag, tossed a fifty-dollar bill on the shelf beneath the bar so the daytime bartenders wouldn't have a short drawer at the end of their shift, checked the lock on the front door, and turned off the remaining lights.

"We'll go out the back," he said, navigating through the dark room, only the streetlight and a few neon signs lighting his way.

We stepped out the door and I immediately fell onto the bike rack. "Good thing we're close," I conceded while pulling the motorcycle key out of my pocket.

He looked at me leaning on the rack. "You'll kill us both on that thing."

"I can always drive, you pussy."

"Yeah, maybe a boat."

"You gotta boat?"

"Sure. Which one you want?" He swung his arm widely toward the many boats in the bay's marinas just behind him.

"How about a Scarab?"

"Hmm, let's see." He walked toward the inner harbor's edge and pointed to a boat about ten slips down. "How about that Whaler?"

"Too slow."

"Fuck you, speed racer. It's got a 115 Mercury on it. She'll fly."

"Okay. I'm drivin'."

We walked onto the gangplank and with every step, he's telling me to be careful as he's stumbling worse than me. We climbed aboard the boat; it was a seventeen-foot Boston Whaler with a center console and a bench that formed two seats.

I hopped in the captain's spot, ignoring his search for the hidden key. "Let's go skiing."

"Here. Don't start it yet." He handed me a red and white floating key chain.

"Cool! Let's go."

"Just wait." He untied the ropes and pushed us off from the dock. "Okay but go slow. It's five miles per hour here." He sat down next to me and put the garbage bag of beers between us at our feet.

I turned the key and it started immediately, startling me. "Wow! It works."

"No shit. Let's go. Remember, easy."

I pushed it into forward gear and cruised through the waterway southward. "Can I go fast now?"

"Not 'til we're out. Have a beer and relax."

The water was like glass as we idled past the many yachts and multi-million-dollar homes of Newport, Balboa, and Corona Del Mar. "Where are we goin'?"

"Let's go to Avalon for breakfast cocktails."

"Is this your boat?"

"No."

"Where'd you get the key?"

"People usually stash one on their tender."

"Tender?"

"Yeah, the little boat they use to ferry to their yachts."

He pointed to a few huge yachts moored in the harbor.

"Won't we get caught?"

"We'll dock the boat in a transient slip and take the ferry back."

"Ferry?"

"Yeah, from Catalina."

"Oh. How far is it?"

"Twenty-six miles across the sea." He sang like The Four Preps. "It's actually about thirty-two from here."

"Really?"

"Yeah. Go straight off that jetty and you'll see it."

"Can I go fast now?"

Stihl surveyed the inlet. "Just be careful."

I pushed the throttle wide open, sending the bow high up in the air.

"Watch what you're doing!"

"Fuck you, I'm driving." The bow settled and we charged out of the inlet.

"Go right of the bell buoy!"

"What?"

"That thing! Go right!"

"Sure." I yanked the wheel right; the boat flew off the tops of waves, crashing down hard in mighty splashes.

"There! Do you see it?" He pointed over the console windshield while holding on to the grab handle with the other hand. I could see the lights on the horizon as we rose on the waves.

"Is that Avalon?"

"Yeah. Head straight for it."

The motor screamed each time it came out of the water, and I cheered with each splash of the bow.

"Don't stuff it."

"What?" I couldn't hear him over the noise of the boat.

"Watch what you're doin'!"

We ran full throttle for a few minutes until the motor began to break up and stalled out.

"What happened? Did it blow?"

"Reno, we're outta fuckin' gas."

"So, now what?"

"Well, he doesn't have an electric trolling motor, so we float."

"Can't we row back?"

"Look." He pointed behind us at the beach; it was a few miles at least.

"Well, it's not like we can swim it."

"No doubt. You'd be lucky if the sharks let you live long enough to drown."

"Sharks?" Even I didn't want to be eaten by a shark.

"Yeah. This is the Pacific Ocean, remember?"

"Okay. Let's float."

"Have a beer while I think. I wish we had a flashlight." He grumbled while looking around the boat by the flame of his lighter that the wind repeatedly blew out.

I opened another beer and it spewed all over me until I got my mouth over the top. He rejoined me at the console, saying, "Gimme' one of those," and we polished off the beer and passed out soon after with a little help from the gentle swaying of the ocean. It was a couple of hours later when his "Get up, dude" woke me. I felt nauseous as I sat up and tried to orient myself.

"You gotta hold this gas can; it won't balance on top of the other one and I've gotta hook up the fuel line."

"What? Where are we?" I glanced at the Pacific's expanse before focusing on wedging the can into a spot where the fuel line could reach so it wouldn't fall over and break the connection. It all came back to me as the motor started and I climbed onto the seat as Stihl put the boat in gear.

"Where's land?"

"It's straight ahead."

I looked around, shivering from the dampness of the cool morning air. "All I see is fog."

"Exactly. That's the coastal marine layer."

"Are you sure Newport is that way?"

"No, but it's my best guess and the compass says east."

"Where'd you get the gas can?"

"There was a spare in a baitwell, usually is somewhere, I just didn't see it last night."

"Is there any beer left?"

"No, but I'm glad you're so relaxed. I've never seen anyone like you. You're like a thousand miles per hour even sittin' still."

"Fuck it. What're ya gonna do?"

A few minutes went by before Stihl spoke again. He was watching intently as we pushed through the foggy sea at a slow but steady pace.

"I don't believe it!" He snapped upright from his slouch, clearly pleased with his nautical prowess.

"What?"

"It's a bell buoy."

"What's that mean?"

"Land hazard."

"Oh. Good. Let's crash."

"Shut up. We're not gonna crash."

"Is that Newport?"

"I don't know but it's a jetty. We gotta lose this boat."

"Just pull up to it."

"Then we will crash. We've gotta swim for it."

"Look, seals!" I pointed to several seals sleeping on the buoy's edge.

"This is Newport, dude." He shut off the engine.

"What are you doin'? Let's go."

"The harbor patrol will see us if we go through the inlet, and I don't know whose boat this is. I really hate to do it to the boat, but we've gotta bail and swim to the jetty."

"That's kinda far, isn't it? And what about sharks?"

"It's only a hundred yards or so and no shark is gonna risk swimming near the jetty at the wedge."

"Are you nuts man? And what's the wedge? And what do you mean sharks are afraid of swimming by it?"

"I don't want to scare you but we've gotta do it, just stay with me."

"What? Wait." I pulled the Ziploc bag out of my pocket, checked the seal, tucked it in my shorts, and said, "Let's go before I change my mind."

We both jumped off the stern of the boat.

Stihl screamed, "Damn, it's fuckin' freezing," when he surfaced.

"No shit, metal man. Even I knew it'd be cold."

We settled in for a minute; Stihl was bobbing in the water just feet away from me. "Okay. We've gotta land on the right side of the jetty or we're fucked. Don't swim hard. The tide will bring us in from this distance as long as there's not a rip current."

I started to pass him as I hurried toward the warmth of dry land, but he cautioned, "Slow down. Save your strength for the jetty."

It felt like an hour, but four or five minutes later I asked if we could rest.

"Okay. We'll rest but float on your back. Don't tread water."

"Why?"

"Saves energy and you won't attract sharks."

"But you said..."

"I lied."

"Okay. I'm ready to go."

"I thought so."

After another break, about a hundred yards from the jetty, Stihl said, "Okay, this is the hard part. Are you ready?" in an exhausted tone.

"What now?"

"We've gotta swim hard to the right of the jetty, okay?"

"Why not just go to the beach?"

"It's too far and either the riptide would keep us out or the wedge would crush us."

A few minutes later, the water was pushing me quickly toward the huge boulders that made up the jetty. "Cool, a free ride." I floated along with an easy backstroke.

"No! You've gotta fight it! Swim away!"

"Are you nuts?" I was tired and wanted to let the ocean do the work.

"You'll get there! Just swim away!"

Stihl was right. The waves pushed me into the rocks while I swam against the current. We both got a little beat up trying to climb the slimy rocks, but once safely out of the water, we rested on a flat spot about halfway up the huge pile. We couldn't speak for a full minute, each trying to catch his breath.

"Where's the boat?" I scanned the horizon without sitting up.

"You did good, man. I thought you'd kill us both."

He ignored my question, so I just said, "Let's not do that again."

I pulled the Ziploc from my crotch and was pleased by the bag's uncompromised condition.

"Reno, you had your shoes on?"

"Yeah. You've got your sandals?"

"I used them for paddles on my hands."

"Yeah, well I like these shoes, and they kept my feet warm."

"You are crazy, aren't you?"

"Totally."

He shook his head in amazement, stood up, and said, "Let's go."

"No. Let's rest."

"I need a drink."

"Okay. Let's go."

We walked along the hard sand at the shoreline, joking about sharks not wanting to eat us and surviving the long swim when the boat became visible, bobbing in the distance. Stihl said something about calling the harbormaster to report the boat so it could be recovered, but I was reflecting on the journey.

"I can't believe how long that jetty is."

"Well, you don't have to do it again." He was probably still a little pissed that I slowed us down by wearing my shoes.

"You do need a drink."

"You don't?"

"Of course I do. Where are we going?"

"What time is it?"

I looked at my watch. "About 9:15."

"Sweet. The store is open."

"A bottle?"

"Yeah."

"Works for me."

We bought a bottle of Seagram's Seven and a twelve-pack of Bud, walked to The Pub, and drove the bike to his place.

<hr>

"Go slow. We're almost home," he said as we pulled out onto the boulevard.

"Nag, nag, nag." I taunted him, revving the engine.

"So, it's pretty fast?"

"Dakota and I pushed it to one-forty on PCH."

"I figured as much."

"I had to open her up to see what she had."

"Who? Dakota or the bike?"

"The bike. I knew Dakota came race-ready."

Tammi shouted, "Where have you been?" as she opened the front door.

I climbed off the bike and asked, "Does she ever lighten up?"

"Not ever, dude. Welcome home."

He pushed past her at the top of the stairs; I stopped. "Hi, Tammi. Where's Dakota?"

"Don't I get a hug?"

"What?"

"I watched your money after she left."

"When did she leave?"

"Do you love her?"

"Get real. When did she leave?"

"A while ago, maybe nine o'clock."

I walked in and slid down the wall to a sitting position next to Stihl. "I'll tell you a secret if you gimme' that bottle."

He handed me the bottle of Seagram's and pulled two beers from the bag.

"Tammi, put this in the fridge." He slid the bag to her feet where she stood over us, hands firmly on her hips like some displeased drill sergeant. "So, what's your secret?"

"Oh yeah. You're sittin' on the wet spot."

"What?" He rolled over me spilling beer on both of us as he went.

Tammi said, "You two need help," after observing the rolling maneuver.

"So, why don't you help us?" Stihl responded, holding his groin.

"Because he hasn't asked."

"Okay, Tammi, help him." I teased while we both laughed in exhaustion.

"Very funny boys. He's like my dad."

"I'm not your dad. Stop saying that!"

"I just mean, I think of you like a dad."

"I can't believe this is my life, surrounded by little babes who call me dad?"

"Must be, man. It sure ain't mine."

"Were you guys swimming or something?"

"Why?" Stihl's tone indicated he was losing patience with her interrogation.

"Well, you're wet, and you smell like fish, so there's that."

"It's bad pussy."

"You're gross!" She shot him a look and stormed out of the room.

"I'll have to remember that one, Stihl; it works pretty well."

PART X

Destiny's Soldiers

Destiny's Soldiers

Stihl and I squinted against the California sunshine that flowed unobstructed through the windows of the rickety shack on a million-dollar postage stamp of land. Someday the owner would get smart and demolish this place in favor of a viable beachfront, but until then it was an overpriced but affordable spot within walking distance of all that Stihl needed.

"I hate daytime." Stihl was looking out the window at the day dweller's world.

"Yeah, we should go to Vegas; I hear it's always night there."

"When?"

"Whenever."

"I'm off 'til Tuesday."

"Really?"

"Yeah!"

"How far is it, if you drive, I mean?"

"About six hours in the Cougar."

"Hmm, that's three on the bike." I calculated out loud, taking into consideration his driving style.

"No way am I goin' that far that fast."

"Well, at least we wouldn't have to swim back."

"Good point. Have you ever been?"

"Nope."

"Oh, man. You were born for Vegas. It's anything you want, twenty-four hours a day."

"Sounds good to me."

"How much can you afford to lose?"

"Why would I lose?" I asked sincerely.

"I'd say you're ready." He responded with a tired smirk.

"Is ten grand enough?"

"You'd be king for a day with that kinda cash."

I tossed the coke on his lap. "Cut up some energy, I'm taking a shower."

"You got it!"

I looked over my sea-ravaged clothes. "Shit man, I need the girls to do another beachwear run."

"No worries. There's plenty of clothes in my room; help yourself," he offered without looking up from the baggie, adding, "We should get some breakfast; Huevos Rancheros would really hit the spot."

"All my nutrients come in the bottle."

"Ya gotta eat, brah, or you'll rot from the inside out."

"One could only hope."

After a shower, I was still singing a weak rendition of "Viva Las Vegas" when I walked into the living room. "You're up, dude."

He struggled to his feet like a guy who just swam a quarter-mile in the Pacific. "Coke's on the picture and Tammi's getting clothes for you. I'll be right out."

"Cool." I snorted the lines he left, grabbed the baggie, and headed down the hall. As I walked through the open door into her room, the door slammed behind me. "What the...?" I spun around just as Tammi yanked my towel off. She stood holding my towel without a shred of clothing on. "What are you doing?"

"I know you fucked Dakota and I'm gonna steal you back."

"That's cute, Tammi, but I don't have time for this."

"Don't you think I'm pretty?" She sounded crushed.

"You're very attractive, Tammi, but I've got to get ready."

"You'd be with Dakota."

"Not right now I wouldn't."

"Really?" My words seemed to uplift her.

"You two are a real mess, you know that?" She dropped to her knees, taking me in her mouth before I could react. "Hey, hey, not with braces." Her body slouched, still holding my half erection in her hand. "Why do you want to have sex with me so badly? You know sex doesn't mean love, right?"

"You think I'm ugly, don't you?"

"Does it really mean that much to you?"

"Yes!" She bopped up and down on her knees like a puppy wanting a treat.

"Fine. Let's do it."

"Really?"

She rolled on her back, legs spread widely like some low-budget "porno flick" while I watched her in amazement. I settled on top of her, thinking, "I can't believe this shit." She was so tight I came almost immediately. I was surprised and started apologizing, "Sorry. It was good and I..."

"It was?"

"Yeah. You're tight and..."

She cut me off. "Let's do it again."

I grabbed the tropical print muscle pants and shirt she selected for me. "I'm outta here. This little game of yours is too much."

Stihl was headed down the hall carrying my shorts and shirt from the bathroom. "I rinsed the saltwater out of these so they're not ruined; you oughta hang them over the porch rail so they'll dry out." He handed them to me as we passed.

"Thanks, bro'."

I heard him laughing after he opened the bedroom door, followed by Tammi berating him for his response to her obvious activities and refusal to stop looking at her naked on the floor. I just shook my head, hopped back in the shower, and quickly rinsed off before dressing and heading outside.

I was putting money in the emptied tool bag compartment under the seat of the bike when Stihl came out the front door. "I don't even want to know," he said, coming down the stairs.

"Those two are certifiable, man."

"No doubt. What are you doing?"

"Stashing some money and coke under the seat."

"Good idea."

"If it'll fit, it is." I was having a problem fitting both bags in the small space even after removing the little tool pouch.

"You can leave somethin' in the Cougar. Nobody's ever touched it out here." It was parked at the end of the front walk.

"Put half of this in the car, okay?" I handed him the bag of coke with about eight grams still in it.

"Okay."

"Wait. Can you get the good stuff here?"

"I can set you up but not with that shit."

"I know, but you're sure we can get ounces of some good stuff I can sell?" I checked him for confirmation.

"Positive."

"Gimme' that and take this." I traded him ten grand for the bag of cocaine, stuffed five thousand and the bag in the little tool pouch compartment, and shoved it back under the seat. "You almost ready?"

He double-checked the door handle of the Cougar. "Ready."

"Well, I guess it's Viva Las Vegas." I slipped the key in the ignition.

"Oh yeah!"

"Be careful," Tammi yelled from the porch, waving.

I pulled a wheelie off the curb.

"Holy shit!" Stihl gasped, squeezing the wind from me while hanging on.

I turned around to head north on the boulevard, glancing over my shoulder at him as we settled in.

"How do I go?"

Stihl thought about it and decided he didn't want to be on "The 405" on the bike. "This will become the 55 North; follow it to the 91 East, then stop in Yorba Linda for gas so we don't end up stranded." Stihl didn't know how far the bike could go on a tank of gas, but he knew for sure that running out of gas in the desert could be even worse than in the Pacific.

"55, 91, Yorba Linda, got it." I rolled the throttle back, grabbed second gear, and took a deep breath as we accelerated away from the beach heading for the desert. After we passed through the stoplights of Newport and Costa Mesa, I saw the sign and yelled, "Freeway!"

Stihl screamed, "Ho-ly shit!" as we thundered down the on-ramp, hitting fourth gear crossing all six lanes in our merge.

"Hang on, dude." I snapped it into fifth gear, blistering through traffic at over one hundred and forty miles per hour.

"Slow down you fuckin' maniac!" His fingers dug into my ribs with fear as Southern California's fast lane fell behind us in a blur.

We pulled off the 91 Freeway in Yorba Linda for gas and the cold one I knew he needed. "How 'bout a beer?"

"Fuck you!"

"Okay. We'll gas and go."

"Bull shit! I need a drink." He stepped off the bike, clearly weak-kneed.

"You okay?" He flipped me the finger over his shoulder as he walked toward the station store. "Get five bucks on number nine, okay?"

He came out a few moments later, saying, "You got five bucks worth. Pick me up over there." He walked past me and crossed the lot towards a strip mall. I filled the tank with super no-lead, put back the fuel nozzle and gas cap, releasing the ignition key, and then went inside and bought a pack of smokes.

I was sitting on the bike smoking a cigarette, enjoying the sunshine until I saw Stihl coming. I drove over to him and asked, "You okay now?"

"Yep." He was holding a pint of Jack Daniel's high for me to see.

"You'll never be able to drink that on the bike."

He took a drink and then handed it to me. "You just watch me, speed racer."

I took a big swallow before spinning the cap back on it. I would have preferred to chug the whole bottle, being fine with pulling a James Dean on the desert highway, but I needed to keep my head clear so I didn't take an innocent soul with me. I pulled out onto the road saying, "Next stop Vegas!"

Stihl drank nearly half the bottle in one swig and let out an "Oh yeah" as it washed over him, a numbing protection for the ride. "Okay Knievel, get back on 91 and I'll show ya from here."

"Got it. Just hold on; we've got to make up for lost time."

As I shifted into fifth gear on the Freeway, I heard him yell, "I'd rather swim!"

The desert is so beautiful, with its mountain ranges rising from nowhere, defying the flat landscape, its passage to the unseen land beyond them. I wondered if Laurie looked down from above as I raced through the great Mojave, alone in my quest for self-destruction.

"How fast are we going?"

I looked down and saw she was just below the red line. "One thirty-seven."

"No shit?"

"No shit."

"I feel numb."

You oughta try it in my seat, I thought, as we blew past Whiskey Pete's like a shot on the final stretch into Vegas.

I shut off the bike under the huge overhang at the Stardust Hotel and Casino. "Dude, that's gotta be some kind of record."

"Yeah, great. Who do I see about frequent flyer miles?"

It was good to see he still had a sense of humor somewhere in that cramped body he was stretching.

I was taking the stash out from under the seat when I got another one of those cold feelings in my core. "Hey bud, come over here." I called out to the valet. "Here's a hundred bucks for letting me park here, and this hundred's for keeping a very close eye on it." I needed to know it was safe and handy for a quick exit if necessary.

"Yes, sir!" He grinned and took the money as if I'd made his night complete.

"I'll keep the key."

"No problem, sir, it's not in the way over here." He hurried away towards a Ferrari that pulled up with an old guy and a spectacular twenty-something blonde.

I was blown away by the sea of neon and glittering buildings. Las Vegas makes Atlantic City look like a Parsippany strip mall.

Stihl put his arm around my shoulder after we entered through the revolving doors where you're immediately confronted by the overwhelming sight and sounds of bells and lights that fill the massive spaces for as far as the senses can observe. "What do you think, brah?"

"It's more than I imagined."

"Welcome to Sin City." His arms stretched as wide as his smile.

Staring out at the endless rows of slot machines, I just couldn't shake the uneasy feeling in my bones.

"Stihl, you check us in, okay?" I didn't want to use my ID, so I handed him three hundred dollars and turned to look around at the incredible diversity of the crowd. Every walk of life was represented, from bikers and street hustlers to yuppies and blue-haired old ladies, all sharing the same dream: Beat the house at its own game. I had to laugh at myself for being so spooked. What could I possibly have to fear in Las Vegas?

Stihl came over just as I was lighting my second smoke. "Let's go check out our room. I wanna show you something." He was like a kid on Christmas morning as I followed him through several expansive rooms, up and down stairs, escalators, and past countless gaming tables on our quick tour. Finally, we got to the elevators; he looked at our key card envelope as the doors opened. "We're on the eighth floor."

We got off the elevator at eight and walked for what seemed like forever again until we reached our room: Eight-Forty-Four. He swung the door open wide revealing a room with two queen beds, a large dresser with a mirror, bedside nightstands, and a small round table with two chairs near the window. The whole room was done in burgundy and black. Stihl opened the drapes, providing a great view of several other casinos and the mountains in the distance. I stepped to the window for a better look when a knock at the door stopped my heart. "What the fuck?"

"Chill out, brah. It's room service." He opened the door for a guy in a Stardust uniform carrying a tray of cocktails. He paid the guy and then directed him to bring four more right away. "I got us Jack and Coke; maybe I should have left out the Coke?"

"Sorry, man, I must be tweaked from the ride over or somethin'. It's all good."

I felt an eerie presence surrounding me as we were speeding

through the barren land, like a weight, or maybe a chill you just can't shake. I pushed it aside as the result of sleep deprivation mixed with drugs and booze, but it had been palpable from the moment we exited civilization on our journey.

"No problem. That ride almost did me in too."

I downed the first drink without stopping. "I feel better already."

"Good. Let's split the room, okay?" He handed me one hundred dollars.

"Stihl, how much money do you plan to blow tonight?"

"I brought a grand to roll, but I could go either way. I've left a few grand down many times, but over ten grand up once. Ya just never know how the cards will fall."

"I brought five G's to blow tonight; it's on me." I handed him back the money.

"Okay, bud, thanks, but I've got the drinks."

"Please, you're the most hospitable guy I've ever known." He'd been so good to me since the moment we met, I wanted to at least try to show my appreciation, but he'd already succumbed to the gambling bug and turned on the TV to watch Keno numbers being called, which is like watching bingo at an old folk's home, but he'd bet on the number of ice cubes in a cocktail if there was a line.

"Hey, Stihl, can you call down and tell him we want the bottle and forget the soda, okay?"

"Sounds like a plan. It's too early for real gambling anyway." He scoffed at the numbers not aligning with the set he played in his mind.

After he hung up the phone, he pulled out the phone book from the nightstand between the beds. "Dude, you've gotta see this." He motioned me over and then changed his mind. "No, wait, stay there. You should be sitting down for this." He brought it over and sat it on the table in front of me.

"What's this?" It was pages of full-color photos of beautiful women in various percentages of attire, ranging from evening gowns to bikinis and lingerie; below each one was a phone number. "Are these hookers?"

"Yeah, and that's really them."

"No way. They're models."

"No, that's them! A buddy of mine comes here every weekend; I swear he's working his way through the book. I thought you could appreciate that."

I thumbed through the pages and saw there was every kind of girl from all over the world; there were even guys. Hell, there were even guys dressed as girls. "It's some kinda crazy fuckin' menu!"

"Exactly."

"Yeah, but where's the prices?"

"I don't know. Maybe it's a la carte."

"Damn, they're really hot. How could ya choose one?"

"I guess ya pick a fantasy and go with it."

"What's your fantasy, Stihl?"

"I'm a gamblin' man. My fantasies are in the chips, and 'Lost Wages' is my home away from home."

"Lost Wages?"

"Yeah. The newbies may call her Las Vegas but us regulars know the real deal."

"Copy that, metal man." I threw the phone book onto the bed next to him as he lay watching Keno numbers on the TV. "Show me the hottest one in the book."

"Why?"

"Well Superman, I wanna check out your Lois Lane." He was still looking when room service showed up again. "I'll get it. You keep looking."

I paid the guy with Stihl's one-hundred-dollar bill: fifty for the bottle, forty for the drinks and I sent him on his way with a twenty-dollar tip, including a ten from my pocket. I chugged two drinks back-to-back, put the other two next to Stihl on the nightstand, grabbed the bottle and sat back down at the table. "So, who is she?"

"I've got it narrowed down to two."

"Take your time." I dumped half the bag of coke onto the table, chopped about twenty lines out of the pile and spun a one-hundred-dollar bill into a straw. I snorted a line up each nostril and sucked a third line into my mouth; the body rush immediately swept through me, and I thought, "Mmm, that's some damn fine powdered death; I'm gonna miss it."

"Okay, I've got her." He got up with the book flopping in his hand.

"Let's see our winner." He handed me the book and bent over to do a line. "Take two. They're small."

"Your idea of small could kill a horse."

"God, I hope so."

He did another line, dropped the bill on the table, and pointed to an exquisite strawberry blonde on the right side of the page, saying, "That's her," while pinching his nostrils, and then snorted some whiskey off his fingers after dipping them into his drink.

"That's quite a woman, Mr. Metal."

"I'll say."

"Says here her name is Whitney."

"Works for me."

"Good. Get me the phone."

"Why?"

"Christmas is coming early this year."

"No way, man. I don't want to..."

"You don't want her hanging out just to please you?"

"What?"

"Yeah. One night, this girl, all to yourself, and she lives just to please you."

"That's quite a concept, I must admit, but I hear the tables calling."

"Get me the phone."

"It's too early."

"Oh, did you want her after some other guy?"

"No!" He looked at me like I just farted.

"Then get me the damn phone."

The phone cord was too short, even the handset only reached to the edge of the bed, so I turned my chair around to grab it and propped my feet up on the bed. I asked Stihl to dial the number since he was standing next to the base of the phone.

"What about you?"

"Just dial, I'll worry about me."

"Okay, what's the number?"

"555-5477." I read from the caption below her name.

"Hello." A soft voice answered after several rings.

"Hi, Whitney?"

"Yes."

"This is Reno over at the Stardust."

"Hi, Reno. Kind of a funny name for this part of the world." Her voice was now clear and sensual.

"Yeah, I get that a lot. Anyway, I asked my friend to find the most beautiful woman on those special pages in the phone book and he chose you."

"Well, thank him for me, won't you?"

"Well, I thought you could do that yourself if you were so inclined."

"Hmm, and at what time would this be?"

"It's seven now; how's eight-thirty sound?"

"Nine's better."

"He's your first stop, right?"

"Yes, my only. I'm just getting up now."

"Good. We're at the Stardust, room eight-forty-four."

"Now, it's just him, right?"

"Well, I thought you could do me a favor?"

"What would that be?" She asked with a suspicious tone.

"I want you to choose the most beautiful woman you know and have her accompany you as my guest."

"Well, I can do that, but you do understand there is a fee for our company?"

"Yes, of course. What is it?"

"Well, it's two hundred dollars an hour just for our company, plus tips for any special attention you might desire."

"Will this friend be as extraordinary as you are?"

"Oh, she's much prettier than I am."

"That being the case, I'd like to make you an offer."

"All right, I'm listening."

"I can offer you each two thousand dollars, in cash, for the entire evening."

"Hmm. At what time would the evening end?"

"I'd think by one, but it's at your discretion after two."

"May I call you back? I have to check with my girlfriend."

"Fine. We'll be here for an hour or so, okay?"

"One hour, I've got it. Good-bye, Reno."

I hung up the phone and told Stihl they'd be calling back within the hour. We sat in relative silence, him watching Keno and me staring out the window as the daylight began fading, the lights growing more brilliant with each degree of light lost.

It was nearing 8:00 PM when I took a long drink from the bottle of Jack. "Man, that's good." The burn of the whisky felt like poison as it ran down my throat into my gut, and the thought of a poison bringing me another moment closer to an end brought me peace.

Stihl watched my facial expression after the drink and asked, "You're really on a mission, aren't you?"

"Ya gotta devour every moment you can steal in this fuckin' world."

"You act like you're dying of some incurable disease."

"Stihl, my choices have ended quite a few lives, a beautiful girl among them. I've gotta believe justice will be severe when it comes."

"You think they'll come after you?"

"Who, the cops?"

"Whoever. It's quite a mess."

Ignoring his comments, I memorialized Laurie. "You should've seen her, Stihl. She was more radiant than a sunset over a ball of fire." He was silent as I spoke, looking out the window, like me, at the ghosts of yesterdays gone forever. "All she asked of me was not to leave her."

The phone rang, and then rang a second time.

"Get that would ya." I was still looking out the window, and then spoke softly to the sky as it turned many shades of pastel colors. "I saw you in the desert, Laurie. I saw you in the sunset that first night too. I'm comin' home soon; too bad you'll be somewhere else."

Stihl hung up the phone. "They'll be here at nine. Man, does she sound bodacious!"

"Nice. Let's get a couple bottles of champagne, two perfect roses, and another bottle of Jack," I said, without looking away from the window.

"Hey brah, are you all right?"

"Stihl, tonight will be among your top ten best nights when you look back; that's a big deal."

"Yeah, but..."

"I'm right here, dude, and I'm very excited." I turned to face him as I finished.

"Well, all righty then." He picked up the phone and dialed room service.

I turned away, looking out over the city once again. Why was I still here, still living the insane existence I reveled in without any retribution being levied against me? I believed I owed a huge debt for my actions and couldn't understand why it hadn't been collected. I was intentionally dancing on the razor's edge along a cliff and just wanted to fall and burn up in a blaze of glory, but the winds of change always held me up from a fatal step at each turn, and I just don't know why I was being spared from my suicide-by-recklessness. It couldn't go on much longer; surely the end was near.

"It's all set." Stihl hung up the phone.

I came back to the room from my thoughts of eventuality while still looking out over The Strip. "How old do you think she is?"

"I don't know. Mid-twenties maybe?"

"That sounds about right."

"How old are you, dude?"

"You saw my ID."

"Yeah, well..."

"I'm eighteen, and MacNab's my name, not West." I turned from the view of sweeping, abstract waves of color that now crept in to paint the desert sky.

"I thought so. Nice to meet you, Reno MacNab."

"How'd you know?" I wondered how I tipped him off.

"Because after a certain age, love is diminished by history."

"That's very profound. Is it true?"

"Unfortunately, it is."

"That's too bad, my friend. I guess David Gilmour was right."

"Right about what?"

"He said, '*You don't really fall in love unless you're seventeen.*'"

"Hmm. What song is that?"

"*All Lovers Are Deranged.*"

"I'll have to check it out."

"Ya know Stihl, I'm much older than my years, too fuckin' old."

"That's why I served you, that and your high-quality, out-of-state ID. Plus, you looked pretty damn serious gettin' outta that cab; made ya wanna see what would happen next with a dude like that in the place. Considering what the tourists want out of their trip to "Zooport," we've got to try and oblige. At first, I thought you might be some young rock star that snuck outta the Four Seasons for a round before the show, which happens more often than you think in that town. The long hair, piercing eyes, totally inappropriate high-dollar yet disheveled outfit combined with the overconfident strut through the door screamed frontman, until you spoke; then I knew you were pure gangster, which is even more of a novelty."

"Oh yeah? Well, I'm no gangster, just fucked up."

"You're okay, Reno, just lost like the rest of us. I'm gonna take a shower and get the road off me." He patted me on the shoulder before turning toward the bathroom. "The stuff should be here soon."

"I'll handle it, and you do stink."

"Reno, you may not believe this, but you will get over her."

"Not if there's any justice in this world I won't, and besides, it's not getting over her in particular, she was only mine for a moment and the moment's gone. It's coming to terms with my role in so many things. I told you before, I'm just no fuckin' good, and the ones I love get the worst of it."

I didn't look back and heard the bathroom door gently close. I took a drink from the bottle and snorted two more lines. The sky was turning brilliant shades through the tinted glass as the night wore on. The ride gave me too much time to think, bringing up pain I suppressed for days. I reached for the stationery and pen on the dresser behind me for a little poetic release. Tommy was gone, Laurie was gone, Missy was crushed, my parents were disappointed, and they didn't even know of the latest disasters. It was all too much, and hope was inconceivable. I thought maybe a quick death is too good for me. Perhaps a long, slow decay in prison would be more suitable. I wondered which prison is worse, the one behind bars or the one I'd already been sentenced to within my mind? I was sketching a solid black, broken and bleeding heart tattoo concept with a poem started around it when the knock on the door startled me.

"Who is it?"

"Room service."

I slipped the pen and paper into a drawer and let the man in. He was pushing a stainless-steel cart with a white cloth draped over its surface; on it were two bottles of champagne wrapped with white cloth inside stainless-steel ice buckets. Two roses lay next to the bottle of Jack Daniel's; they were long-stemmed and had little water tubes on the base of their stems. He handed me a bill for three hundred and fifty dollars.

"It must be good champagne."

"It's Korbel, sir."

I handed him four hundred dollars.

"Thank you, sir."

"Have a good night."

Stihl called out from the bathroom. "Are they here?"

"Nah, it's only quarter of."

I pushed the cart over to the dresser by the table, put the bottle of Jack on top of the dresser, and placed one rose on a pillow of each bed. I looked out the window from between the beds, saying, "Glittered gates await arrival from your star, a moment's light seen from oh so far," as my eyes welled up. I'm no good at pauses; I need full speed ahead or it all catches up. Tommy and Laurie were gone and there wasn't a damn thing I could do about it. It felt like forever since I'd seen her face, and the devil's justice had already stolen the sweet memory of her touch. I know people make their own choices in life but it's hard to assign responsibility to those who've passed on, right, wrong or indifferent. I'm sure that in any case, her fate was most assuredly altered by crossing paths with my collision course of a life.

When Stihl came out of the bathroom, I was looking out the window at the Circus Circus Casino, thinking how appropriately named it was. The whole town was like a huge circus under the desert's starry big top.

"When are we going out tonight?"

"No need, Stihl, the city's coming to us."

"I guess you're right, but I am a gamblin' man and the tables are callin' me."

———

Lori Ann stood beside Whit at the door to room eight-forty-four, glancing back at the long hallway and the exit sign which led to the elevators. It was all she could do to not sprint away in retreat from this awful mistake. If she was wearing more comfortable shoes, she might've made a break for it.

Whit looked her over. "Just breathe. We're just hangin' out with a couple of guys in a casino; the only difference is they're giving us two grand each for the privilege of our company."

Lori Ann took a deep breath, exhaling slowly. "Okay. It's fine." She was lightheaded. Anything could be on the other side of that door, but no matter what it was, it was her destiny, so she reached down deep for all the courage she could muster and smiled as it opened.

———

We were sitting at the table, sharing the last of the first bottle of Jack and reminiscing about our swim when a soft knock came at the door.

"That's them. Remember, her name is Whitney."

"Brah, that's one name I won't soon forget." He opened the door with an unmasked Cheshire grin and a warm greeting. "Hi, come on in."

"Thank you," Whitney replied as they passed him entering the room.

I rose from my seat. "Hello, ladies. I'm Reno and that fine gentleman is Stihl, as in 'The Man of,' but he's also the best damn bartender in Southern California and is at your service."

Lori Ann felt all the apprehension wash away as she absorbed the vibe of the room. It was just as Whit said: a couple of guys that seemed to be normal enough; and maybe it was the cocaine but she thought one of them was cute.

The girls smiled warmly, followed by Whitney's friend asking, "Does everyone in California have a cool name?"

"Nope. Just us." I winked at her.

"Well, I'm Whitney and this is Desiree."

"Nice to meet you ladies. May I offer you a line?

"Sure." Desiree responded with a traffic-stopping smile directed towards me.

She was tall, probably five feet ten inches or better in her heels. Her gently-styled hair was sandy blonde and hung halfway down her open-backed evening gown. As she approached, I noted her eyes were as light and piercing blue as my own, and God must have worked overtime on her well-tanned physique.

Whitney sat down on the edge of the bed nearest me, her legs crossed stiffly as she got the lay of the land. "You sounded much older on the phone."

I disregarded her left-handed query. "And your taste in women only accentuates your own beauty."

"Thank you." They spoke in stereo as Desiree rose from the table, releasing her hair from a careful grasp so as not to disrupt the remaining lines. She started to say something about the color of the cocaine on the table but brushed it off thinking there must certainly be more than one source of the pink coke in the world, and the product Marty found was probably only a fraction of the stuff that came in on that day alone.

Whitney said, "It seems we have a poet in our midst," with a practiced charm.

"Well, he's mine." Desiree leaned down to softly kiss my cheek while the familiar Peruvian euphoria swept through her body and mind.

"And a willing captive at that," I added, pulling a wad of money out of my pocket.

"Well, we know of Stihl's skilled endeavors, but your occupation is?" Whitney inquired while looking hungrily at my fist-full of hundred-dollar bills.

"I'm gainfully unemployed." I locked eyes with her as I spoke in casual defiance.

Stihl sat down next to Whitney on the bed, handing her the rose from the pillow nearest him and said, "He's the original crazy diamond and absolutely destined to shine on," which brought a grin from me.

Stihl was pleased by me catching him referencing another of the great songs for which David Gilmour has a writer's credit. He'd been thinking of Pink Floyd while in the bathroom, following my David Gilmour quote, and settled on an image of me that included the bittersweet lyrics of "Shine on You Crazy Diamond." It was as if they'd written it for the lost soul that was his new friend.

"Thank you. That's very sweet." She accepted the rose with a demurely bowed head.

"So, should I assume the terms are as discussed?" I asked while holding four thousand dollars in one hand, putting the remaining cash into my pocket.

"Yes, but I anticipated two rooms."

I got up and pulled a bottle of champagne from the ice. "Well, to be honest, this gathering wasn't our intention when we planned the trip, so we can get a second room if need be."

Desiree said, "It's okay, Whit." She was now seated at the table, taken aback by how attracted she was to this guy. She'd been so hesitant to come but was settling in.

I punctuated her sentiment with, "Perfect," before popping and passing the champagne to Stihl and retrieving the other rose for Desiree. "This is for you." I handed it to her in cordial fashion.

"Thank you, Reno. He's got my eyes, Whit."

"I see that." Whitney stowed the money, post-counting, in the glittery bag that matched her gown.

"Who's wearing Lauren perfume?" I asked, enjoying the fragrance.

"I am. How old are you?" Whitney was direct in her tone, holding a glass as Stihl filled it.

"I'm twenty-one; Stihl is twenty-eight. And you are?"

"You know better than that." Desiree teased with a slight Southern accent.

"No, that's fair. I'm twenty-five."

"I'm twenty-three." Desiree jumped in on the moment.

"Thank you, Stihl. You are good," Whitney said after sipping from the flute of champagne.

"Thanks, hon," added Desiree as he filled her glass.

"So, what's on our agenda, Stihl?"

"Actually, Whitney, I'd like to do a little gambling." He answered while pouring some whiskey into a glass before handing that bottle back to me to put on the table.

"That could be fun. Would you two like to join us?" asked Whitney.

I looked at Desiree for feedback and she said, "I'm not much of a gambler, but if you like we can."

"No, thank you. I think I've already hit the jackpot."

Desiree blushed, covering her face with a slender hand accented by two gold rings. She was dazzling. I couldn't understand how such a girl ended up in this occupation.

"Well then, shall we go?" Whitney directed more than inquired while rising from the bed and carefully setting the glass on the dresser before her.

Stihl replied, "Sure, let's hit it," after downing the remaining half-filled glass of Jack he was holding.

"You take it easy on that stuff." Whitney warned Desiree as she leaned in to do another line.

"I'm okay, Whit."

I said, "Good luck," as they departed with one more over-the-shoulder glance from Whitney. I grabbed the remote from the bed and switched from Keno to MTV just in time to catch the tail end of "Rock You Like a Hurricane."

Desiree chimed in with, "Sweet jam," as the Scorpions sang, "Come on, come on, come on. Here I am. Rock you like a hurricane."

"Desiree, can I ask you something?" I spoke while pouring some champagne into her glass. "It's kinda personal."

"I guess so."

I put the bottle in the ice bucket and sat down at the table, looking at her affectionately. "I was wondering why someone of your incredible beauty and obvious intelligence would be in your line of work?"

"I'm not really an escort. I'm a dancer. Well, I've been dancing for a few weeks because I need the money. I'm actually a waitress, I guess. I owe Whitney a lot for helping me since I moved here, and she needed someone to come with her on short notice so I said I'd help her out one time, but she promised I could leave any time I wanted and I didn't have to touch the guy if I didn't want to. Plus, I guess I decided it was worth trying the escort thing once because I'm saving to buy a condo, but not the sex part; I never agreed to that."

"Well, I guess money talks louder than anything else, doesn't it?" I asked with a sense of further disappointment in humanity.

"I guess, but I'd go out with you anyway, Reno, so it works out pretty well."

"Hmm. Why would you go out with me?"

"Well, I mean, you're good-looking. I can't believe you're paying for a date."

"What if I was some weirdo?"

"Whit promised I could leave if you were creepy, so I figured I'd help her out if I could."

"Well, I'm glad you're here."

"Me too. Where are you from?"

"Huh?"

"I'm sorry, it's just that nobody's from here. I'm from Florida and Whit's from Illinois."

"What part of Florida?"

"West Palm Beach." She lied; it had become second nature since LA.

"So, why Vegas?"

"Do you mind if I take off my shoes? They really hurt."

"Of course not. Please make yourself comfortable."

She slipped off her shoes. "Oh, that's much better. I don't usually dress like this."

"Well, I'm pretty casual, as you can see." I was, of course, still wearing the borrowed tropical print muscle pants with a surfer T-shirt.

"You look great. I like your butt." She blushed, surprised by her forwardness. She hadn't met a guy who was nice enough for conversation since Florida, let alone sex, and the pink coke and alcohol were working overtime on her inhibitions.

"What size do you wear?"

"What?"

"Sorry, I meant like pants size?"

"I wear a three-four."

"Can ya convert that?"

She blushed again. "I usually wear a size small."

"How tall are you?"

"Five foot seven with bare feets."

"What size bare-feets?"

"Six." She giggled again at my repeating her "feets."

I walked over to the phone and pressed the guest services button. When the woman answered, I explained that I needed a comfortable, size small outfit for a young woman who is five feet seven inches tall with size six "feets," sparking another round of giggles, and I needed it all sent to my room as soon as possible.

"I can't believe they'll actually bring clothes to your room."

"I'll bet they'd bring a car to my room if I had the cash."

"Isn't this town crazy?"

"It's a crazy world, sweet Desiree."

"That it is."

"So, why did you come here?" I asked again as I returned to my seat.

"It's your turn. Where are you from?" She flipped the script, not wanting to continue telling me lies. It was too wonderful to be around someone nice and she didn't want to adopt her newly developed dancer persona.

"I'm not sure anymore." I answered sincerely while admiring her natural beauty.

"I feel like that all the time."

"I guess we've got some things in common." I was warming up to her and trying not to compare her to Laurie.

"We do." There was a glow in her smile as she rose to her feet and stepped toward the window. "Have you seen the sunset tonight?"

"Yeah, it's picturesque, to say the least."

"I love the sunsets here."

"Have you been to California?" I was now standing a couple of feet to her left looking out the window as well.

"Only to LA with my boyfriend."

"You have a boyfriend?"

"Not anymore. He left me in LA a while ago."

"Why would anyone leave you?" I choked on the words and tried to continue. "I'm sorry. I'll... Fuck!" I looked away, turning my back to her.

She wrapped her arms around my waist from behind. "Are you okay?"

"I promised I'd never leave her." Tears welled up without permission.

"I'm sure you couldn't help it. What happened?"

"I sent her out with my friend. They, they died in a crash. I couldn't go. I had to leave. It all happened so fast." It was like the dam had broken and my emotions just blew through and flooded out.

She spun me around, held my arms in her hands and looked into my eyes. "We can't change destiny; you have to believe that."

I threw my head back and spoke to the wind. "God, I'm so sorry Laurie."

"What?" She pushed me away, startled, looking at me as if she'd just seen a ghost. "How did you know my name?"

"I, I don't, I mean, it's Desiree, right?"

Her facial expression shocked the sadness from me.

"My real name is Lori Ann; you said Lori."

I sat on the edge of the bed. "Her name was Laurie."

"That's too weird. How did she spell it?"

"L-A-U-R-I-E."

"Mine's L-O-R-I. When did this happen?"

"Thursday."

"Thursday? No wonder you're a wreck."

"Thanks."

"No, I didn't mean it like that. Was this in California?"

"No."

"When was the funeral?" She appeared agitated.

"I don't know."

"But it just... Why didn't you...?"

"I had to leave."

"I don't understand." Lori Ann suddenly felt like it was a mistake to let her guard down as feelings about Stephen leaving her rushed into her chest. She struggled to organize her thoughts and control her emotions.

I spent at least fifteen minutes telling her the whole story, even going all the way back to New Jersey; when I finished, she looked at me like I was a mirage, as if she could blink and I'd be gone. She seemed to garner great meaning from my experiences, almost becoming part of the story, and then she told me of her trip to California with Stephen. Someone they knew in Miami found four kilos of cocaine and they were in LA to sell to men she didn't know. She described how she waited for hours in the hotel before running to Las Vegas in fear of the people Stephen met up with, but she had since come to consider that her boyfriend may have taken off with the money or drugs to pursue a life it could finance. She became a waitress and then ultimately a dancer for fast cash and met Whitney at the club where she danced. I sat quietly, captivated by the story but missing the connection she was trying to impress on me.

"Do you believe in destiny?" she asked.

"Yeah, of course I do."

"Don't you see, we're like destiny's soldiers. The plans have been made and we just stumble through life surprised by every turn, but it's been preordained for eternity."

It hit me like a freight train. Laurie sent me to Vegas; I followed the sunsets right into my destiny. The cold feelings and fears were her leading me right where I had to be.

"Laurie brought us together, right?"

"No. It's much more than that." She grew increasingly excited as she spoke. "It's not Laurie or Stephen or even us. It's pure destiny."

"You and me?" I struggled to see the big picture she was painting.

"All of it! You, me, Stihl, Whit, and a million other people. Don't you see how it all came together? How could we have ended up here tonight? Think of all the things that had to occur to put us in this room together. We're perfectly broken tiny pieces in an infinite puzzle that an unimaginable force moves to align per a master plan that we can't begin to conceive of. It's amazing. Yes, it's our destiny, but also so much more, and for everyone." She trailed off and a touch of melancholy came through in her tone. Looking at her angelic presence and hearing her words, I realized she was exactly where I was in life, trapped by our pasts and fearing our unknown futures.

"I don't mean physically, not even earthly, I mean, I'm talking about our souls." She got down on her knees, taking my hands in hers, gazing to the deepest depths of my soul within the window of my eyes. "You see it, don't you? How only an amazing force could've moved so many pieces to put us here in this room together, tonight, right now."

Someone knocked at the door. She squeezed my hands, hers trembling slightly. Her eyes were locked with mine while saying, "If it's them, let's leave so we can talk, okay?"

"Who is it?"

"Room service."

"Hold on. I'll be right there." I kissed her gently on the forehead, feeling connected to her in a way that seemed impossible. My blood pulsed warm again for the first time since our arrival in Vegas, maybe for the first time since the phone call from Missy. "I believe you, Lori Ann."

I let the man in long enough to exchange two hundred dollars for the clothes in a Stardust bag before returning to kneel by her side. "What's your last name, Lori Ann?"

"It's Morgan. Lori Ann Morgan. And yours?"

"MacNab, but my ID says Reno West, so that's what I've been going by."

"Reno MacNab. Hmm, I like that. You must have cool parents."

"Here. You can get out of that dress; it can't be comfortable." I handed her the bag and she rose without a word, dumped the bag on the bed, and I watched from my knees as she undressed, exposing her entire body to me without hesitation. She put on the silk jogging suit, covering one of the most flawless works of art ever to grace this world. She put her original clothes into the bag and emptied the small matching purse on the bed before tossing it in the bag as well. I looked at the contents from the purse: lipstick, the condom Whitney made her take, "just in case," a small wad of money, a bank card, and a little vial of coke with a spoon attached by a fine gold chain. "Where did you get this vial?"

"From my boyfriend."

"Do you know where he got it?"

"No. Wait. Yeah. He got it from the guy in Florida. I remember when he came home with it. I thought it was cute." A few seconds later she asked, "Why?"

"Never mind, it couldn't be. I'm just getting paranoid again." I'd only seen two people with the vials with gold chains: Laurie and Carlos. I placed the vial with her other things on the bed, and then I kissed her passionately as if we shared years as opposed to moments together. She held me close as we instinctively turned again to the window and looked at the city below, the neon lights splintering the darkness and merging with the remains of a painted desert sky.

"I don't want to be here. This place is changing me into someone I'm not."

"We'll go in the morning," I replied without hesitation.

"I'm afraid to go back to LA."

"Me too," I said, trying to lighten the moment.

"I mean it." There was a tremble in her voice.

"Don't worry, you'll never be out of my sight; and we're going to Mexico, a little town called San Felipe. How would you feel about a 'Blue Lagoon' lifestyle, just us in a straw hut on a little strip of beach?"

"That sounds amazing. Promise me."

"No more promises. You'll just have to know."

"I know I need a drink."

"You must be my destiny."

I softly kissed her cheek as we moved toward the table to sit down; she slid her chair over by mine and asked, "Do you mind if I share that instead of champagne?" She hated champagne and had to drink the stuff at work for money. The men would buy way overpriced bottles and the bar would split the money with the girls. I handed her the bottle of Jack Daniel's and watched in amusement at her expression as she drank straight from the bottle. "I'm used to soda in it." She confessed with an "I just bit a lemon" expression.

"Do you want some soda to cut it down a bit?"

"I don't want anything watered down, ever again."

I took the bottle from her, sat it on the table, and leaned over to kiss her. She pushed me away, stood up, and pulled down her pants seemingly all in one motion.

"Stay there," she ordered when I started to get up.

She took off the rest of her clothes and pulled down my pants with little assistance. I removed my shirt as she turned my chair away from the table.

"I told you not to move."

"Sorry."

Lori Ann had only been with one guy in her entire life, but recent experiences emboldened her; she felt so alive, so connected, that she pushed her fears and all that would inhibit her to the side as she moved. She leaned down and flicked at me with her tongue, instantly snapping me to full attention. She straddled me and lowered herself, absorbing me as she descended. The shock, emotion, and fiery temperature of her body sent waves of enchantment pulsing through my entire being until we climaxed as one, tears of joy filling our eyes as our bond fused like welded steel.

"Don't think I'm crazy, Reno, but I feel completely connected to you."

"I know what you mean. I feel it too."

I kissed every inch of her body within my reach. Maybe it was just two people needing someone so desperately, or maybe she was right about being destiny's soldiers. Either way, it felt so real, and I needed just one more chance to get it right. Maybe she was the last of my guardian angels on earth, or maybe you can only fall in love when your heart isn't looking or doesn't even know it's possible. Like a third-grade boy falls for the pig-tailed girl sitting beside him in class; or the seventeen-year-old boy falls for the angelic girl spied across a parking lot when his tangled life has been uprooted, again; or the young man caught off-guard by the welcoming gesture of kindness from a stunning beauty who appears from nowhere in a smoking lounge on the first day in a new world; or the lost soul, seemingly without hope, surrounded but alone, at the cliff's edge in a Las Vegas casino, who sees a beautiful light where there had only been darkness. She was still sitting on my lap in a shared embrace when the telephone rang.

"Should I get it?" She whispered the question while nibbling my ear.

"You'd better; I certainly can't."

"Hello? Yeah? Wow, really? Okay. Just drop mine off; I'm staying here. Yes, he is. Bye." She hung up the phone.

"Well, what's up?"

"Stihl won five thousand dollars on the slots so they're 'comping' him a room."

"No shit?"

"Yeah. I've never won anything." She said it sadly as if it was more than a monetary prize she was referring to.

"You won me."

"That was destiny and we both know it."

There was a knock at the door and my eyes widened.

"That's her; don't worry. She was calling from their room down the hall."

I told her I'd get it and pulled up my pants before walking toward the door. She quickly slipped into the bed nearest the window, covering herself from head to toe before peeking out to say, "Okay, ready."

I opened the door. "Hi, Whitney."

"Hi there, Mr. Wonderful. Still in bed, huh?" Whitney teased Lori Ann as she crossed the room.

"Yep."

"Here's yours." She offered Lori Ann two thousand dollars in an outstretched hand.

"Give it to him. I don't want it." She held her hand up in a stop motion.

"Are you sure?"

"Yes."

"Okay. Here's your dough, lover. That thing must be magic."

"Whitney?"

"Yeah, honey." She turned to face Lori Ann after handing me the cash.

"Thanks for everything."

"You bet. And you take care of her, Reno."

"I will." I thought of Debbie's words and got a chill.

"Okay, then. Bye." She headed for the door.

"Whitney, ask Stihl to call me, okay?"

"Sure, Reno. Later kids." She didn't look back and the door closed behind her.

"I'm not taking any chances. Let's go tonight."

"Why?" She sat up waiting for my response, her gorgeous breasts again exposed.

"Please. I just need to leave tonight."

"Sure, but don't let your ghosts get you down."

"The last time I waited I lost it all."

"Okay. I've got to get my stuff though."

"We're on a motorcycle, so it's cash only."

"I've got a car."

"Is it here?"

"No. I came with Whitney."

"Is there cash at your place?"

"No. I've got money in the bank, but not much."

"Is that a bank card or a credit card?"

"Bank card. I've never had a credit card."

"Good. We'll leave now. A brand-new start, just you and me."

"You're crazy."

"I know, but humor me, okay?" The dark feeling crept into my bones again as destiny's fingers pressed cold against my nerves, and then the telephone rang again. Lori Ann picked it up from the night-stand at her side.

"Hello. Okay, hold on. It's Stihl."

She handed me the telephone while getting out of bed. I told Stihl I was leaving with Lori Ann, trying to explain our feelings of destiny while she got dressed.

"Hold on, buddy. Hey, Lori Ann?"

"Yes?" She looked up from tying her new sneakers.

"I just wanted to tell you how amazing you look right now."

"Thank you; you're beautiful too." She refocused on her shoes with a wide, sweet smile.

"Okay, Stihl. I'm back."

"Well, I can catch a plane home if you're leaving tonight. Will you be there?"

"I don't think so, man. I'll get the money from the Cougar."

"I left a key with Tammi in case I lose mine; it's been known to happen."

"Thanks for everything, Stihl."

"Come by before you go. We're in room…"

"Bro', I've gotta go now while I still can."

"No worries, brah. Call The Pub sometime; I'll be there."

"It's a ten best, Stihl. Don't lose focus."

I could hear his voice getting weak as he said, "Love ya, man."

"Me too."

It's amazing how some people can impact your life so dramatically in just an instant while others you can know for a lifetime and never share the same kind of bond. Stihl was a man of character and spirit unmatched by most and was a true friend from the moment we met. Destiny can be cruel and yet so kind it would seem, or is that simply life, perhaps its very definition?

Seeing she was dressed, I said, "Let's go."

"What about all this stuff?" She pointed to the table.

I took the bag of coke out of my pocket and held it up to the light. "Let's thank it for the role it's played and leave it for some other lost souls."

I was going to add that Stihl would be coming to the room to get his stuff at some point, and he'd be thrilled to find it, but she jumped into my arms and said, "I knew you were my destiny! I knew you were out there and I'd have someone to love."

"It's amazing to think this could be real." I wanted to believe she knew something I couldn't wrap my head around yet. In life, at a young age, a summer can be an eternity and a moment can change your perspective on everything; but what's more, love can be born in an instant, and regardless of the past, it can last forever.

She broke our embrace but held my hands. "We're gonna make it, right? Aren't we?"

"I think so," I grabbed the bottle of Jack Daniel's. "But let's bring 'Uncle Jack' for moral support."

"Absolutely!" Lori Ann hid the bottle under her jogging suit top as we walked through the casino and out the doors to the main entrance.

"That's her." I pointed to my bike as we passed the valets under the massive overhang.

"She's perfect." Lori Ann ran over and climbed on the back of the seat with the excitement of a child finding her first bicycle under the Christmas tree.

As I started the bike, a super-stretch hotel limousine pulled up to the main doors.

"I love those crazy long limos, don't you?" She wrapped her arms around my waist.

"Yeah, I do like 'em." Before the words left my mouth, I felt the cold steel in my chest again. I dropped the bike into gear and pulled out from the hotel entrance.

"GOOD EVENING, MR. MONTELLO, MISS DEBORAH. IT'S A PLEASURE to have you with us again." The senior concierge held the door for the couple to exit the hotel's limousine.

"Thank you, Bruce." Carlos took Deborah's hand after handing him a fifty.

"I want him now, Carlos." She was squeezing his hand firmly, nails digging into his skin.

"I told you I'll find him, now try to relax; that's why we're here, Deborah. You must try and allow yourself some peace."

She ignored his plea. "Antonio won't kill him until I see him, right?"

"Of course, Deborah, now please relax. Laurie wouldn't have wanted you so upset."

"Laurie wouldn't have wanted to be dead either, but he fuckin' killed her, didn't he?"

"Deborah, please restrain yourself until we are in our suite. I'm sure you understand that this discussion would be best continued behind closed doors." Carlos returned her grip with an assertive grasp of his own as the sound of a racing bike pulling away echoed under the canopy.

"Look, Look," shouted Lori Ann until I finally pulled over.

"What's the matter?" I turned to look behind us where she pointed so franticly.

She hopped off the bike, saying, "It's an upside-down sunset!" The lights of Vegas glowed orange in the distance like the sun had landed in the middle of the desert and now resided there.

"It's beautiful." I got off the bike and joined her to enjoy the view from the side of the dark highway.

"Let's watch the sunset every night in Mexico."

"I'd like that." I pulled her into my arms but she pushed free of my hold.

"Reno?"

"Yes."

"I've got to tell you something."

"Fine, but then let's go, okay?" I climbed back on the bike.

She admitted, "I'm only nineteen," as she climbed on behind me. "Are you mad?"

I burst into laughter as I started the bike.

"Hey, you're not mad, right?"

I pulled onto the highway, shifted into second gear, and then yelled, "I'm only eighteen myself."

She smacked me playfully on the shoulder before resuming her tight grasp as we raced down the dark desert road, stirring destiny's winds as we traveled toward whatever it held in store.

PART XI

Memories' Garden

Memories' Garden

The pavement seemed to be washing away the sins of years gone by as it vanished beneath the tires of the speeding bike. The very same sights and sounds appeared different from just hours before. It was more than just the darkness; the air was lighter as we pushed through. Laurie would always be etched deep within me, but I felt the pain subsiding as a sense of hope transposed its gnawing hold on me. Once again, like an unseen bolt of lightning, an opportunity for the happiness pursued by all presented itself to a person who had become some shred of his original being, torturously lurking in the shadows of his own existence.

I could feel the warmth of Lori Ann's embrace through the chill of the desert night, and within it I found an offered peace that carried me as we slipped through LA unannounced, wrapped in the security of a shared vision between new lovers surfing upon destiny's wind. Newport was quietly sleeping when we idled up to Stihl's Cougar parked on the peninsula's main boulevard.

"Is this your place?" She asked as she massaged her thighs, easing the tension from hours on the bike. She looked so innocent and sweet hunched over near the curb in this twilight scene.

"No, it's Stihl's. My money's in the car. I'll go get the keys and be right back, okay?"

"Okay, my prince. I'll await your return."

I examined her playful expression, winked, and then placed my hand over my heart with a pat before turning to focus on quietly climbing the stairs and entering the unfurnished home. I didn't have time to endure the type of scene Tammi might create.

"Okay. Now, where would she put the keys?" I looked in the kitchen drawers, cabinets, and even in the refrigerator, hoping I wouldn't have to go into the bedrooms. As I closed the fridge door, I saw the paper bag in the garbage can. "See Stihl, they can be taught," I whispered fondly, finding the keys in the bag like I'd shown Dakota such a short time ago, a period that now seemed like a lifetime. With keys in hand, I just couldn't resist peeking into the room at the end of the hall for a last glance at yet another road not taken. It occurred to me as I watched them sleeping in a blanket of youth's innocence that inside of a week, mine would be just another memory or perhaps a notation in some diary to be cast aside like the forgotten adolescence of a million forlorn adults. Having stolen a moment's pause, I quietly retreated from the house.

Lori Ann had assumed the position of a provocative model in some racy motorcycle ad. She was seated backward with feet on the buddy pegs and head resting on the fuel tank, her back arched dramatically in what looked to be uncomfortable at best. "That can't be comfortable, but it sure does look good."

"Yeah, yeah. I'm trying to realign my back. Did you find the keys, Double-O Seven?"

I jiggled the keys for her view as I walked to the Cougar's passenger door; in no time, I was out of the car with cash in hand. "Okay. I've just gotta put the keys back and then we'll get out of here."

"How long before Mexico, sweet prince?"

"Stop calling me that." I warned with mock conviction. "We're just a couple hours from the border."

"Well let's get to it. I wanna be on the beach by noon."

She did a spin to face frontward on the bike and looked straight ahead as if she could see the border. I wondered if Mexico was a wise move considering its potential ties to Carlos' Cartel, plus I wasn't yet sure how we'd make money without selling coke.

"Lori Ann, maybe Mexico's not the answer."

She had a puzzled expression. "Where then? I'm afraid to stay in California."

"I have family in Maryland; nobody would look for us there. My cousin Artie is a cool guy; we practically grew up together, and his sister Bogie's a holy terror. They're both around our age, and the Eastern Shore of Maryland is about as far from anywhere as you can get while still being somewhat close to cities." A smile crossed my face at the thought of seeing some family. It had been quite a while, but the memories of my youth were as fresh as the morning's dew.

The sound of her voice saying, "What would we do there?" interrupted my reminiscence.

"Well, I've got over nineteen grand plus whatever you've got so we can go anywhere. I just thought Maryland might be a good place to lay low for a while."

"Okay. So how do we get there? I'll go anywhere with you, sweet prince."

"We'll fly like two birds from this gilded cage, my fair maiden."

"Okay, okay. No more 'sweet prince' if you drop the 'fair maiden' stuff."

"Agreed. I'll call my cousin and see if he can pick us up at the airport, okay?"

"What about the bike? And I'll have to deal with my car and apartment in Vegas at some point."

"Yeah. We'll figure it out. I'll just leave the bike with Stihl; he'll take good care of her 'til we get settled and then I'll have her shipped, maybe the car too."

"Works for me."

It's amazing how certain situations can bring people together, like Stihl and me, or more to the point, Lori Ann and me. I do believe that for whatever complex reasons, I was bonded with her from the instant of our meeting, much the way Laurie had been ever-present in my thoughts after our brief encounter on that first day of school, her warmth and kindness even more alluring than her outward beauty. In every case, connections grow exponentially deeper when sharing from soul's depth.

I put the keys to the bike in the Cougar's glove box and snuck back into the house to replace Stihl's keys in the bag from the garbage can. As I turned to leave the house, Dakota's voice startled me from the edge of the hall. She was half-asleep, wearing only panties and a T-shirt from an OP Classic Surfing event.

"Why are you guys back so soon?"

It took me a second to get over the shock and reply. "Go back to sleep. I'll see you soon."

"Who's she?" Dakota was looking out the window while rubbing the sleep from her eyes.

"A friend. I've gotta go, Dakota. We'll talk later, okay?" I tried to sound reassuring.

"No. I know we won't, but I'm glad I met you, Reno." She hugged me. "I knew you'd go, but not so soon." Her touch was warm and sincere. I started to respond but she rose to her toes and kissed me softly on the lips. She said, "Be careful," and then disappeared down the hall.

I stood in awe of yet another young woman who deserved much more credit than I had been willing to award.

As I came down the stairs towards Lori Ann, she asked, "Is everything all right?"

"Just fine." I knew Lori Ann saw Dakota through the window and assumed correctly that she would let it go. "There's a payphone a few blocks from here. We'll call a cab and be on our way."

She took my hand as we walked southward down the peninsula. The marine layer was so dense and the shore break so loud that we joked about anticipating an earthbound wall of water that never came to crush us.

We crossed the street heading toward the Last Class Lounge and past the ferry launch, each lost in our respective reflection until she saw the Ferris Wheel. "I wish we could ride it. I bet ya can see everything from the top."

I looked at her soft face moistened from the dewy air and kissed the perfect line of her cheekbone. "We could stay if you want to." I whispered into her ear as I pulled her into a quiet embrace.

"Thank you, Reno, but California just doesn't feel safe to me. I truly believe our destiny awaits far from here." Her voice was distant but not notably distressed.

We only knew each other for about nine hours, but in that period, we bared our souls and found an incredible connection that some may never experience during years together. I felt as though I knew her intimately and believed she heard the same whisper of destiny's double-edged sword; one side the unseen boulder careening toward us as individuals; the other a dream of a peaceful existence with a true partner in all things, surrounded by palm trees and blue waters bathed in pastel magnificence at each day's end. The problem with the latter image is it creates a glorious yet false sense of security leading one to believe that once perfection is attained it will last. Nothing lasts. This is all temporary and none of the images we behold and embrace offer insight into the eternity that is revealed in His time alone. However, destiny, or the predisposed master plan that began before time and extends beyond human existence, is perfect in every way with the possible exception that we are not privy to its big picture until our time here has passed. In our hearts, we found peace within the shelter of each other; within our souls, we trusted that destiny had perfection in store for us.

"It won't always be like this. We just need to buy some time and plan our direction. Maryland will do us good. We'll rest up so we can think clearly."

She looked into my eyes and I knew she believed in me. I just hoped I was worthy of her trust. After all, my plan was of the usual sort, every move driven by urgency rather than a thoughtful endeavor.

"I think we'll be happy anywhere, Reno, and I'm sure Maryland will be exciting with you at my side."

Her casual sincerity was incredible, a beauty born from something flowing deep within, masked only by perfect teeth and lips so pouty that they somehow distracted from the bluest eyes I've ever seen. She was captivating. Lori Ann was right about one thing: life was never boring around me, but I hoped this move would bring more peace than excitement.

We joked about being farmers, or worse yet, politicians in the nearby nation's capital as we walked through the Fun Zone and up to The Pub's outdoor payphone.

"Okay. If it's 5:00 AM here, that's 8:00 AM Eastern Time. Artie's gonna be pissed if they partied it up last night."

"Why don't you call him from the airport? That'll give him a little more sleep anyway."

"Wait a second. He's probably got a real job. We may have already missed him." I grabbed the phone and started dialing. First, I dialed four-one-one and got his number from directory assistance, and then I dialed zero to get an operator to place the call collect under my name since I didn't have enough change for the cross-country call.

"Reno?"

I could hear the surprise in Artie's voice.

"Hey dude, thanks for accepting the call. I'll buy ya a six-pack when I get there."

"When you get where? Where are you now?" Artie grumbled in a raspy voice.

"I'm in 'SoCal'. Do ya mind some company on the farm?"

"Fuck you. I've never lived on a goddamn farm, and you know it. Are you comin' my way?"

"If ya don't mind the company. By the way, I'm not alone."

Artie warned, "No lunatics. You're bad enough without your crazy-ass friends around."

"Chill out, dude, she's a girl." I quickly added, "And not a lunatic at all," before he could point out that the gender of my companions rarely indicated better behavior. I felt a little embarrassed that he was right about my usual compadres.

"A girl? Is she coming of her own free will?" Artie was amused with himself and laughed out loud.

"Very funny. So, will you pick us up or not?" I snapped, aggravated by Lori Ann being privy to this conversation.

"No problem. What airport are you comin' into?"

"I'll call ya in an hour with our flight info. Will you be home?"

"Holy shit! It's after eight. No, I won't be home 'til after five. I can get ya around six at BWI or seven at National. Don't go to Dulles; it's a pain."

I heard him fumbling with clothes, trying to get dressed and talk at the same time.

"Look bro', just tell me where you're living these days and I'll see ya there tonight. Okay?"

I whispered to Lori Ann. "We'll just get a cab."

She said, "Or a limo," with a child-like grin.

"I don't mind pickin' y'all up but if ya want I'll leave the key under the mat. It's the apartments behind the Acme; you'll see 'em from the 404 bypass. It's the first Denton exit. Okay?"

"What apartment number is it?"

"Huh? Oh yeah. One-thirteen. I gotta go. Call if y'all need a ride."

"Thanks, bro'. I'll see ya tonight."

"Cool. Bye."

I hung up the phone with warm thoughts about seeing family, and amusement at his oversleeping.

"It's a good thing I called, or he'd probably be lookin' for a job. He's never been much of a mornin' person."

I patted the bottle of Jack Daniel's she held under her zipper top. "You'll like Artie; he's a long-time friend of 'Uncle Jack.'"

"Me too. Are ya ready for a shot?"

"You read my mind, honey. How much is left?"

After calling the cab company from a sticker on the phone booth, we sat on the curb and finished the bottle. The cab arrived within fifteen minutes, and I found myself back at John Wayne International Airport a short time later, in awe once again of how much perspective can change in such a short time. I stood in the same spot less than a week ago, broken and in shock, devoid of hope and the desire to live. Now, I hoped that like some feline predator, I'd be granted yet another of many undeserved lives. The only difference was I desperately wanted to straighten up my act this time, no false promises to the God of fools and lost souls who protects those such as me.

"Are you gonna miss this place?" Lori Ann asked as she looked at the transplanted palms that begged to the sky.

"We'll come back someday and take over this fuckin' joint; then it'll be worth missing."

"I'll bet you will. I just hope I'll be here to see it." She was still looking at the trees outside the glass walls that encased the front of the building.

I was reading the departing flights' screen as we were speaking. "I told you, you're not getting out of my sight. Now let's get ticketed. There's a flight into BWI departing in less than an hour."

She smiled thoughtfully at my words, but at that moment I realized she too could feel destiny's darker hand reaching out in her direction, the chill within her almost palpable. We were alike in so many ways that it was almost eerie, but it only drew me closer to her, especially in what was seemingly a war for our survival.

"I want the window seat." Her teasing tone ignited an incredible lust for her affection.

"I know somewhere you can sit; there's two choices, in fact." I pulled her tightly against me and slipped my tongue in to meet hers for a passionate exchange.

She pushed me away with one hand on my chest while countering with a tug of my pants back toward her with the other. "If you don't stop we'll never catch that flight, and then I can't make love to you at thirty-thousand feet."

It was only minutes later that we sat patiently at gate three waiting for our non-stop flight to Baltimore's BWI Airport. It's worth noting that the same day "coach seats" were over nine hundred dollars each, making me appreciate Bobby's generosity all the more.

We arrived in Maryland at 2:07 PM Eastern Time, our buzz heightened from eight mini bottles of "Jack's" best, only two hours of sleep, and one incredible mile-high-club session in the plane's lavatory.

After locating a phone booth with a directory, I called a local limousine service that agreed to take us to Denton for two hundred dollars.

"The limo driver will meet us outside the baggage claim doors in about an hour. I thought we could pick up some local color at the shops in the main terminal. Is that cool with you?"

"Sure. What's the weather like here?"

"Hot and humid, just like Florida. Definitely shorts and T's."

Each of us bought some nice shorts and several shirts. I called my other cousin Bogie at my aunt's house, and after finally convincing her I was really in town, she agreed to come over to Artie's place later.

The limo ride was boring, mostly due to our eighty-year-old driver. I told Lori Ann stories about Bobby as we made our way to Maryland's Eastern Shore, and she seemed excited when we crossed the Chesapeake Bay and passed through the Kent Narrows area.

"This is really pretty. Is Denton like this?"

"Not really. It's kinda small-town living but it's close enough to hang out here if you like."

"Does Denton have water?"

"Yeah. It's got the Choptank River runnin' right through it. We're not far now."

I wondered what we'd do for transportation. It was clear to me already that Lori Ann would not be content being stranded in Denton even in the short term.

Denton hadn't changed much since my last visit. It was still a sleepy little town mostly inhabited by generations of farmers and the few businesses it takes to support that type of community. The only entertainment available on a nightly basis was a couple of tiny bars and one makeshift "night club" that was housed in a closed down Methodist Church now called The Robin's Nest. This was a controversial establishment, to say the least, mostly because of its location on Main Street in the center of town; lest we forget, Denton's geographical location is just a whisper away from a notch in the Bible Belt.

We arrived at the apartment around 4:30 PM and made ourselves at home with the remaining couple of beers from the fridge. Lori Ann had been quiet since our arrival, unsuccessfully masking her tentative feelings in silence.

"Don't worry, honey, it's more fun than it appears."

I certainly understood her apprehension when looking at this place in contrast to the places we'd been in the last twenty-four hours, but I always had great times with my cousins and saw no reason this trip should be any different.

"I'm sure you're right. Besides, it's not forever, right?" Her tone was positive but also reserved, leading me to question my decision to try out Maryland even as a temporary home.

"How about if we give it a few days and then we'll go if we're not completely satisfied. Either way, it's temporary for sure. Okay?" I leaned over and sat the oddly sized ten-ounce Budweiser can on the small coffee table in front of the couch before kissing her softly on the ear. "If you're not happy I promise we're outta here."

"Thanks, but I'm sure everything will be just fine."

The earnest expression on her face made me believe everything would be just as we hoped. We finished the last of the ten-ounce Buds, unique to the Eastern Shore, and were in search of a phonebook for a cab to the liquor store or the bottle of Jack I felt must be present in any place my cousin called home when he walked in. The door swung open with Artie declaring, "Fifty bucks says y'all drank all my damn beer!"

I said, "You're damn right I did, and you don't have a drop of 'Gentleman Jack' in this whole place," while embracing him in a bear hug. "This must be the only house south of the Mason-Dixon without a bottle of whiskey. Some redneck you are."

"I ain't no fuckin' redneck but the 'JD' is under the sink you fuckin' Yankee, and I brought more beer knowin' you'd be here drinkin' all mine."

He smiled widely and handed me a paper bag containing a twelve-pack of ten-ouncers as he swiped the door closed behind himself with his foot. It was only then that he saw Lori Ann, who'd been just outside his view, essentially blocked by the door. Before I could introduce them, she said, "Hi, I'm Lori Ann," while shaking Artie's hand, greeting him with a Southern charm so elegant it stunned me. There was so much more to know about this angel on earth.

"I don't have to hear another word to know you can do better than this guy. Here's my keys. Make a run for it while ya still can." He was digging into his pocket in a phony effort to retrieve his car keys.

"Nice, Artie. Thanks for the vote of confidence." I punched him in the arm to punctuate the sentiment.

"Look at this girl. Where'd you find the lamp, Aladdin?"

Lori Ann spoke up, saying, "I found him and I'm the lucky one," while squeezing my arm.

"He does have that effect on people. Hell, I love him too; God only knows why."

We grew up together raised as brothers, spending most summers of our childhood together, forging an unbreakable bond.

"Okay, okay. I've heard enough. Let's have a beer and plan the evenin's entertainment." I took the bag into the kitchen, leaving them alone in the living room. I returned a few minutes later with three beers and the bottle from under the sink. Lori Ann was speaking as I entered the room.

"So we decided to come to Maryland instead of Mexico." She shared a very abbreviated version of our meeting in Vegas, taking the bike to Newport Beach and hopping a plane this morning.

Artie was looking at me as I entered the room. "It's never boring in your world, is it?" He was declaring more than asking, once again amazed by my adventures.

"No, but just once I wish it would be."

I joined them on the couch. We sat and talked until the beer and whiskey were gone and then decided to take Lori Ann on a tour of her new surroundings and replenish our supplies.

Las Vegas did not provide Deborah with the kind of rest Carlos hoped for; her focus remained firmly on avenging Laurie's death. She continuously prodded Carlos for updates on the progress of the search for Reno MacNab and swore no rest until she personally killed the man she held responsible.

"You kill people for less on a regular basis. This fucker killed my sister. I want his ass," she screamed across the table in the Minneapolis mansion.

"Deborah, I know how you must feel but you must be patient my love." He tried again to assuage her fury by assuring her of the inevitable capture of this elusive young man. If he could only find this fugitive, he would gladly hang him from the nearest tree just to satisfy her hunger and return to business as usual. As for his personal feelings on the matter, this kid's guilt was not so clear, but he had no reason to spare him either.

"How can you know what I feel? My sister is dead and the little bastard who's responsible is running free. You can't even find that chick from Florida. One day she's gonna see the cops about that boyfriend of hers ya know."

"Why do you think we went to Las Vegas instead of Hawaii? We received a tip that she was dancing at a club there, but she's since disappeared without a trace. I've got people looking for her in Las Vegas and Los Angeles, and I have men in Florida watching the boyfriend's and her parent's houses. She'll turn up. And now I've got to have a small army looking for your Mr. MacNab as well. It's difficult timing but we'll resolve it shortly."

"Difficult timing? You fuck! This ain't some drug deal gone bad; it's my sister! Now you help me or I'll find someone who can." She stormed out of the lavish dining room leaving Carlos alone to contemplate the weight of her words.

He deliberated aloud. "Sweet Deborah, please don't force my hand against you. There's so much you cannot understand." Later, he made a series of calls inquiring as to the progress in the searches for his newfound antagonists. None had any success yet, but Rafael revealed that Mr. MacNab had also been to the west coast and possibly even Las Vegas recently.

Carlos' tone became cold. "So, what does that mean? I don't care as to where our friends have been, my concern is regarding their present whereabouts. I fear I may have entrusted these issues to the wrong man in you, Rafael. Do you require replacement?"

The man spoke with a shudder in his voice. "No sir. I will double my efforts and produce results. Please be assured we are on top of this matter, Don Carlos." He knew replacement within the organization meant a permanent type of termination.

"See that you do succeed, Rafael. My faith in you has become tiresome."

"I understand, Don Carlos. Voy a triunfar!"

"Bien, Rafael. I don't need this young Charro running around loose right now." Carlos hung up the telephone and sat back in his chair, speaking to the air. "See that you do. Viejo amigo. See that you do."

After surveying Denton, we settled in for a cocktail at The Robin's Nest. It was nice to be in Artie's company after so long apart; he was as enjoyable as ever. After several drinks, we adjourned to the interior balcony for a friendly billiards match. We were profoundly competitive with each other. He beat me two out of three games but, in my defense, Lori Ann was shooting me panty shots throughout the entire match.

"I told Bogie we'd be at your place; maybe we should head back."

"So much for sleeping tonight. Wait'll ya meet my sister. She's hell on wheels, especially where this one is concerned," Artie shared with Lori Ann as we made our way from the infamous pub, referring to my close relationship with Bogie. He was right; we're extremely protective of each other.

We bought two cases of ten-ounce Budweiser, one liter of Jack Daniel's, and various snacks en route to the apartment. It was no surprise to find Bogie waiting in the parking lot when we arrived. As usual, her bubbly aura greeted you three steps before her physical embrace.

"Hi, honey. What the hell are y'all doin' here? How long can you stay? Are y'all moving here? Do ya need a place to stay? Mom said you can stay with us. Well, tell me everything."

Bogie's tremendous hug almost made me stagger as I tried to introduce Lori Ann to her. "Okay, honey, settle down. It's great to see you. I want you to meet Lori Ann."

After introducing Bogie to Lori Ann and a lengthy inquisition right there in the parking lot, we ambled into Artie's apartment and settled in the kitchen. Artie and I sat at the table and began a shot-for-shot contest of alcoholic endurance while the girls stowed the supplies. Lori Ann waded through the final barrage of Bogie's typical query of any woman who entered my life; this culminated with Bogie declaring, "I approve," as she and Lori Ann joined us, each with a glass of the imported beer Bogie brought. Looking across the table at my cousins, I saw the changes two years had on their physical characteristics.

Bogie was more beautiful than ever. Her carefully styled blonde hair surrounded her soft features, and her big brown eyes distracted just enough from her athletic physique to allow her intelligence and wit to take center stage. Artie had grown into manhood with the broad shoulders and deep voice that women long for. Masculine indeed, but none exist with a warmer heart, eyes a deeper brown, and such a ready smile.

As we sat talking of each other's unique journeys over our time apart, I was reintroduced to Lori Ann again and again. Her life, although hardly deprived, had more than its share of trials. She was raised like many "Navy brats." Her father was a non-commissioned officer stationed at all points of Florida and beyond during her formative years. Being an only child afforded her no comrade during the frequent moves. It's of little surprise she took to the first young man who promised stability to this beautiful gypsy. I hoped I could provide a more favorable fellowship than her misguided first love.

Those who were familiar with my frequent flights of fancy would indeed question the validity of my monogamous quest, but nonetheless, my intent was as pure as my desire to move forward without narcotic inducement. Such are the fantasies buried deep in the addict's soul, only ever realized by the grace of God.

Melancholy waves rushed through my body like ghosts on parade as being with family turned my thoughts to the Tokyo crew, and of my real father whom I hadn't spoken with in way too long.

We sat and talked until dawn's presence was cast through the kitchen windows that framed our silhouettes against the wall. Artie headed off to cheat the biological process of rest, trading an hour once again where eight should have been spent. Bogie had less of a demanding schedule; high school being her principal occupation.

Bogie said, "Why don't we head down to Ocean City and show Lori Ann there's something fun to do here?" hoping to increase the odds of our visit becoming permanent.

"And do what? Let me guess, you've got a fake ID too? Is that how ya got the beer? I thought this place was wholesome. We're leavin'!"

Bogie smacked my arm with a backhand.

"Listen to his holiness. Maybe we should go back to your favorite church, The Robin's Nest," Lori Ann said, feeling much better about our trip since meeting my cousins.

"Aren't you two tired?"

In chorus, the new pals responded, "Hell no!"

Although I didn't regret leaving the devil's candy in the Vegas hotel room, I would have loved a little Peruvian pick me up. I hoped Lori Ann would help me avoid the mighty marching powder that had brought so much pain into my life.

"I'm taking a shower first though. Ya never know who you'll meet at the beach." Bogie trotted off to the bathroom leaving Lori Ann and me alone at the table.

"She's cool, huh?"

She reached over the table, taking my hand in her own, and said, "I like them both. It's like home, hangin' out all night with friends," and then kissed and sucked my fingertips in a loving token of thanks.

"If you keep that up, you're not showering alone."

She eased around the table. "You'd better not let me shower alone. Who'd do my back, or my front for that matter?" Her lips and tongue met mine in a sweet foray. Intimate moments with Lori Ann were like standing within a tropical waterfall, enveloped and caressed by the cascading water. I experienced chills simultaneously wrought with hot body rushes that culminated into fervid and lusty desire.

"Shower nothin', I want you right here." I pushed her backward onto the nearest chair and wrenched her shorts to her ankles while burying my face deep in her thighs in the same movement. Only after her wriggling got beyond my control did I rise and release myself before thrusting vigorously into her depths with the voracity of an untamed animal. The intense rapture combined with exhaustion created a euphoria unmatched by any experience available to man, including narcotic inducements. We nearly collapsed following our climaxes. Only the sound of Artie's scorn towards Bogie's waking him kept us conscious long enough to dress before falling off to sleep in a heap of sodden flesh on the floor.

Artie turned to Bogie as they viewed our spent bodies at their feet.

"Let 'em be. If I know him, they haven't slept in days." After covering us, he tossed a second blanket over Bogie who surrendered to the couch in his absence. He mumbled, "Lucky fuckers," as he closed the front door behind him and headed off to work.

I woke first. The spasms in my neck from our contorted sleeping position got the better of me. As I staggered around the apartment, stretching my tormented spine, I thought of my absentee relationship with my family. A personal promise was made in those moments. After we settled somewhere on a more permanent basis, I would contact them all again. For now, I wandered in memories' garden longing for simplicity in my ever-complex existence.

PART XII

The Last Sunset

The Last Sunset

Artie lost his job for crawling into work hungover and late one too many times. He arrived back at the apartment within an hour of his departure. His griping about being chewed out and fired, again, woke the girls; so, after showers and a mostly liquid brunch, we headed to the beach, a trip that took the better part of the day due to many detours including a strip joint. The girls were surprisingly and humorously rowdier than Artie and me, and as such, caused our premature, escorted departure from the topless establishment. Lori Ann was enjoying Maryland more with each new adventure, pleasing me immensely. Now, I just had to find a legitimate means of income.

We arrived at the beach just in time for the day's surrender to the night, its finality present in the amber glitter of lights on the surf.

I said, "Somehow, I always feel complete, connected to something larger yet simultaneously reminded that I'm totally insignificant in the presence of the sea," to Lori Ann as we looked out over the vast expanse of the Atlantic.

"I know what you mean. It's like God is right here but still just out of reach." She responded without looking away from the surf.

"Okay you lovebirds, let's check out the boardwalk." Artie spoke from several yards away while he watched the masses of swimsuit-clad tourists milling along the wooden planks, their sand-covered towels draped over shoulders and stowed within overstuffed bags from the day on the beach.

I leaned over and kissed Lori Ann lightly on her temple. "Let's go see what awaits us on this coast."

"Is Artie really all right about the job thing?"

"No worries. He'll be back to work in no time. He works for his father, my uncle, in a specialty construction business, so it's just a matter of time before he's forgiven and back on the clock."

***

It was after 2:00 am when the private line in Carlos' bedroom rang, waking him like a shot in the night.

"This had better be good."

"I'm sorry to wake you, Don Carlos, but I might have some information on that Florida transaction."

The nervous voice on the line admitted to breaking the orders given by Carlos. He apologized profusely for leaving Florida with a woman he met while searching for the girlfriend of the man Raul killed in Los Angeles. Antonio and the woman he met went to her home in Ocean City, Maryland for the weekend but only after weeks of surveilling the LA girl's parents' house with no sign of anything. He thought a night or two away wouldn't make any difference after so long, especially when so many others were looking for her too. They were enjoying a drink in a bar on the boardwalk when he believed he spotted the girl Carlos was hunting down. She was drinking with what seemed like friends.

"It took great courage for you to confess your indiscretion, Antonio. I will keep this in mind when deliberating your personal situation. Are you sure it's her?"

"I can't get that close, but I'm pretty sure it's the girl in the picture and they called her Lori Ann." Antonio felt nauseous, still fearing instant retribution for his disobedience.

"Do not lose sight of her, Antonio. I will personally be there later today. You are carrying your phone, aren't you?"

"Si, Don Carlos, I am, and I will not let her from my sight."

THE WAITRESS INTERRUPTED OUR LAUGHTER AT THE TABLE TELLING us it's time to go; they'd announced last call about twenty minutes before. We were gathering our things and gulping the last of our drinks when Lori Ann asked, "Did you ever have the feeling someone's watching you?" I know it's crazy, I don't even know anybody here, but I just feel like I'm being watched."

"Everybody looks at you Lori Ann, you're beautiful." I attempted to calm her as we walked out of Brass Balls Saloon.

"You've been hangin' around Reno too long. He always thinks somebody's after him." Artie chimed in with intoxicated commentary.

Bogie was too drunk to weigh in on the subject. Instead, she slurred some inquiry as to why we were asked to leave the last bar.

"They closed. It's after two." I gave her a hug to ease her disappointment.

"Let's get outta here before the cops start handing out beds for the night." Artie was speaking from experience.

We eventually made our way back to the car and began the journey home to Denton. At the first stoplight, Artie saw a guy he knew from Kent Island who always has great coke. After a brief conversation, I decided to buy an ounce of his bulk product to try and improve our financial situation. I told Lori Ann that with the estimated twenty-five hundred in profit, we could have the bike and car shipped to us. She wasn't happy about selling coke but agreed we could use the extra cash, and a vehicle was certainly a must. I still had about sixteen grand and we hadn't touched her money yet, but it was going fast, and I needed the pick-me-up.

"DEBORAH, I'VE GOT TO TAKE CARE OF THIS SITUATION MYSELF AND then I will devote all my efforts to finding Reno." Carlos reiterated in an increasingly frustrated tone.

"Why can't someone else take care of her?"

"I've told you, Deborah. She may have seen me; she's definitely seen Raul and can connect me to something I do not wish to be associated with, so I must be sure that it's handled this time."

Carlos resumed packing his overnight bag, hoping she'd understand and provide the needed time to resolve this critical issue, but she exploded. "I can't believe you don't see the importance of avenging Laurie's death. You fucking mobsters are always talking about the importance of family and killing anyone who interferes with your precious agenda."

"Deborah, you know I find that to be offensive and I've told you I'll find him for you and that you may do with him as you please, but I'm not even sure he's directly accountable for Laurie dying in that crash. He wasn't even there, and she was pretty wild, you've said so yourself."

"Fuck you! I'll get him myself. I do have other connections ya know. Fuck it. I'm gonna use them since it's not a priority to you." She screamed and threw her fists toward the floor as she turned to leave the bedroom.

"Deborah, I can't have you and your so-called connections creating controversy and possibly implicating anyone in my organization. You must wait for me to handle the situation; there is no other alternative." Carlos' voice was stern and direct.

"I'm not in your fucking boy's club, Carlos, I'll do whatever I want." She stormed out of the room cursing his lack of support.

He glanced at the various personal items of hers scattered about the room, softly saying, "I wish I didn't believe that Deborah, but I know you're right and you must choose your own path," as he reached into the bag to retrieve his cell phone. He was still dialing as the Bentley tires squealed exiting the driveway.

After several rings, a raspy voice answered. "Hola, que deseas?"

"Migel, I'm afraid there's a problem we must address. Deborah is in the car and will not return; she was never in the house either. Do you understand the situation?"

"Si, Don Carlos. Entiendo."

Carlos hung up, tossed the phone back into the bag, and continued packing in silence.

By some miracle, we made it back to the apartment without being arrested for drunk driving. Artie weaved in and out of the traffic lanes the entire trip. Once inside, I began chopping up the coke into a fine powder to be cut with baking soda since there was no head shop in the area to buy a quality cut. When I finished, twenty-eight grams had become forty-five bringing its street value to over four thousand dollars, not bad for a fifteen-hundred-dollar investment, including the cut. Artie made a list of people we could call to move the stuff and we all did a few lines just to get us through the night. We waited as Artie called a few of his more derelict acquaintances to see if they had a late-night need for our supply. None of us were pleased about having possession of all this stuff, therefore, we agreed to make an all-out effort to be rid of it as soon as possible.

Carlos swapped seats with the pilot and landed his private jet in Easton, Maryland, thirty minutes after an in-flight call to Antonio who told him the current location of the target. Antonio greeted him on the tarmac in a rented Lincoln Town Car.

Antonio asked, "How was your trip, Don Carlos?" putting on a brave face despite his deep-seated fear of his present situation. He had never killed someone before and wondered if he would be killed soon after completing the task at hand.

"Why are you here?" Carlos was disgusted, looking right through Antonio as if he already didn't exist.

Antonio stammered and stuttered as he tried to explain that he was picking him up, but Carlos wasn't listening.

"Donde esta la chica, Antonio?"

Antonio knew he was in a terrible position when Carlos spoke in Spanish but was pleased to have a concrete answer to the question: "She's in a town called Denton. It's only about fifteen miles from here."

Carlos was now standing so close that his breath brushed Antonio's face. "How do you know she is there when you're here talking with me?"

"I uh, I was just there and uh, she was there, so I uh, came here to get you and..."

His heart was in his mouth.

"And if she is not there then what would you propose we do?"

"But she..."

"Do you think I'm incompetent, Antonio? That I don't know how to arrange simple transportation for myself?"

"Well, no, but..."

"Do you realize how important it is that this situation is in our control, or perhaps you want me to be implicated in some ugly incident?" Carlos interrupted and continued without allowing a response. "I'm becoming concerned, not only about your intelligence but your loyalty as well. We will have some things to discuss after the business at hand is resolved. Don't you think so as well, Antonio?"

"Si, Don Carlos. Should I go back to the location now?"

Antonio was terrified and his knees threatened to give way. Carlos just stared at him with a trademark, vacant gaze that few had lived to describe.

A second black Lincoln Town Car appeared and pulled up within a few feet of them. Carlos walked over to the car and spoke briefly to the driver who stared intently at Antonio throughout the exchange. The car slowly pulled away as Carlos walked over to Antonio's rental car and got into the passenger seat without a word. Antonio hustled over to the car, hopped in, and asked, "Are you ready?"

Carlos just shook his head in obvious disappointment at another foolish inquiry. Antonio was sweating so profusely that he could hardly see to drive through the stinging of sweat in his eyes.

THE CAB DROPPED STIHL OFF AT HIS PLACE AT ABOUT 5:00 PM; before he could pay the driver, the girls exploded out the door.

"Where's Reno? Is he with you?" As usual, they spoke in stereo.

"None of your business and no, he's not with me."

"They're after him. We've gotta warn him. Two guys were here looking for him and they said they'd be back later."

"What guys? Who were they?" Stihl looked around as a chill ran down his spine.

"They didn't say who they were. They just said they needed to know where Reno was. They were scary looking, dressed in clothes like Reno's but darker, and snooped all around the house," Dakota lamented while Tammy scanned the area tearfully.

Stihl noticed the bike and asked, "Was he here when they came?"

"No. He left the bike yesterday and disappeared with some girl." Dakota answered as she followed him into the house.

Stihl wandered throughout the house trying to piece together what happened and why the bike was still there. "Did he say anything while he was here?"

"He..." Dakota started to respond but Stihl interrupted.

"Where are the keys to the Cougar?"

"They're in the garbage," Dakota replied.

"What?" Stihl was sure he misunderstood her.

"Reno taught me to hide stuff there; he said it's the last place people would look for valuables." Dakota drifted off tearfully.

Stihl thought about it and concluded, "He was somthin' else, huh?"

"Is, not was. He'll be back," Tammy insisted, breaking her silence.

Stihl retrieved the keys and headed out to the car without another word. His heart sank when he saw the motorcycle keys in the glove box. "Where are you, dude?" he asked softly of the onshore breeze that now chilled him at eighty-two degrees, and then a sense of peace pushed the uncertainty aside. Stihl imagined nothing and no one could catch up to the kid he'd known. Reno moved so fast he was even ahead of himself. "Good luck, my friend." He spoke aloud as he placed the keys in his shorts' pocket. Stihl stepped back from the car, looked down the boulevard, and then up at the girls standing on the porch and let out a slow sigh before heading down the sidewalk to buy a bottle of Seagram's Seven.

AFTER JUST THREE CALLS, ARTIE STRUCK GOLD. A SMALL PARTY morphed into an all-nighter, and we had the solution to their 4:00 AM dilemma: more cocaine. We agreed to bring a quarter ounce to them for the bargain price of six hundred dollars, so we loaded back into the car and headed off to some farm outside of town. The group in the small outbuilding consisted of six guys in their early twenties and four girls in their late teens and early twenties. I immediately noticed the level of their intoxication and cheerfully agreed to join them for a beer, feeling no threat.

Bill Barnette was the group's apparent leader and did all the talking regarding the purchase. After the typical rhetoric to determine that no one was a cop, we started the negotiation; Bill commenced the exchange.

"I'm used to payin' four hundred for a quarter."

"No, you're not. This town has nowhere near the competition for that kinda pricing, but I'll go twelve on a halfer if ya can hack it."

Bill looked me up and down and said, "I'll go a grand on that half but no more, city boy."

His expression let me know he enjoyed looking like he knew what he was doing in front of his friends, so I played along.

"You know I can't go below eleven hundred. Hell, I'm breakin' even here."

Pleased and pacified, he agreed. "I'll do your 'leven hundred but next time try buyin' lower, city boy."

I accepted with a nod as we exchanged bags for bucks while the first morning's light began to alert the farm's livestock of the coming day. Lori Ann, Artie and Bogie looked on in silence, each computing how much money we just made.

***

ANTONIO TURNED OFF THE LIGHTS BEFORE PULLING INTO THE parking area of the Denton apartments where he followed the group earlier that evening. Carlos looked around and inquired, "Which one is it?"

"One-thirteen. It's in that building there. Do you see it on the left?" Antonio was relieved to see the lights still on, knowing his fate would have been sealed if they left in his absence. Carlos ignored Antonio's question.

"Which car did they arrive in?"

"The red Firebird by the front door, see?" Antonio's voice trembled. The four-door car they had been in was gone; he noticed it only while being questioned. Antonio struggled not to vomit as he scanned the parking lot for the sedan. Where could it be? "Wa-what should we do now?"

"Now we wait until I say otherwise, Antonio, and you shut up." Carlos sensed Antonio's fear and wanted to settle into the surroundings before making any moves. He was sure he would recognize the girl from the picture if he saw her in person and wanted as little commotion as possible during this exercise; sloppiness was what brought him to this circumstance in the first place.

Antonio sat wondering what would be worse: to have the girl drive up right in front of them or not show up at all. If she doesn't return, who's to say she didn't slip out a back door; if she does return, there could be another uncontrolled incident like the one he heard about in LA. He decided to tell Carlos the truth just as the sedan pulled into the lot. Carlos snapped to attention.

"That's her, Antonio! She's in the back of that car."

Before Antonio could reply, Carlos added, "They've got two cars; you should have known that."

"I'm sorry, Don Carlos. What should we do?"

Antonio couldn't believe his luck. If they hadn't returned, he would never have left the parking lot alive.

"Don't move. If she sees us this whole thing will explode."

Carlos gasped. "Ay, Dios mio. That's Reno MacNab. They're together? How can this be?" Carlos was baffled. Antonio started to offer an opinion but was again interrupted. "Did you know this man was with her?"

"Well, I thought..."

"You thought what, that you shouldn't examine the pictures you've been provided? Your incompetence is overwhelming." Carlos stared at Antonio with a glare that caused physical pain in Antonio's head as his mind raced for something to say. As Carlos scrambled for his cellphone, he said, "Watch them, Antonio. Your life depends on this."

"Si, Don Carlos. I've got them."

Antonio hadn't noticed Reno as the one in the description and newspaper mugshot the soldiers were given but thought perhaps this event might spare his life. Carlos dialed frantically, calling his Bentley's car phone in Minneapolis; Migel answered in silence. Carlos knew Deborah would've spoken if she picked up the phone, so he reluctantly asked, "What is the situation, Migel?"

"Ah, Don Carlos. Es como dices. El auto esta' arreglado y lo a casa ahora."

"Was all of the work done, Migel?"

"Si, Don Carlos. La mechanica se ha ido a casa tambien."

"Gracias. Adios Migel." Carlos pushed end on the cell phone and told Antonio, "They must all be eliminated. This has gone far enough."

Antonio sat looking out the window in silence. After a few moments, he asked, "Are we waiting for a mechanic, Don Carlos?"

"Antonio, you are such a child. What does the adult world hold for you? No. I will see to this myself."

"But sir, I thought you never..."

Carlos looked disdainfully at Antonio. "Are you so naive that the word 'never' remains in your vocabulary?" At that moment, Antonio knew he, too, would be killed; much more than that, he knew any plea for leniency would only disgrace his name and place his entire family under a dark shadow.

Carlos stared out the windshield watching the group go into the apartment like an eagle watches a mouse slipping into its burrow; his eyes were fixed on the window blind as if it were translucent.

ONCE INSIDE, WE ALL PLOPPED DOWN ON THE COUCH IN A SILENT daze of exhaustion, booze and drugs. I broke the silence. "Well, we're three-hundred from break-even. So, at this rate, we'll rake in over two grand on the deal, not bad for a couple hours work."

"I wish we didn't have to do this but it's fast cash and that's tough to resist," Lori Ann added in a tired voice.

"Scares the hell outta me. I mean, all this shit in my place. Jus' 'magin' if the cops walked in right now, man, we'd be done," Artie said in a tired slur before announcing his intentions for sleep and lots of it.

Bogie, on the other hand, had enjoyed Bill's generosity and was mentally amped out. "Come on you guys, let's party. I'm not tired."

Her tone betrayed her words and gave away her physical exhaustion regardless of her brain's belief.

I said, "Honey, you're wrecked; it's just your head doesn't know it. We all need some sleep and tomorrow's another day, so let's rest up for it."

Lori Ann began frantically scanning the living room. "Damn! I left my purse at that guy's house."

Bogie was heading into the kitchen when she said, "Take my car. I'll bet they're still up," with a tone condemning our decision to call it a night.

"What's in your purse?"

"A lot of stuff, Reno, including my bank card and license. I've really gotta get it."

"Maybe it's in the car," Bogie suggested from the kitchen.

"It's under the chair I was sitting in, I'm sure of it."

"So be it. Bogie, we're takin' your car. I'll see ya in a while."

Bogie reappeared, whining. "I wanna go."

"No, you want more coke. But instead, you're gonna sleep, right?"

"Fine. My keys are by the door."

Lori Ann started to take Bogie's side but I interrupted her and asked, "Do you want to get stuck at that party for another couple of hours?"

"No, but..."

"Honey, sleep will mend these wounds, I promise." I ran my fingers through her hair and kissed her softly. "We'll be back in twenty minutes."

"Okay my prince, our chariot awaits."

"All right Cinderella, let's go before it turns into a pumpkin." I swatted her ass before reaching for the door.

CARLOS HAD BEEN SILENT SINCE MAKING HIS CALL, FEELING DISGUST for having his hand forced against Deborah. Antonio sat imagining his eventual demise. How could he have been so stupid to leave his post for even a moment? Hell, he'd done it twice; there was no coming back from his mistakes.

"Antonio, this is how we'll handle the situation: We will wait ten more minutes, then walk up to the door and knock."

"But..."

Carlos stopped him mid-sentence. "Silencio! If they answer the door, we push our way inside and very quickly, quietly, and cleanly eliminate the entire group. Then wait five minutes and leave."

"But..." Antonio tried again.

"Callate! If they don't answer the door..." Carlos froze mid-thought and uttered, "Que chingados," as he saw Lori Ann with me exiting the apartment.

"Can I drive?" Lori Ann asked as we approached the Firebird.

"Are you okay to drive?"

"I'm fine, just tired of being driven."

"Okay then."

I flipped her the keys, we got in the car, and I sparked a cigarette as she adjusted the seat to her liking.

"Ready?" She asked as the car roared to life.

"Let's go, speed racer, but try to keep it on the hard stuff."

"Cute." She replied while backing up the car, looking over her shoulder for other cars.

I glanced out my window to check the maneuver and saw a dome light come on and quickly off in a Town Car at the far end of the lot.

"Man, I guess everybody around here pulls all-nighters."

"What're you talkin' about?" Lori Ann asked as she swung around to shift into drive.

When I looked at the car again it was dark, and no one was around. I scanned the lot; it was the only car near that caliber in the whole place. I patted my pockets reflexively to be sure I had all the coke in case it was a cop who was going to hit Artie's apartment.

Lori Ann watched me frisking myself and asked, "What's the matter?"

"Cops don't drive Town Cars, right?"

She brushed off my paranoia. "Not where I'm from. Only snow-birds and gangsters from Jersey do."

"Hmm. Drive over by that car so I can see some gangsters."

"Let's just get my purse. You can play with the gangsters when we get back."

Feeling embarrassed, I agreed, and we pulled out of the lot.

Carlos had a tight grip on Antonio's neck, with his thumb on the man's windpipe. Through gritted teeth, he said, "If they had seen us, I would have shot you first and then handled them." After a minute that felt like an eternity, he released his grip leaving Antonio gasping for air.

"Should I follow them?" He struggled to ask as the pain nearly prevented words.

"If they escape, I'll kill you where you sit."

"Si, Don Carlos, I'll be careful."

Antonio pulled slowly out of the lot and then waited until the Fire-bird turned the next corner before proceeding. Carlos checked the silencer on his pistol and set it on the seat next to him, his hand resting on it with a tapping finger.

After retrieving the purse from the farm, we hopped in the Firebird and headed back to Artie's, this time with me behind the wheel.

"Those guys really party. I can't believe they're all still goin'. It's after six."

I started to respond to Lori Ann when I caught sight of what looked like the Town Car from Artie's lot with its lights on in a pull-off area ahead. "I think that's the same car."

We looked closely while passing the car and simultaneously shouted. "Shit!" We looked at each other, shocked by the other's response, and then again, in unison, said, "You know them?"

"They look like the guy who chased me in LA!"

"That's Carlos, Laurie's sister's boyfriend. What the fuck is he doing here?"

I accelerated hard down the road; the Town Car lunged into the street in a cloud of dust behind us.

"Carlos? That's gotta be the guy from LA. He's one of the buyers of the coke we got from Miami. They've gotta be the Spanish guys who met Stephen." Tears filled Lori Ann's eyes as she trembled, looking out the back window.

"Are you serious? Why would Carlos need to buy coke from your boyfriend?" My mind raced in confusion.

"This was special coke, Pink Peruvian Flake, the same kinda stuff you had in the hotel. Where'd you get it?" she asked, trying to sort out my connection to all of this. "They're gonna catch us. Go faster!"

"I'm goin' as fast as I can." I wondered how Carlos would know Lori Ann and Stephen but concluded he couldn't be the same guy. "I got the pink stuff in Minnesota from Carlos himself; he must be after me because of Laurie. They blame me for her death."

"No. They're after me because of Stephen."

"Is this even possible?" I asked of myself, puzzled by the possibility that this man could be connected to us both. I glanced at the speedometer that read ninety-five miles per hour and checked the rearview mirror; they were gaining ground. "I hope we've got more gas than them 'cause this fucker's not that fast."

"We've got less than a quarter tank, Reno. What are we gonna do?"

I couldn't help thinking this is what it must have been like for Laurie and Tommy in the last moments of the chase, so I slowed down to seventy.

"You're slowing down?" She was incredulous.

"I can't kill you. I've gotta think of what to do."

I watched the big car catching up in the rearview mirror as Lori Ann frantically turned front to back with fear in her eyes.

"They're gonna kill us both! Please go faster." She pleaded, almost hysterical.

I slammed on the brakes and slid through a hard-left turn onto a more rural road heading towards Ridgely. They somehow managed to make the turn as well, so I floored it through the ensuing corners of the country road, hoping they would have to slow down to make it in the big car.

Antonio knew if he lost us, he'd be killed immediately, so he pushed the car beyond its capabilities in hopes of any error on my part.

The Lincoln skidded wildly around the turns and was just about to lose control when Carlos yelled, "Policia!"

We were approaching an intersection when Lori Ann screamed, "Look out!" I was watching the car behind us and didn't notice the stop sign. I swerved sharply but clipped the nose of a police car as we barreled through the intersection. I yelled, "Fuck," as the cars impacted and we spun into a drainage ditch and bounced into a field, ultimately grinding to a stop in the dirt. Antonio managed to maneuver through the scene without getting tangled up in the crash. He slowed as they continued away from the wreckage and asked Carlos for direction.

"Just get out of here."

"What about them?"

"They're not going anywhere; we'll simply wait for them to be released from custody."

"Are you okay? Lori Ann?" I grabbed her arm and gently jostled her.

"Huh? Did you see that?" She had been dazed for a second but was basically fine. A rising bump on her head was the only visible injury on her body.

"Thank God you're all right." Tears filled my eyes as I took her in my arms.

"I'm okay. Are you all right?" She asked as she brushed the hair from my face.

"I'm fine. Let's get outta here." I tried to start the demolished Firebird. "The car's shot. Will your door open?"

My door was jammed. Lori Ann opened her door, climbed out, and then reached back in to help me exit the wreckage.

"Holy shit. Look at the cop car." I pointed after noticing its position, nose in a ditch across the intersection. The two of us stood taking in the entire scene when it hit me. "Where are they?" I was frantically scanning the surrounding area for the Town Car.

"They musta bolted after the wreck," Lori Ann replied after looking around again.

The cop crawled from his car and was hobbling in our direction with his gun drawn. He was way overweight and had a beard that covered his whole face, obviously a town cop. His uniform was disheveled, and a profound limp hampered his movement.

"Let's go." I simultaneously grabbed Lori Ann's hand and started to run across the field.

"What about Bogie's car?"

"We stole it. She's at home in bed. We've gotta make it outta here so I can stash this coke."

Before I finished the statement, a police Bronco and two more squad cars appeared on the scene. The sirens wailed at a piercing volume, and the Bronco entered the field with a heavy bounce heading right for us.

"I'm sorry, Lori Ann, I tried." We stopped our futile dash and waited for the inevitable.

"It's not your fault." She took me in her arms with an embrace that ended only when a policeman ordered our separation at gunpoint.

"I said face down, arms away from your sides, hands open. I mean right fuckin' now," an angry voice ordered, followed by, "You are under arrest. You have the right to remain silent," as they put handcuffs on me with a knee in my back.

Carlos called the Ridgely Police Department from a payphone, posing as a concerned citizen. "So, the officer is all right. Well, that is good news. I hope you caught that reckless driver. Did you?"

"Yes, sir, and we appreciate your concern. Sir, did you witness the accident?"

"Oh, no, I just saw the terrible aftermath and was concerned for the officer. What will happen to that other driver now that he's been caught?"

"That's up to the Judge, sir. He'll be arraigned tonight in the 5:00 PM court session. Is that all then, sir?"

"Oh yes, and thank you, officer."

Antonio started to ask a question but was interrupted by Carlos' hand raised to indicate silence.

"You're going to court tonight Antonio and finding out the fate of our friends."

"What if they recognize me?"

"Yes, that is a problem for you to address, Antonio. My recommendation is that you be reasonably disguised and seated in the back of the room."

Antonio felt his significance as a soldier losing its last ounce of value while Carlos reveled in nearing a solution to both problems. Carlos had Antonio drop him off at a charming Bed and Breakfast but instructed Antonio to get a low rent room near the courthouse and to call as information became available. Clearly, Carlos wanted no affiliation with Antonio if something should go wrong. Carlos also needed some peace and quiet to plan his next move, to deal with his feelings regarding Deborah, and of course, to consider just how these two thorns could sprout from the same rose.

I used my one phone call to tell Artie and Bogie what happened, so they'd know where we were, and to report the car stolen. I only looked forward to seeing Lori Ann in court during our arraignment. The police found over a half-ounce of cocaine in my possession; that, in combination with nearly six thousand dollars in cash and a stolen car gave the District Attorney a massive hard-on. I wondered if the Minnesota file would be located during their criminal check on me, hoping they'd run the name on my license instead of my fingerprints, and if Lori Ann would be charged with the cocaine and money as well. I also instructed Artie to use the ten thousand dollars I left at his house for Lori Ann's legal defense, less the deductible on Bogie's car. A man I presumed to be a lawyer arrived to see me at around 2:00 PM.

"Hello Mr. MacNab, I'm John LaChance."

We shook hands and I sat back down on my concrete cot.

"My name is Reno West. Are you a public defender or did my cousin send you?"

"No, I'm not a public defender, and we can dispose of the aliases."

I was so stunned by him already knowing my name that I didn't pay any attention to his demeanor.

"Well, I told my cousin you were supposed to defend Lori Ann not me, so why are you talking to me?"

After a momentary stare, Mr. Lachance replied, "May I ask why?"

"Because I want all available funds used to defend her. She has no knowledge of the cocaine found in my possession, doesn't know I stole the car, and should be released immediately."

"Well now, there-in lies the rub. You see, Ms. Morgan also claims the drugs are hers and that you took them from her just before the arrest to protect her from prosecution."

"Look, she's lying and you've gotta get her outta here. I'll fly with the public offender."

"That's 'Defender,' and unfortunately, you're both being charged on all counts ranging from a hit and run and assault of a police officer to possession with intent to distribute."

I looked pointedly at the lawyer. "If you can have us both walk outta here on any kinda deal in the next few days, even for a day or two, then do it. Otherwise, I'm authorizing that my defense be forfeited and requesting that all efforts be directed toward defending Lori Ann and in setting her bail. I know you can get her outta here once she cooperates against me with the local yokels."

"Well, that would have to be the case because there's no way you're going anywhere based on what I've seen so far."

"So be it. You tell her to play ball and let me rightfully take the fall for this. And Mr. LaChance, you tell her I love her too."

I turned away from the lawyer and faced the wall as tears filled my eyes.

"Very well, Mr. MacNab. I wish you much success with your kamikaze approach to life."

The next sound I heard was the cell door closing. In the following hours, absent of drugs and booze, I felt more alone than at any other time in my life. I acknowledged that I was unworthy of love, happiness, and the stability so many others take for granted. The words of "Me and Bobby McGee" echoed through my head: "Freedom's just another word for nothin' left to lose," and in those words, I found the truth about my life. I had run so fast and for so long that I never had a chance for something good in my life. In my haste to grow up, I let my childhood slip by without even a glance at what should be a time to see the world with an innocence that is stolen soon enough. Now, at only eighteen, I'd entered my favorite Pink Floyd song's lyrics: "Traded a walk-on part in the war for a lead role in a cage. Oh, how I wish, how I wish you were here." I was still wallowing in self-pity when another man arrived at my cell, this one dressed in a black leather jacket, grey T-shirt, black jeans, and black running shoes.

"Mr. MacNab, I need a word with you. Please step out of the cell." His voice was deep and raspy, his eyes cold and absent of life. I did as he requested but was stopped at the cell door by a police officer's stiff arm.

"Look, this kid needs shackles to be walkin' around or it's my ass," the cop told the ominous man.

The enormous man in black looked at me and then at the guard while grabbing my shirt and said, "Son, if you so much as breathe without my permission, I'll snap you like a twig. Are we clear about that?"

I believed his words and nodded yes without a verbal reply.

"Good. Now, get out of my way officer, and stop wasting my time." He pulled me past him and down the hall.

I couldn't believe my eyes. Lori Ann was seated in a room at a table with John LaChance at the opposite side. Her eyes were swollen from crying and she looked exhausted, but I'd never seen a more beautiful sight.

"Lori Ann, are you all right?"

Before she could answer, I was poked in the ribs from behind. "Remember our deal. Not even a breath," the harsh voice reminded me as he pushed me toward a chair.

Lori Ann's face showed the pain I felt being jabbed but she was silent in her misery.

LaChance spoke after I was seated. "Thank you, Agent Reece. Would you excuse us for a moment?" The big man lumbered from the room, giving me one more warning look as he closed the door behind himself. As soon as the door shut, LaChance continued, "I am Deputy Director LaChance of the United States Drug Enforcement Agency, or DEA if you like."

My face flushed and stomach churned as he finished. "What the fuck? You said you were our lawyer?"

"I said no such thing and am not responsible for your assumptions. I am, however, here to discuss your situation and possibly make you an offer. Do you both understand what I'm saying?"

We nodded in silence, stealing a glance at each other as we responded.

"I will tell you that the local authorities want stringent sentences for both of you, and this feeling is shared by the Minnesota officials as well, Mr. MacNab. Mr. MacNab, you are facing no less than fifteen years in each state, while you, young lady, could serve a minimum of five years in the Maryland Penal Facility for Women. Do you understand what I have told you both so far?"

Again, we nodded in unison.

"I'm going to need a verbal response at this point, for the recording."

He gestured toward a tape recorder as we responded, "Yes," in stereo.

"Good, now we can move forward. I have had several Agents watching you both for some time since you came into contact with a man you may know as Carl Montello, Carlos Ramirez, or any number of other aliases. He has been meticulous while in this country to not get involved personally in any illegal activities, but for various reasons has risked a great deal to see the two of you eliminated. Are you aware of this situation?"

"Yes sir." We were becoming more at ease with the man.

"Fine. Now this is what I need for you to consider, and you must both agree or it will not work. I believe that you are in love, although you appear to have only known each other for a brief period, which is good for my purposes and, in part, for yours as well."

Lori Ann and I felt a glimmer of hope from within the darkness we experienced over these last hours while he searched for how to articulate his next statement. He straightened in his chair and continued. "Our desire to indict this man has put you in a position to be of assistance to your government. Thus, we propose the following: First, if you agree, you will be released from court on a bond that will be posted by your government under a fictitious name, and at that time we believe Carlos will make an attempt on your lives. This is the only way I can seal his fate; whether or not he succeeds is not of great relevance to the case."

We looked at each other and then at him in amazement.

"I should say that if everything goes as planned, you would not be harmed in any way. However, there is that possibility and you must be prepared for that reality."

Lori Ann and I were reeling in deep thought and did not respond to his statement.

"Are you ready for the good news now?"

His words were lighthearted but his expression was unchanged. We didn't reply, so he continued.

"Second, if we are successful and he is not, you will be placed in our witness protection program and relocated to a safe environment where you will be productive individuals in society."

"Together?" Lori Ann perked up as she was thinking the same thing I voiced.

"We don't feel that you are a manageable risk as a team and since you're not married, we have no moral obligation to your union. Therefore, you would never see each other again under the terms of this deal."

My heart sank in despair as I wondered if retribution for my actions would ever be fully paid.

"Well, I imagine you two would like a moment alone to talk with each other at this point, and of course, to decide on my offer, so I'll be back in five minutes. I do apologize for the length of time you're allotted for deliberation, but we have a narrow window to work with and there are many characters in this play."

He got up, picked up the recorder, and started walking from the room. He stopped at the door and added, "Oh, and Mr. MacNab, your situation in Minnesota would be unchanged, although you would only be at risk of incarceration if you were so foolish as to be identified at some point within that jurisdiction; otherwise, your new identification, including fingerprints, would supersede the existing data on file." He nodded to himself as if agreeing with his statement before turning to walk through the door.

I looked at Lori Ann and winked; she frowned at my pleasure and asked, "How can you smile? We'll never see each other again."

I leaned closer and whispered into her ear. "Wait one month and contact Stihl at The Pub. You remember it, right, where we used the payphone?"

Her eyes glowed as she reached out to take my hand. "I love you, Reno."

"I love you too. We'll have Stihl arrange a room for us down in San Felipe in six months and then we'll have our sunset."

We stole an embrace over the table and were still in each other's arms when LaChance returned and asked, "Well, do we have a decision?" while sitting the recorder back on the table.

"Yes. We've decided to accept your offer."

He looked at us carefully before asking Lori Ann, "Do you also agree with this decision?"

"Yes. I'll do it."

He contemplated our responses and then stated flatly, "If you fuck this up, you'll be right back in here and with much bigger problems I assure you."

I looked at Lori Ann and then reassured the man. "We won't blow it."

"Well, that being the case, let's get to it."

He went on to explain what steps would come next and had us each sign agreements; they were essentially disclaimers of liability. We were to be released via bail being posted and then journey to a motel in a nearby town where we'd wait for Carlos to make his move. They would report us as deceased to the pertinent government agencies and media, regardless of the outcome, thereby terminating our current identities. I assumed that's how he would seek a life in prison sentence for Carlos without parole regardless of what happened to us. We would be taken to separate locations and given new identities including complete records from birth. We would also be assigned jobs and housing in a community where we must live for at least ten years, and even then, we would need permission to relocate. Lori Ann was surprised that the Government would go to such lengths to set up one man, and it made her feel even more afraid of the entire situation. My main concern was it seemed that it would be easier to just let Carlos kill us, thereby wrapping up the whole package neatly in one move, but our options were few, so I kept those thoughts to myself.

Antonio was seated in the last row of benches when court began. Ours was the first case and notably swift in its disposal. He was in the car and on the phone with Carlos within an hour of his arrival. He wore tattered clothing, a baseball cap, and tinted glasses; it worked on Lori Ann and me but the Agents on the case were well aware of his presence and watched closely as he exited the building.

Antonio explained the developments in our situation to Carlos, who in turn directed him to follow us until otherwise instructed. Carlos acquired his own rental car so he could have transportation without Antonio ever losing sight of us, plus he had another man hanging back in the area in case he needed backup or an escape hatch.

We were given two hundred dollars and the address of a Budget Motel on Route 50 in Easton where we were to wait for the inevitable attack from Carlos. A taxi was parked out front waiting for us; this was painfully clear when he didn't bother to ask our destination before pulling out of the lot. Lori Ann and I sat silently, waiting for the moment we'd again be alone, holding hands and stealing the occasional kiss.

"That'll be fifty bucks," was the only thing the driver said upon our arrival; I paid him and we walked into the lobby. The front desk clerk wasted no time directing us to our room after the requested fee of one hundred dollars was quietly handed over to him.

"How much ya wanna bet dinner is fifty bucks?"

Lori Ann laughed uneasily but did not respond.

Once inside room one-fifteen, I closed the door just in time for her to leap into my arms.

"I don't wanna lose you. Can't we run for it? Please, let's just go."

She squeezed me so hard I could barely answer.

"We wouldn't make it two steps out the door before they grabbed us. This whole place is crawling with Agents, Lori Ann, so let's just make the best of it and hope they keep their end of the bargain, okay?"

"Are we gonna die?"

I whispered, "We'll be fine, honey. Just keep thinkin' about the sunset in San Felipe." I made a sweeping motion with my arm trying to indicate the possibility that the room was bugged. Her eyes overflowed with tears, and I held her until the phone rang, startling us both terribly.

"Hello," I answered tentatively. "Yes. That would be fine, thank you," I replied to the voice asking if pizza would be satisfactory for our dinner. "Well, it looks like pizza's on the menu."

"I'm not hungry, I just want you close to me."

She looked so isolated and like she could fall apart at any minute, so I whispered into her ear, "If I see a chance we're gone. Otherwise, I'll see you six months from this moment in Mexico, I promise."

"But you said no more promises."

"Just this one, baby. We will find a way to be together, okay?"

"Please make love to me now while there's still time." Her words trailed off as if she were making a last request.

"Let's wait until the pizza arrives, then we'll be uninterrupted."

She agreed with a silent nod and sat on the edge of one of the two beds, staring at the door as if the Grim Reaper himself would pass through it at any moment. I sat beside her and watched, holding her hand, largely waiting for the same event.

Antonio called Carlos' cell phone from his rental car, now parked in a used car lot adjacent to the motel.

"Hola," answered Carlos.

"It's me and I have a location, sir."

"Good, I'm on Route 50 in Easton. Where are you?"

"The same. Go west out of town toward the airport and you'll see the Chesapeake Motel next to a used car lot; I'm in that lot."

"I'll see you shortly."

Carlos pressed end and exhaled some of his tension. "Now we finish this the old-fashioned way." He was pleased with the thought of the police helping him pin down his prey. Within minutes, he located the lot and was parked next to Antonio amongst the used cars. Carlos studied the area and then put down his window. After a brief conversation specifically describing where they each should park, Antonio pulled to the location in the lot as directed to await further instruction.

The pizza was brought by a Dominos delivery guy; he was the cleanest-cut forty-year-old delivery person in history. I was shocked when he only charged us ten dollars for the crappy pizza. Judging from his frosty demeanor, he may have been The Reaper after all. I placed the pizza on the small table by the window and locked all three locks on the door before joining Lori Ann on the bed.

I started to undress the angel at my side. "Don't worry Lori Ann, we'll be fine." We made love for what seemed like both a lifetime and an instant until a knock jolted us; it came from the door connecting our room with the adjoining one.

"Hold on a minute." We scrambled to get dressed. Lori Ann had terror in her eyes, but I calmed her, saying, "Don't worry honey; gangsters don't knock."

I let the raspy-voiced Agent from the police station into the room.

"This is the door he'll probably choose to enter through to limit his time in view to the public, so lock the bolt and the chain and don't sit in clear view of the opening. This room is bugged so we can hear any unusual noise indicating his presence in the room, thereby alerting us to enter ourselves and make the arrest. Then, we'll take you both to the local airstrip and you'll be on your way. Understood?"

"If he's here, won't he know we're not dead?"

He looked agitated by Lori Ann's question. "They gave you the caps, right?"

I said, "Yeah, but what if they don't align with shots he fires?"

"Look. You slap them against your chest as soon as he makes a move; they go bang and splat fake blood all over you. Didn't they go over this with you? It doesn't matter anyway; we doubt he'll be alone, so everybody thinks the other guy did the shooting, and that's where we come in. Then, there's total disarray for the poor bastard."

Lori Ann's "Okay" was less than convincing. I just nodded.

"Remember, lock this door." He reminded us as he exited through it.

Lori Ann said, "Wait," and asked him, "Do you think we have a chance?"

"Well, there's enough of us to stop an army; I just hope he's stupid enough not to notice."

He closed the door behind him.

"Let's try some of that government pizza," I suggested, trying to change the subject.

"Okay."

I locked and chained the door and brought the pizza box to the bed behind the swing of the adjoining door, as per instructions. Lori Ann moved over to the bed I was sitting on and said, "I sure would hate for us to die in this dive."

I didn't respond but took a good look at the room for the first time; it was of average motel size and arrangement with dark green carpet, tropical green print bedspreads, and green bamboo print curtains. The furniture appeared to be grained wood at first glance, but closer observation revealed laminate peeling from most edges. A four-channel TV set took up most of the space on the small dresser facing the beds, and cheap track lighting was mounted on the walls behind the beds. The door to the adjacent room was between the two beds, but on the far wall, opposing the foot of the beds, and the bathroom was at the back of the room next to the bed we were sitting on. The building was so narrow that each room had a front and back door to a row of parking spots.

After we ate, I decided to better our odds in any way I could, so I placed a nightstand one foot behind the presumed gangster entrance door, placed the TV on it, and then tied the television's power cord to the bottom dresser drawer handle, setting up a trip cord between us and any who entered through that door. I hung a sheet from the other bed over the mirror, so our reflections wouldn't reveal our location if they came in through the main door or could see through the edge of the curtains. "That's as good as it gets," I said while inspecting my work.

"I wish we had a gun, but you did a great job of booby-trappin' the room, honey, and I feel safe as long as you're here."

"Well, I appreciate your vote of confidence but James Bond woulda got laid for his efforts."

"Oh, I see, and it will be a while, so why don't you get that reward right now."

Her eyes twinkled as she pulled her shirt over her head, revealing the flawless exterior I missed already. Seeing her nude in front of me took me back to the first night in Vegas. How could I exist for six months without her at my side? I'd become so comfortable around her and would have done anything to escape into uncertainty as opposed to the other alternatives. As I got undressed, I had to wonder if I'd ever hold her this close again.

"How do you know the rooms are joined?" Carlos quietly asked after calling Antonio on the phone. He limited the discussion when they were parked next to each other for fear of drawing attention to their presence, but now needed more detail.

"I called under an assumed name and asked what they have available on the ground floor. I was told that all of the rooms on that end of the building are joined to be used as double rooms, so I figured it must be joined because it's on that side."

"Good. So you will go into room one-fourteen on its left."

"Si, Don Carlos. What time should I go?"

Carlos looked at his gold Rolex and said, "It's nearly 8:00 PM now, so you will go at nine.

"Okay."

"Good. Now keep your mind focused on the task at hand and by 10:00 PM we'll be on our way home."

Antonio sat quietly watching the building from his car, wondering how many bodies would be found in the aftermath.

Deputy Director LaChance sat in a van just across the highway from the motel, giving instructions via a multi-link radio that only connected to the group in this operation so a police scanner couldn't pick up their conversations. He was joined by a technology expert right out of the academy who was listening to every sound in our room, and another Agent who stared out the tinted side window with infrared binoculars for night vision.

Though Carlos summoned Antonio to his car, he was dumbfounded by him walking almost directly through the open lot to get there, but the other reasons for Antonio's imminent retirement were so much more egregious that he just dismissed this latest fuckup without comment. Carlos ignored Antonio's greeting as he got in the car. "Antonio, it must be tonight while we have the opportunity."

Antonio sat silently by Carlos' side in the car wondering if he would live to see the morning's light, or if his body would be found in the room as well. Perhaps Carlos called him to his car to kill him now, even before killing the others?

"Antonio, I want you to go through the woods behind the building and then enter the room next to theirs. Do you know if the adjoining room is vacant?"

"It should be. There's hardly anyone in the whole place." Antonio was relieved to still be part of the plan.

"If it's not, be quick and silent in your activities. We can't alert them to our presence. You'll turn the lights on and then off again to let me know when the room is clear. I'll then join you in a matter of minutes. Do not enter their room until I am present. Do you understand?"

"Si, Don Carlos, I do."

Antonio felt sick; he hated the thought of killing innocent people, so he silently prayed for the adjoining room to be empty. He accepted that his last act on earth would be to take a life because it was the only way to preserve his family name, although no priest would accept it as an excuse for such a sin.

"Why can't we just go in through the back door to their room?"

"Antonio, this will allow us to enter through an interior door as opposed to one that might be witnessed from the lot. Just do as you are told. Your disobedience has severely tried my patience already."

Antonio's mouth was so dry that he couldn't respond.

LaChance watched the men sitting in Carlos' car, requesting an update from his men through the handset.

"This is Alpha. All units check in."

The first to reply was an Agent with the team in the room to our left, the one beyond the building's opening, on the side without adjoining doors. "Alpha, this is Bravo. No activity, sir." He had almost no sightline outside the room due to the curtains being closed to conceal their presence. Their primary role was to storm the rooms once the order was given.

The next team was in a van in the car lot next to the motel, parked just one hundred feet from Antonio's car. The Charlie unit reported the previous activity of Antonio moving on foot to get into Carlos' car, and now reported, "Alpha, this is Charlie. Confirm two actors, actor two is on the move toward number two vehicle." Antonio was exiting Carlos' car and heading back to his own.

The last group to check in was in an SUV parked in a spot along the back of the motel. "Alpha, this is Delta. No activity, sir."

LaChance responded, "Copy, Alpha out," before looking over his shoulder to say, "Look alive men. We're close."

In unison, they replied, "Yes, sir."

I couldn't believe Lori Ann was able to doze off in my arms, and once I slipped free of her embrace, I took a moment to look at her resting in silence. She slept with the innocence of a lamb on the eve of its slaughter while I paced the floor letting her get just a few more minutes of desperately overdue slumber. Eventually, the fear of an attack with her unprepared got the better of me, so I gently kissed her. "Lori Ann, you've gotta wake up. Honey. Please wake up."

She stirred and opened blurry eyes to the reality of our situation, mournfully saying, "I thought maybe it was just a bad dream."

I held her close and quietly reassured her. "It's gonna be all right. Remember the sunset."

I thought surely retribution has been collected by this point, at least for any sins of hers.

She whispered, "I hope destiny has more to offer us than just the precious short time we've shared."

I looked into her beautiful eyes. "It must. How could we come so far just to be separated so soon?"

The thought of my brief time with Laurie flashed in my mind and that icy feeling crept back into my bones as I got up from the bed and handed Lori Ann her clothes.

The young Agent monitoring the surveillance equipment in the van asked LaChance, "Sir. Do they know they're going to be separated as soon as it's over?"

LaChance looked over his shoulder to make eye contact with the rookie.

"Don't get caught up in other people's problems or you'll never make it in this job."

The young man nodded and returned his focus to listening for encroachment within the rooms.

At 9:00 PM, Antonio took a shallow breath before opening the door to exit his car and move toward the woods. Carlos' words echoed in his mind: "You must do exactly as you've been instructed Antonio, or we will not succeed."

The Agents were alerted.

"Alpha, this is Charlie, we have movement. Actor two is on foot and headed toward the rear of the neighboring building. Actor one has relocated sedan one to one hundred feet north and is parked on the north end of the subject building lot. Actor one is our target."

Lori Ann and I sat quietly on the bed, staring at the unplugged television as if it might have some ability to convey what was occurring around us.

Carlos waited patiently for the signal from Antonio, now parked just steps from the room with his prey.

LaChance responded, "Copy Charlie, this is Alpha; we have a go situation. All Agents on ready standby. Only critical 'comms.' Await my signal."

Antonio scanned the motel for any sign of cops before slowly stepping out from the tree line, praying for the adjoining room to be empty as he crossed the narrow lot.

The rear SUV team advised, "Alpha, this is Delta; we have movement. Actor two has exited the woods at the western side of the building and is approaching the rear of the motel."

"Copy that Delta. This is Alpha. We are live."

Carlos listened closely to the portable police scanner next to him on the seat of his car while watching Antonio cross the tunnel-type corridor near the room. Agent's surrounding the area made another safety check of their equipment, their hearts pounding in anticipation.

"Did you hear that?" Lori Ann froze after she finished speaking; her eyes were wide like a deer in a spotlight.

"No, honey. Try and relax."

Antonio slipped into the empty room after picking the lock, his brow soaked with sweat, breath held until realizing the room was vacant.

Delta team's spotter watched Antonio enter the neighboring room.

"Alpha, this is Delta. Actor two has entered room one-fourteen through the western door."

LaChance followed with, "This is Alpha. We have lights in neighbor room. Ready. Ready."

Carlos saw the lights turn on and then off again signaling the room was secure. He carefully surveyed the area before stepping out of the car, putting his pistol under his shirt and tucking it into his pants. He moved slowly with the predatorial instinct of a puma, stopping often, repeatedly scanning his environment.

LaChance held his breath and watched Carlos' progress through night-vision goggles, and then spoke into the microphone. "This is Alpha. Actor one is on the move. Reposition on my mark." He glanced at the young Agent and reiterated, "The first sound. You tell me on the first sound."

The young Agent was so focused now he could hear Lori Ann and me breathing in the room.

Carlos reached the neighboring room and looked back cautiously as he turned the knob and slipped silently through the doorway. He raised a finger to his lips, indicating absolute silence to Antonio who was standing next to the connecting door with his gun drawn and ready.

"Alpha this is Delta. Actor one has entered room one-fourteen through the western door."

"This is Alpha. Reposition now. Check-in ready."

The teams exited their vehicles and staging room, moving quickly and silently to positions surrounding the target rooms, reporting in whispers.

"Bravo in position."

"Charlie in position."

"Delta in position."

LaChance responded, "Copy. Ready intercept."

Carlos eased the pistol from his pants and indicated they would burst through the door on the count of three.

Lori Ann and I sat side by side, holding our blood-caps in clammy hands, acutely aware of someone watching us. Electricity filled the air, and all involved seemed to charge at once.

Antonio kicked the door open; Carlos was positioned behind and to his right, gun drawn. The door jam and chain scattered across the room, and the young Agent gave the signal to LaChance and all teams. "They're in!"

LaChance ordered, "Go! Go! Go!" as his team leaped from their van and sprinted to join the others at the scene.

The doors burst open, and the television tube imploded as heavily armed soldiers of the drug war flooded the rooms from in front and behind Carlos and Antonio while I tackled Lori Ann violently to the floor from the bed where we were sitting. Our blood caps exploded from the impact as shots were fired from every direction and voices screamed in multiple languages within the small room. "Freeze," "DEA," and "Madre de Dios," resounded among the chaos. I felt a sudden burn in my arm and held Lori Ann beneath me even tighter until finally, someone shouted, "Clear. Clear. All clear!" There was moaning coming from several locations in the room and I wasn't sure who won until I heard a raspy voice command, "Get up now," as a powerful hand grasped my shirt and yanked upward.

I was pulled from Lori Ann and realized there was blood covering us both as another Agent grabbed my shirt and helped lift me from the floor, bringing new heights of pain shooting down my arm.

"We're goin' now!"

He dragged me from the room so fiercely that my exit was a complete blur. I cried out, "Lori Ann, Lori Ann, are you all right?" but the Agents pulled me into an SUV and sped off, holding my head down toward the floor. In what seemed like seconds but was in fact three minutes later, I was pulled from the truck and dragged up the stairs of a private jet. I continued pleading for Lori Ann and to know if she was all right, but everyone around me was too busy to pay attention. Finally, the jet door was pulled closed, and a man said, "She's fine, calm down," as he strapped me in the seat and pulled at my clothes looking for wounds. We taxied and took off moments later, but just as we took off, I saw another black SUV pull onto the tarmac and stop next to a similar jet. I couldn't see faces through the tinted windows on the dark runway and could only hope Lori Ann was among them.

I WAS HELD FOR NEARLY TWO MONTHS WITHOUT TELEVISION OR radio. The only people I came into contact with were Agents and they told me less than nothing about anything. One day, LaChance came to see me and advised me that some things had gone wrong that night.

"What do you mean, 'gone wrong?'"

He sat down and began to explain. "You see, Carlos didn't get hit until he fired several shots himself, and among the four casualties was your friend."

I vomited on myself and choked on the tears of shock, hyperventilating in a panic attack until I fell to the floor, almost completely losing consciousness. When I regained brain function, a nurse was asking me how I felt and wiping my forehead with a cool towel. I jumped up, hysterical, saying, "But I was on top of her. How could she have been shot?"

"The bullet grazed your arm and entered her chest, killing her instantly. I doubt she even felt it. I'm sorry, but those are the facts."

I sat in shock trying to piece it together in my mind. "What? Where is she?" My voice trembled in pain that had no masking from drugs or alcohol after the months of forced abstinence. I rubbed the scar on my left shoulder and tried to imagine the odds of the bullet taking such a remarkable turn into Lori Ann below me, a Magic Bullet kind of trajectory at best. My mind raced. Why would fate be so cruel? Why not simply put the bullet into my back? She had done no wrong. I am the one who should've died. How could a bullet hit my left arm and her left chest to kill her instantly when I held her so tightly beneath me?

"Where she has been taken is irrelevant, Mr. West. Because Carlos was killed, we cannot place you into the government's protective custody; I would therefore recommend that you not contact anyone you've known in Minnesota, specifically because your charges there are still pending."

I was bewildered by the onslaught of reality. All I knew was I wanted out.

"So, I can go?" My voice was that of a man who, although breathing in front of you, could not be any more dead if his heart stopped an hour ago.

"You will be given a one-way flight to anywhere you choose; this will be at no cost to you in gratitude for your service to your government. Also, the charges in Maryland have been dropped, and the damages to the vehicle and officer paid, again, in thanks for your service to your government. The clothing you were wearing the night of the incident was ruined and so you were provided the clothing you've been wearing here as a courtesy. You may take any or all of it, and a bag can be provided upon request. Your alias ID for Mr. West that is, in fact, a valid Minnesota driver's license, through means that are unclear to us, and all other personal property that were in your possession, including the five thousand eight hundred and forty-six dollars in cash you had when you were arrested is being returned to you because you are not being charged with a crime. However, the illegal drugs and contraband you possessed have been confiscated and destroyed per federal law. You might wish to alter your appearance in some manner if you choose to visit certain locales. And again, I strongly suggest that you do not return to Minnesota at any time."

My hair had grown longer and kind of unruly over the months since my capture, but I refused offers to cut it.

"I appreciate your advice, but I just want out of here, man." I stood up and wavered slightly, and then collected myself. "Where's my money?"

LaChance looked me over. "None of this ever took place Mr. West, and to some extent, because your only identification is the ID you've procured, Mr. MacNab may as well be dead. We should let him rest in peace and try to use this new beginning to the best of our abilities. Understand that once you walk out the door here, your government will have concluded its obligation to you, and we too will consider these events as having never occurred."

I looked at him in amazement. How could someone be so callused? But then I thought of my own incredible balls. How dare I judge anyone from where I stood? The months of imposed abstinence had cleared my mind; that, combined with restriction from TV and radio made room for forced reflection leading to excruciating emotional pain and regret beyond my wildest dreams.

"Mr. LaChance, I realize this was not your doing. If I could have a ticket to Orange County, California, I'd appreciate it greatly."

I was sincere and he saw it.

"Very well, Mr. West. This Agent will bring you to the Missoula airport. You are currently in Idaho; it's about an hour's drive to the airport and the ticket will be in your name at the United Airlines ticket counter. When you arrive at the terminal, Agent Ward here will give you the balance of your personal property. I wish you the best of luck. Goodbye."

LaChance turned and walked from the room without looking back.

The Agent who drove me to the airport was silent until we pulled up at the terminal. "Mr. West, in this envelope you'll find your wallet, driver's license, and your cash with a receipt, and the plane ticket you requested can be retrieved at the United Airlines counter."

I emptied the manilla envelope onto my lap, jammed the contents from it into the inside pocket of the denim jacket they gave me and stepped out from the car. I only accepted the clothes I was wearing; I didn't see the point of encumbrances. I heard the car pull away but did not look back. At the airline counter, I retrieved my coach ticket and learned that my flight departed in about an hour. I reached into my pocket and pulled two twenty-dollar bills and my ID from the wad and tossed the wallet into a garbage can without looking at its contents. I felt a sharp pain run through my body and fought hard not to cry as I walked into the lounge nearest my gate.

"I need a double Jack and you can keep the ice."

"I'm gonna need some ID partner," the bartender said, gesturing to the sign behind him on the wall that read, "We ID everyone. You must have been born before 9-27-1965," in red LED numbers that could be updated each day.

I put the license and two crumpled twenties on the bar without comment.

"Ok, Mr. West. Double Jack comin' up."

I looked at the license and had to shake my head, thinking, "Boy Pete, you really are good." After the drink, I had another just like it and then left two dollars from my change on the bar and headed off to my gate.

The flight was short; I only had time for one more cocktail

onboard to brace myself for yet another return engagement at John Wayne International. I wished for a fiery crash but the landing was perfect, so I disembarked with the rest of the sheep and found myself standing in the same damn spot again. I processed the Twilight Zone version of my life as I looked out the glass walls of the terminal. The buzz from the alcohol was quite a bit more than usual after the months without it, and it was already working on my mind. I felt the weight of my sadness increasing with each drink, the booze magnifying the negativity and hopelessness. This time, there were no cabs around when I exited the building, so I just started walking; I walked for hours, not minding at all after so long in relative captivity. The time and air were clearing my head as the whisky worked its way through my system, which was not a good thing. I stopped periodically, asking for directions at businesses along the way, and bought a pint of Jack Daniels at a liquor store when I started to feel too sober. When I neared the beach house where this last tragic leg of my journey had begun, I stopped and stared from half a block away before sitting down on the curb to take a drink and think about my situation. Lori Ann was gone, Stihl didn't need my resurrection from the dead in his life, and I didn't deserve to have the bike back, which was still sitting right where I left it, so I crossed the boulevard and stuck out my thumb. Within a few minutes, a Vanagon full of kids not much younger than me stopped.

"Where ya headed, dude?"

"South, man. I'm headin' south." I had thoughts of Lori Ann and our San Felipe sunset filling my mind as I contemplated the journey still ahead.

"Sure, dude, c'mon in." He extended a hand, and as I stepped into the van, scanning the faces that warmly greeted me, I heard a bootleg version of "The Stones" singing "Dead Flowers."

I suddenly realized in a flash of nausea, retribution for me would never be a quick or decisive penance. Instead, more suitably, it would be an eternity filled with the knowledge that I had brought on my own suffering and must now live its reality with each and every breath that remained. To paraphrase Cat Stevens: I always believed that when I looked back on the times I cried, I'd laugh; but I never thought that when I looked back on the times I laughed, I'd cry.

PART XIII

The Long Journey
Home

The Long Journey Home

Another tear drifted silently down her cheek as she held Stihl in their parting embrace. Lori Ann knew the dreams of shared sunsets with Reno would never be realized, but her love for him left her no choice. She'd venture to San Felipe in search of the sunset he described, even if it meant experiencing it without him. She and Stihl had a strong bond born of their love for Reno. The brief but profound relationship each had with Reno and their mutual love for him brought them closer than some lifelong friends.

She wondered where they would have taken his body and wished she could visit his place of rest. The Agents, of course, offered no information beyond the fact that his life was lost in the motel room, lost saving hers. Lori Ann was rendered unconscious during the first moments of mayhem in the room. She suffered a blow to her head when Reno tackled her to the floor, only briefly recalling his weight and embrace taking the breath from her. Regardless, her last memory was being wrapped in the arms of the man who died protecting her, using his own body as a shield. Reno told her no harm would come to her with him in the room, and he kept that promise – if only the promise of shared sunsets in San Felipe could have come true as well.

Freedom was now her prison. She would spend her life with the memory of a brief time when she had a chance at love, an opportunity for two lost souls to start anew; now that dream had to be pushed aside like all the others she allowed herself.

Against Stihl's considerable warnings about going to Mexico, she started Reno's motorcycle, still parked where he left it such a seemingly short time ago; it was merely a flash in time but also an eternity. She and Reno had been through so much in just three days, destiny's wind sweeping them together at the perfect moment only to tear them apart.

She hadn't ridden a motorcycle since the summer between sophomore and junior year and that was a dirt bike, not some high-performance street machine where her feet barely touched the ground. Lori Ann was scared but the bike was all she had to remember him by and her only means of transportation. The government closed her Las Vegas bank account but gave the money to her when they released her, so thirty-eight hundred dollars in cash was all she had. She accepted a flight to San Francisco when the DEA offered a one-way ticket anywhere, after over ten weeks in their Utah facility, still afraid to fly into Los Angeles. She took a bus and found her way to The Pub and Stihl who took her in with open arms, but she only stayed one night in his unfurnished room before explaining she had to head south. She had to see the sunset they held onto in those last moments together in the motel.

Tammi and Dakota were merciful in limiting their questions to a dozen or so with a little help from Stihl, but Lori Ann was the only one who knew of Reno's last days and they were starving for information. Lori Ann was struck by how much of an impact Reno had on everyone he encountered, including herself.

She squeezed the clutch in with her left hand, pushing gently at first and then sharply with her left foot on the shift lever until the grinding crackle of first gear engaging was felt as much as heard. She eased the throttle on with a twist of her wrist and slowly released the clutch as the bike began to move. The motor strained under the weight, causing the bike to lurch and lean hard to her right. She held on tightly as she rolled the throttle towards herself, simultaneously hopping with her right foot to try and level the listing cycle. Finally, she accelerated the machine to an upright forward motion and was merging onto the boulevard. Stihl watched in silent fear from the sidewalk, willing the bike to straighten up and not crush her beneath its weight. All he could do was look on with tears in his eyes as he watched the amazing young woman manage the U-turn and glance his way before heading north off the peninsula. He knew she was truly Reno's girl. Who else but his other half would have such blinding dedication and courage regarding the journey toward a single sunset on a lonely beach in a foreign land?

Stihl gave her directions and insisted she take all his on-hand cash, about a grand, after pleading with her to stay and think a while about the journey she planned. He felt a sense of understanding as she drove away, his heart heavy but confident there was no other choice for her. They were modern-day poets, the both of them. Stihl took a last look at the only reminders of the wildest wave that had ever crashed into his over-hyped town, Reno MacNab, as Lori Ann disappeared from view. He was a young man tortured by his sins in a world that offered him no quarter for the choices he made, all the while maintaining a sense of humor and his brand of honor under the crushing weight of the pain and guilt so few knew he carried.

Stihl said to himself, "Well, at least he got to check out like he dreamed. Crazy fucker went out in a blaze of glory beyond even his own imagination." He went inside, slumped down against the wall in the barren room, held up his Seagram's Seven bottle in salute, and made an out loud toast to his fallen friend. "Here's to the ten best, buddy; I know you lived 'em all."

Fear overshadowed Lori Ann's overwhelming sadness during those first moments on the bike, but that anxiety faded as she grew more relaxed with driving the powerful machine. Her heart ached, seeing only loss as she viewed the coastline passing by below Pacific Coast Highway. She knew her destination was filled with unknowns and danger, and that it wasn't a destination at all, simply the beginning of what was yet to be known, but she had to see the place she and Reno dreamed of during their final quiet moments. She needed to know if her mind had painted the picture accurately from Reno's description. More than anything else, a promise had been made and she would see it through. It was surely a safer scenario to stay with Stihl, and help getting a job and a roof over her head were infinitely better options than any other at this moment. Going back to Vegas certainly wasn't an option; Reno helped remind her she was better than that.

She told Stihl she would likely return after the trip but had no real plans for anything beyond a tiny strip of beach in an unknown country. When they agreed on her eventual return, both carried the truth in their hearts. Newport Beach was beautiful, but it wasn't home for any of them, just a pit stop along the way regardless of how long they'd been there.

The trip down took its toll on me. Since my arrival, I spent the majority of time walking silently along the coastline, laying low under the cover of foliage and abandoned vessels along the beach at the south end of town where the last of the paved roads end and the dirt roads begin. I lost weight but had no hunger for sustenance. I was free at last of so many things but paced like a caged animal until the pain took me apart, again and again, each time leaving me balled up in a heap of flesh existing only to reflect on my errors, mourning for my losses and wishing for an end that wouldn't come. The setting sun was the only time I knew as filled with certainty, and that was the hardest part of the day. I pleaded with God to help me understand how this became my reality. How could they both die? How could I be such a fool to think I could protect Lori Ann, that I could save her when I couldn't even save myself? Why did they trust me and how could they love me? All my actions were based on fear in the moment. I didn't act, I reacted, and self-preservation was always the goal. I no longer prayed for another chance as I once had, nor did I seek forgiveness any longer. I simply waited, watched, and waited. Surely my sins were enough for me to be removed from this world, and soon my life of hell on earth would be replaced by the eternal hell that follows.

Lori Ann arrived at the border in San Diego just before dusk on Thursday, tired and knotted from the three-hour ride. Her thoughts scrambled for continuity as she looked at the gateway to Mexico. Greenish-gray tollbooths lined the entrance to the modest bridge with armed guards in like-colored uniforms who questioned those seeking passage to either side. She contemplated turning back, for just a moment, and then twisted the throttle as she snapped the bike back into gear and eased back into the parade of travelers. A tedious balancing act from toe to toe kept her upright as she inched closer to the large man with an almost audible scowl on his face.

"Is this your vehicle Ma'am?" he asked without a sign of inflection in his voice.

"Yes." She replied in a practiced calm tone.

"What's the purpose of your visit to Mexico?"

"Vacation."

"Are you transporting any drugs or fruits or vegetables?"

He seemed to look through her with the aid of his mirrored aviator sunglasses.

"No, sir."

"How long will you be staying in Mexico?"

Her mind fogged over. The question didn't seem applicable to her even as she casually replied, "A week or so."

"Do you have proof of US citizenship in your possession?"

"Yes." She had her Florida license but felt nauseous knowing it wouldn't cover her riding the motorcycle.

"Enjoy your vacation, Ma'am."

"What? Oh, thank you." She pulled away and merged into the southbound caravan on the bridge, watching for a sign indicating the 1D Highway, and then she need only find the other odd signs as Stihl said. "One, Three, and Five and you'll arrive. Just stay on the odd numbers heading south and you'll be fine." She didn't let fear break her concentration as she glanced at the locals shouting at her in Spanish. Their gestures and outcries made her second-guess the trip again. Finally, a sign: 1D-Ensenada-75Km. She knew she was on the right track when the road became four lanes; Stihl told her it was the only four-lane highway on the Baja Peninsula.

She looked down at the speedometer and realized she was doing eighty-five. After glancing in the mirrors and feeling sure no locals decided to follow her, she eased off the throttle and backed it down to sixty-five. As she watched the road for potholes that could be a serious hazard, she tried to do the math in her head to determine the time it would take to travel seventy kilometers at sixty-five miles per hour.

Working the metric conversions in her head started to frustrate her, so she rolled the throttle a bit to increase her speed to seventy and felt satisfied that her estimated time of arrival in Ensenada would be less than an hour. Stihl told her San Felipe was only a couple hours from Ensenada and the entire trip should take about five hours. She settled into a zone from the droning sounds and vibration and began to daydream that Reno was driving and she need only to hold him as tightly as she pleased. The setting sun drew her deeper into the fantasy she entertained as the high-pitched whine of the engine numbed her into a lull. Tears filled her tired eyes as the reality of her situation was jarred to the forefront of her mind by a crack in the asphalt. The bike jumped and she pulled with equal strength from both weary arms to settle the wobble it created. Now was not the time for daydreams.

The sunset was particularly brilliant this evening, and though the painful reminder was ever-present, I felt a strange sensation that somehow Lori Ann shared it with me. I spent three US dollars on yet another bottle of local tequila and felt the dizzying effect of its poison in my mind as the last drops went down along with the setting sun. I had enough money to buy a better brand but was sure the local liquor would burn through my liver and brain more quickly.

The sand was an irritation on every inch of my body, and the quick dips in the California Gulf seemed to only bring a burning to exaggerate the discomfort of sun and sand burns. I smelled of cheap booze, saltwater, and body odor but the locals endured my unkempt state in exchange for the few dollars I spent each time I emerged from the dunes and foliage. The sparse palms were located by the hotels and bars, so I ventured to the less desirable stretch for solitude during the day, only walking among the palms occasionally at night when few ventured to the water's edge. I hadn't eaten in more days than I could recall. When I vomited on the surf line, I found no difference in content within the foamy water that swept it away after each failed charge toward land. The sea was winning of course, but a brief observation would always indicate the land's superiority in the timeless battle. I imagined myself as a tiny island being eroded from existence by the relentless pounding of the choices I made, a constant washing away of the dreams I foolishly anchored to, and proof that a greater force rights all in this world that begins and ends in a way beyond our conception. Perhaps tonight's swim with the foolish hope of relieving even the physical pain would dissolve the last grains of the corrupted island I'd become. Those final grains of existence that kept me visible to the world would wash away to be used in the construction of another island beginning a thousand miles away. I staggered into the surf and fell into its arms as if to accept the outcome I visualized so clearly in my tortured mind.

———

SANCHEZ LISTENED INTENTLY TO THE CONVERSATIONS TAKING PLACE at the grand table in the Minneapolis mansion. He was pleased to be recognized as an individual who could handle the central operations but knew he was not at all like the man he would replace. Carlos had been feared for good reason; Sanchez was admired more than feared within the organization. After many discussions among the men, Don Suarez addressed him directly. "Young Sanchez, this is a great responsibility. You will make many decisions in the future and the impact of those decisions will affect us all. Are you prepared to own these responsibilities and lead the men in your trust?"

"I am, Don Suarez."

"And young Sanchez, are you prepared to accept the weight of this responsibility knowing it may one day cost your life?"

"I am, Don Suarez."

"Then it is done. You will be forever known as Don Sanchez."

Don Sanchez rose after the ceremony and greeted the small parade of men who either briefly rested a firm hand on his shoulder or kissed his hand in recognition of his authority. Sanchez had been a good soldier, was educated, and proven loyal beyond question during a time of considerable strain when he silently faced the possibility of a Panamanian death sentence. Six months later, all charges, including the murder of a political figure had been dropped. The fact that he didn't kill the man in question had no bearing on the trial's outcome.

Don Sanchez took in the room again in silence, listening as the last of the family powers departed the home. His rule would be strict but the hatred at soul's depth would never control him as it had his prede-cessor. Carlos had been angry at the world since his youth and lived as if some unclaimable vendetta had driven him to madness. He'd become ineffective in business dealings and was only followed due to his over-reactive internal justice and drug-induced paranoia reaping fear in those around him. Some believed the relationship with his American lover caused him to lose touch with the traditions of Columbia and maybe the family. Sanchez vowed that he would live by the family ways and not be tempted by the American apathy that to him was pestilence in its most grotesque form. He knew of the situation regarding the problematic children that sealed Don Carlos' demise, but after consid-ering the options and the weight of their existence with regard to his affairs, he concluded they were no more dangerous than any other child might be and dismissed the situation completely. In his opinion, they were merely another indication of bad judgment by his predeces-sor, plus the only information they possessed was now public and concerning a dead man. His sparing their lives would be his first signal that business always takes precedence over personal matters, a move designed to show that Don Carlos' actions, in the end, were not worth defending. Don Sanchez sat again, this time more deeply in the wing-back chair, looking at the many books on the walls, and decided that a short rest was in order.

Lori Ann passed through Ensenada without stopping, carefully following the signs for Highway 3 and the upcoming stop in Ojos Negros. Stihl advised purchasing fuel in the small town of Ojos Negros instead of risking the potential perils of nightlife in cities such as Tijuana or Ensenada. He further informed her that Mexico is full of many dangers, but the small-town locals are typically a very warm and hospitable culture yet to be corrupted by the vile western influences of greed and perversion. They are spiritual and family-oriented and possess a work ethic beyond the memory of most societies. Stihl believed they would provide her with fuel and kindness absent of treachery.

She pulled into the tiny, single-pump service station in the center of Ojos Negros just after 10:00 PM. The sky was filled with a million stars; each seemed to represent a lost dream and each cluster a place that must be better than this world and its flaws.

"Como esta, Señorita."

"Huh?" She jumped back into the moment as if a leap from a thousand feet had been required. "Oh, hello," she replied, looking at his patient expression. "I need gas."

He said, "Petrol," with a gentle tone. His face looked to be made of battered, heavy leather, and his hair was thick and glistened black like the night sky. He was small in stature but had an overwhelming presence, a paternal presence that reminded her of the few moments when her father relinquished his military scowl to show love for her as his daughter.

She pointed to the gas cap, opened it with the key from the ignition, and offered a weary smile while repeating, "I need gas."

"Si. Bien. Petrol. Gracias."

He reached for the pump, removed it, and turned a bar on the side to activate the counter. When he finished filling the tank and placing the nozzle in its receptacle, he looked at the amount and back at her with a smile that conveyed they could not come to terms through verbal communication.

She handed him a five-dollar bill. "Is this enough?"

He accepted the bill and dug in his pocket, retrieving a handful of pesos, first counting out a small group of them and then offering them to her.

"Gracias, Señorita."

She accepted the coins without knowing their value and felt a bit like Jack with a handful of beans but smiled and replied, "Gracias."

The man gave a half-wave to her as he turned and headed back toward the tiny, dilapidated structure, adding a sweeping motion to disperse the gathered children at the station's screened doorway. They vanished in a wave of tiny giggles and whispers that even if she had heard clearly, would not have been decipherable.

The bike roared to life the instant she touched the starter button, and the crack of first gear engaging was enough to indicate it was no worse for the journey. She glanced at the tiny faces that had already returned behind the tattered screen door and watched their eyes light up as she snapped the throttle twice before easing the clutch out and heading toward coastal highway five. She was going to make it, but make it where? What was the real purpose of this trip anyway? Perhaps just another beach to cry on, or maybe it was something more, something destiny's wind would only reveal in its time. Maybe it was her journey home. After all, home can mean so many things.

I watched the cloudless sky hold the endless sea of stars in perfect position as the evening waves raised me like an offering to the heavens, each time returning me in rejection over and over again. I floated in my mind, just as my body floated on the cap-less swells of high saline water that rendered me so buoyant. There was no sound beyond the surf, no disturbance, just the waves and the sky. If my mind could only stop reliving the past, sleep could come and the future would be halted by a gulp of the sea, or so I believed.

Lori Ann knew they must be the Sierra Madres, just as Stihl described, but the ominous, dark peaks rising from the desert shot a chill through her just the same. The air was crisp and filled with gulf coast moisture, but she knew that once off the bike, it would be no less than a tepid evening. Stihl told her to stay at the Hacienda, it was just across the street from the beach and was not as much of a party spot as the beachfront places. He further advised that she wait until morning to walk the beach alone, as it is rarely occupied late at night, and she might do best to avoid anyone who would be wandering the sand alone at such an hour.

It was nearly midnight when she passed the sign welcoming her to the village of San Felipe, population 846. The archway that stretched across the road at the diminutive town's entrance was merely offering a prelude to a small series of consecutive cantinas, curios, and of course, the modest hotels that dotted the coastline. She looked forward to seeing the shrine to the Virgin of Guadalupe, but she decided to heed Stihl's advice and stay in this evening.

The impact with the boat wreckage startled me so intensely that I thought a shark decided to try my leg for a late-night snack. The sea rushing away from beneath me was all that kept me from drowning. I had run aground just like the rotting vessel that had taken my leg as its last victim. As I lay surrounded in the subsequent rushes of the sea's challenge to overrun the shoreline, I felt the sting of the saltwater within the formidable gash on my calf. "Fuck" was all I could muster in response to this most recent development before staggering to my feet, struggling while my equilibrium played catch-up and taunted me with the chance of another spill to earth. I slept in one of the beached wrecks the first night in San Felipe, but between the crabs jockeying for position and the mist of the salty surf invading my sleep, I decided that higher ground in the dunes was a better place to escape consciousness in the weeks that followed. I looked up at the lighted windows on the third floor of the Hacienda and wondered what it would have meant to be checked in awaiting the arrival of Lori Ann, but then stopped short in my dream, saying, "What a fuckin' joke this life is," as the slur of my words became evidence of my returning state of inebriation. Sand filled the wound on my leg and aided the coagulation of blood while every twitch of my muscle sent a dull ache up my thigh. I smirked at the thought of dying of some bullshit infection after all I'd been through.

Lori Ann opened the door to her room and was greeted by a musky smell that only a warm gulf shore can create. She pulled aside the drapes and opened the double windows displaying a view that brought an ache to parts of her heart she never visited before. Countless stars illuminated the sky while the surf reflected the moon like a mirror for self-admiration. The palms swayed gently at the base of the hill her hotel occupied while locals mingled with a few well-seasoned, returning visitors in the cantinas. If only he had been more concerned with his own wellbeing. Why would he lay like an open target on top of her, exposing himself to fire from any direction? He could have been here enjoying this perfect evening, just like the one he described as they dreamed of escaping all that haunted them. What was she going to do in this place? Was it a fool's errand without reason or perhaps her indulging the fantasy that his spirit might somehow embrace her while here?

She drew the light linen drapes back to obstruct the view and turned to look over the villa she inhabited. The desk clerk referred to the rooms as villas, but he was overstating the glamour of the establishment. The room was maybe twenty feet by fifteen feet in dimension and had a queen-size bed with overhead framing to support the mosquito netting that veiled it to the floor. A small table with a chair was in the farthest corner with no television or telephone to be found. The bathroom was small but clean with thick terrycloth towels hung and folded from a suspended shelf unit. The clawfoot bathtub looked inviting after her grueling ride, but sleep was becoming a priority over comfort as she unwound from the journey's physical stress. Her shoulders and triceps ached so badly that the lower back fatigue was largely overshadowed. He would have massaged her weary muscles and made love to her so tenderly in this moment. Thoughts of how he cared for her during their time together brought tears from eyes she thought again and again couldn't possibly muster another. She contemplated the conciliatory words of her mother amidst the third relocation of their family during her high school years. Her mother said, as many do, "What doesn't kill you, makes you stronger." It was as useless in retrospect as it had been at the time; and even if this theory is true, inner strength can be damaging as well. People who have lived through incredible hardships and emotional trauma will often close themselves off completely, abandoning love and hope, ceasing to truly live by society's definition of life. Some others in similar circumstances will seek comfort through extreme involvements in religious pursuit or within complex philosophy, ignoring the trivial routines of life entirely; still, others will hide within a fog of drugs and or alcohol, living in an empty shell that pre-medicates any would-be emotions. Either way, strength comes from within, and each person's version is his or her own. However, strength is just tolerance to pain, so getting more of it by surviving isn't a desirable pursuit. Inner peace is what's truly of value, but the only earthly source of such serenity doesn't specifically come from within, it comes from something greater than us all.

As I laid in silence on the narrow strip of sand that remained uninvaded by the tidal swell, I allowed myself to focus on the pain in my leg. I tried to overcome its presence by sheer will, forcing a mental numbness to cloak its throbbing reminder. The management of the pain in my leg was merely a game of control, another game being played alone while I awaited some divine intervention that would bring an end to my tortured soul. The fact that I was losing my mind to cheap tequila and sorrow was probably of great benefit in the task.

Exhaustion claimed victory over Lori Ann and sleep brought temporary peace to a heart that knew none in consciousness. The morning would bring light, and she would leave this place without the sunset of a stolen dream. Stihl was right that she shouldn't have journeyed here. She had no business in this place. It was Reno's and perhaps it was to be theirs, but it was not hers alone. Even a heart as large as hers had limits to the pain it could absorb, and a sunset in San Felipe would be filled with more sadness than she could imagine or perhaps endure.

The morning air was stifling at minimum and the sun burned a reminder of the previous night's mishap in the wound. Insects of all shapes and sizes scrambled about the carnage that was their opportunistic meal. Twitches of pain brought forced awareness to the feeding frenzy that devoured my wounded limb, but it was the reflexive slap of my hand that brought me instantly to my feet in the midst of garbled profanity and horror from the scene. I dashed into the sea, finding strange solace in the familiar pain of its stinging rush. Soon, the shock wore thin in my mind, and I sat hard into the whitewash while examining the menacing gash in my limb. As I urinated in the swirling waters that bathed my submerged lower extremities, I pondered my course of action. I hated to waste money on medical supplies because I knew I'd never earn another dollar beyond the soggy mush in my pockets, but a bandage would be the only way to fend off the onslaught of irritant carnivores. I thought a bottle of tequila would be multi-purposeful and perhaps a bandana from a local curio would serve as bandage enough to bide my remaining time. I scanned the beach but saw no inhabitants. I wondered how long it would take for this place to be discovered by the greedy slobs that ruined Cabo San Lucas and so many other beautiful locations. They would come bringing invitations to mass tourism and construction to accommodate the plague of society as it destroyed another mile of God's splendid creation. "How will you forgive us for such sins?" I asked of the clouds above; and like so many other questions, it was carried off in the wind without reply.

Lori Ann awoke feeling slightly nauseous from the clammy air that filled her room. She looked around until she focused on the glimpses of sea and sky as the breeze parted the drapes in a succession of silent ruffles. She moved to the bathroom without allowing deliberation of the view and ran the water to temperatures few could bear in such climates. The small tub filled quickly with her body reducing the available space allotted for water. She submerged her head again and again as she worked her fingers through the knots in her hair from the wind. She decided to stop by the closest curio to purchase a bandana or something to restrain her hair during the long ride ahead. She could wait until she reached San Diego for food. Her appetite was weak at best, and the fear of botulism was certainly realistic.

I wandered to the street looking for signs of life as I ventured but saw no one around. I looked overhead at the sun's position and assumed it to be 8:00 or 9:00 AM at the latest. I threw my watch into the sea many days before for haunting me with the reminder of time. The curios would soon be open, if they weren't already, but it was early enough to avoid any tourist who might wish to befriend a crazed-looking gringo.

Lori Ann checked out and walked from the hotel's insignificant lobby feeling relief that the motorcycle made it through the night without change of ownership; it didn't occur to her last night that it was an issue to be contended with. Reno would have probably found a way to bring it into the room with them. She was warmed by the thought of him arguing with the manager as he prepared to ride it up the stairs. She stretched for a minute and then swung her leg over the seat and settled into her balancing act as she turned the key and depressed the starter with her thumb.

I heard a racing bike roaring to life in the distance as I entered the curio. I missed my bike and the feeling of the wind in my hair at high speeds through the desert and along the coastline. Most of all, I missed the feeling of Lori Ann's arms wrapped tightly around me as we moved in perfect synchronicity with the machine. She was the only one who seemed to understand the natural movements of a bike in corners and never fought the feeling of falling over.

"Como esta?" the store owner offered in salutation.

"Bien. Tequila?"

I scanned the small room for observers as I asked. They sold everything, but it was, in fact, illegal to sell liquor without licensure.

"Si. Esta bien." He pulled an already bagged liter of the local brand from behind the counter and offered it to my view; it was my daily supply although I'd gone through two bottles on occasion.

"Bueno."

I selected one of the bandanas that were imprinted with the Mexican flag; I sat it on the counter and offered a soggy handful of currency totaling ten US dollars for the transaction. They love US dollars, and he cheerfully accepted the mess while placing the bandana into the bag with the liter. He said, "Gracias," as I turned with bag in hand, ignoring any change that may have been due. The coins he'd have offered have little value, even in Mexico, and they would have just rubbed my leg raw through my pocket or been lost in the sea.

Lori Ann gazed up and down the street as she balanced the bike at the foot of the small hill and then eased out toward the left and chose a curio just a few doors down. She did a large, sweeping U-turn and pulled over to the northbound side of the road, nosing in toward the curb, but hadn't noticed the buildup of sand and struggled to keep the bike upright as it slid toward the raised concrete. The handlebars snapped from her grip as the tire wedged against the curbing and forced the weight of the bike to overwhelm her strength as it fell to the street. "Shit." She cursed as she rolled onto the sidewalk, narrowly avoiding the bike pinning her leg. She sat up and considered the likelihood of being able to lift it from such a precarious position when an American voice spoke from behind her.

Just as I stepped out from the curio, I witnessed a young girl tumbling from a motorcycle onto the sidewalk. I moved toward her and asked, "Are you okay?" Her back was to me; she was looking at the downed machine.

"I'm fine. It only hurt my pride." She responded while brushing off as she rose to her feet. "But I could use a..." She froze mid-sentence as the air left our lungs simultaneously and our eyes locked in astonishment, neither able to jar the moment's revelation into reality. The bottle I held smashed within the involuntarily-released bag as it struck the ground, tequila flowing like so many tears streaming from the swollen eyes of mournful bodies as emotions raced through our hearts, souls, and minds. Words could not be formed into speech as images from the past flashed desperately in an effort to lock in identities. Reason was replaced by wonderment and then again by disbelief. We stood on shaky knees just feet from each other but couldn't move to close the distance. Finally, Lori Ann spoke in a voice broken and trembling with pain and hope. "Is, is it really you?" Her hands rushed to her face as her sobbing became uncontrollable.

In just three fumbling steps I reached her, took her in my arms, and spoke in both question and statement. "They said you died." I trailed off into a thousand sunsets that had been banished from existence. The projected memories of a lifetime were shaped in fantasy creating an impossible future; these, along with the hopeless desperation and longing over the months since I'd seen her exploded into technicolor waves of disillusionment. The horrors that filled my mind in the knowledge of her death competed for space and questioned this new reality.

She reared back, looked at me through flooding eyes, and slapped my face twice in quick succession. "Where have you been? I thought you were dead!"

I felt the sting of the slaps in delayed reaction and flinched a moment later under her ensuing embrace.

"I knew God wouldn't take you from me. I just knew he couldn't take you away. How could he steal such beauty from my heart?"

I could only offer the words, "I love you," and "I've missed you so much," in return as I held her in an embrace that a lifetime could not prepare one for.

The sun shined that day in San Felipe as brilliantly as it ever would again. The world and life itself had come full circle. We were tested by severance, lied to, and crushed of all hope and spirit but our love was greater than the evils that would divide us. We were allowed the promise kept by grace and beauty in the universe that is bigger than all it encompasses: Destiny, so pure and powerful, it overcomes all adversity and opposition.

Love is the greatest gift of all; its origin and strength are beyond this world's comprehension. We must cherish love that is given so freely, returning it as we are able, for the spirit in which it is offered is the only way it can be shared while awaiting destiny's sunset on our long journey home. Our paths are forged indelibly but by forces unknown and beyond our control. All that is understood is that while plans are made, destinations change.

About the Author

S.B. Gilfillan is a recovering alcoholic with over thirty-one years of sobriety at the time of this book's release. His goal in this publication is not to glorify, but rather to candidly portray the lifestyle he miraculously survived.

He wishes to remind us that no matter how deeply a person has fallen into the grasp of drug and alcohol addiction, there is always hope if it is sought.

Destinations Change represents his first published novel. He currently resides in New Jersey and is working on his second book.

Website: DestinationsChange.com

facebook.com/SBGilfillanAuthor

twitter.com/Sbgilfillan

instagram.com/Sbgilfillan